CWMARDY

CWMARDY

THE STORY OF A WELSH MINING VALLEY

BY

LEWIS JONES

LAWRENCE and WISHART
London

First Published 1937

This Edition, with Introduction
by David Smith, 1978

© Lawrence and Wishart

ISBN 85315 468 6

AG1

This book has been republished with
the support of the English-language
Section of Yr Academi Gymreig

Typeset by William Clowes & Sons Ltd
This Edition printed by Redwood Burn Ltd,
Trowbridge & Esher

DEDICATION

To the architect, without whose inspiration, practical help, and patience in extremely difficult conditions even this little attempt at building would have been impossible.

INTRODUCTION

by David Smith

Lewis Jones was a Communist. This was the central fact of his life, the philosophical pivot around which his stormy political career and volatile temperament revolved. His politics shaped his life and coloured his writing because of his deep ideological commitment to them as the only release for a trapped society. His place and his time, he considered, allowed no other real choice. In every other respect, although hemmed in by extremely restricting public and private circumstances, Lewis Jones personified individual choice.

The argument on his lips was for collective action disciplined by political organisation, but he could never abandon the chaotic welter of individual types which made up his 'people'. He tried to combine the two elements in himself, often with disastrous results in the shining eyes of those who believed the tribunes of the people should be exemplary ambassadors of their proletarian constituents. Yet his wilful bohemianism never removed him from those he felt, with a sure instinct, he could succour through both his cockatoo personality and his tempered intelligence. The two novels he left, as a bonus from a lifetime of giving, are revealing of a public experience whose density of meaning for the literature and the history of Wales are only now being unravelled. For Lewis Jones it was the only world he knew.

He was born, in 1897, in Clydach Vale, mid-Rhondda, the pulsating heart of a South Wales whose economy and population occupied a strategic niche in the British Empire. Being orphaned early in life and so raised by his grandmother were direct signposts for the mitching schoolboy to enter the Cambrian Colliery of D. A. Thomas, later Lord Rhondda, and the model for the novels' Lord Cwmardy. That was in 1909.

Around the Cambrian Combine pits in mid-Rhondda flared the virulent strike of 1910–11 and the Tonypandy riots which, as a collier boy, Lewis Jones would have witnessed. From this couldron of turmoil came, by 1912, the pamphlet—*The Miner's Next Step*—denouncing all leadership not rooted in the men themselves. A number of idealistic leaders emerged who sought to turn theories of workers' control into practice.

Like so many other South Walian thinkers in the first half of the twentieth century, Lewis Jones was marked by the vigorous democracy evident in *The Miner's Next Step* and by that anarcho-syndicalism which, in its instant promise, framed so well the aspirations of a society as bewilderingly new as any found by an Andalucian peasant enticed to Barcelona. It was the milennarian possibilities of this topsy-turvy world that Lewis Jones glimpsed and sought to harness.

His early mentor was the sagacious Noah Rees (on whom Ezra is based), a man wise in pit ways and educated, through Ruskin College, in fundamentalist Marxism. Clydach Vale had its own Marxian Club and Institute long before, in 1909, the Central Labour College was specifically established, as a breakaway from Ruskin, to provide independent working-class education. This too was the mulch on which the boy would feed as he sped, through an early marriage at sixteen to being, before the First World War ended, the youngest ever Chairman of the Cambrian Lodge. That war had shown the bargaining strength of a mining work-force which was in excess of 250,000 in South Wales by the early 1920s. Lewis Jones tied himself to it further by relinquishing his studies in mining engineering for headier visions. He attended the Central Labour College in London, on a scholarship, between 1923 and 1925. At this time, like Len his main fictional protagonist who is an amalgam of himself and other close friends, he joined the youthful Communist Party. During the lock-out of 1926 he was sent on a speaking-tour of the shaky Nottinghamshire coalfield: this led to his prosecution for seditious speeches and a three months' prison sentence.

After the collapse of the General Strike all struggle was defensive. The work-force was halved, non-unionism set in again, unemployment rates in Rhondda went over forty per cent, and a rival, non-political union was supported by the coal owners.

Lewis Jones did not know how to defend: his refusal to work with blackleg labour led to his dismissal as check-weigher in 1929 and to the start of his final decade of work amongst the unemployed whose wretched condition now symbolised the coalfield in a grim reversal of its pre-war buoyancy. By this time he was an orator of unrivalled gifts, able to articulate the emotions of people with whom, in all other ways, he merged. He became a Welsh organiser for the National Unemployed Workers' Movement under whose auspices he led three Hunger Marches from South Wales. Within the coalfield he was active in arranging demonstrations and meetings, culminating in the huge protests against the Means Test in early 1935. That these were all-party demonstrations based on the entire community confirmed his belief in the potential for total, political involvement inherent in his society, if only the scales of illusion and mutual suspicion could be permanently removed.

To the end he argued for unity within the Labour movement and, in the heyday of the Popular Front, shared many platforms with Labour politicians. At a by-election in 1936 he was elected, from mid-Rhondda, to the

Glamorgan County Council as one of only two Communist County Councillors. The international struggle against Fascism was seen as an extension of the daily fight against exploitation at home; his speeches had him bound over by the law yet again.

He volunteered to go to the Spanish Civil War but was considered more valuable as a domestic propagandist. Besides, his earlier brushes with the conventions then considered proper in a leading Communist party member did not augur well for the kind of harsh political discipline required in Spain. As if to quell all doubts about his political drive, he worked unstintingly in the cause of Spanish Aid and it was in this cause that he died when his heart gave out after addressing over thirty street meetings in a day. That was the week in January 1939 in which Barcelona fell to Franco.

Lewis Jones was no martyr, however, if martyrdom suggests passivity, resignation in the face of overwhelming odds, the victim's brave acceptance of his fate. The point of his life, on the contrary, was its aggressive activity, its breezy, vital lustiness that refused, in the name of others, to be graceful. This is the legacy, too, of the novels he managed to write despite his intensely packed life.

Cwmardy first appeared in 1937. It is exclusively set in the Rhondda and is, at one level, a straightforward attempt to present a dramatised chronology of events from the 1890s to the early 1920s. South Wales had been either investigated through the dehumanising prose of government reports and surveys (in 1910, in 1917, in 1929, in 1932, in 1934, in 1937) or conveyed through the cliches of romantic novelettes. Lewis Jones was a part of that first Welsh generation who, with no appropriate literary tradition behind them, tried to capture their highly charged history of boom and slump in novels and short stories. He was distinct from other writers in that his intention was primarily to set the record straight from his inside knowledge.

Introduction

A lot of the factual material in *Cwmardy* is in details inaccurate, but it remains essentially true to the significant trends of the history. What is more worrying is his inability to escape the convolutions of a highly literary prose in the narrative or to put more convincing dialogue in the mouths of his characters. There are passages (the death of Jane, work in the pit, the explosion) where the force of the event breaks through limitations of style and technique, and there is much humour and frank sexuality scattered throughout. Nevertheless no one could claim attention for the book principally on its literary merits. Its crucial quality, apart from considerable documentary value, is the skilled and knowledgeable manner in which the evolution of a political consciousness, with many checks and balances on its understanding, is shown as intimately related to a particular place and a special work experience.

We are, perhaps, told too much and not shown enough for the intimate lives of individuals to come into clear focus, but their ultimate shaping by social, cultural and economic pressures which are connected (through wages, work, commerce, school, pit and religion) is lucidly conveyed in an understanding more skilled Welsh novelists have sometimes lacked. The novel is akin to archaeological remains where patterns of a vanished life linger, both hauntingly elusive and brusquely present.

April 1978   *University College, Cardiff*

FOREWORD

IF anyone is to be blamed for this book it must be my friend and comrade, Mr. Arthur Horner, President of the South Wales Miners' Federation, whose fertile brain conceived the idea that I should write it.

He suggested that the full meaning of life in the Welsh mining areas could be expressed for the general reader more truthfully and vividly if treated imaginatively, than by any amount of statistical and historical research. What I have set out to do, therefore, is to " novelise " (if I may use the term) a phase of working-class history. All the events described, though not placed in chronological order, have occurred, and each of them marks a milestone in the lives and struggles of the South Wales miners. The present volume covers the period of thirty years up to 1921, and I hope to complete the story up to the present day in a second novel which I have already started.

The work is really collective, in the sense that my fellow workers had to fight the battles I try to picture, and also in the sense that I have shamefully exploited many comrades for incidents, anecdotes, typing, correcting and the multifarious details connected with writing. We found many difficulties confronting us, not the least of which was the fact that, book or no book, the mass struggle must go on and all of us had to play our part. The jumpiness of certain portions of the book is evidence of this. It was written during odd moments stolen from mass meetings, committees, demonstrations, marches, and other activities. But I do not advance this as an excuse for the shortcomings, which no one better than ourselves knows it contains. Rather do I state it as a reason.

LEWIS JONES.

CONTENTS

CHAPTER   PAGE

I. AN EVENING IN CWMARDY I

II. LEN GOES TO SCHOOL 18

III. THE CHAPEL EXCURSION TO THE SEASIDE . 27

IV. THE DEATH OF JANE 41

V. THE EXPLOSION 68

VI. THE INQUEST AND BURIAL 91

VII. LEN STARTS TO WORK 105

VIII. THE PIT CLAIMS ANOTHER VICTIM . . 129

IX. CWMARDY PREPARES FOR ACTION . . 144

X. CWMARDY GOES INTO ACTION . . . 153

XI. ACTION DEEPENS 163

XII. SOLDIERS ARE SENT TO THE VALLEY . . 193

XIII. THE PIT THROBS AGAIN 216

XIV. LEN AND MARY ORGANISE THE CIRCLE . 230

1*

Contents

CHAPTER		PAGE
XV.	War	246
XVI.	Len works for Peace	269
XVII.	The War draws to an End . . .	288
XVIII.	Cwmardy teaches Len a New Lesson .	304

CHAPTER I

An Evening in Cwmardy

BIG JIM, known to civil servants and army authorities as James Roberts, stopped abruptly and let his eyes roam over the splendour of the mountain landscape. A coat hung uncouthly from his arm and a soft breeze played on the hairy chest that showed beneath his open red-flannel shirt.

His small son, Len, stood near by wondering what had caused this sudden halt. He saw Big Jim open his mouth as if about to say something, but instead of words came a smacking sound and a large mass of tobacco-stained saliva.

The lad, whose wavy hair shadowed his sad eyes, watched the spittle twirl in the air before it fouled the grass at his feet. Len looked at the massive body that made his own feel puny, while Big Jim remained pensively motionless.

Father and son remained silent for some minutes, the former looking like a Wild-West desperado with the red silk scarf dangling loosely from his neck. His soap-stiffened moustaches gave him a fierce, reckless appearance which Len thought romantic.

The lad eventually grew impatient with the silence. " What be you waiting for, dad ? " he asked, his wistful eyes searching for the face that towered above him.

The plaintive voice rose to Big Jim's ears like a bubble. He looked down on his son and sighed. " I be just thinking, Len bach," he started, his deep voice tinged with pathos, " 'bout the days long ago, when I did use to walk the fields of the North before ever I come down here to work in the pits."

The man sighed again, bit his moustache, and sat on a

little mound nearby. Len wormed his way to his father's knee, and the pair silently looked before them at the miles of undulating highland which buried itself in the shimmering haze that marked the encircling distant sea. Here and there the landscape was splashed with patches of purple heather and rich brown bracken whose blended colours stood out boldly in the telescopic clarity of the midsummer evening.

Browsing sheep languidly chewed their way from patch to patch, while larks lifted their song into the blue recesses of the sky. Even the clear air conspired to produce an aspect of tranquil serenity on the mountain top. Rising and falling in tiny semi-visible globules of heat, the air played an irresponsible hide-and-seek with the bladed grass.

The two solitary humans were affected in different ways by the pacific scene. It softly recalled to the rough, toil-scarred miner the days of his youth. But young Len had no such solid memories to be awakened. In their place he felt a vague emotional hunger that made him sad. He turned on his stomach and lay full length on the grass before his father, who was meditatively moving a huge lump of tobacco from cheek to cheek, occasionally spitting its gravy-like juice into the air.

The lad strained his eyes towards the distant channel. He wondered what the ships it held looked like, and vainly tried to magnify the black spots that dotted the ribbony gleam. A hoarse grunt from Big Jim brought Len to his haunches. "Huh," said the former, trying to twist the reveries from his mind by twirling his moustaches, "this bit of mountain by here, Len bach, is where King Rhys did have his head chopped off." The statement was resonant with rolling r's. Big Jim waited in confident anticipation of a comment from his son.

Len looked at him with wistful interest. "For what did they chop his head off, dad?" he asked.

"Oh," was Jim's slow reply, "I be not quite sure now, boy bach, but I 'spect they did do it 'cause he was a bad man and that was the only way to bring him to his senses."

Len thought a moment before asking, " Well, how was he a bad man and who did chop his head off for it ? "

This put Jim out of his depth, but he tried to recover the position by saying as he scratched his head, " I don't hardly 'member now, boy bach. You see, it did happen a long time ago, ay, hundreds of years ago, and I can't pull things back to my mind these days as I used to."

He turned the subject sharply. " Do you see that red grass over there ? " he asked, pointing a huge forefinger vaguely into the distance. Len looked into the desired direction and fancied he saw the red patch.

" Ay," he said, " you do mean that place where the sheep is, dad."

" That be it. Well, by there a big battle was once fought between the Cymro and the English. A awful lot of blood was spilt that day and the grass have been red with it ever since."

Len wanted to ask further questions, but Big Jim lifted him to his feet before they could be made articulate. " Come," he muttered to his son, " it be getting late and your mam will be wondering where we be." The pair sauntered slowly across the mountain-top that was already crimsoning in the rays spread by the setting sun. Len watched the deepening hues and wondered where they went when darkness fell.

Father and son soon reached the mountain crest, where they again sat down so that the former could have another smoke before descending into the valley. Len knew his father took some time to enjoy a pipeful of tobacco and resigned himself to the consequent wait. Lying on his stomach the lad surveyed the valley beneath.

His eyes looked down upon the belt of smoke that hung half-way up the mountain like a blanket blotting out everything beneath. The lad watched the billowing cauldron break and twist into ever-changing forms in the clutches of the evening breeze. They swirled into bubbling eddies that brought to his mind thoughts of the broth he had often seen his mother make over the open fireplace of their home.

" Look, dad," he uttered excitedly, " i'n't it like the cawl mam do make if soot was to fall in it from the chimley ? "

The analogy tickled Big Jim. " Ho-ho ! " he guffawed. " That be good, muniferni. When I do tell your mam what you have said her belly will shake with laughing. Ho-ho-ho ! "

Len could not see the joke, and let his eyes follow the sheep-track winding its way down the mountain breast like a tortuous vein. He saw where it buried itself in the murk and hid as if ashamed of its eventual destination. It was just there, Len knew, that the grass ceased to be green.

Big Jim still showed no signs of moving, although the sun had already dipped half its red orb behind the mountain and was now sending scarlet gleams across the black blanket that was the valley's sky. Father and son gazed at the changing panorama in silence, their bodies tingling to the palpitating throb of the pit engines that came to them from below. Its vibrant rhythm broke through the air with the monotonous regularity of a ticking clock, and Len felt the vibration soak into his flesh. A muffled hum of voices muted in an incoherent chorus mingled with the throb.

For long minutes the pair lay while the glow from the dipping sun melted into the black pall and became a deeper red. At last Big Jim knocked the burning ashes from his pipe and rose to his feet. " Come," he commanded the entranced Len, " I got to see Dai Cannon, my butty, so we will go down the long way, past the pits." Len followed obediently, being always eager to get near the pit that stood at the top end of the valley.

Carefully threading their way down the steep path, they entered the belt of smoke and were soon standing at the foot of the mountain against which the grimy pit-head machinery, buildings, and gear stood out with grim grotesqueness.

Len's eyes widened at sight of the forbidding black power-houses and the lake of feeding water near them. A score of pipes with tiny holes intersected this latter and sent bubbling sprays of boiling water into the air, where each became a miniature rainbow before falling back into the lake.

Len could not take his eyes from this effervescent, sparkling cascade. " Is all the colours in the world by there, dad ? " he asked wonderingly.

Big Jim coughed and blew his nose. " Ay, I think they all be there, boy bach," he answered doubtfully. " But," he added, " you did ought to see it first thing in the morning when the sun be rising. Ah, that be a sight for sore eyes."

Len thought a moment before saying, " When I grow up and start to work I will be able to see it in the morning, 'on't I, dad ? "

" Ay, ay, my boy," answered Big Jim ; adding under his breath, " When you start to work you 'on't want to see it." Len did not hear this.

The thought of working in the pit sent ripples through his flesh and made him anxious to grow up quickly. He looked at the trellised iron-work of the pit-head frames, to which the power houses made such an appropriate background, and sighed longingly. The gleaming rail-tracks which radiated from the pit-head down the valley towards the invisible sea seemed, in his imaginative eyes, to be like veins of quickly coursing blood. Big Jim broke into his thoughts with the command, " Follow me, and be careful how you do tread."

Len followed the imprints of his father's feet in the powdery coal-dust which thickly coated everything. He passed great piles of logs, some of which were covered with reddish rough bark, while others, slippery and smooth, looked indecent in their nakedness. Big Jim replied to his query on the contrast : " Those big heavy uns, with bark, be Frenchmen. You know, those who do bring the onions every year," he exclaimed. " The other ones, that do look like wet sausages, be from Norway."

Without another word the pair made their way carefully past the numerous obstacles that cluttered the colliery surface. In a short time they reached the straddling pit-frames, whose huge wheeled heads broke into the dark shadows which sat on the red-streaked haze of smoke and steam surrounding the pit-shaft.

Big Jim allowed Len to look over the little gate into the cylindrical hole that seemed to dangle like a black blob from the wire ropes that threaded it. The immensity of the drop made the lad draw his breath sharply. It was the first time he had been so near to the shaft. Big Jim said, " Watch this now," and spat a mouthful of saliva half-way across the shaft, where it remained suspended for a moment before beginning its twisting fall into the hole that swallowed it from sight. Len watched it as long as he could, straining his eyes to follow the falling object into the depths of the pit.

His eyes became sore, and he turned to his father to ask in an awed voice : " How deep be it, dad ? "

The latter answered casually, " Oh, 'bout two thousand feet or thereabouts, I s'pose."

The lad stood amazed for a moment, then asked, " Be it the deepest pit in the world ? "

" Duw, duw, no," replied his father. " It be the deepest about here, but there be pits, mun, that do go down for miles in some parts of the world. I 'member myself," he continued reminiscently, " when I was in South Africa, a pit that go down half a mile. Of course," he added apologetically, " it be only niggers that do work down there ; us white men be the bosses."

Len thought deeply over this as they made their way towards the long wooden bridge that separated the pits from the rest of the valley. Half-way across he stopped and looked over the parapet at the oily river far below, which noisily gurgled in angry whirlpools around every rock that stemmed its progress. " It do look like it is quarrelling with itself," he commented. Big Jim said nothing, but led the way over the bridge to the long wooden building near its end, one half of which was a stable and the other half the home of Dai Cannon.

The lad felt his feet sink with a squelch into the dust-blackened manure that covered the ground. The stench of this and of hot horseflesh stung his nostrils after the clean air of the mountain. He sneezed, then stretched himself and peered through the little window into the stable. The sweaty horses stamping their feet and clanging their head-chains, thrilled him. He flattened his nose on the pane to get a better view, and would have remained there indefinitely had not Big Jim shouted sharply, " Come on, Len bach. You be hellish nosey to-day, in't you ? "

Len reluctantly left the window and followed his father to the doorway of the house. Jim rapped the door with his great knuckles. His knock was answered by a short, round-shouldered man with dark hair and a dough-coloured face. The heavy, dropping moustache that hung over his mouth failed to hide the thick, moist underlip. One hand was thrust down his trousers between the heavy belt and stomach, while his black-rimmed eyes gave the face a sepulchral appearance.

This was Dafydd Jones, known to all the workmen as Dai Cannon, a name given him because of his explosive eloquence. A self-taught man, he could quote the Bible chapter and verse, and although he spoke the idioms of the pit with his workmates, he possessed an extensive vocabulary that enabled him to talk on equal terms with anyone when the occasion demanded. Each Sunday he occupied the pulpit in the little tin chapel, and his rusty clothes redolent and shiny with the drippings from upturned tankards, did not detract from the pungent vehemence of his sermons.

Dai stepped into the manured roadway, where his pot-bellied rotundity and humped shoulders contrasted queerly with the erect bulk of Big Jim.

" Huh," he grunted, " I had give you up and was thinking to prepare my sermon for next Sunday. S'pose I will have to leave it there now that you have come at last." Jim gruffly started to explain the delay, but Dai airily brushed him aside with the remark : " Tut, tut. Don't waste your breath, mun, you will want it later on."

He invited Jim and Len into the wooden shack while he put his coat on, but the former refused. " Me and Len will wait by here," he declared. Dai did not argue the matter but went inside and shortly returned with his coat on.

The queerly contrasting trio then made their way to Main Street, that led from the pits down the hill to the village of Cwmardy. Main Street was the shopping and social centre of the village that had grown with the pits. It contained the few shops, the numerous chapels, and the three drinking-dens that the village boasted of. The turreted church was jostled on one side by the police-station and on the other by the Boar's Head public-house. There were no pavements, and the roads in winter were slimy with black mud, while during the summer they were heavy with powdered coal-dust.

Len had to quicken the pace of his short legs to keep up with his father and Dai. The occasional people they passed with a sibilant " Nos-da " salutation looked like black shadows in the deepening dusk of the unlit street. For some distance the three walked in silence before Dai muttered : " It do look as if they 'on't clear that fall for another couple of days, Jim." Len cocked his ears interestedly. Talk of the pits and work always excited him.

" No," replied Big Jim morosely, " and no bloody wonder. I never seen such a fall in all my born days. It come down like water, and nothing on earth could ever stop it. I was 'specting every minute to see the grass from the mountain mixed up in the stones."

Dai grunted acquiescence and added, " Ah well, it's a bad boot that have got no leather at all. You will be able to take the old 'ooman out and make up for what you done at the school opening yesterday."

Big Jim stopped and looked down at his mate in amazement. " Well, muniferni," he grunted, " that be a dirty back-hander ! After me saving you and Bill Bristol from simpling yourselves before all those people, you do turn round and blame me ! Huh," he spat into the road, " that be the thanks a man do get for looking after his butties."

Dai said nothing to the charge made against him, and the three proceeded on their way without further conversation until they reached the village square, in the centre of which was a brick structure known as " The Fountain," although the only water it ever held was that which fell on it from the clouds.

One corner of the Square was occupied by the general stores and bakehouse of Mr. Evans Cardi, while on the opposite side of the street stood the shop of Ben the Barber. This was where the villagers shed their hair and their viewpoints. It was the local parliament, where the problems of the pit and the village were debated by the miners.

Ben the Barber welcomed everyone to his shop. He had a tongue as sharp as his razors and delighted in provoking arguments among the men. This was not a difficult task, and Ben participated in the numerous debates with a kind of gleeful vindictiveness, pouncing with cunning skill upon all weak points.

Big Jim and Dai remained outside this shop for a little while before the former bent down to Len and asked, " Be you 'fraid to go home by yourself, Len bach ? " The lad looked at the dark opening at the side of the general stores. It led up the mountain at right-angles to Main Street until it reached the eight houses called Sunny Bank.

It was in one of these houses that Big Jim and his family lived. To Len the tiny twinkling lights from the windows looked like far-away stars.

He swallowed a nervous lump that had risen in his throat before replying, " No, dad, I be not afraid to go up by myself if you will wait by here till I be half-way."

" Good lad," replied Big Jim, digging his hand deep into his trousers pocket. " Here, take this ha'penny and me and Dai will wait till we know that you be safe." Without another word Len turned and started his way up the hill. The darkness swallowed him before he had taken ten strides.

Big Jim and his friend waited in silence until they heard a shrill long-drawn shout, " I be all right now, dad. So-long." Satisfied, both turned and walked into Ben the Barber's.

The echoes of Len's voice had hardly died in the night when its stillness was broken by another, harsh and piercing : " Len-n-n," it wailed, " where be you ? Come to your mam quick."

The lad recognised his mother's voice. " I be coming, mam," he shouted back reassuringly.

In a few minutes he reached the doorway of the house, where his mother awaited him, her head wrapped in a heavy woollen shawl. She had been on the point of searching for him when his voice reached her as he shouted to his father. She now caught the lad fussily to her and hurried him indoors. Here she removed the shawl that hid her haggard face and big-boned body, with its slightly stooping shoulders. Care-dulled eyes made her look older than she really was.

Len sat on the chair facing his sister, who was toasting bread before the open fire. " Where have you been so long, Len bach ? " asked his mother, her usually harsh voice now soft and husky. " Mam have been awful worried 'bout you." Len told her of the trip round the mountain and the pits. When he had finished the recital she asked sharply, " Where did your father go after you did leave him ? "

" They went into Ben the Barber's," replied Len, " and dad did say he 'ood'n't be long."

" Long, indeed," Shane snorted ; " it is time for every decent man who do think anything of his fambly to be in his own house this time of the night. Much he do think of his home and his children," she went on with rising temper, " to leave a little innocent boy like you to come up the black hill by yourself. How do he know," she demanded of no one in particular, " that you have not fall into the gutter and broked your little neck ? Huh ! Call hisself a father indeed ! "

Len said nothing. He looked at Jane, his sister, five years older than himself. Even in the candle-light she had a vague charm. Her fair, clustering hair enhanced the brightness of her eyes and the paleness of her thin face. Jane was her parents' first-born. She now rose to her feet and pulled the toasted bread off the fork, saying to her mother, " There now, mam fach, don't upset yourself. Dad will be home all right. Now jest sit down while I do make supper for you."

Len watched her take down the ill-assorted dishes from the huge box-like dresser that hid one side of the small kitchen. The cracked mirror in its centre grinned at the candle-light. One of the three shelves which constituted the dresser was filled with loose fortnightly volumes of "The History of the Boer War." These, despite their finger-soiled pages and torn covers, were sacred to the family. No visitor could leave the house without first being shown the three separate places in which the name of Big Jim was mentioned.

Big Jim had joined the militia just prior to Jane's birth and immediately the Boer War was declared had volunteered for active service, becoming batman to an officer whom he always declared to be a certain general.

Shane, left to take care of young Jane the best she could, washed and sewed clothes for other people. When Jim returned she had a home of sorts awaiting him, but the toil and worry of this period had left ineffaceable marks upon her body and her temper. Strong-willed and faithful, she was proud of the fact that her people belonged to the valley before the pits were ever thought of.

Jim had courted her with whirlwind impetuosity, his magnificent body sweeping away all her preconceived notions of love-making. Many people asserted that he ran away to the war to escape from Jane, the consequence of his courtship, but Jim always repudiated the suggestion with indignation and offered to fight anyone who repeated it.

After his return from the war Shane often begged him to " clean " her by marriage, but he always evaded this issue by asserting that the children tied him to her with stronger bonds than any marriage lines. Shane, however, never accepted this plea. She never tired of reminding him that he had " dirtied " her and was not man enough to do the right thing in the eyes of God. Big Jim, arrogant and tempestuous, feared nothing on earth except Shane in her tantrums.

Len waited patiently for his supper. He crouched nearer the large open fireplace that sent heat up the chimney and smoke into the kitchen. At last supper was ready, and the three drew their chairs to the table.

Meanwhile Big Jim and Dai Cannon had entered the shop of Ben the Barber. The lather boy, Charlie the Cripple, smiled widely at their appearance. The lad, being more or less a prisoner because of his disability, enjoyed the company of adults, and liked nothing better than to listen to the older wags exchanging reminiscences of the days when the valley was a place of wooded beauty with just one street, Sunny Bank, looking down upon it.

Charlie would sigh when the old men lauded the green-plastered slopes now buried beneath monstrous conical masses of pit residue. Some of them remembered the sewer-impregnated river, shining with oily outpourings from the pit, when it was a sparkling stream nursing trout in its cobbled bed. These tales were romance to the crippled lad, but he also liked to listen to the boisterous breeziness of Big Jim's quaintly spoken English

Everyone in the crowded and smoke-filled room moved up when the newcomers entered. Ben the Barber paused, holding an open razor over the lathered face of Will Small-beer. When the pair were seated Ben coughed before saying, as he went on shaving his customer, " To continue where I left off when we were interrupted, stupid as you workmen are, you nevertheless provide the real power in the world to-day. I know," he added quickly, his sharp, thin voice rising when he saw Dai Cannon squirming on the bench, " that no one looking at your dull faces would believe this. But there, seeing is not always believing."

Will Smallbeer rubbed his nose vigorously with the back of his hand. " What in hell be you talking about, mun ? " he croaked hoarsely. " Do you mean to tell us that old T. I. Williams, the coalowner, who have now been made Lord Cwmardy, have got no power or brains ? Tut ! Where be your bloody sense, mun ? Look at Mr. Hicks, our general manager. Do you say that he be not a clever man ? Huh ! Where be the power of a man who do work in the pit all the week and then haven't got 'nough to have couple of pints on a Saturday after he pay his lodgings ? Huh ! " he snorted in conclusion and with a triumphant glance around. " If you do call that bloody sense, I give in."

Ben turned to Dai Cannon with a sneering smile. " There," he said, " the oracle has spoken and he's knocked you all flat."

Dai knew the symptoms and accepted the challenge. He gave a retching cough, wiped the product into the sanded floor with his boot, then spoke in a ponderous voice. " Power and brains are not the monopoly of any people or class," he said. " We must admit there are some brains among the masters, and certainly a lot of power, but there are also brains with some of the workmen, although they have no power. Take myself or Ezra Jones, our leader," he went on. " Both of us are workmen and both of us are clever. This doesn't mean, however, that all workmen or all masters are clever. You have only to look at Will Smallbeer to see that."

The latter jumped to his feet with a snarl. " Don't you try to simple a better man than yourself can ever be," he shouted. Little lumps of saliva mixed with the lather on his moustache. " I might look a bit tup to you beggars," he continued, " but I can hold my own with any of you in the pit."

Big Jim immediately bridled up at this. He was regarded as the strongest and best-skilled man in the pit, and took pride in the fact. " What nonsense you be talking, Will bach," he growled patronisingly. " Why, mun, I could work the hands off ten men like you any bloody day, muniferni, and you do all know it well. There be no man in Cwmardy can take a tool out of my hands."

Ben swept his razor across the strop as if he was slicing a man's head off. " Huh," he grunted. " Hark at the brains oozing out ! There'll be a hell of a mess on my floor after this unless you're more careful. Here you are, bragging how clever you are, and all you can brag about is how much work you do. Ha-ha ! Not a word about the money you get for your work ! Now I know why you come to me on Sunday mornings for a haircut and shave on tick. It's men like you the masters want. Give them men with brains from their shoulders down and they have no need for any brains themselves. Ha-ha ! Huh, you make me sick." Saying which he spat contemptuously on the floor.

There was silence for a while after this outburst before Bill Bristol, his thin face quivering, took up the argument. " There be'ant no need to get excited," he declared. " To me it seems us have got to have masters and us have got to have workmen. Without masters us cawn't have pits, without pits us cawn't have wages, and without wages us cawn't have beer and baccy and grub. That's how I see the business," he concluded. The argument continued for some time longer until Big Jim and Dai left to make their way across the road to the Boar's Head.

Long before his father had left the beer-stenched bar Len was curled up in the bed he shared with Jane. He watched her slowly undressing, his own small body hidden beneath the bed-clothes. In many ways he was a queer lad for his age. He had neither the physique nor the desire to participate in the boisterous games of the neighbouring boys. His greatest pal was Jane and his greatest pleasure he found in the occasional rambles over the mountain with his father. Apart from this, his natural tendency to introspection made him seek solitude, where he could allow his vivid imagination to wander without interruption.

These practices made him older than his years, and he

thought more than he spoke. He was, however, devoted to his parents. He loved and respected his mother's quaint, affectionate firmness and thought his father only one step removed from God and Bob Fitzsimmons the fighter.

As he watched Jane undressing his mind again traversed the mountains. He wondered how many were really killed in the battle his father had mentioned, and if it were true that the grass was dyed with blood ever since. Drowsily he moved up for Jane and nestled closely to her warm body. Imperceptibly he floated from thought to thought until he was suddenly brought back to the bedroom by a loud rattle at the front door. He sprang to his haunches in alarm, but lay down again when he heard his mother patter to the door to open it for Big Jim.

Jim looked worried and irritable as he made his way past Shane into the kitchen. He sat heavily on the stool near the fire and looked around slowly. The flickering candle-light sent hot grease down the sides of the brass holder. The dimness got on Jim's nerves.

" I'n't there no oil in the house, Shane bach," he asked, " that you have got to use corpse lights ? " Shane paid no heed to his surly question. In a short while he continued, " Here I be in the dark of the pit all day and now I can't get light in my own house. Muniferni ! No wonder men do go to the 'sylum before their time." He spat into the fire. Shane heard the spittle sizzle in the flames.

A few minutes' silence followed before Jim asked, "Where be our Jane ? Out gallivanting, I s'pose," he answered himself.

Shane replied sharply, " No, she be not out. The gel is in bed, where you ought to be long ago instead of sitting on your backside in other people's places, then coming home here full of grunts."

She paused a moment, swallowed hard, then went on with increasing bitterness. " That's how all you men be. Always thinking of your own comforts. Never do you think of me, slaving my fingers to the bone trying to keep the children tidy and the house clean."

Jim made no reply.   He was sorry now for what he had
said, because he knew Shane was getting into her stride.
He stretched his long body towards the table and picked up
a piece of toast.   Before he could recover his position the
stool overbalanced and he lay ignominiously on the sanded
floor with his head under the table.   This was too much
for his dignity.   " Argllwydd mawr, venw ! " he roared as he
scrambled to his feet.   " Be you trying to kill me or what,
pulling the stool from under me like that ?   Do you think I
be a crot of a boy to be played with, eh ? "

Shane gave him a blistering glare before muttering in a
gloomy tone, as if she were pronouncing a curse : " Sure as
God is your judge, James, you will be sorry for your words
one day.   You sit by there like a great bear and do not
move a finger to help me or yourself.   Not satisfied with
this, when you be too drunk to sit on the stool you put the
blame on me for falling off it.   Ach," she continued, her
voice rising higher with every sentence, " out all night I
ought to leave you.   That 'ood be good enough for the likes
of you.   Fine man you be, indeed, to rear a fambly of
children who haven't got a shirt to their little backs while
you do spend your money in the public-house and put silks
and satins on that slut of a landlady."

Big Jim shook his head at this sneer and started to plead.
" Leave me alone, Shane bach," he begged ; " don't go on
to me no more now."

" Don't go on to you, indeed," retorted Shane, continuing
her indictment.   " Oh, God bach," she wailed into the air
" what for did I ever take a man like this ?   Here I be, day
in and day out, trying to rear my children clean and
'spectable so that no one can point a finger at them, and
after it all this lout do bring disgrace and shame on us all.
Oh dear, dear, what have I done ? "   She turned to Big
Jim with flashing eyes.   " Pity the good Lord didn't strike
you dead when you was in Africa ! " she cried.

Her last words brought tears to Len's eyes.   He heard
no more after this and knew his father had fallen to sleep in
the chair.   The lad cuddled closer to Jane and was himself

asleep when Shane crept upstairs for blankets with which to cover her snoring spouse.

Her naked feet squashed the black beetles that plastered the kitchen floor at night, but she paid no heed to these as she again ascended the stairs to her bedroom.

CHAPTER II

Len goes to School

LEN woke earlier than usual next morning. He sat up in bed and shook Jane by the shoulder. "Come, Jane," he said, "I've got to start school to-day and it be time for us to get up."

Jane slowly shook the sleep from her eyes in response to his request. She rose and dressed while he remained squatting in bed. When she had finished they both proceeded downstairs, Len clad only in his shirt. The contact of the cold stone stairs with his bare feet sent shivers up his spine, and he was glad to get near the kitchen fire. Big Jim and Shane were already down, the latter busily preparing breakfast.

Half-way through the meal Big Jim, his mouth full of toasted bread, muttered to Len. "Well, boy bach, you be a big man to-day, starting school, eh?" The lad merely nodded his head in reply. He was not over-excited at the prospect of attending the school which had been built across the gutter that separated Sunny Bank from the village. He had spent much of his time in this gutter, driving tunnels into its sides at the risk of his life under the impression that he was acting like a collier. Or sometimes, for a change, he had transformed the hole into a "tent," by simply putting a piece of sacking across its mouth, and on these occasions he would peer carefully through the sacking to look for imaginary Red Indians.

During the winter, snow often filled the gutter, and Len loved to impress his " photo " in its soft, alluring surface by lying prostrate in the snow with his arms and legs spread-eagled. This made him soaking wet, a fact that disturbed Shane much more than it did her son, but all her pleadings

18

and threats had failed to rob the lad of this exquisite pleasure, and now the school had effaced his beloved gutter.

After breakfast Jane helped Len to dress in the new velvet suit specially bought for the occasion. The blue material showed up the boyishness of his long face and clustering brown hair. Shane's eyes filled with tears as she looked at the lad. Pride in her son quickened the beats of her heart and, turning to Big Jim, she remarked : " Duw. Our boy do look fine to-day, don't he, James bach ? "

" Ay," replied her spouse. " He do that, my gel. But what can you expect from the son of Big Jim, eh ? " And twirling his moustaches arrogantly, he continued : " Some day you will be so good a man as your father, Len bach, and that be saying something, i'n't it, Shane ? " turning to his partner.

The flattery helped to lift Len out of his despondent mood, and his spirits became more in accord with the boisterous excitement of the other lads who accompanied him down the hill for the first day at the new school. His dislike of the building that had robbed him of the pleasures of the gutter was permeated with a faint curiosity. He wondered what would be expected of him in the school. But neither Jane nor any or the inhabitants could enlighten him, because this was the valley's first school.

When Len reached the school-yard he was paraded with the other children and marched into the class-room. He was surprised to find girls present. This possibility had never entered his mind, and the fact made him resentful, an emotion which increased when he found that the teacher was a young woman who did not look much older than Jane.

The lad was told to sit at the same desk as Ron, the son of Mr. Evans Cardi, who, as Len later found out, was about the same age as himself. But all resemblance between the two lads ended there. Ron was robust, ruddy, and well-fed. He kept boasting to Len with boyish candour that his father only intended him to remain at the school until he was old enough to go to college. Len was suitably thrilled at this information, although he had not the slightest idea what a college was. His initial nervousness had evaporated in the bright freshness of the class-room, with its interesting pictures of battles and kings.

During the days that passed Len took a greater interest in his class-mates. Among them was one who particularly attracted his attention. Her sombre eyes, frail body, and dark, wavy hair fascinated him, and he discovered that she was Mary, the daughter of Ezra Jones, the miners' leader in Cwmardy.

In the months that followed Len proved he had a capacity for absorbing his lessons. He was particularly fond of history, and revelled in the stories of the conquest of India and America by the British. But nothing gave him greater pleasure than to read and hear of the Boer War. He felt he had a living link with this through his father. His natural quickness soon took him ahead of the other pupils with the exception of Mary, who in a quiet, unobtrusive way, seemed to devour the lessons and tenaciously retain all the knowledge she gathered. The mutual mental alertness brought the two youngsters into closer bonds of friendship, and often, accompanied by Ron, they spent the evenings after school hours scouring the mountains for birds' nests. Sometimes the two lads failed to present themselves for school although they had left home for this purpose, and on such occasions they would go for long rambles through the murk of the valley into the clear air of the country a few miles away.

Once away from the valley and the school Len and Ron, with boyish exuberance, thrilled to the joys of exploration. The fact they were missing school without their parents' knowledge or consent put an edge to the pleasure they found in exploring the many noisy little streams. Sometimes they caught little tiddlers which they proudly imagined were trout, and with a kind of patronising pride they always showed these to Mary, who refused to accompany them on their illicit expeditions.

One day, unknown to Len, the schoolmaster sent for Shane, who, donning her woollen shawl, obeyed the request with some trepidation. At the school gates she paused a while to gather her breath before entering, her mind full of queries.

It appeared that the master had been waiting for Shane, because immediately she knocked at the door he opened it for her. " Good day, Mrs. Roberts," he said, his face grimmer than usual. " Come in." The manner of his invitation increased Shane's nervousness. She sensed that it had something to do with Len, but had no idea what it could be.

After ushering Shane to the chair opposite the master seated himself at the desk and immediately came to the point. " I have asked you down, Mrs. Roberts," he said, " to discuss Len, your son."

Shane stiffened a little in the chair, but made no reply. " Yes," he went on, " I am very worried about him." He looked at her quizzically for a moment before saying : " I hope I am right in believing that you want him to be a good scholar and a credit to yourself, his father, and the school, Mrs. Roberts ? "

The flustered woman nodded her head dumbly. " I thought so," asserted the master ; " and, this being the fact, I cannot understand why Len loses school so often."

Shane bridled up immediately at this. " Lose school ? " she asked incredulously. " Who do say my boy lose school ? Why, he be here every day like a clock ever since he started. Huh ! Be very careful what you do say, my man ! 'Member there be still a law, even for the poor."

Mr. Vincent, the master, was taken aback for a moment by this indignant outburst. When he had recovered he tried to placate her. " Now, now, Mrs. Roberts," he exclaimed, " there is no need to get excited or angry. You have confirmed my suspicions that Len has been absenting himself from school without your knowledge."

Shane's lower jaw dropped in astonishment, but after some seconds she snapped her teeth together. " I don't believe my boy 'ood do such a thing," she asserted definitely. " I 'oodn't believe no man, not even if he went down on his bended knees before my eyes."

There could be no mistaking that all argument would be futile, and the schoolmaster said no more. He rose and left the room. In a very short time he returned with Len at his side, obviously frightened. Shane drew the lad to her and both of them stood facing Mr. Vincent. Len looked scared, but his mother's whole demeanour was defiant. " Well," she demanded, " what do you want, now you have got my boy here ? "

Mr. Vincent looked at Len. His eyes were hard and cold. " Tell your mother," he said, " where you were yesterday." Len shuddered at the question and his face went white. The silence became heavy and the room oppressive to mother and son. Shane's eyes misted during the prolonged silence, but her cheek muscles twitched although no word was said till Mr. Vincent instructed Len to go back to the class-room. The boy shivered coldly as the door closed behind him. Slowly, with his head bent, he took his seat in the class, blind to the eyes that stared at him curiously.

At the first opportunity Ron whispered, " What was the matter, Len ? "

" It is about our mitching from school yesterday," the downcast Len replied. " My mother is in the master's room."

Ron chuckled, " Yes, I know," he said, " the master was in our house last night, but my father told him not to worry because I wouldn't be here much longer."

This was small consolation to Len, who was conjecturing what was happening between his mother and the master. He paid little attention to what the teacher was saying during the next ten minutes, but lifted his head with a start when he heard the door open.

Mr. Vincent stood framed in the doorway, his face grim and hard. He carried a long cane in his hands, the sight of which fascinated Len. He wondered if his mother had gone home, and hope kindled in his heart as he thought she might have remained in the master's room.

The boy hardly heard the harsh command, " Len Roberts,

come out here. Let the whole class see you." When he responded, he seemed to rise from his seat without personal volition, and equally automatic was his stride as he walked to the front of the class. Something cold clutched at his heart. He knew with increasing certainty that he was about to be punished before all his schoolmates.

Never in his life had he been physically beaten, and the immediate probability that it was about to happen appalled him. Only five yards separated him from the master who had become his tormentor, but it appeared five years to the lad as he slowly walked forward. He tried to shout for his mother, but no sound left his mouth. His face was strained and set when at last he reached the master's side, who turned him round to face the class. Len kept his head down, and Mr. Vincent began to address the pupils.

" You see before you," he said, " a boy who has lied to his mother, not in words but in deeds. He led her to believe he was coming to school when he already knew he had no intention of doing so." The silence in the class-room was made more deadly by the sharp voice.

" What can you think of a boy who deludes his best friend, his mother ? " the master went on remorselessly. Each word stung Len like a lash. He felt they were unfair and untrue. All he had done was in a spirit of adventure, with no thought of lying, and the consciousness of this steeled him and determined him not to cry.

As Mr. Vincent went on, " A boy who can do a thing like this will grow up a vagabond and a man without honour unless he is checked in time," Len looked at Mary, and her eyes seemed to shine with disbelief as she returned his glance.

The master ended his homily with the words, " Hold your hand out, Roberts," and Len dazedly did as he was bade, his eyes fixed on the rising cane.

He saw it suddenly stop ascending and heard it swish as it swept down upon his outstretched hand. Without conscious thought he withdrew his hand a split second before the cane reached it. The stick met Mr. Vincent's shin-bone

with a resounding thwack, and he clutched the injured
limb. Suddenly Ron began laughing, and in a few seconds
all the children in the room had followed suit. The teacher
vainly shouted for order, fluttering between the seats
and cuffing everyone who came within her reach, but Len
remained standing, aghast at what he had done. He looked
apologetically at Mr. Vincent as the latter continued to rub
his leg. Then suddenly, without a word of warning, the
master began to slash the cane across the boy's face,
heedless of where the blows fell.

The children's laughter died as suddenly as it had started.
Each of them watched with increasing childish horror
the flash of the quivering cane as it rose, to fall in quicker
and heavier slashes. Mary rose to her feet and shouted,
" Stop it, you coward ! Hit someone as big as yourself."

After the first unexpected blow on his face, Len bent his
head, only to feel the back of his neck burn with the next
slash of the cane. Spontaneously his hands went to his
head. The burning pain spread from his neck to his
knuckles, and in a short time his whole body felt as if it
were on fire. Whimpering and only half-conscious of what
he was doing, Len staggered about in an effort to escape the
twirling cane. " Oh, mam, mam," he shouted, " come
and stop him ! He's killing me ! " In the pain of the
blows he failed to see Mary fling an ink-bottle at Mr. Vincent. It caught him behind the ear, and the ink spattered
all over his face and collar. Spluttering with anger, the
master stopped chastising Len, and slowly wiping his hand
over his face, looked around at the class. Every pupil sat
motionless and every eye looked straight in front. Mr.
Vincent started forward towards the boy nearest him,
hesitated a moment, then, without another word or glance,
left the room.

Immediately the master had left the children jumped on
the seats and desks, singing and shouting, and it was a considerable time before the harassed teacher could restore
quiet. Throughout the hub-bub, however, Len remained
silent. He was wondering if his mother had authorised the

beating, and the very suspicion, although it was unfounded, hardened the lad and determined him to say nothing to his family. He felt he was doubly hurt, by the cane and by his mother, for before he left the school for home he was firmly convinced that his mother knew what the master had done, and the thought stung him much more than the cane.

Len's mother did not speak to him that night, and he went to bed earlier than usual. His mind was a turmoil of emotions that kept him turning and tossing for hours. He saw the school in a new light. It had become a monster that was going to rob him of his mountain rambles and the free existence he was accustomed to, and memory of the hiding he had received filled him with a hot resentment. For hours his brain was confused with conflicting thoughts, until imperceptibly they became focused on chains. He saw chains all round him. They seemed to hold him down and fetter his every movement, and he broke into perspiration. He thought of books. They floated before his eyes through the links in the chains, in a multiplicity of shapes and colours, and he saw in the open, flashing pages pictures of ships and engines, cowboys and kings. The fast-moving leaves slowed down and changed to canes. Long, sinewy sticks that bent and twanged. They fell on his back with stinging slashes at each of which they quivered and hummed with laughter. He jumped up in bed shouting, " Oh, mam, mam, stop him. He will kill me ! "

Shane rushed into his bedroom and caught him in her arms. " There, there, boy bach," she crooned into his ear, " don't cry no more at those old dreams. Mam be with you, and you can venture you be safe so long as her eyes be open." She remained with the lad till he fell asleep.

In the weeks that followed Len came to hate the school and everything connected with it. Despite this, at the end of the first year he shared top place with Mary. He read his report sheet to his parents that evening.

Big Jim and Shane were rather awed by this educational achievement of their son. Jim prophesied that one day Len would be a " big scholar."

" Ay," replied Shane, " I knowed that before he started school. Let us hope he 'ont forget his poor old mam and dad when he be up in the world."

Jim snorted at this. He regarded it as a reflection upon himself. " What ? " he exclaimed. " Think you that the son of Jim the Big will ever forget his people and his butties ? Never on your life, my gel."

Shane looked at him sharply, then said, " You do know full well, James, that my words did have no such meaning as you do put into them. But there," she added, " talking to you be like talking to a sledge. I do only waste my time by saying anything to you."

She turned to Len before the surprised Jim could reply. " You must keep pitching in, my boy," she told him ; " then perhaps one day you will win a scholarship and go to college like Ron, although his father be paying for him."

Len looked at her with alarm in his eyes. " No, mam," he said slowly, " I don't want to go to any schools after I finish this one. What I want is to go to work with dad in the pit as soon as I be old enough."

" That be the spirit ! " declared Jim. Shane only sighed.

CHAPTER III

The Chapel Excursion to the Seaside

USUALLY on Sundays Jane woke Len early. The whole family, with the exception of Big Jim, regularly attended the service in the little tin chapel at the end of the street on the Sabbath. The services were conducted by Dai Cannon, and Len enjoyed them.

He liked to see the preacher's moustaches quiver as he thundered of blood and brimstone. It was known to all the villagers that Dai's sermons were always better and his vehemence greater the more beer he had consumed on the Saturday night.

His lurid language and flowing eloquence always lifted his listeners into ecstasies of fervour, which found vent in the singing of hymns. The blended harmony of the voices gave Len special pleasure, although the hymns often saddened him.

One Sunday at the conclusion of the service, Mr. Evans Cardi, who was the senior deacon, announced that the chapel anniversary fell during the following week.

" We expect," he stated, in his ponderous manner, " that all our brothers and sisters with their children will attend for the procession through the streets. We shall take our collecting boxes with us and all the money we gather will go towards our excursion to the seaside in the summer."

This announcement was received with great excitement by the congregation. During the few days that remained before the anniversary the womenfolk patched and cleaned their dresses in readiness. Those who could afford it bought new ones.

When the great day arrived Shane arrayed herself in the black cape she had bought twenty years before. This and

27

Big Jim's " best suit " were only brought from their hiding-place in the box under the bed for special events. Jane dressed herself in a flower-patterned linen frock whose simplicity set off the firm beauty of her body. Excitement put a colour in her cheeks and a glow in her eyes that outdid the colours in her dress.

The two women, Len accompanying them, made their way to the little chapel, where most of the other people were already gathered in little groups, chatting and slyly eyeing the dresses of the new-comers.

Len's inquisitive eyes were immediately attracted to the great silk banner that rested against the wall. Imprinted in yellow on its scarlet background was the representation of an angel looking with piteous eyes upon a box that looked like a horse-trough. Above this touching scene were the words " Cwmardy Primitive Methodist Church " and beneath it " Glory be to God."

The preliminaries were soon completed. Four young men took the banner and carried it to the front. Dai Cannon and the deacons fell in immediately behind, followed by the remainder of the congregation. The procession of brightly clothed figures made a pretty sight as it slowly wound its way round the village. In each street it stopped and sang hymns to the people who filled the doorways, and who always gave liberally to the collectors when they came round after the singing.

Before the procession had gone far the light frocks and pinafores were soiled and smudged in the smoke-infested atmosphere. But no one paid any attention to this, least of all Len and Ron, who walked together.

Having circled all the streets in the village, the procession made its way towards the long drive which led to the Big House where Mr. Hicks, the general manager of the pits, lived. This was in the centre of a wooded patch on the mountain breast. It overlooked the valley and the pits. Lord Cwmardy had originally built it for his own use, but had let it as the official residence of the pit manager after his own elevation to the peerage.

Len looked in amazement at the huge house, with its verandas and rolling lawns. He was intrigued by the lake that glistened a little lower down in the grounds.

" I wonder if ships could sail on that ? " he asked Ron.

" Of course they can," replied the latter in a contemptuous whisper, " it's over a hundred feet deep. I know because my father told me."

They had no time for further conversation before the signal was given and the choristers lifted their voices to the lilting hymn which always saddened Len. Mr. Hicks' housekeeper and a number of young people listened from the veranda to the singing. When several tunes had been sung the housekeeper flung down a shilling and ceremoniously shepherded her charges into the house.

On the way home Len heard one of the men who had carried the banner say to his mate : " Stingy old cow! She's well in with Hicks, and I bet he gave her more than that, only the mean bitch kept it for herself." Len edged away from the conversation.

Big Jim was awaiting them when they arrived home. He had supper already laid. Anniversary day was the only one in the year when he regarded it as an obligation upon himself to remain in and watch the house. Although he never went to chapel himself he had a deep respect for the opinions of those who did, which was one of the reasons why he was so attached to Dai Cannon.

The long trudge had tired Len, and he was not sorry when bed-time came and he ascended the stairs with Jane. The fatigue left him when he lay down and the excitement of the day began to quicken his blood. He watched Jane undressing. His eyes shone with unusual interest. For the first time he consciously noticed that Jane's breasts were different from his, and wondered why this was so. He knew his mother had big breasts because he had seen them when she was suckling the little brother who had since died of fits. But this did not solve the problem that was now consuming Len. Jane had not had a baby like his mother, yet her breasts were big.

When the young girl came into bed he cuddled up to her, and soon fell to sleep with his hand on her bosom and his mind full of queries.

The spring imperceptibly floated into summer and the day for the chapel excursion drew nearer. The children became restless with excitement. Shane had insisted that Big Jim should remain home from work on this day " out of respect to the chapel and the children " as she cogently remarked to him. There had been no argument against this, and the whole family became embroiled in the preparations. Shane did the necessary patching, sewing, washing, and pressing. Jane cleaned the house from top to bottom, including the rarely used parlour. Big Jim slyly put aside each week little sums of money of which Shane knew nothing.

Len failed to sleep the night preceding the eagerly awaited day, and responded immediately Shane called him at six o'clock. Excitedly shaking Jane before leaving the bed, he hurried downstairs, where he found his mother preparing breakfast while Big Jim shaved. The latter was nearly bent in two trying to catch a glimpse of his face in the tiny cracked mirror which was the only one in the house.

During breakfast Big Jim kept on making humorous remarks. " It's a lovely fine day for the 'scursion," he said, looking out of the window at the sun trying to force its way through the clouds of smoke and dust from the pits. " Like old times," he added turning to Shane, " when you and me was courting, eh ? Ha-ha ! " He laughed happily. " Do you 'member the outings we used to have then, Shane bach ?" he asked. Before she could reply he turned to Jane and Len with the remark, " Them was the days. Never will be any like them again. Your mam was worth looking at then." He caught Shane's eyes and hurriedly continued, " Not that she be bad looking now, mind you. Only in those days she did have your wavy hair, Len, and her face was 'xactly like Jane's do look now. Eh ? What say you, Shane bach ? " he inquired.

The latter said nothing, although the subtle flattery brought a gleam to her tired eyes.

After breakfast Jim made his way towards the stairs with a mumbled, " Well, I 'spose I must go up the bedroom now to fetch my best boots." His attempt to appear casual was hopelessly lost in the mumbled words.

Shane hastily interjected, " No, no, James bach. There be no need for you to go up. Jane will fetch the boots for you."

Jim gave her a scared look, then pulled himself together to say with heavy dignity : " What think you I be, venw ? Think you I do want a crot of a gel to tend on me ? No, thank you, I will manage to tend on myself." He proceeded up the stairs while Shane put the finishing touches to Len's dressing and Jane cleared the table.

Some little time later, when they were all ready, a noise overhead reminded them that Big Jim was still upstairs. Shane flurriedly called out : " Come on, James. You be a long time putting on your boots, i'n't you ? We will be late unless you do hurry up." A wicked little pucker twisted her mouth when she added as an afterthought : " You haven't lost anything, have you ? "

Back came the answer in a gruff, shaking rumble : " Lost, muniferni ? Lost ? What think you I have got to lose, venw ? "

The shuffling went on for a little time longer, and Shane was on her way up the stairs when they heard Jim slowly and heavily descending. His white face was haggard when he entered the kitchen and the ends of his moustache drooped pitifully. The buoyant spirits that had preceded his entry into the bedroom had been left there.

No one said a word as Shane straightened his tie and brushed the dust from the knees of his best trousers. Jim submitted meekly, although the flesh on his cheeks twitched as if invisible strings were drawing it into tiny knots. Little drops of perspiration dripped from his chin on to the high collar, which he had only worn as a special concession to maintain the dignity of the family in the eyes of the chapel deacons.

Having made all ready, Shane took a final look around the
2*

kitchen. Satisfied with what she saw, she dug her hand into the bosom of her dress and pulled out a purse. Carefully concealing its contents from Big Jim, she withdrew some silver, which she handed him with the remark : " Here, take this, James bach, not for you to go 'bout with your finger in your mouth to-day."

Jim looked at the money in his hand. His eyes were bulged and glassy. A deep suspicion began to shape in his mind that this was the money he had been looking for but failed to find. He half opened his mouth as if about to say something, then closed it again with an audible snap.

Swallowing back the lump in his throat, he caught Len by the hand and gruffly said, " Come on or we will lose the train."

It was over two miles to the little railway station, but the little family, each one consumed with different thoughts and emotions, covered the distance before they were aware of it.

At the station they fell into the long queue of people who were slowly filing past the two chapel deacons at the doorway, who exchanged their vouchers for tickets.

Big Jim kept mumbling to himself at the delay. Shane asked, " What be the matter with you, mun ? Do you 'spect the deacons to deal special with you and let you go on in front of all the people who have been here before you ? "

Big Jim made no reply other than to glance at her with glaring eyes. Shane took no notice of his surliness.

She caught Len's hand and bent down to murmur in his ear, " Your father be in a awful state all of a sudden, i'n't he ? "

Len had noticed nothing out of the way but answered, " Perhaps he be bad, mam." Shane chuckled wickedly at this.

In a short time they passed the deacons and entered the little hut which was the railway station. It was packed with people, bags, and baskets. Each family carried its own provisions for the day. The excitement in the crowded room affected the little children. The bigger ones laughed and chattered, while the babies struggled and cried in the woollen shawls which held them to their mothers' bodies. Numerous breasts were openly exposed as women tried to quiet the cries. The atmosphere became increasingly hot and moist as the people overflowed from the tin hut on to the platform.

Shane suddenly missed Jane. Urging Len and Jim to follow her, she went out and paraded up and down the platform until she eventually found her daughter and Evan the Overman's son sitting close together on a fish barrow.

Near them a number of young men were playing " devil's cards " as Shane called them. She turned Len away from the scene and called Jane to her with the words : " Come from there, Jane. I'n't you shamed of yourself, sitting there brazen as brass ? Time 'nough for you to sit with men in a railway station when you be married." Jane pouted, but obeyed and left the young man sitting sheepishly alone.

The people began fussily to gather their bags, baskets, and children in readiness for the train that was now due. It arrived puffing and blowing as though impressed by its own importance. The wooden-seated carriages were soon full of perspiring people. Young couples sat on each other's knees while the older children sat on the floor.

After much running about by railway officials, who were unaccustomed to so much traffic, the train slowly rattled out of the station.

Len remained standing at the window, his nose pressed flat against the cool glass that soon was streaming with moisture. He watched the country fly past, while miles of coal wagons seemed to float by like a river.

It was the first time he had ever left his home in the valley, and the amazing newness of the experience, together with the splendour of the ever-changing countryside, made him oblivious to the terrific heat in the over-laden carriage.

The train ran some distance along the coast before reaching its destination. The vista of sea and ships thus exposed sent Len's blood coursing madly.

Never before had he seen ships, and his only sight of the

sea had been the glimpses he occasionally had from the mountain-top of its glistening ribbon-like winding round the coast. Its close proximity now gripped him like a dream. When the train arrived at the seaside station the sweat-soaked people poured out on the platform as if emptied from a steaming oven. Little children howled in the misery of damp clothes as their already wearied parents hurried them through the irritating sands to the beach. Here everyone sat down. The glare of the sun, flung back by the sea, blinded pit-darkened eyes for a while and forced tears where none were meant.

A nearby steam organ started to play. It filled the hot air with raucous noise, but the people soon caught its vague refrain and accompanied it with lusty singing. This stimulated their flagging spirits, and in a short time the receding tide was followed by bare-footed adults and children.

Big Jim and his family spread a newspaper on the sand and began eating the food that Shane had packed. Len thought he had never tasted anything so delicious, although the sand gritted in the tinned meat and bread beneath his teeth. After the meal Len commenced undressing. He wanted to play naked in the water, but Shane stopped him. " Duw, duw, boy bach," she asked, " do you want to catch your death of cold ? "

The disappointed lad had to be content with paddling his stockingless feet. He played at this for some hours, his eyes longingly wandering across the waves whose edges swirled in cooling bubbly frothiness about his legs. He sensed the power of the ever-recurring sweep and felt an aching urge to ride its crests and hollows, which he mentally likened to his beloved hills and vales. The illimitable distance of the rolling sea awed him, and he wondered what the horizon was hiding. The occasional black stripes on its surface, which he knew were ships, seemed to cling to the dim distance as if stuck there.

His mother called him away from his thoughts and he returned to where his parents and Jane were sprawling on the sand. Shane wiped the moisture from his legs with the newspaper they had used as a table-cloth. Big Jim rose ponderously to his feet and announced he was going for a walk. Shane knew where he was going, but, since it was a holiday, contented herself with saying : " All right. Take care of yourself, and watch you o'n't get drunk. Member the deacons be all eyes."

Jim glanced back and replied : " You trust me for that, my gel. Think you I have got no sense, mun ? Huh ! " Saying which he went on his way and was soon lost to sight.

Jim had been gone some time when Jane asked her mother if she also could take a stroll. " Certainly," answered Shane. " You have been a good gel, to-day. But mind you don't go far." Jane rose, arranged her disordered dress, and casually strolled off, the sun playing on her fair hair and pink-clad body.

For some time after the departure of the pair Len lay motionless at his mother's side, his mind still centred on the ships he wanted to explore. He noticed that they all made their slow way past the headland that jutted into the sea on the right. Wondering if they were all gathered there, he suddenly sat up.

" What be the matter with you, boy bach ? " his mother inquired.

" I wish Ron was here," was his enigmatic reply.

Shane looked at him a moment in bewilderment before asking, " Why, Len bach, i'n't you satisfied to have your old mam with you ? "

Len felt the reproach in her voice and hastened to explain that if Ron were present they could walk across to the headland that hid the ships. Shane sensed his mood and struggled to her feet, saying, " Come, my boy, you and me can walk so far as that. Huh ! I 'member the time I could walk thirty miles without flinching and then carry a sack of coal from the tip."

Len joyfully jumped to his feet. He picked up the empty basket and followed his mother through the soft sand that soon filled their boots and burned their feet. It was late in the afternoon and the sun, free of clouds, focused its rays upon the beach with sleep-inducing intensity. Len's youthful exuberance, however, invigorated Shane. They steadily plodded around the recumbent people who sprawled about the shore. In half an hour they had left the sands behind and were walking alongside the golf-links and green-clad dunes. Courting couples took advantage of the seclusion offered by the latter.

Len's enthusiasm kept him ahead of Shane, even though her feet were now free from encumbering sand. He peeped into the dunes. What he saw set his brain whirling with questioning thoughts. He remembered Jane undressing and saw her panting breasts. The conjured picture sent little tickling ripples through his flesh. He thought he had unravelled the problem of the difference between girl's breasts and his own. What he had seen demonstrated that the former were larger so that men could play with and caress them.

This train of thought robbed his feet of direction and he wandered aimlessly from dune to dune, his musings accelerated by the occupants of each. Immersed in a tumult of emotions, Len paid no further heed to his surroundings until he stumbled sharply and heard a small scream followed by a flash of something white. Thus suddenly brought to himself, he glanced into the dune over whose edge he had nearly tumbled, and saw a young girl twist hurriedly from the embracing arms of her companion while she vainly tried to hide a pink garment behind her back. The lad's eyes were drawn to the disarranged dress that partially exposed the warm breast which the young man had been caressing. Len looked at the white face and recognised his sister.

An instantaneous stab like a hot flame burned through his body, bringing tears to his eyes. For a moment he remained motionless, then burst out, " Oh, Jane bach, what be you doing ? " His embarrassed sister made no reply and turned her head away. The lad's mind suddenly turned to his mother trudging along behind. " Quick," he said, " mam is coming." The girl sprang to her feet as if impelled by an electric current. She hurriedly arranged her clothes, then remembered the pink garment behind her. A quick blush spread over her white face. Her companion felt the urgency of the situation and turned his back to her.

Trembling in every limb, Jane hastily pulled the betraying garment over her sand-encrusted shoes while Len gulped back his tears and helped to arrange her dress. The toilet was hardly completed when Shane came panting to the edge of the dune. The loss of Len from her sight had put her into a quiver of nervousness. Perspiration poured down her face as she slowly recovered her breath and took in the scene beneath her.

Turning her weary eyes from Len she looked at Jane and immediately noted the pallor of the girl's face. Half unconsciously she noticed the impression of bodies on the soft crushed grass. The fidgetting youth near by attracted her attention. She recognised him as Evan the Overman's son, the young man who had sat with Jane in the station while they were waiting for the train.

Jane felt years roll away before she heard her mother's voice float quietly down from an interminable distance. Something seemed to quiver through its customary harshness and mellow it. " What have you been doing, Jane bach ? " Shane asked plaintively.

Len edged closer to his deathly white sister as she replied in a frightened whisper, " Nothing, mam, nothing." Shane stood motionless for a moment, her eyes full of fear. Then she beckoned the young people to her with an awkward gesture.

The agitated youth had been silent during the scene, but he now jumped forward. " There is nothing wrong, Mrs. Roberts," he blurted out hysterically. " Me and Jane only come here to have a little chat away from the noise of the crowd. Don't think wrong about us. You have been young yourself once."

His demeanour belied his plea, and Shane knew he was lying. Choking back her tears, she replied, " All right, boy bach, all right. May time prove that you be speaking the truth."

No more was said. Shane beckoned Len and Jane to follow her, and the trio left the young man where he stood. During the slow trudge back to the sands Shane tried to beat back the fears that tumbled to her mind with increasing torment. The day for her had come to a sudden end. Mentally she battled with herself whether she should communicate her fears to Big Jim.

Len, holding his mother's hand, walked dumbly by her side. He wondered what had happened to make her look so sad and old. Unable to find an answer, he turned his thoughts to Jane. The hot flame again seared his body when he remembered the bared breast and the young man caressing it. The fact grieved him, although he had not the slightest knowledge of its import.

Jane, tight-lipped and with nerves twitching hysterically, looked piteously at her mother. But the latter, absorbed in her own misery, paid no attention. Immersed in themselves yet thinking of each other, the three eventually reached the spot where Big Jim lay fast asleep, with his mouth wide open and his legs spread loosely in an obscene sprawl. His cheek was cut, while one eye was swollen and discoloured.

Shane glanced over her mate quickly, noting the contented twist on his face. She stooped and lifted Jim's huge hands and saw the knuckles were torn and blooded. Hazily Shane wondered what had happened, but her mind still wrestled with the main problem. Should she tell him? Perhaps, after all, she thought, nothing had really occurred between Jane and the youth. Even if it had, perhaps nothing would come of it. Thus she argued with herself. Her thoughts tore and gashed her infinitely more deeply than the wounds did Jim's hands. Shaking him gently, she called, " Wake up, James bach, wake up."

Turning on his side and drawing his knees up, he drowsily murmured, " Plenty of time, nghyariad i, the hooter haven't gone yet. Let me be for a bit."

" No, no ! " burst out Shane frantically. " I want you, James bach. You must wake up now." The urgency in her voice jerked him out of his beer-laden slumber. Rubbing the sun glare from his undamaged eye and licking his damp moustache, he sat up with a grunt.

He immediately sensed something was wrong with Shane and assumed it had to do with the fight he had engaged in during the afternoon. He started an apologetic explanation. " It was not my fault, Shane bach," he began, " I didn't want to fight, but I couldn't leave my butties down, could I ? " The last was a plaintive query.

Shane sadly studied his face. Already she felt stronger and more confident. " Did you win ? " she asked.

" Win ? Of course I did," he replied, as though the very question were an insult. " Have anybody ever seen Big Jim losing ? "

Heedless of the boast, she quietly dragged from him all she wanted to know of the afternoon's events. The recital helped to deaden the pain in her heart and decided her to tell him nothing about Jane until something transpired.

They still had some time to wait before the arrival of the excursion train to take them back to the valleys. This they spent on the sands with the rest of the people, most of whom were already worn out. The air resounded to the noise of screaming children, which helped to further irritate nerves already frayed by the excitement and fuss of the gruelling day.

At last the time for the return train arrived. Perspiring parents dragged and carried howling children to the railway station and packed the waiting carriages. Len, feeling himself stifling in the breath-laden compartment, tried to open the window, but was stopped by Shane, " for fear of the draught " as she said.

The journey home was agonising, and everyone was glad when the train eventually puffed into Cwmardy. Len felt the smoky, noisome air of the valley to be the sweetest he had ever breathed. The walk up the hill to Sunny Bank was a silent one. None of them wanted supper that night.

Len and Jane went to bed before their parents. The lad watched his sister stripping off her clothes. Her audible sighs sent the memory of the events of the day surging through him. Without knowing why, he felt a vague pity for her that seemed to deepen when she dropped the white nightdress over her slender body. His tear-misted eyes saw a thousand rainbows dance around the dim flame of the candle. Speechless, he waited until she came to bed and pressed the hot wick of the candle into the oily grease with a piece of paper.

Len gathered courage in the ensuing darkness. He nestled his body to her warm flesh and said, " Don't worry, Jane bach. I 'on't tell mam what I seen." Jane made no reply but he felt the heavy sobs that shook her shudder through him beneath the bedclothes. They broke down his boyish restraint, and he jumped up in bed, tears rolling down his cheeks.

Jane reached up in the gloom and drew his wavy head to her bosom, which he clasped with a loving tenderness. The dormant mother-love rushed in waves over her body at the touch of his sweat-moistened hand. Twisting on her side she huddled him back under the bedclothes, taking care not to remove his hand. In this posture they both cried themselves to sleep.

CHAPTER IV

The Death of Jane

FOR many months the events of the excursion day dominated young Len's mind. Since their return home he fancied the house had become gloomier. His parents spoke in whispers whenever he was about, and he could not escape the tormenting thought that these changes were in some way due to Jane. He began to observe that his sister was each week becoming more mopy and haggard. At night his wandering hands stole over her stomach and breasts, and he noticed that the former was swelling while the latter were growing heavier. Watching like a cat, he noticed that Jane spent a long time in the lavatory each morning and he sometimes heard her retching painfully in sickness.

Deep in his immature heart Len felt something terrible was happening, and an undefinable fear began to grow on him. One night, some months after the excursion, he fell to sleep in the armchair near the kitchen fire. He was awakened by a soft murmur of voices. Without raising his head Len slyly opened his eyes. The only light in the kitchen was a deep glow from the fire, around which his parents and Mrs. Thomas, the next-door neighbour, were sitting. Shutting his eyes again, the lad listened to the conversation. "Yes," he heard his mother say bitterly, " I am 'specting it to happen in six weeks from now." She groaned, then continued, " To think my poor gel have got to go through this and he have not been near her yet. Anybody would think she was muck."

She stopped again while Mrs. Thomas tried to console her. " Don't worry, Mrs. Roberts bach," she said. " God will pay him back."

There was a moment's silence before the neighbour

41

asked, as if seeking a loop-hole, " Be you sure of your dates ? "

" Sure ? " burst out Shane passionately. " Was I not there the day it did happen ? " She stopped, then moaned in a sudden spasm of grief. " Oh, God bach, I would sooner if you did strike her dead at my feet the day she was born, than for her to come to this. The first of my children, too. Day in and day out have I slaved to rear them 'spectable and to put the fear of God into their little hearts. And now to come to this." Her voice broke in a pitiful wail.

For some minutes there was another deep silence, which was broken by Shane. She sprang to her feet and shouted in a voice vibrant with passion and hate, " Be a man, Big Jim ! " Jim sat up as if jerked by a rope at her words. " Yes," she spat at him, " be a man for once. You can fight in a public-house for other people, fight now for your own flesh and blood." Jim sat silent and motionless, his eyes staring into the fire as she continued tauntingly : " But no. You would sooner sit on your backside by there, biting your nails. It is easier than hiding your only daughter from the storm Evan the Overman's son have made for her."

Big Jim's continued silence enraged her. " Have you no tongue that you do not answer me ? " she howled, heedless of her words. " Why don't you rise from your backside and go to Evan the Overman ? Get out, Big Jim. Go, tell Evan the Overman that his son have dirtied your daughter." Her voice softened a little as she beseeched, " Be a man, James. Put on your coat and make Evan's boy do the right thing by our gel before it be too late."

Big Jim looked up from the fire to her haggard face, the lines in which were so deep that they appeared to have been chiselled in. A deep, impotent grief filled his heart. He understood Shane's anger but wondered how he could ask another to marry his daughter when he was himself not married to her mother. He loved his children with the blind devotion of an animal and it hurt him to the bone that this thing had happened. The disgrace which the event would bring upon the family disturbed him very little. What he feared was the possibility of something happening to Jane. " Don't worry, Shane bach," he muttered, his puzzlement evident in his tone. " I be not dead yet, and I can still keep my children without asking other men to do it for me."

Len choked back the sobs that gathered in his throat as his father went on. " These hands that have stood the biggest timbers in the pit, this body that have lifted the heaviest trams, are still strong enough to work to fill another mouth. Yes," he went on, while his tear-glistened eyes looked directly into Shane's, " Jane's baby will be so dear to me as is Jane herself, whether it be made on a mountain or in a bed."

Shane began to sob. Mrs. Thomas attempted to console the grief-stricken woman. Taking Shane's bowed head into her arms, she murmured, " There, there, Mrs. Roberts bach, don't take it so hard to your heart. Everything will come all right in God's good time."

The weeping woman raised her head, and the red glow from the flames turned the tears trickling down her cheeks into blood. Turning to Big Jim she said softly, as though talking to a child : " I know, James bach, that it will never have a better father than you. But think of the shame on our daughter, on all of us. In God's eyes she is not clean and people will point on her baby and say ' Look at Big Jim's gel, she have got a bastard by Evan the Overman's son.' "

Jim's huge frame stiffened and quivered at the words, which acted like an electric current. For some seconds he fought silently to control himself, then, rising slowly from the chair, he stood erect before the two women. He breathed quickly and his voice was harsh as a saw when he said, " If ever I do hear another living body say that, it do mean that my life will end upon a hangman's rope." Saying which, he brought his fist down upon the table with a crash that startled Len from his feigned sleep.

No more was said until the lad had finished supper and

was sent to bed. Here he strained his ears to listen, but nothing reached him other than a faint indistinct murmur. Disappointed, he turned to Jane and woke her from her restless sleep. Nestling closely to her in the semi-darkness of the candle-lit room, he mumbled hesitantly, " I know what be the matter with you, Jane. You be going to have a baby bastard."

Jane sprang to her haunches, the nightdress slipping from her shoulders, and glared at the frightened lad. For a moment it seemed she was going to strike him, but she suddenly caught him in her arms and pressed his face to her naked, palpitating bosom. The smell of her flesh and the pulsing of her heart tingled Len's senses as her tears moistened his hair. " Oh Len, Len," she moaned rocking him backwards and forwards in her grief, " what shall I do ? I have got a good mind to go up the feeder and end it all." He tried to soothe her, but Jane continued fatalistically, " Mam will kill me when she knows."

Len had been alarmed at her despairing outburst, but he brightened up at this. " Don't worry 'bout that," he told her confidently, " mam do know 'bout it already, Jane bach."

Frantically the girl probed every word of the conversation from him. When he repeated his father's statements she burst into sobs again, saying, " He is too good for me. Many fathers would put me out on the streets."

Len started convulsively and raised himself on his elbows. " Oh no, he 'oodn't," he retorted vehemently ; " and if he did," he added manfully, " I 'ood keep you. I will be starting to work very soon now."

She cuddled him to her and sighed, " There now, Len bach, go to sleep ; it will soon be all over." Sleep, however, was out of the question for both of them. Jane sobbed softly all night, while Len wondered how the baby that was coming would be born. The definite knowledge of what was wrong made his mind a little easier, though he could not understand how it happened or what it meant. The surreptitious manner in which he had obtained the information determined him that the matter was a big secret and must not be mentioned to his schoolmates. With this thought in his mind he dozed off.

Big Jim returned from work the following morning without making his usual call at the Boar's Head. While he bathed Shane fetched his best clothes from the box under the bed. Preparing herself as he dressed, she warned Len and Jane : " You two children stop in till me and dad come back. We 'ont be very long."

Jane looked at her mother. Her eyes were appealingly pitiful. She sensed where they were going, but did not have the courage to ask them to desist.

Len noticed the look and a gnawing pain tugged at his heart as he wondered what was the matter. Big Jim, carefully soaping his moustaches, appeared too preoccupied to observe anything. As he picked up the bowler hat and followed Shane to the door, he huskily muttered over his shoulder : " Don't you worry, gel bach ; everything will come all right in the end."

His head bowed, like a man on the way to the scaffold, he accompanied Shane down the little street that led to Main Street. He inclined to lag behind as they drew nearer the house of Evan the Overman, and several times Shane had to urge him to walk faster. Her eyes glistened wetly.

When they eventually reached their destination there was a momentary pause before Shane timidly lifted the bright brass knocker which adorned the door. Big Jim stood in the muddy roadway, his whole demeanour betraying the awkward misery he felt. At the second rap the door was opened by the young man who had been with Jane on the day of the excursion. It was the first time Shane had seen him since the incident on the dunes. His sudden appearance now drained the blood from her face and her eyes seemed to grow bigger and wetter.

Speechless with emotion, she listened to the stuttering words of the youth, who was obviously as upset and surprised as herself. " Hallo," he stammered, " come to see me, I 'spose ? " He hesitated while her sunken eyes bored a sharp, nervous pain into his head. Turning his head away from the burning gleam, he gathered his thoughts and blurted out, " I believe I know what you have come about. It is about your Jane."

Neither Jim or Shane replied. " Well," continued the disconcerted young man, " it is no good coming to me. I am not the man you want to look for. Jane have been courting dozens before me." He stooped again, his eyes still averted, and then burst out as if the words were boiling in his throat, " I am not the first chap who have been with her."

Big Jim, who had been silently fidgeting in the roadway during this monologue, stepped sharply towards the door at these words. His body was taut and his moustaches twitched. " That will do," he said curtly, in a quivering voice. " Me and my wife have not come here to see you, and we want to hear no more from you. We have come to see your father, Evan the Overman." The young man paled at the threat in Jim's voice. Stuttering more than ever, he hastily retreated into the passage, saying, " Oh, all right, Mr. Roberts. I didn't mean any harm. I will tell my father you want him." Shutting the door behind him, he left the old couple in the roadway.

Shane looked at Jim's set face and warned him, " Now, 'member, James bach, no nonsense. You keep your temper and leave the talking to me. We have come here to get justice for our gel and not to use our fists." Before Jim could reply the door opened.

Facing them stood a short, thickset man with a sallow face and heavy, overhanging eyebrows. This was Evan the Overman. He was an official at the pit where Big Jim worked. In common with other officials, his function was supposed to be that of watching over the workmen's safety, but the colliery company regarded this as secondary to output, and the ability of the officials was measured by the amount of coal they could wring from the area and the men in their charge.

Evan the Overman's attitude was domineering when he said, without any preamble, " I understand you want to see me particular."

Shane replied to him. " Yes, Evan," she said, " we do want to see you very particular." Without another word he beckoned them in and led the way to the parlour.

The old couple carefully wiped their muddy boots on the coconut mat before entering. The mat bore the word " Welcome." Even in her perturbation Shane noted the gaudy brassiness of the room as she sat gingerly on the edge of the plush settee. Big Jim remained standing until Evan invited him to sit. This Jim did, precariously perching the unaccustomed bowler hat on his knee.

When they were all seated the official opened the conversation. " Hmm," he began ponderously, " I believe I know what you have come about, James. I believe I am right in saying it is about your Jane, isn't it ? " Receiving no reply to his question, he continued, " I have been told Jane is going to have a baby and that she do blame my son for it."

Bridling at the sneer in his voice, Shane interrupted him. " Yes," she said, " that be quite right. Jane be going to have a baby by your Evan."

The outspoken assertion and the manner in which she made it startled the two men for a moment. Shane went on in a softer voice : " We have come to ask you, as a God-fearing man, Evan, to make your son clean the gel he have dirtied. You have knowed me and James for many years now and, although James is only a collier and do like his drop of beer, you do know us to be 'spectable people not ashamed to look nobody in the face. Yes," she went on proudly, " we don't owe a penny to no man and nobody do need to be ashamed to have our Jane for a wife. I know we be poor, but she have been reared 'spectable and clean, thank God." She paused a moment to swallow, then continued : " Yes, Evan, we have come to ask you to make your son do the right thing." Her voice faltered on the last sentence and it sounded like a plaint.

For some moments nothing else was said. Then the overman rose heavily to his feet and walked slowly to the door. He opened it and shouted, "Evan, come here." In a very short time the young man entered, sheepishly avoiding the eyes that scanned his face. "You know what we have been talking about," his father began. "James and Shane do blame you for the baby that is coming to their Jane, and they want you to marry her. What have you got to say about it ? " His words were a command.

Seconds elapsed before the youth made any response. The three parents anxiously watched him, each seeming ready to catch the words when they dropped from his lips. At last he started speaking. His voice was low and he kept looking at the floor. " I do admit I have been with Jane," he started, " but only once and that was when we went away with the chapel." He stopped a moment. No one moved and he continued, his breath quickening. " She was courting regular with another chap before that. I have got witnesses to prove it." He raised his head and looked at his father. Encouraged by the quick gleam of interest he saw in the latter's eyes, he failed to notice the horror in Shane's or the spasmodic twitching of Big Jim's face muscles. The young man choose his next words like bullets which he shot venomously at Jim and Shane. " You can't trap me with this," he rattled out in jerks. " You have got the wrong bird this time. You are only blaming me because my father is an official. But it is no good looking for the right man in this house ; he don't live here."

Each word struck Shane with an impact that quivered through her body. She hid her drawn face in her hands. Hot tears trickled like molten glass through her fingers. Immersed in her own grief, she did not see Big Jim spring to his feet, his panting chest emphasising the magnitude of his bulk.

He stood motionless, the pallor of his face giving greater heat to the glow in his eyes. When he at last spoke the deep tremor in his voice made Shane shudder and raise her

tear-stained face. " Oh," said Jim, with callous delibera-
tion, " so the son of Evan do class my gel a whore. Eh ?
The man who have used my daughter do now call her a pros-
titute." He paused to battle with his passion, then spat
out, " Look well to yourself, man, before talking 'bout
other people. Before you start to run other women down,
look well to your own mother."

Shane sensed the drift of his words and tried to stop him.
She wailed through her tears, " Don't say no more, James
bach, for the sake of God."

Jim waved her aside and paid no attention to Evan the
Overman cowering in the chair. Completely dominating
the situation, he nailed the trembling youth with his eyes
and went on : " Too late now. Too late. When you hurt
my gel, you do put poison in my heart. Poison that have
got to be spit out. And if it do kill anyone, who am I to
try and stop it ? " He paused again with a visible tremble,
gulped hard and then continued : " You say that your
father is an official. Yes, that is true. But you don't tell
us how he came to be one. Answer that, Evan bach,
before you open your mouth again. But, there," he went
on raspingly, without waiting for a reply, " perhaps you
don't know."

Apart from Jim's voice the room was silent. Shane sat
rigid, her bottom jaw hanging loosely. Evan the Overman
had buried his face in his arms, while his son stood motionless and helpless before the glaring eyes of Big Jim.

The young man trembled as Jim continued : " Let me
help you. Do you believe your father was made an official
because he was a good workman. Ha-ha ! " The laugh did
not sound out of place. It was deep and bitter, giving
coherence to the words that followed. " No, of course not.
I could work his hands off, but I have not been made an
official. No; my boy, it is not *that* you have to brag about.
Your father did not have the job of overman because of the
work he have done himself." Jim's voice began to rise as he
said, " No ; it is not there you will find the answer. Your
father was made an official because when Williams, the

under-manager, come here first he did lodge with your father and mother. Yes," he burst out passionately, his voice palpitating with the contempt that consumed him, " your father did sell his wife's body for an overman's job."

The usually arrogant colliery official slumped forward in the chair. His heaving shoulders betrayed what his covered face was hiding. Young Evan cowered, with staring eyes, against the door post. Big Jim lifted Shane from the settee and stood with her in the middle of the room.

Pride and passion deepened his voice : " You do tell me to look somewhere else. Yes, I can. But you look first, my boy, to your own face and see if you can find the likeness of Evan the Overman there. Huh. That is one thing you will never see. I am sorry for you. The son of such a man as your father is not fit to enter the family of Jim the Big. I would sooner find the father of my gel's babby in the gutter than in this house."

Jim's voice became softer as he said : " But there be no need for me to look anywhere. I am man enough to father my daughter's babby as I have fathered her. I ask no man to make or to keep my children."

Neither father or son opened their mouth as Jim made his terrible indictment. The room became cold as a vault of resurrected corpses. Shane, almost overcome by the ruthless, devastating words of her mate, trembled from head to foot. She was thankful when his great arm encircled her waist and he led her to the door, saying aloud, " Come, Shane bach. Let us leave this painted muckhole and the rubbish that do live in it. Our Jane do still belong to us and her babby is ours."

Big Jim paused as they passed the young man at the door. His voice vibrated with a sudden spasm of passion and hate. " Do you hear me ? " he shouted.

Neither of the stricken, shamefaced men looked up as he went on : " Now both of you 'member this. The father of Jane's babby do not live in this house. If ever I hear a word that it do, that day will I come back and pull it about your ears brick by brick." With this he slammed the door, sternly bade Shane dry her tears, and with his arm through hers proudly marched past the neighbours who had seen them enter the house and had waited in anticipation of a rowdy scene.

Words were not necessary to explain the result of the interview. Shane's tear-stained face told it.

The couple found Len and Jane awaiting them when they arrived home. Jane looked in her mother's eyes and burst into sobs when she read the message they contained. Jim turned at the pitiful wail. " That will do," he said abruptly, " there is to be no more crying in this house." He waited until Jane had somewhat controlled herself, then added more softly, " Sit down and wipe your eyes, my little gel. Now, listen to me. The little babby you are going to bring into the world belong to no one but the people in this house. It will be ours and no one else's. There will be no wedding before it is born, and its father is not Evan the Overman's son. Do you understand my words, Jane bach ? " he queried, a world of love in his voice.

Jane's face went ghastly white and her eyes dilated, but she made no reply other than to nod her head dumbly.

Shane went to the girl. " What your father do tell you be quite right," she told her. " Your sin will fall on all of us, but the good Lord will help us to carry it."

She gathered her daughter into her arms, murmuring as their tears melted together, " Don't cry, nghyariad bach i. Mam be with you." Rocking the weeping girl in her lap like a baby, she broke into a soft haunting Welsh lullaby. She crooned the words into her daughter's ears as she had done seventeen years before, when suckling her :

>Cariwch medd Dafydd
>Fe nelyn i mi
>Ceisiaf cyn maro
>Roi tone arni i.

>Bring to me,
>Said dying David,
>My harp,
>That I may play another tune
>Before I die.

The mournful words, clothed in minor tones, soaked into Jane's pent-up emotions, soothing their pain and calming their tumult.

She pressed her body closer to her mother's and sank slowly into a soft sleep interspersed with irregular sighs. Big Jim, with infinite tenderness, lifted the girl from Shane's lap and carried her to bed.

All the while Len had looked and listened in bewilderment. He did not understand what marriage was, but that Evan the Overman's son, whom he now knew had done something terrible to Jane, would not marry her struck him as an affront to the family. Whatever had happened to transform his sister from a happy girl to a morose, malformed young woman, Len did not know. But he knew from what he had heard that Evan bach was responsible and that he was now evading the consequences. The knowledge that all the family was suffering as a result tormented Len for a long time. At school he became even more taciturn than usual, refusing all Ron's attempts to draw him into a conversation or a game. He began wandering the mountains alone, boots and stockings slung around his shoulders. He roamed aimlessly through the grass while his mind pondered the problem of Jane.

In this way the weeks went by. Each week he observed her body become more misshapen and her face more haggard. Her eyes alarmed him. They were dull and full of impatient grief. Len felt the atmosphere in the house change. His parents no longer quarrelled, and when they spoke it was in quiet whispers as if they were afraid the walls would hear what they were saying. Jim no longer burst his grumbling way into the house. Neither did he frequent the Boar's Head with his mate, Dai Cannon. When he came home from work he moped in the armchair near the fire until it was time to go to bed.

Shane was the only member of the family who maintained the ordinary routine, and even she, Len observed, did more sewing than was usual. The changed domestic environment affected the lad deeply and developed in him a hatred of the man he thought responsible. In his mind the problem now appeared perfectly simple. If Evan the Overman's son married Jane everyone would be happy, he thought. The simplicity of the solution made him wonder why Evan did not apply it. During the nights when he lay alongside his sobbing sister, he clenched his fists and wished he were big enough to force the cause of all the trouble do the right thing.

The snatches of conversation he picked up in the kitchen from his mother and Mrs. Thomas, the neighbour, led him to believe that the only thing that prevented young Evan marrying Jane was the fact he was an official's son and not an ordinary workman like Big Jim. This idea grew on Len. He pondered long over the distinction between officials in the pit and workmen. It struck him as monstrously unfair that this distinction in status should break up his home life and make his people sad. The hatred he felt for Evan the Overman's son slowly diffused itself into a hatred of all those classed as officials. He began to regard them as enemies. He was too young and immature to appreciate the subtle divisions deliberately developed between the colliery staff of officials and the workmen, and came to believe that all officials had, of necessity, to be cruel.

Jane no longer went outside the house. Occasionally and for no apparent reason she burst into hysterical sobs that shook her body. In her eyes grew the dull glazed look of a hunted animal that, even as it runs, knows there is no escape.

Very early one morning, when the sun still had some hours to travel before it peeped over the mountains into the valley, Len was awakened by his father. He vaguely heard Jane toss and moan as Big Jim wrapped his trembling form in a blanket and carried him down into the kitchen. Len was placed in the armchair while his father sat on the stool near the fire. Big Jim bade the lad go to sleep, but the strangeness of the proceedings brushed all sleep from Len's eyes. He looked about him. The kitchen was full of shadows and the big boiler on the fire only added to the

number. Len saw the water it contained bubbling and
sparkling in the beams from the oil-lamp. He wondered
what it was for and where his mother was.

The front door opened with a sudden clang and Shane
came in accompanied by Mrs. Thomas. The former's head
and shoulders were swathed in the big woollen shawl, but
Len's eyes did not see this. They were riveted on the
black bag Mrs. Thomas carried. He had often heard that
babies came in such bags as that.

Shane muttered something to the crouching Jim, who
immediately got up from the stool and began pacing the
kitchen with bent head and hands behind his back. Len
watched his mother dip an unlit candle into the fireflames
and heard her hurried footsteps shuffle up the stairs. Mrs.
Thomas remained downstairs and filled a large pan with the
hot water from the boiler. In a short time Shane returned
to the kitchen. She took up the pan of hot water and with
a whispered " Don't worry, James bach, everything will
come all right," accompanied Mrs. Thomas back up the
stairs.

Big Jim stopped his restless pacing. He stood still, while
his huge body began a soft, regular swaying as though
trying to soothe a child cradled in his arms.

The silence and definiteness with which everything was
done frightened Len. He felt like crying. The black bag
had made him aware that the unusual happenings had to do
with Jane. Lying perfectly still on the armchair, he let his
mind drift. He saw Jane as she was prior to the excursion ;
then before his eyes drifted a picture of her horribly
bloated body as he had seen it the previous night. Tears
blurred his vision and coursed down his cheeks. The
hatred he felt for officials ran through his blood like fire,
and he began thinking of the form his revenge would take
when he grew up.

Closing his tired eyes, the lad tried to ease the torment in
his mind, but the continual shuffling overhead made this
impossible. His active imagination likened it to the sound
of doom walking through the darkness and slyly sweeping

up its victims. Suddenly a dreadful scream brought him in one leap from the chair to his father's side. Whimpering and trembling, he clung to Jim's legs, the quiver of which mingled with that in his own body. Len's upturned, pitiful eyes asked mutely what was wrong, but Big Jim, himself seared with anguish, made no reply other than to stroke the lad's hair. The action pacified Len somewhat. The scream died down in gasping moans, through which he heard Jane's pain-drenched plea : " Oh, let me die, mam. Let me die." The lad felt his father's legs stiffen at the words, but he did not feel the tear that fell on his hair.

Shortly after this Mrs. Thomas came down for more boiling water. Her return to the bedroom was followed by more screams and their culminating moans. This went on for hours, and Len felt the night would never end. He longed for daylight to steal its way through the drawn blinds. Every second became an embodied nightmare.

The sound of his mother's harsh cough as she came down the stairs eased the tension. Her sweaty face was a lump of shiny shadows. She murmured tiredly to Big Jim : " You had better get ready for work, James bach. The time be going on. You have got nothing to worry about," she said as an afterthought. Without a word Jim drew from under the table the box that contained his working clothes.

Len went back on the armchair while his father dressed and Shane toasted some bread. The pit-grimed clothes which Jim drew on his naked body filled the small kitchen with dried coal dust, which settled in layers on everything. The bubbling water in the boiler lapped up the black dust and made it into soft mud.

When he had finished dressing Big Jim drew his chair to the table and poured the hot tea Shane handed him into a saucer from which he sucked it in audible gulps. He left the flame-scorched toast untouched. After the second cup of tea he rose and without a word made for the door. At the foot of the stairs he hesitated and squared his drooping shoulders to the sigh that seeped up from his heart.

For a moment he stood motionless, then, with a muttered

3

" Good morning," turned towards the doorway that led to
the day then being spawned. His eyes were blind to the
black-bordered red streaks that ran across the sky at the
bottom of the valley. They resembled the blood-streams of
birth. His ears were deaf to the loudly shrieking pit
hooters that raped the early morning air with violent echoes.
He paid no attention to their frenzied demand that he hurry
to the pit. Imperceptibly his body melted into the silent,
shadowy line of men that wound its way up the hill to the
colliery.

After Jim's departure Shane sat on the stool before the
fire. She rocked herself backwards and forwards, quietly
groaning with every movement. Len watched her for some
time. He wished she would stop the rocking that
threatened to put her head in the flames with each forward
motion. Thought of this possibility unnerved him, and he
was on the point of speaking when he heard her murmur to
herself : " Oh, Jane bach, Jane bach, it will be all over on
you, nghyariad i, very soon now. You will never come
through this. Ah," she went on softly, " it do seem only
yesterday you was suckling on my breast." The memory
brought tears to her eyes. She stopped her rocking and
sobbed despairingly, " O God, what have I done that you
should make my little gel suffer ? " Receiving no answer
to her supplication, she resumed her rocking until a sound
overhead took her hurriedly up the stairs.

Len eased his legs on the chair and sank into an uneasy
doze. When he woke daylight had already yellowed the
undrawn window blinds. His mother sat at the table, her
head pillowed in her arms and her shoulders shaking convulsively. Len looked in amazement at the tall, cadaverous
man who stood near. He knew it was the doctor and
wondered what he was doing in the kitchen. The lad
turned his eyes again towards his weeping mother. The
connection between the tears and the doctor suddenly
flashed into his mind. Panic-stricken he rushed towards the
man, shouting and weeping, " What have you done to our
mam ? Oh, mam, mam," he wailed, " what have he done ? "

Shane took the hysterical lad on her lap. His frenzy calmed her own grief. "There, there, Len bach," she crooned, "you must be quiet or you will wake Jane." The last words were more a sob than a statement. The doctor beckoned Mrs. Thomas to accompany him to the door, which they closed behind them.

Very shortly Mrs. Thomas returned and fussily put her arms round Shane's shoulders. "It be no good worrying now, Mrs. Roberts bach," she said. "The good Lord do always know what is best. Poor little Jane is out of her pain now, and is resting safe where there be no temptation." Shane did not reply. Mrs. Thomas continued: "Don't you bother 'bout anything. I will see to the laying out and James can go to the undertaker's when he come home from work. I will take all the dirty clothes with me now and have a couple of hours' sleep, then I will come back and put things in order for you." Shane nodded her head, dumbly acquiescent.

When Jim returned from the pit late in the afternoon the drawn blinds in every house of the street told him what had happened before he reached his own. Speechless with grief, he bathed and donned his clean clothes. Shane appeared oblivious to his presence until he carried the tub into the backyard. When he returned to the kitchen he caught her to him and kissed her hair. She broke down completely under the caress, and it was some minutes before he could calm her.

He succeeded eventually and remained silent while she stared into the fire. Presently she raised her head and began speaking in a low sing-song tone: "Our little Jane have left us, James. Yes. Left us for ever and we will never again hear her voice in this kitchen." She paused a moment and swallowed hard. When she continued it was more to herself than anyone else. "Often have I been harsh to you, Jane bach. But I did never mean it." She turned to Jim, who was getting alarmed at her attitude. "She was our only gel," she said, peering into his tear-misted eyes. "Yes, our only gel. And now she have been taken from us. O God," she burst out in sudden passion, " why for did you make her suffer so much before taking her ? Could you not have spared her pain ? " She paused again, as if afraid of her thoughts, then went on challengingly : " You did desert my little gel when she needed you most. You have done the same as Evan the Overman's son done. You left her when she wanted you. Ach," she went on harshly, " what have our little Jane done that she should be deserted by everybody ? She have never done no wrong. And yet Evan bach do go happy and free on his way while my little gel is stiff and cold upstairs."

There was silence for a while and Jim thought the outburst was over, until Shane gave another sigh and continued her slow, despairing monologue : " Our little gel did mean no harm that day at the seaside," she moaned. " She was young and clean as the driven snow. Yet look what she have had to suffer, while him who was the cause of it did lie safe and sound in bed sleeping through her agony. And now all her pain have been for nothing."

Shane grasped the silent Jim by the shoulders. Slowly and deliberately, letting every word soak into his ears before proceeding with the next, she said, " All my life I have prayed to my God. Every Sunday I have gone to His chapel. In everything I have tried to live in His ways. Yes. I loved him. And yet the first time I do ask Him for mercy He do turn against me."

Her voice was cold and her face was bitter as the clash between faith and anguish tore at her vitals. She gave a deep sigh and said as though resigned to her fate : " When God do desert his children there be nothing fair in this world and nothing more to look forward to."

Jim sensed the impending breakdown implied in the last words. " Sh-h-h," he warned her soothingly. " This do come to everybody in their turn, Shane bach." She looked at him sadly, her eyes already dark with mourning.

Later Len saw his father don the best suit and go out. No word was said or explanation made. Mrs. Thomas came in during his absence and occupied herself in the little parlour at the side of the kitchen. Len tried several times to make his way upstairs with the intention of seeing Jane, but on each occasion he was prevented.

When Big Jim returned to the house he was accompanied by a tall, thin-faced, black-coated stranger. Mrs. Thomas gave Len a penny and told him to go out for a while until the strange man left. The lad made his way up the mountain behind the house, stamping a tear into the sod with each aimless stride. Darkness was beginning to blanket the valley in a black shroud when Len came back to his home. The light in the parlour window surprised him. He had never seen one there before.

He found the house full of neighbours, all of whom were talking in subdued whispers. Len went straight to his mother, who sat crouched on the stool, and asked what was in the parlour. Shane looked at him dazedly for a moment before replying : " Nothing much, Len bach, nothing much. You shall see in the morning." Her voice sounded empty as an upturned bucket.

After supper Mrs. Thomas took the lad upstairs to the bedroom. Len looked at the empty bed. A peculiar smell rose from it. He asked Mrs. Thomas, who was fussily arranging the clothes, " Where be our Jane then ? I thought she was in bed."

The woman readily replied, " You go to bed, Len bach, and don't bother your little head. Jane is safe enough, you can venture."

Len was not satisfied, but he said no more as she tucked him beneath the bed-clothes. The peculiar smell seemed to be thicker here and he thought it hung more heavily around him. Weary, his mind full of worrying notions, he soon fell to sleep.

Next day Len found the house even more silent than it had been during the past few months. In addition he felt something eerie creep into his bones. Tiny bubbles of perspiration covered his body ; each one felt like the icy point of a needle. Mrs. Thomas was still there. She seemed to be in complete charge of the household. Whenever Len tried to get near his mother, the well-meaning neighbour always prevented him. "Don't bother your mam now, Len bach," she said ; "she have got enough on her plate as it is." The lad could not understand the reason for this, but he obediently submitted.

After dinner Mrs. Thomas told Big Jim, "We can go in now, James. You had better take the boy with you." Jim rose from the table and caught Len's hand. As they approached the parlour door the boy felt he was on the verge of some great adventure. His heart missed a beat, then jumped more quickly into action at the sound of the raised latch. He thrust his perspiring hand more deeply into the engulfing fist of his father as they entered the parlour.

Len noticed immediately the two long candles wasting their flames in the daylight mellowed by the drawn window-blinds. The white-covered chairs puzzled him even while he wondered what the long yellow box on the table in the centre of the room was for. He instinctively knew that the funny-shaped plank of wood standing upright near the fire-grate belonged to the box. The shining shield near its top stared at him like a lonely, glaring eye.

The lad pressed his body more tightly to the rigid leg of his father. He turned his head away from the shield and waited. Len knew something else was to come, but had no idea what it was until he heard Mrs. Thomas murmur quietly, her apron to her eyes, "Don't she look lovely, Mr. Roberts ? "

Like a flash Len knew what was in the box. Before he could say anything Big Jim bent down and lifted him from the floor. With awestruck eyes the boy looked down into the interior of what he now knew to be a coffin. Jane lay there, more still and silent than he had ever seen her.

Her body was clothed in a white lace and looked longer than when Len had last seen it. Her hands were waxy mirrors reflecting the blue tracery of all their veins. They were folded across her breast. One hand grasped a bunch of red roses that cast a blush over her smooth, white face, which seemed to smile into Len's downcast eyes.

Cuddled to Jane's side was the body of the baby that had killed her. Its tiny face looked like a blob of paste. Len felt a sudden urge to again caress Jane with his hands. He wanted to run them over the smooth contours of her breasts. Lumps of saliva rose to his throat. He swallowed them back in gulps and began to struggle hysterically in his father's grip. No tears came to his eyes as he continued the vain fight against Big Jim, but the feeling of impotence eventually conquered him and the emotional storm abated, leaving him panting on his father's shoulder.

Jim let him recover his breath, then slowly lowered him to the coffin until his lips touched those of his silent, smiling sister. Len shuddered at their cold clamminess. He tried to warm them with his breath. Jim saw the boy's hands wander through Jane's hair, and lifted him away before he could clasp her head.

Together father and son looked down for a few moments longer. Neither said a word. Their tears fused before reaching the dead face, whose smile seemed to soften at the burning touch. Big Jim turned away at last and the pair went quietly out, followed by Mrs. Thomas, who closed the parlour door softly behind them.

Five days after Jane had died Len was again taken in to see her. This was to be the last occasion before they screwed the coffin down ready for the funeral next day. As before, Big Jim lifted his son above the edge. Len looked down and a look of horror filled his eyes. Jane's beautiful face was gone. In its place was a dirty yellow mask with snarling lips that curled back from shiny white teeth. A blackened penny grinned at him mockingly from each of her eyes. The roses had died and were now withered blotches on the white lace of her shroud. Dark blobs filled the places where her cheeks had been. The tiny shrunken form at her side was covered. A fusty smell rose from the coffin and reminded Len of the odour in his bed the night after Jane had died. An acid-tasting lump rose to his throat. It made him feel sick. Turning his head away he hid his burning face on Jim's neck. In this manner both went back into the kitchen.

All that night the horror of what he had seen sunk more deeply into Len's mind. The awful face chased him in his sleep. Always it was grinning before his eyes. It refused to go away. Fumes came from its mouth and entered his nose. He felt himself choking and screamed to Jane for help, pressing tightly to his body the pillow on which her head used to rest. But the horrid face with its coin-covered eyes and drawn lips followed him. He started fighting it away when he heard it say, " Don't you know me, Len bach ? I am Jane, your sister. Why do you drive me from you ? "

Len stopped his frantic struggles and looked again.

The pennies melted and made way for bright blue eyes. The lips closed in and the cheeks filled out. Len's heart thrilled. He laughed happily and pressed the face of his sister to his lips. The short stiff hair on it hurt him. He looked again and found he had been kissing Evan the Overman's son. His body quivered with disgust and he threw the face from him with all his might. It rebounded back upon the bed and again it was the face of the coffin.

Len heard his father's voice ask from an interminable distance, " What be the matter with you, Len bach ? Perhaps you had better come to sleep with me and your mam." Jim felt the steaming body of the lad dampen his flannel shirt as he carried him into Shane's bedroom. Finding comfort in his parents' presence, Len fell into a deep, lethargic sleep.

Next morning he was awakened early. " You must get up now, Len bach," said Mrs. Thomas, shaking him gently.

Len looked around and asked bewilderedly, " Where be mam and dad, then ? "

" They be downstairs," was the impatient reply. " Come now, there's a good boy. It be the day of the funeral to-day and we have got a lot to do."

Len rose sluggishly and went down the stone stairs to the

kitchen. He was followed by the exhortation, " Don't you worry your mam to-day, boy bach. She have got plenty to go on with as it is and she do want plenty of quiet now."

As the day wore on relatives, friends and neighbours crowded into the small kitchen. The women all began weeping sympathetically when they saw the dry-eyed Shane sitting silently on her stool. The black apron she wore deepened the pallor of her face. Her dull eyes looked vacant, giving the impression that she had given up searching for something she wanted urgently to know. But Big Jim, who had somewhat recovered his composure, twirled his moustaches in the old bombastic manner and tried to put everyone at their ease by assuming a nonchalance that deceived no one.

Everyone, apart from members of the family, ate dinner with a quiet, respectful gusto. When this was over Len was dressed in a brand-new black suit, which, like Big Jim's mourning suit, was to be paid for later out of the insurance money. He noticed that everyone now became excitedly expectant in a subdued way. Hushed whispers filled the kitchen with a droning sound, and he wondered what was the matter, but did not like to ask anyone.

The lad pulled the drawn window-curtains a little to one side so that he could see into the street. He saw a large number of men about the house. Most of them he knew to be his father's workmates and drinking pals. They were all dressed in black or blue suits which had obviously been taken from long hiding in drawers and cupboards, and above the starched linen collars their necks were red and sweaty.

When Len heard the door-latch rattle he turned his head from the window and saw Dai Cannon walk in. The people in the house became momentarily silent as Dai entered. He wore his " pulpit costume," as he called it. Long wear had rusted its original blackness. The lobes of his ears were pressed upwards by the high collar. His face was sombre when he approached Big Jim.

3*

He shook his mate's hand with a muttered " Hard luck, butty," then made his way towards Shane. The hitherto dry-eyed woman began to sob as soon as she saw him. The tears overflowed and streamed down her face. This visible agony made all the other women present weep, while the men, swallowing hard, looked on awkwardly, all of them trying to appear unconcerned.

Dai patted the grief-stricken Shane on her head. " There, there, my gel," he consoled, " it have come to you as it must come to all of us some time or another. Try to bear up the best you can, Shane bach, you still have the others to think of."

With this he turned away and asked Mrs. Thomas for the Bible. She told him it was in the parlour and that everything was ready to start.

Dai led the way out of the kitchen, followed by Big Jim, Shane, and Len, then the relatives and as many of the neighbours as could squeeze into the little parlour. Len kept close to his parents at the head of the coffin, while Dai Cannon undid the heavy brass clasps of the family Bible, which contained the written history of the bereaved family. With sure fingers the preacher found the page he wanted. His ponderous voice started in a hoarse undertone, gaining in volume and in tempo as he warmed to his theme. With the skill of an Inquisition torturer Dai Cannon used the poor, covered body as a claw with which he tore the hearts of his listeners. He left them red-eyed, gasping with pain and grief, and when he had accomplished this he finished. There was a brief hush, broken only by an occasional sob, then they all slowly made their way back into the kitchen.

Dai went to the door and beckoned to some of the waiting men, who immediately came forward. The undertaker opened the parlour window and the men pushed the coffin into sight of the people who crowded the small street. Here it was grasped by willing hands and placed upon a trestle.

The people gathered round while Dai Cannon, his sleek

black hair shining even in the foggy murk of the valley, mumbled a few hardly audible words. A voice began the rising cadences of a hymn. Other voices followed and soon everyone had joined in the mournful lay which was their farewell to Jane and her baby.

The last husky notes had not finished floating in the thick atmosphere before the men filed off in twos before the bier, leaving six of their number to carry the bare box and its contents on their shoulders.

Big Jim, holding Len by the hand, walked immediately behind the coffin. Following father and son came the other male members of the family in the order of their relationship, and in this fashion the long line began its slow trek down the valley towards the distant cemetery, Len carrying the little bunch of white flowers thrust into his hand by Mrs. Thomas.

As the mourners left the street they shivered to an unearthly wail that followed them, and seemed to hammer the air into sharp points that stuck in their quivering nerves. " Oh, Jane bach, Jane bach, come back to me. They be taking you from your mam for ever." The wail died down for a moment, then rose to a horrible scream. " Bring her back to me, you jawled ! " it demanded. " Don't rob me of my only gel. Oh, Jane, Jane."

Len looked at his father, but Big Jim's face was hidden in the shadows of his drooping shoulders. As the funeral slowly made its way down Main Street, men coming home from the pits stayed their weary feet and doffed their caps till the coffin had passed. The coal-blackened faces made their eyes appear like white, liquid balls.

Evan the Overman and his son ran up a side-lane when they saw the funeral approaching. Ben the Barber and the landlord of the Boar's Head had drawn the blinds of their establishments out of respect for Big Jim.

At regular intervals the men who carried the coffin were changed by others who fell out from the front. Len walked like a person in a dream. His mind failed to co-ordinate impressions until he reached the cemetery gates and the single, sonorous " dong " of the bell shook him from his stupor. His dazed eyes singled out the marble monuments each the symbol of a corpse, an advertisement of decay. He stared hard at every coffin-shaped earth-mound whose only ornament was a withered bunch of flowers dead as the body it marked.

Len knew now that Jane and her baby had gone for ever, but he still wondered what was going to be done to them. The cortege stopped while he was thinking, and Big Jim led him through the silent ranks of bare-headed men to the edge of Jane's grave.

Still clasping his father's hand, Len looked down into the freshly dug, water-sogged hole. He began to cry, and throughout the ceremony that followed he only dimly comprehended the beautiful panegyric that Dai Cannon was pouring out upon the dead daughter of his mate. After the hymn that followed the closing words Len looked again into the hole. This time it was not empty. The coffin seemed to float in the water that reached half way up its sides. Len threw the little bunch of flowers into the grave. He wanted them to drop on the coffin, but they fell into the water surrounding it. This turned his tears into sobs and Jim hurried him away.

Len never remembered going home. He sat moping in the corner while the relatives and friends busily consumed the ham and other food specially bought for and peculiar to the occasion. When the repast was over the relatives and friends quietly took their leave, each whispering a few condolences to Shane as they went. Then Len and his parents were left alone with their thoughts and their memories. The tears that fell on the sanded floor did not break the silence that followed, but at last Big Jim rose and, tenderly lifting the worn-out Shane to her feet, led her upstairs.

Len followed with scarcely a sound, and that night he missed Jane more than ever as he pictured her warm body and recalled conversations with her. During the months that followed he dreaded remaining in the house. Incidents and words constantly brought Jane back to his mind, and he would go off to the mountains and wander aimlessly over their slopes. Often he would lie down on the mountain and cry himself to sleep, waking when the coldness of dusk pierced his clothes, but he no longer found any pleasure in the rambles down the valley after and during school hours. The death of Jane had marked the end of his boyhood.

CHAPTER V

The Explosion

THOUGH the death of his daughter had shaken Big Jim, he soon took up the usual routine of his life. When he had money he spent it in the Boar's Head, more often than not finishing the night with a fight. When he and Dai had no money they spent their evenings arguing in Ben the Barber's shop, and the main topic of discussion sooner or later always centred around the pits. It appeared that conditions were becoming worse. Mr. Hicks, the general manager, was pressing the men for more coal, while the officials, under his direction, were refusing to pay for work the men claimed they had already done.

Len heard the repercussions of what was happening in the pits each alternate Saturday, when his father brought home the pay for the preceding fortnight's work. When Big Jim had what he regarded as a good pay, he always enjoyed a little smoke after dinner and before bathing. But when he had a smaller pay packet than he expected or thought he deserved, he would bath first, then after dinner casually throw his wages on the table with an offhanded remark, " There you be, Shane bach. That be all I can do for you this week, my gel."

On one such occasion Shane slowly counted the money over, while Jim carefully soaped his moustache. After the first count her lips tightened ominously and she went over the coins once more. Then she looked up. " Some little mistake by here, i'n't there, James bach ? " she asked quietly.

Jim looked at her with feigned surprise. " Mistake ? Of course not, my gel," he replied. Then he added, " Not that I know of anyway. Let us count it again ; perhaps it is you that have made the mistake. Ha-ha." He laughed lamely, in spite of a big effort to appear unconcerned.

Together they recounted the money scattered on the table. When this was done Jim looked at Shane uneasily. "There you are," he said with forced jocularity. "What did I tell you? It is you who have made the mistake, my gel." He stopped a moment, then finished with, "I knowed there be nothing wrong with the pay."

Shane bridled up. "Nothing wrong?" she exclaimed incredulously. "Nothing wrong, you say? Man alive, if there be nothing wrong with the pay then there must be something wrong with you. Or," she added slyly, "perhaps you be starting your 'scursion tricks again."

Jim coloured up. "For shame, Shane bach," he said reproachfully. "You didn't ought throw that up to my face. You do know it was only a little joke on my part." His temper began to rise. "What the hell can I help if the pay be small?" he burst out vehemently. "Arglwydd mawr, I do work hard enough for it."

A short silence followed this outburst. It was broken by Jim, who began to wheedle. "Come, nghyariad i, give me my pocket-money. I have promised faithful to meet Dai Cannon to-night on very 'portant business."

Shane interrupted him brusquely. "Ah, I did think so," she said. "Dai. 'Portant business. Anything but your home. How do you think I be going to keep all of us on this money? Bah, boy's money! I 'ood be shamed to bring it home if I was you."

Jim dreaded the bitter onslaught of her tongue, but he braved it for the sake of his pocket-money. He tried blustering. "Come, come, venw," he uttered sharply, "there be no need for all this fuss and nonsense. You can't always 'spect to have big money. I will have a good place next week, then things will be better."

Shane took no notice of his bluster. "Big money! Next week!" she twitted harshly, her eyes beginning to glitter. "You will say next that I have been squandering the pay.

If anybody did hear you, man, they 'ood swear I had put you ears over heels in debt."

She began to weep into her canvas apron. " What good be next week to me ? " she asked plaintively. " We have got to live till then, and don't forget, James," she put in as a final shot, " that you be a big-eating man."

Big Jim looked at her, his eyes at once desperate and despairing. He was ashamed of the pay himself, but was too proud to admit it. Shane had beaten him in the argument and he had no more to say. He put on his coat with a hopeless gesture and walked to the door, making as much noise as possible on the way.

Shane raised her head from the apron. " Where be you going ? " she asked.

The tone of her query put new hope into Jim. Quietly, as if weary and overcome with care, he replied, " Not far, Shane bach. Only just down the road to have a shave from Ben the Barber."

" But you have got no money," she retorted.

Jim saw his opportunity and jumped at it. " No ; I do know that well 'nough, nghyariad bach i," he said ; " but Ben be very good to me when he do know I be down and out."

Shane pricked up her ears at this. Her face reddened. " Don't you dare, James Roberts, to simple me before any man," she commanded. " We have gone through worse times than this and we still be alive."

Jim knew he had conquered and gravely murmured, as she handed him some money, " I did know you 'oodn't leave me down when it come to the push, Shane bach. You be so good as gold, though your words do come so hard as brass sometimes."

With this he went out, promising he would not be late.

Shane remained at the table planning how best to share the pay between the various debts that had accumulated during the past fortnight. Len wrote the items down at her dictation. Several times she made him change them, but at last she seemed satisfied and rose to her feet. Len fetched

the heavy woollen shawl from behind the door. She
swathed this round her head and shoulders and bade Len
follow her.

Both of them enjoyed these Saturday night shopping
expeditions. The women of the village used the general
stores of Mr. Evans Cardi to retail gossip while the obliging
Mr. Evans attended to their requirements.

This night the chief item of gossip was the bad times.
" Yes, my gel," Mrs. Thomas told Shane, loud enough for
everyone in the stores to hear, " things be getting worse
from day to day. How they 'spect people to live on the
money they pay our men, the good Lord alone knows."

A murmur of assent spread round the counter.

" Ay," responded Shane, " you be quite right. I
'member the time we could put a few shillings by our side
every fortnight, but we have to pay it out now as it come in,
and then we haven't got 'nough to go round half our time."

The conversation became general. One woman who had
a houseful of children remarked, " It be 'bout time our men
did something. What with small money and the children
coming every year, life be not worth living. The pits is
going to pieces," she added bitterly : " they will never
again be like they used to."

After a while Shane gathered up the groceries Mr. Evans
had placed in a big paper bag for her. She handed this to
Len with the remark, " We had better go now, boy bach,
to make supper ready against your father come home."

The street looked dark and forbidding after the warm,
glaring oil-lamps in the stores and a slight drizzle made the
road muddy underfoot.

Len and his mother had reached the lane that led up the
mountain to Sunny Bank when they heard an uproar in
Main Street, which they had left behind. " Some drunken
men fighting again, I 'spose," commented Shane casually.
" Fitter if they went home to their famblies."

She continued on her way. Suddenly she pulled up short
and turned her head towards the street. Above the uproar
rose the great voice of Big Jim. " Let him come on," she

heard him roar. " Think you I be 'fraid of any man, let alone a bloody Bristolian ? "

Shane hurriedly retraced her steps, Len following with the groceries. Outside the Boar's Head they saw a crowd of people stretching across the street, swaying spasmodically to the accompaniment of excited shouts. " Fair play there ! Keep the ring clear ! No up and down."

Shane pulled the shawl more tightly round her head and forced her way towards the centre, Len following closely at her heels. He heard a woman scream at the top of her voice : " O God, they be killing each other. Police ! Police ! "

A man near her growled, " What the hell be the matter on you, venw. Get off home if you don't like to see a fight. Don't worry 'bout the police." He added, " I 'spect he is snooping round the back-streets looking for burglars that are not there, ha-ha. You can venture you 'on't see him here," he concluded.

Smacking thuds followed by loud grunts frightened Len, and he would have run away had it not been for his mother. When she stopped pressing through the crowd he drew to her side and saw the ring made by the people. In the centre his father and Bill Bristol, both naked to the waist, were punching away at each other with every ounce of energy concentrated in their fists.

Len saw the blood spurt from Bill's face as Big Jim's fist caught him squarely on the nose. A gasp went through the crowd, echoing the impact of the blow. Bill Bristol staggered back, and willing hands held him erect. Someone offered a knee as a stool, and Bill was made to sit on this while the blood was mopped from his face with his own shirt.

Meanwhile Big Jim had turned to Dai Cannon. " That have finished it," he said : " you might as well leave me have my shirt and coat now."

He began to pull on his shirt when he heard a sudden shout : " Good old Bill ! That's what you want, guts ! Play for his belly and you'll soon have him down. The bigger they are the harder they fall."

Like a flash Big Jim twisted the shirt off his head and half turned to meet his antagonist. But he was too late to check the headlong rush of the recovered Bill. The latter dodged the fist flung at him like a thunderbolt and buried his lowered head deep into Jim's belly.

Big Jim's mouth was forced open with an agonising gasp by the violently expelled wind. The quivering knees slowly contorted themselves into a subsiding movement and Jim's body collapsed like a deflated concertina, but his brain remained perfectly conscious and clear although his muscles were paralysed by the impact. He tore at the air with his lips as he tried to gulp it into his lungs, where it rattled like a bag of marbles.

Shane bent over her fallen spouse and reproachfully taunted him. " What be you doing down by there, James bach ? " she asked him. " Fancy lying in the gutter with the only decent suit you have got. Ach ! Call yourself a man ! Why, I could buy your sort for ten a penny."

The gibe sent an electric quiver through Jim's body, giving it new and sudden life. He sprang to his feet with a bound and a muttered curse.

Bill Bristol, surprised at the quick recovery, sprang forward and met Jim half-way. He tried to repeat the same tactic as before, and literally flung himself, like a bullet, head first at Jim's body. But the latter had learned a bitter lesson. He stepped a little to one side as Bill reached him and his huge fist streaked in and out once like a snake's tongue. The thud of the terrible blow clotted the blood in Len's veins. He saw the horrible jerk that seemed to tear Bill's head from his shoulders. He watched the body straighten like a released spring and flatten itself on the wet earth.

The excited people in the crowd knew the prostrate man would fight no more that night, and anxious hands helped him to recover while Dai Cannon helped Jim don his shirt and coat.

Shane, her eyes shining, kept nagging. " For shame, James," she said. " Do you call yourself a 'spectable man, fighting like a blackguard on Main Street ? Just the same the blood of Bill Bristol could be on your head this night. What do you think people will say 'bout me ? I will be too shamed to raise my head in chapel again."

Jim grunted an inaudible answer and walked over to the recovering Bill, who after some further assiduous attention, stood dazedly on his feet. Jim caught his arm and led him back to where Dai Cannon was earnestly talking to Shane. The latter was saying when they reached her, " All right, David, I will give James half an hour. William did ought to be better by then. But 'member," she exclaimed, turning to Jim, " no more nonsense. If butties can't have a pint together without fighting, then they better left it there altogether."

Without more words Dai and Jim made their way through the open door of the Boar's Head, and most of the men in the crowd followed them.

Len and his mother trudged quietly up the black hill. The oil-lamps shining through the windows of Sunny Bank invited them to hurry through the drizzle, and both were glad when they reached the house. Shane busied herself fanning the dying fire into flame while Len sat moodily in the corner, and as soon as he had finished his• supper he went straight to bed.

Next day in chapel Len watched his mother carefully. He expected to see her with drooping head after the events of the previous night, but both she and Dai Cannon appeared to have forgotten what had occurred.

The sermon was based on the text, " If he strike thee on one cheek, turn to him the other." In deep tones Dai rolled out his message to the congregation, and at the end of the service the women declared to each other that they had never heard such a beautiful and inspiring sermon.

Throughout the day Len failed to tear from his eyes the sight of Bill Bristol's blood-spattered face. Physical brutality was repugnant to the lad. He tried to imagine how Bill felt when Jim's fist smashed into his nose.

The thought made him shudder coldly, and for the remainder of the day he remained silent and aloof.

Since Jane's death Len had become increasingly morbid and introspective, and that night in bed his thoughts ran riot. He pictured Jane as he used to see her and wondered how Evan the Overman's son had done to give her the baby from which she died. His warm body tossed restlessly about the lonely bed as his imagination fluttered between mental images. Pressing Jane's pillow closely to him, he longed again for her presence, but this only made him think of the muddied grave, and as his mind drifted from one morbid thought to another he fell at last into an uneasy sleep.

He slept for some hours before waking to the roar of a thunder-clap. The intense darkness made him doubt if his eyes were open. In the act of putting his fingers to them he saw the blazing flash of lightning that filled the bedroom with a ghostly blue haze. It went in a second and left the room darker than ever. The pursuing thunder frightened him, and he tried to hide from its crackling roar by burying his head beneath the bed-clothes. But the thunder followed.

The fitful lightning flashes and the rising tumult quickened Len's emotions. He felt afraid. Quivers ran up and down his flesh and he broke out into a sweat. He wound the bed-clothes more tightly about him, thinking their warmth would provide protection from the noisy storm, but, though the school books told him that thunder was harmless, he was more afraid of its clamouring roar than of the knife-like flashes that cut the night in two.

Swathed in the blanket, his nerves tense with anticipation, he waited for the next crash. He heard the initial ear-shattering crack, but the usual rolling rumbles that chased it were drowned in an unearthly roar that made the house tremble and for a moment the air was full of little flaming bubbles that suddenly spluttered out and left the world dark and still as if all existence had ended.

Len sprang out of bed and rushed screaming to his

mother's room. He found her moaning as she tried to light the candle with a match that quivered in her hand, while Big Jim, clad only in a shirt, stood peering through the window as if the universe were centred in his eyes. The glow from the sputtering candle filled the bedroom with moving shadows, and Len stopped screaming. The hushed silence that followed was broken by a hoarse groan from Shane.

" Oh, James bach, James bach," she muttered in a shuddering undertone, as if scared of her own voice, " the pit have blowed up."

Jim, still at the window, did not answer. He saw the lights that suddenly appeared at every window in the street glimmer like corpse candles upon the rain-drops, and suddenly springing towards the bed he snatched his trousers from the rail, and with frenzied fingers began pulling the garment over his naked legs.

Simultaneously Shane got out of bed, still moaning to herself. As she also began hurriedly to dress, she asked him : " Where be you going ? " Receiving no reply, she cried out : " Oh, God bach, you be going to your death, James."

By the time she had wrapped the woollen shawl about her head Jim had already rushed down the stairs. Turning to Len, she lifted the terror-stricken lad into the bed. Then, with a murmured, " Be a good boy, Len bach ; mam 'on't be long," she tucked him in and followed Jim down the stairs and out of the house.

The street was already full of half-clad, white-faced men and women. They paid no heed to the driving rain that beat on to their shivering bodies or the lightning that sizzled through the air and bathed the valley in sulphuric blue. Each street was a tributary, pouring men and women into the main stream of people rushing madly up the hill to the scene of the explosion. Only children, hysterical with fear, were left behind in the houses.

The rain slashed savagely at streaming faces, while the thunder cracked and rumbled in angry roars, but the people were oblivious to the cruelty of the elements. As if drawn by magnets, they flung themselves into the storm, defeating all its attempts to prevent them from reaching the pit. At every street the living stream of distracted human beings gained impetus and numbers, and the clang of their hob-nailed boots challenged the jealous mumbling of the thunder.

No words were spoken now. Nothing mattered but to reach the pit. Slowly the long, uphill drag against the storm began to take toll of the weaker and the aged. Gasping and coughing under the terrible physical and emotional strain, they had to give way to the stronger and more agile, who forged to the front. Big Jim, who had burst his way through the querulous crowd, was at the head of the long-drawn, hurrying procession. Shane, panting and spitting thick clots of saliva that filled her mouth, was close on his heels. For every stride he took she had to take two.

Her legs dragged on her thighs like lead. The pain in her body reminded her of the times when she had to carry sacks of coal on her back. Then she had felt her body being squeezed into her feet. Now she felt her feet tearing her body from her head. She stumbled and moaned, but, closing her eyes, she followed her feet, which automatically rose and fell and drew her on. She felt her body go numb from the exhaustion, and was glad, because her brain cleared as a consequence. When Big Jim led the rush over the flimsy wooden bridge that spanned the ravine separating the pit from the village, Shane was still close to him.

The crude structure became a bridge of sighs that echoed the trampling feet stumbling across it, and the thin cordon of police and pit officials at the end was brushed aside like soot by the rushing people. Mr. Hicks, the general manager of the pit, howled, " Keep back. Keep back. Everything is all right." His howls became wails and were lost in the storm. None of the rain-drenched people heard what he said, as with deadly certainty they plunged towards the pit, from whose mouth belched the fumes generated by the explosion.

When they reached the pit-head everything became

confusion for some minutes. The storm redoubled its efforts to dominate the scene. Men shouted incoherently to each other, women screamed and moaned. Everyone gave orders that no one obeyed.

Ezra Jones, the miners' leader, who was already on the pit-head, beckoned Big Jim to him. Ezra's short, thick-set body and stern face looked as hard as the coal from which he forced a livelihood. Jim forced his way forward, Shane still following. "Jim," said Ezra, his cold voice quivering a little, "we must get these people away from the pit-head." Big Jim nodded agreement. He looked around the excited crowd and realised if something were not done quickly the women would become hysterical and panicky. He went back into the thick of the crowd, urging men here and there to the front. When he returned he found the biggest men of the village circling the pit-head, keeping the others behind them.

The storm gave added terror and significance to the scene. Its crooked lightning cynically blinded the staring eyes, then played in blue streaks round the trellised steelwork of the pit-head gears. The lightning used the red glare from the open furnaces as a frame for itself, then mockingly withdrew for a moment into black obscurity, to return unexpectedly a moment later with ten times greater ferocity. Thunder wantonly joined in the game. Its unholy laughter rolled and crackled, tearing the air in a devil's chorus of reverberating echoes, that died down the valley only to be born again, with greater vigour, at the pit.

Heedless of the clamour, Big Jim and Ezra strengthened the cordon of men around the pit. Mr. Hicks, putty-faced and panting, was allowed through. Shane kept near the rim of the cordon, never taking her eyes from Big Jim.

The three men held a hurried consultation with certain of the other workmen, and when it was ended Big Jim's great voice rang out above the storm.

"Rescue brigade and first-aid men to the front!" The ring immediately opened to admit the men who obeyed the command. Scores of volunteers rushed to carry out the next order that someone should fetch the rescue apparatus from the stores, where it had been rotting unattended for years, but apart from an occasional moan no voice could be heard except that which was giving the orders.

It was now discovered that the pit cage had been smashed into the side of the shaft by the force of the explosion, and the splintered steel was dangling like ravelled cloth from the threaded rope that held it.   After another hurried conference it was decided that the only thing to do was to make use of the discarded sinking-bucket, rusting a quarter of a mile away from the coal screens, and soon a score of men were pushing and rolling the bucket towards the pit, while others disentangled what remained of the cage.

Suddenly a woman's piercing scream rang clear through the turmoil. It rose in ascending, agonising shrieks. " O God, spare him for me !   Let him come back home."

Shane shivered icily as a crash of thunder swallowed the pitiful plea.   For the first time that night she forced her eyes away from Big Jim, and looked at the distraught young woman near by, who had fallen on her knees into the black mud and was tearing loose her rain-soddened hair. The woman's mouth opened and shut like a frog's, but no sound came from it.   Shane flung her shawl over the woman's heaving shoulders and, bending down, tried to lift her from the mud.   " Come, my gel," she murmured, " don't take it like this now.   Perhaps everything will come all right for you and all your tears will be wasted."

The woman appeared not to hear, and began screaming again.   Shane shook her roughly, at the same time blinking back the tears from her own eyes.   " That will do," she said.   " You must act like a 'ooman, not like a child, at this time.   'Member, you might need all of your strength before this night be gone over your head."

Other women came to Shane's assistance.   They lifted the shaking form bodily from the mud and led her gently away, leaving the storm to silence the gasping wails that bubbled wetly from her lips.   Once more Shane turned her attention to Big Jim, flinging back the wet hair from her eyes and wringing it into a knot at the back of her neck, but Big Jim and his mates had paid no attention to the incident. Franticly they continued their efforts to fix the bucket to the rope, and finally the sure, hurrying fingers completed the transference.

Ezra began drawing the weird-looking rescue apparatus over his head, but without a word of explanation Big Jim and some of the other men took it from him. Sharp words followed between them, Ezra claiming the right to go down the shaft with the first group. They did not argue, but hurriedly taking a vote, decided that Ezra had to remain on the surface.

The bucket was now dangling over the fearful, steaming hole, slowly circling round itself and round the shaft at the same time, like a ghastly pendulum, the dual motion being caused by the absence of guide ropes to steady it. Soon a number of men, wearing rescue apparatus and led by Big Jim, wormed their way across the black gap that separated them from the oscillating bucket, and climbing in stood jammed erect, their masks making them look like inhuman creatures from some abysmal world. Then, as the bucket slowly sank into the fuming mouth of the pit, Shane forced her way through the cordon. Her face shone white even through the black grime that covered it. Both hands were pressed with tense hardness to her chest. Her voice came in gasps as she shouted : " Stop a minute ! Stop a minute ! "

Someone caught her by the shoulders and held her back. Shane turned round with a snarl. " Keep your dirty hands off me ! " she shouted. " Who be you to dare stop me going with my man ? " Her eyes were too misty to see who gripped her. She wasn't even aware there was more than one.

Shane battled grimly to break away from the impeding grasp. " Let me go," she screamed, kicking out wildly, " my place be with my man."

But finding her struggles were of no avail, she suddenly

relaxed. " It be all right now," she announced. " Please forgive me, I know I have done wrong ; " and her eyes were dry and hard, as they stared at the bucket that was now nearly out of sight.

Its slow descent was followed by a soft groan from thousands of parched throats. The groan became a mass moan which kept time with the motion of the bucket and its human cargo as it slithered out of sight, leaving nothing but the snaky rope to mark its existence. Imperceptibly the moan took shape, was given form. Deeper than the sea, it nestled a path through the voids in the thunder. Sometimes it was subdued by the fiercely crashing roars, but it always returned to ride their crests, until at last it swept a clear road of domination above the storm. At once a prayer and a challenge, the old Welsh hymn burned its fiery way into the hearts of the grieving men and women on the pit-head, melting their sobs into music which mastered the tempest and rang down the valley of doom. Mournfully the cadences of the hymn, harmonised in the common agony, broke the air into emotional vibrations.

> Beth sydd ymi yn y byd
> Ond Gorthrymderau mawr o hyd.
>
> What in this world for me
> But great grief and agony.

The pit had become in one night a crematorium surrounded by thousands of mourning people.

In the meantime Big Jim and his rescue brigade, speechless under their rescue gear, were swinging giddily from side to side of the shaft. Thick, swirling fumes gave them the impression they were slowly falling through dense clouds, and during the descent the bucket swung with exceptional force into the side, nearly tumbling two of the men out into the black depths beneath. As it was impossible to give vocal orders Big Jim did the next best thing, and placed his hands out rigid before him over the side of the bucket. Each of the other men followed suit, and their hands made a buttress between the bucket and the sides.

Slowly, shrouded in a green halo spread by the gleam of the safety lamps hanging from their belts upon the fumes that enveloped them, the rescue men sank into the pit. Although they appeared cool and calm, inwardly they quivered with dread of what they were about to see, for everyone of them was an experienced miner who had practically been reared in the pit and knew all its moods and powers.

At last the bucket bumped sharply on the shaft bottom and the interminable descent was over.

The lamp lights seemed to fling the foggy fumes back into their eyes and made them blinder than the darkness. The men shut their eyes tightly and lowered the lamps until they nearly touched the floor. After some minutes they opened their eyes again and were able to distinguish objects.

Big Jim walked in front, while the others lined themselves across the breadth of the roadway so that nothing should escape their joint observation, and in this way they proceeded, with infinite slowness, further into the pit. After about ten minutes of this, during which the atmosphere got more dense and hot each second, Big Jim called a sudden halt. His lips formed themselves into a " sh-h-h " which no one heard. He realised this, and raised his finger to his mouth as if seeking to enjoin silence where all was still. The men, however, understood what he meant and stood rigidly erect, straining their ears to catch any sound that should break through their masks.

From a seeming distance of miles they heard a crackling noise as if some huge fire was feeding itself on an incalculable supply of what it needed. Sweat poured down the men's strained flesh in streams. It was hot, like boiling water.

One of the men could stand the strain no longer, and dragging the helmet from his head, heard for one second the roar of the fire. Then everything was lost in the cough that tore his lungs. He gasped for air, every gasp choking him more firmly. He felt his lungs tearing and tasted the blood that rushed to his throat and mouth. But he never knew that Big Jim had sprung forward and jammed the helmet back on his head.

When Big Jim raised himself from the prostrate man he shook his head sadly, and the small group, now one man less, walked slowly on. Here and there they had to clamber over falls of roof and hot steel girders, their hearts pumping madly and their heads bursting inside the helmets that covered them. They inhaled the putrid air inside their masks with gasping swallows, like sufferers from tonsilitis.

When they reached the stables Big Jim again halted. Falling on his knees he began to feverishly turn over the black blotches that lay in queer heaps upon the ground. The other men followed suit. When they stood erect again their legs were trembling and their stomachs felt sick. They had found the first victims of the explosion.

At the pit-head the people waited. Every eye was focused upon the rope that had ceased moving long before. Its stillness told the people that Big Jim and his men were still searching. For all who watched it it had become the centre of creation, as hour after hour they waited, their voices becoming mute and their faces set into unnatural hardness. Patience lost meaning and time had no existence in the common urge to know what was happening in the black depths of the pit.

The sun was struggling to push its new-born rays through the cloud-crusted murk of the valley when the iron knocker at the pit-head suddenly clanged. The dead silence that instantly followed the solitary knell was more eerie than the thunder rumbling dismally in the distance.

At the second clang the people shivered as if icicles had pierced their flesh. The tension was eased by the spontaneous quiver, and a tremor of suppressed excitement ran through the throng. A warm glow stole over their cold bodies, and anxiously the waiting people strained their ears to catch the third signal announcing that someone or something was ready to ascend from below. When the sharp command came everyone shuddered with sudden apprehension. They dreaded that the ascending bucket contained someone belonging to themselves.

Shane drew the rain-shrunken shawl, which had been returned, more tightly around her shoulders. The hair again hung loose in wet wisps about her face. Fixing her eyes upon the rope that was slowly beginning to move, she mused audibly, " I wonder what it be bringing up ? "

A gleam flashed in her eyes as she thought, " Perhaps my James be dangling from its end."

She felt the rope was moving too slowly. She wanted it to hasten so that everyone could see what the bucket held, but in the same instant she banished the thought from her head. " No-no," she murmured, " bad news do travel quick enough without us wishing it to come quicker."

The same impulses filled the other people, as the rope weaved a slow path around the huge wheel above their heads. Men mentally measured the rate of the rope against the depth of the pit, and unspoken thoughts told everyone that the bucket was near the surface. A restless, impatient movement again ran through the crowd like quicksilver. Face looked at face in mute appeal and saw nothing but the black-grimed shadow of itself. The ring of men around the pit-head closed in nearer, and stood ready to grasp the bucket and whatever it contained immediately it reached the surface.

Sensing the developing panic, Ezra called out in his cold, harsh voice, " Steady, boys. Cool heads now." The calm, sensible words eased the tension and soothed hysterical emotions, and when at last the bucket broke through the black void of the pit-mouth willing hands hurriedly pulled it to the side.

The sole human occupant was gently lifted out. While some men unstrapped the encumbering rescue apparatus from his shoulders, others removed the misshapen, brattice-covered lumps dumped in the bottom of the bucket like sacks of red cement. Eight of these were drawn out, tenderly straightened on the waiting stretchers, and immediately carried to the manager's office on the other side of the bridge. Silently the people opened their ranks to make way for the passing corpses, for although not a limb could be seen everyone knew that Big Jim and his men had made sure of the first victims of the explosion.

Sad-eyed women, their wet skirts sticking to their legs, followed the procession of stretchers across the bridge to the temporary mortuary in the office. But most of the men remained at the pit-head where Ezra and Mr Hicks were questioning the rescue man, who had now recovered from his exhaustion. He reported that the stables near the pit bottom were a mass of impassable flames, and that a huge fall of roof further on prevented penetration into the inner workings. The eight men already brought up had been found huddled together near the stables, as if seeking to protect each other from the blast that swept the mine.

When he reported the terrible death of the rescue man everyone present was shocked. They vividly pictured the horrible details of the tragedy.

The rescue man brought them back to the task on hand when he added that it was impossible for Big Jim and his mates to remain below much longer, as the after-damp was already beginning to intrude its poisonous breath inside the gas-masks.

To stress his warning the iron knocker clanged an urgent message to the surface. Ezra hastily strapped the rescue apparatus to his own shoulders and stepped into the bucket. The rope again commenced its twirling motion as it dropped the bucket with its solitary occupant into the shaft.

Police and extra rescue men, hurriedly drafted in from other places, cleared the colliery yard of the people not directly engaged in rescue work.

Shane and a number of other women steadfastly refused to move. " What do you think I be ? " asked Shane when they attempted to remove her. " Think you I be slut enough to go crying across the bridge while my man be down in that hell ? No," she declared with adamant determination, " there be no man or devil in this or any other world can shift me from by here until I see my James safe and sound."

Further unpleasantness was prevented by the appearance of the bucket and all those who had descended the shaft after the explosion.

Shane ran forward and threw her arms around Jim's neck. " Thank God," she whispered in his ear. " I be satisfied now that I know you be all right.

Jim said nothing, but squeezed her tightly for a moment before entering the little shack at the pit-head where his mates and the other responsible people were.

While the police cordoned off all approaches to the pit Big Jim made his report. " We will have to tackle it from two ends," he said. " Some will have to work their way through from the pits the other side of the mountain, while some of us be driving through the fall of roof this end."

" But before we can do anything," he added, " we will first of all have to smother the fire in the stable. It will all have to be done in very short shifts, because the heat and smoke be unbearable."

Ezra and Mr. Hicks now took charge of the operations, while Jim and his mates made their way to the office. Here they found the mass of people who had been urged from the pit-head. Inside the office attempts were being made to identify the bodies already brought up. Jim helped in this. The corpses were stripped stark naked and searched for birth marks, while other means of identification were sought in the clothes. Big Jim, examining the pockets of a pair of trousers he picked up from the floor, pulled out a brass tobacco pouch containing some loose tobacco and a shilling and exclaimed excitedly : " This do belong to Shoni Jones, Cap-du."

The name flew from mouth to mouth until it was stopped by a wild scream when it reached the ears of the widow. Willing and tender hands led her away.

It was agreed by the man in charge that the bodies not identified should be left where they were for a while. The body of Shoni Cap-du was replaced on a stretcher and covered with some brattice-cloth.

Headed by what was left of Shoni Cap-du and the dead rescue man, the wet, grief-stricken people wearily made their way down Main Street to their homes. The frenzied rush through the storm on the previous night together with the agonising wait at the pit-head had exhausted them in mind and body, and their grief was sharpened by the uncertainty of the actual casualties and by the knowledge that it would take a considerable time to clear the pit and find the full extent and effects of the explosion. Families with missing men mourned even while they tried to persuade themselves that remote possibilities were probabilities.

Jim and Shane found Len crouched over the dead embers of the fire. The big, bright eyes that looked into theirs when they entered showed that the lad had cried himself dry in a fury of impotent fears, but neither of them had given him a thought during the terror of the night. Shane was immediately penitent. She stooped down and gathered the lad to her wet clothes, crooning in his ear, " There, there, nghyariad bach i. Don't cry no more. Mam 'o'n't leave you alone never again."

Big Jim interrupted her. " Where be your sense, venw ? " he exclaimed. " You leave him alone to frighten his little self to death all night, and now that you do find him alive after all you do want him to die of pewmonia from your wet clothes."

Thus reminded of her condition, Shane began to build the fire into a huge blaze while Big Jim coaxed from the usually reticent Len a recital of what he had felt during the night.

When his parents had left him, Len, already frightened by the storm, had let his imagination run riot. Like all other miners' children, he knew that explosions meant death and destruction. And once he had gripped this fact it was easy for his fertile mind, egged on by the storm and the horrible loneliness, to conjure up pictures of burned and

4

mangled bodies. He had seen his father among the dead, his body shredded into blood-dripping pieces.

Shane had remained silent up to this point, but she now sensed that the lad was working himself up into an emotional climax. She checked the recital with the abrupt announcement, "Come, the two of you, and have something hot in your insides."

Big Jim ate nothing throughout the meal. Shane mused more than she ate. " There be many a poor dab gone to meet his God before his time this night," she said, half crying. " I wonder, James bach, if there be any we do know among them ? "

Jim did not reply. He knew most of the men working in the pit when the explosion occurred, and he knew from what he had seen that only a miracle could bring any of them from it alive, but he did not believe in miracles. The fall of roof, while big enough to prevent ingress to the workings, had failed to subdue the sound of crackling flames or to prevent the heavy, poisonous fumes percolating through.

As Big Jim's thoughts jumped from name to name, linking each with an incident or characteristic relating to it, he muttered, abstractedly, " Poor old Shoni Cap-du 'on't drink any more pints in the Boar's Head."

He was silent a moment, and Shane looked at him quietly. At length he exclaimed, in a somewhat louder voice : " Duw, duw. Who 'ood think the old pit 'ood blow up so sudden ? But there," he added, as an afterthought, " I have knowed there have been something the matter with her for a long time now."

He ceased his musings, and Shane handed him a cup of tea. " Have this now, James bach," she coaxed. " Then try to have a bit of a rest."

Big Jim took her advice but found sleep impossible, and in a very short time his impatient restlessness took him to Ben the Barber's.

The little back room was crowded with men discussing the explosion and its victims. Ben was unusually silent in face of the catastrophe that had swept the pit. He felt keenly the immensity of the grief that was to follow. The men moved up to make place for Jim's huge bulk. They had already been commenting upon his daring initiative during the preceding night. Young Charlie the Cripple kept close to Jim when the latter sat on the bench.

Big Jim turned towards Dai Cannon, who was sitting in his customary place near the fire. Jim noisily retched some mucus from his chest to his mouth and spat it on the floor before saying, " Well, boys, it have come at last, as it was bound to come sooner or later."

He paused a moment, as if expecting Dai or one of the others to say something. Finding that no one responded, he went on, wiping the back of his hand across his mouth. " Huh. If us all spoke the truth us would all say that we 'spected it to come. Ach ! No man can drag coal from the face like hair, and leave his gobs empty, without something being bound to happen. No ; you leave the gobs empty of muck and they will soon fill with gas."

Jim stopped a moment again, then burst out with a passionate oath, his voice resounding with the vehemence of his conviction. " Argllwydd mawr ! That's all they do think 'bout these days is coal, coal, and still more coal. Blast safety. That don't count. Blow the men to hell, but give the big boss coal."

He was now roaring in his fury, and every word brought more saliva on his moustache. " Don't us all know that the pit have been getting worse every day ? " he demanded. " The officials did know so good as us men, but they never took any notice. Bah ! What do us men count ? We be cheaper than chickens."

Big Jim subsided into silence. After a brief spell during which everyone appeared to be thinking hard over Jim's words, Dai Cannon took up the subject. His deep voice trembled with emotion as he said, " There is much in what Jim says. Yes, very much. But it's no good us talking like that now. What we have got to do is get those boys up as quick as we can, dead or alive, and put the old pit a bit shipshape again. All of our talk or all of our tears 'on't bring our butties back to us."

While this discussion was taking place Ezra, Mr. Hicks, and Lord Cwmardy, who had hurried specially from London to the scene of the disaster, were planning the rescue operations. They divided the twenty-four hours into shifts of two hours each, and allocated the men necessary for them.

Big Jim was allowed to come and go to the pit as he liked. He worked practically night and day. His strength, example, and experience spurred on the other men and gave added energy to their flagging bodies.

The men worked in the most intolerable conditions. Excessive heat and the fœtid atmosphere melted their flesh and left them like empty sacks at the end of their short shifts. The bodies they discovered each day were simply ghastly lumps of greasy putrefaction. Very few could be identified. In a short time it became known to the people of the valley that the explosion had left no survivors.

CHAPTER VI

The Inquest and Burial

THE people of Cwmardy were full of excitement. Sad-eyed women, their arms folded inside their aprons, stood on the street corners and discussed the rumour spreading round the village like wildfire. In Ben the Barber's shop nothing else was talked of. No one seemed to know where the rumour emanated from, but those who were bereaved by the explosion already regarded it as Gospel truth, and the day before the inquest on the first eight bodies brought up the flaming pit, matters reached a head in Sunny Bank.

Big Jim, his legs stretched obscenely towards the fire, was about to doze off when Shane asked him, apropos of nothing, " Do you think there be any truth in it, James bach ? "

Jim looked at her, blank surprise in his eyes, before appealing to Len. " Now what do you think of that ? " he asked the lad. " Your mother 'spect me to read her mind while she do keep her tongue between her teeth and her eyes shut."

Len did not answer, although he wondered what his mother was driving at. Jim turned and addressed himself directly to her, saying, " Now tell me, venw, what exactly do you want me to tell you ? "

Shane took umbrage at his tone. " There you go again," she complained. " I can't ask you a simple question unless you do go and lose your temper. You do talk to me, James, like as if I was a dog under your feet."

This somewhat softened Jim's asperity. The terrific strain of the rescue work was beginning to fray his nerves. " There, there, merch i," he consoled her. " Don't take no

notice of me, mun.   I be tired.   Tell me what you do want
to know."

Shane responded immediately.   " I was only asking you,
James bach, if you do believe all this talk going about."

Jim tried to keep his patience.   " What talk, my gel ? "
he asked.

" Oh, I thought you had heard," she replied.   " They
do say that the 'splosion was made by one of the men who
did open his lamp on the sly to have a whiff."

Jim sprang to his feet with an oath and banged his fist
violently upon the table.   His curses were eloquent
testimony that he did not believe the rumour.

Shane tried to placate him.   " Well, well," she said,
" there be no need for you to go to all this fuss.   I be only
telling you what everybody else be talking about."

" Ach ! " he snarled.   " Fitter if everybody looked
after their own bloody business and let the dead rest in
peace."   Saying which, he flung on his coat and left the
house without more ado.

Next morning Shane opened the box under the bed and
took out the suit she had bought Jim for Jane's funeral.
Ready tears sparkled in her eyes as she put the clothes to
air on the rod beneath the mantelpiece.

Jim, immersed in his thoughts, had recovered from his
temper of the previous evening.   " Last time you put these
on," Shane reminded him, " was when we did bury our Jane
bach.   Nothing have been right since she have gone."   She
wiped her eyes on the canvas apron.

" Ay, ay, merch i," retorted Jim ponderously, " that be
quite true.   But it be no good worrying 'bout it now," he
added resignedly.

Abruptly changing the subject, he asked, more to himself than Shane ;   " I wonder what I will have to say in the
inquest this afternoon.   They do tell me these lawyer chaps
be awful clever and can put into your mouth words you
don't want to say and don't mean.   Ezra did tell me yesterday to be very careful how I do answer the questions."

The nervous tone betrayed his uneasiness.   Shane tried

to encourage him. " Pooh-pooh ! " she exclaimed confidently. " Don't tell me that Big Jim be 'fraid of any man that do wear a frocktail coat and a black wig." She had never been in any court of law, but had been told by her neighbours that this was the uniform of justice. " All you got to do," she continued, " is to speak the truth. Truth will stand before man or God." She hesitated a moment to see what effect this had on Jim, then added : " Don't be 'fraid, James bach, I will come with you."

Jim jumped from his seat. " No-no, my gel," he hastily said. " Don't you worry 'bout me. I will look after myself. And even if I couldn't," he added, " they 'oodn't let you in with me, 'cause you are not a witness, see."

No more was said as Jim prepared himself for the inquest. Shane gave the final touches to his clothes and bade him as he left : " Now, 'member, James, you don't owe a single ha'penny to a living soul and can hold your head up before any man."

The inquest was to be held in the large room of the Boar's Head which, ordinarily, was only used on Saturday nights. When Jim arrived at the public-house a large number of his workmates tried to detain him with questions, but he evaded them and hurried into the large, rambling building. To reach the inquest room he had to pass through the public bar, where Dai Cannon and several more of his mates were drinking beer.

Twirling his moustaches, Jim refused with a pathetic smile Dai's invitation to have one before he went in. " No thanks," he said sadly. " You do know I have got very 'portant business to see to first and Shane have told me you can be had up for contempt of court if you go to a inquest with the smell of beer on your breath."

" Oh, well," Dai replied, " if that be the case you had better go in and get it over as quick as you can."

Jim winked feebly as he passed on through the bar. The policeman at the door of the big room let him through without any question. Big Jim, already damp with nervousness, entered and sat down gingerly on the bench nearest him, and looking around the room he recognised many of the men who stood chatting in groups. Among others he saw Ezra, Mr. Hicks, Evan the Overman, and certain relatives of the deceased men. The pompous-looking, well-dressed men in the front he assumed to be lawyers and clerks.

Jim was heartened by the presence of Ezra, the miners' leader, and was glad when he strolled across the room and sat next to him. In a low whisper, which softened the habitual harshness of his voice, Ezra tried to reassure the perturbed Jim.

" You have no need to be nervous," he said.

Jim swelled out his mighty chest. " Huh," he boasted. " Big Jim be not afraid. Don't forget, Ezra, I fight in the Boer War, and a man who done that have no need to be afraid of a few spaniels like them by there," pointing to the well-dressed men.

Ezra smiled quietly and waited. After a few moments' silence he said, " I am glad to hear that, Jim, because I understand they are going to try to put the blame for the explosion upon Shoni Cap-Du."

He felt Jim move on the seat, but went on as if he had noticed nothing, " You can scotch this effort if you speak the truth and stick to it through thick and thin."

Big Jim had no time to reply before the proceedings opened. He stood on his feet with the others in sympathy for the victims. Then for what seemed ages he hazily tried to follow Ezra's subdued comments on the evidence given by various people. But most of his attention was devoted to swallowing the hard lump that persistently rose in his throat, and this nervous reaction, coupled with his poor grasp of English, robbed him of any coherent knowledge of the proceedings.

He vaguely recognised Mr. Evans Cardi among the twelve sitting to the right of the coroner, and even while he tried to listen, he wondered why it was there were no miners among the jurymen. He heard a far-away voice call for " Mr James Roberts," but it did not occur to him that the name

was his until Ezra nudged him sharply and muttered,
" Your turn now. Pull yourself together ; speak the truth
and watch me."

Jim rose slowly to his feet, his white face set like a man
about to hear sentence of death passed on him. His huge
bulk dominated the room, but he was unaware of this as he
walked towards the important-looking men sitting at the
table. When he reached the table he stood irresolutely for
some seconds with perspiration gathering in little beads
about his collar. It irritated him, and he aimlessly inserted
his finger between his collar and wet neck, while everyone
present gazed at him with interest.

The stern-looking man opposite began asking questions.
Jim replied in a husky, tremulous voice which contrasted
strangely with his usual deep and boisterous tones. He
felt his face muscles twitching, and it was only with great
difficulty that he managed to control them. When he
spoke the words stuck in his parched throat and he had to
cough to get them out of his mouth. The strange sound of
his voice made him even more nervous, and he looked
supplicatingly at Ezra, whose encouraging glance and confident demeanour heartened him.

The coroner, having completed the usual formal inquiries,
was followed by an insignificant looking man who began to
re-examine Jim. He had a squeaky voice and a bombastic
manner, to which Jim took an immediate dislike, and with
every answer he gave his initial nervousness progressively
evaporated.

" Yes, sir," he said in answer to a question. " I be the
first man down the pit after the explosion and the first to
come across the dead bodies." Jim's voice was now nearly
normal and resonant.

His interrogator struck a pose before saying impressively,
" Now, Mr. Roberts, I want you to tell us exactly what you
saw when you reached the bodies."

Big Jim's mind spontaneously flashed back and a shudder
passed through his body. What he had seen again floated
before his eyes like a horrible picture. The contorted bodies

4*

charred and unrecognisable, appeared, like fantastic shadows about the court-room.

Suddenly Jim jerked his great body erect. He remembered Ezra's words and the rumour spreading round the village. " Argllwydd," he thought, " this man be trying to trap me to put the blame on Shoni Cap-du." And he murmured to himself, " Not if Big Jim can help it."

The fact that he was about to defend his dead mates steeled his nerves and gave him greater courage, and giving a quick glance round the room, he began.

" When we reached the pit bottom, me and the other boys did have to go very slow and careful because of the thick after-damp, and we didn't know how the gas-masks would act, because they had been in the stores for years."

He stopped a second, drew in his breath sharply, and continued. " After we had gone 'bout fifty yards from the pit bottom and was just by the mouth of the stable where we first heard the fire, I fancy I see something in front. It looked black and limp, as if a lot of brattice had been blowed into one heap."

Jim swallowed a mouthful of saliva, then resumed. " When we reached it we did find it was not brattice but the bodies of our poor dead butties. They was lying round 'xactly as if they had been struck by lightning. Duw," he added sadly, " it was awful, mun, to see your butties lying cold like that."

He was interrupted before he could continue further. " Ahem. Very good, Mr. Roberts, and no doubt very interesting," said his cross-examiner." But we want to know what you saw, not what you felt. Now tell me. When you came across the bodies, did you see any lamps? "

Jim's dislike for the man immediately increased. He realised that the questioner was trying to get an admission from him, and although he did not mind this, he objected to the method used. Some of the questions appeared to his practical mind as irrelevant and silly, and in answering the last one he made no attempt to conceal his contempt.

" Of course we did see lamps," he said. " Do you ever

'spect to see sensible men in a pit without them ? Huh. Any fool can answer that question and only a fool would ask it."

His opponent was discomposed by this reply and the twitter that circled round the court-room.

" Is that so ? " he commented sharply, his squeaky voice rising to a falsetto. " Then perhaps you will tell us if you examined the lamps you say you saw ? "

Big Jim nodded a brief affirmative.

" Now tell us if you saw something wrong with any of the lamps."

Big Jim hesitated and looked across at Ezra, who sat immobile and detached on the corner of the bench. Ezra's quick eyeflick seemed to flash the message : " Speak the truth and stick to it."

Jim cleared his throat and answered, " Yes. There was something wrong with them."

Everyone in the room held his breath. The cross-examiner looked knowingly at the coroner, as if saying, " He was a bit awkward, but we've got it at last."

Big Jim continued : " All the lamps was in the dark, because their flames had been blowed out by the blast of the explosion."

He stopped at this. The tension in the room eased. The little interrogator was red-faced and angry at being thwarted in this manner. He shot his next questions quickly and viciously.

" Were any of the lamps damaged ? "

" No."

" How do you know ? "

" Because I did examine each of them."

" Did you know John Jones ? "

" Yes. We did call him Shoni Cap-du."

" Never mind what you call him. Tell me if you found anything wrong with his lamp."

Jim's temper flared up at the trend of the questions. " Ho," he shouted, his voice booming through the room like a drum. " So that's the way the wind be blowing, is it ?

Well, let me tell you straight from the shoulder that Shoni's lamp was under his left leg. I did pull it from there with my own hands, and the only thing that was wrong with it was that the handle was twisted a little bit."

A deep silence followed these words, spoken so vehemently in defence of the dead man. But Jim's questioner seemed oblivious of the impression created. He took a paper package from the table and unwrapped it to show a miner's oil-lamp with a twisted handle. He handed this to Jim with the words : " Is that the lamp you took from under John Jones's leg ? "

Jim took the lamp in his hand, turning the pot that contained the oil as he did so. The pot gave under the pressure and Jim, surprise in his whole appearance, kept on turning until the pot came away from the top of the lamp. If the wick were now lighted it would be naked to the air.

He looked at the separated parts, and his eyes halfclosed as he concentrated his mind on the problem. The remorseless voice of his interlocutor pursued him. " Is that the lamp you took from beneath John Jones's leg ? " it asked again.

Big Jim looked once more towards Ezra before he replied. Again he saw the same message in the hard face : " Speak the truth and stick to it."

In a firm voice he answered : " It is the same lamp, and yet it isn't. Something have happened to it since it was in my hands before."

He paused, then went on more confidently. " The first thing a miner will do whenever he get a lamp in his hand is to twist the pot, just like I did with this one. It do come natural to us, and I know I did twist Shoni's lamp when I picked it up from under his leg."

His voice rose sharply. " Somebody have been mucking about with this lamp since I brought it up the pit," he challenged.

The slow, cold smile that crossed Ezra's face seemed to say, " Good lad, Jim. Stick to it."

The lamp was now handed to the jurymen, each of whom

scrutinised it as if he were acquainted with all its parts and secrets.

While they were doing this Jim was pulled back to the issue by a question sharply barked at him. " If you don't think the lamp was responsible for the explosion, can you, as a practical man and an experienced miner, advance another theory as to the probable cause ? "

A puzzled frown puckered Jim's forehead. He shook his head slowly, then asked, " 'Scuse me, 'o'nt' you ? But will you please tell me what you do mean by the last part of your words ? You see," he added apologetically, " I be not much of a English-speaking man and some of your words do come strange to my ears."

The coroner helped him and put the question more plainly. " What you are being asked, Mr. Roberts," he explained, " is, if you don't believe the lamp caused the explosion, then what else do you think could have caused it ? "

Jim thought deeply for some moments, then said very deliberately : " No ; I don't believe the 'splosion started back where we found Shoni Cap-du at all. It be my belief, sure as God be my judge, that it did start somewhere in the face. I do know for sure that there was tons of gas back in the empty gobs, and just one little spark from a mandril would be 'nough to blow the whole lot up.

" However that might be," he added solemnly, " I am so sure as this hand is fast to me this minute," he held his huge scarred hand out for all to see, " that the 'splosion was not made by the lamp."

This answer, which caused a murmur of interest to pass through the room, was followed by another question. " What makes you so positive that the lamp had nothing to do with the explosion ? "

Jim chose his words carefully as he replied : " If that lamp made the 'splosion because the pot was unscrewed, then it 'ood have been unscrewed when I found it. If Shoni Cap-du put the flame to the gas, then he 'ood have been blowed to pieces before ever he 'ood have time to screw the pot back on. More than that," he continued, with rising temper, " no man without the key could open that lamp unless he smashed it open, and here it is as perfect as on the day it was first made."

While the people in the room whispered excitedly to each other at Jim's concluding remarks, the coroner invited that worthy to resume his seat.

When the whispering had ceased the coroner summed up the evidence. " Accidents such as this," he said, " however regrettable they may be, are an inevitable outcome of modern coal-mining. In the present case every care seems to have been taken by the management to ensure the maximum of safety. Yet, in spite of all efforts to keep the pit reasonably free from danger, this terrible catastrophe occurs."

He coughed ponderously before continuing. " Were it not for the open lamp found after the explosion, one could very well consider it to be purely and simply an act of God. But this discovery is of particular significance, and appears to point to the fact that the terrible tragedy was due to the deliberate or foolish action of John Jones. We shall, of course, never know the real truth of the matter, but while I am impressed with the evidence of Mr. Roberts, I cannot for the life of me imagine what interest or motive the management could have in opening the lamp after it came up the pit."

He stopped to clear his throat and concluded, " No ; I cannot accept that theory. In my opinion the explosion was caused by an act of foolish negligence on the part of a workman."

The jurymen had all craned their necks forward as an indication that they were listening attentively, and without leaving the court they returned a verdict in accordance with the coroner's directions.

Big Jim was furious and would have sprung to his feet in protest had it not been for Ezra's restraining hand. The two workmen were surrounded immediately they appeared in the street. Ezra said very little, but Big Jim, his moustaches twitching with indignation, could not curb his rash temper.

" Just fancy," he roared, " blaming a poor dead man, who can't answer back, for the 'splosion."

A cry of " Shame ! " spread through the crowd as Jim went on, " All of us do know what caused it. If the gobs had been pinned as they ought to be, there 'ood have been no blow-up. Ach," he continued dismally, " us don't count no longer. Coal be more 'portant than us now."

" Ay," came a voice from the crowd. " You be quite right, Big Jim. What do hundred men count for 'longside a hundred trams of coal ? Men be cheap 'nough these days, and will soon be dear at ten a penny."

Someone laughed at this quip. But the laugh sounded flat and was not taken up.

Immediately after the inquest the people of the village made preparations to bury their dead. Very few of those brought up the pit could be identified, but this difficulty was easily overcome by those in charge. Each body not identified was allocated to some family on the basis of a button or some such fictitious clue. This method served two useful purposes. It saved unnecessary and useless investigation and it also eased the grief of the relatives, who were led to believe that the inflated, flame-seared mass of rotten flesh encased in an odour-proof shell in the parlour belonged to them.

The first group of fifty-nine bodies brought up the pit was buried together in a common grave.

On the day of the mass burial the atmosphere weighed heavy upon the people of Cwmardy. Each house was a casket of sobs and sighs. All window-blinds were drawn and businesses closed down for the day. The people in each street followed the coarse wooden coffin they believed contained their own relative or friend and the coffins were, covered with crude wreaths that glistened with the tears of the donors.

All the sombre wooden boxes with their flowery coverings were carried to the village square and laid side by side.

When all was ready Dai Cannon lifted his squat body into the solitary bowl of the fountain. His pale face was made whiter by the shiny blackness of his hair. He looked dignified and impressive to the people from the height of his platform in the bowl.

Dai waited a few moments to get a grip on his feelings. Then his deep, sonorous voice began to float over the silent throng who waited, sad and patient, below him.

" The good God has given and the good God has taken away," he chanted. " He has taken loved ones from relatives, husbands from wives, and fathers from children. He has left our valley full of widows, orphans, and grieving parents, all of whom have nothing but sad memories, which cannot ease their pain. The Lord has given the pit power to destroy men's bodies, but has kept to Himself the power to preserve people's souls."

His voice rose till it rang through the black air like the wailing chords of a harmonium.

" O, Lord, you seem so cruel to Your children this day. They, in their grief, do not understand Your infinite mercy and tenderness. They, in their sorrow, do not know that You do all things for the best. They see only the coffined remains of those they love, and cannot see the purified souls now nestling to Your bosom. You have said, ' Through fire to eternal bliss.' The bodies which held the souls you now hold in Your blessed care have been through the fires of the pit and deserve the best that heaven can provide.

" Give strength and courage, O Lord," he exhorted, his voice falling in emotional waves upon the bowed heads of the people, " to those of Your children now suffering the horrors of earthly parting from those they loved best. Give them solace in their grief. Put soothing balm in their aching hearts. Let them feel that their loss has brought them nearer Thee. Cast from the minds of these women and children all thoughts of this week of death and devastation. O God, we do pray Thee to sow again in our valley the peace and happiness that we knew before the explosion."

Tonefully his words wormed their way into tormented hearts, tearing them into agonising shreds. Sobs mingled with moans and made a death-dirge as he continued his plea, and when he finished practically everyone was weeping, open and unashamed.

Len, standing near Big Jim, wept in a fervour of self-pity. The words brought Jane vividly to his mind. He wondered how she now looked in her coffin and shuddered at the recollection of the last glimpse he had of her. Shane, tears streaming down her face, kept rocking her body backwards and forwards, moaning painfully all the while. Big Jim blew his nose throughout the service, wiping it with the back of his hand.

When Dai Cannon finished Len stopped weeping and looked about him. He saw Ezra standing near the fountain. The man's eyes were hard and dry and a cynical smile played around the corners of his lips. Len had seen very little of the miners' leader, although, like all the other children, he had heard much about him.

After the service Ezra quietly took charge. He whispered directions to Dai Cannon, who immediately transmitted them to the people.

Six men, already appointed, took hold of each coffin. Their hard and horny hands seemed to caress the boxes they lifted to their shoulders. The fifty-nine coffins, carried on three hundred and fifty-four broad shoulders, lay head to foot in one long line. Behind each coffin came the mourners who thought it contained the remains belonging to them. All the other people fell in behind this procession of dead bodies and relatives. Men walked seven and eight abreast in the middle of the road, while the women and children walked on the sides. Dai Cannon, Mr. Hicks, Mr. Evans Cardi, and Big Jim walked immediately in front of the first coffin. Len fell in with his mother among the women.

The choir from Dai Cannon's chapel started to sing the hymn that had conquered the storm on the night of the explosion. Its plaintive melody, palpitating and mellowed with grief, rose above the housetops of the village and crept slowly up the sides of the surrounding mountains, whence it drifted back, matured music, to cover the valley with a blanket of shivering sound. The echoes re-entered the throats where they had originated and were reborn, more resonant and rounded, to be thrown again with greater vigour and clarity into the air. Here they hung, harmonising with the slow-moving funeral feet.

Dogs in the side-streets sat disconsolately on their haunches and gave voice to the dread that suddenly consumed them. Len felt the voices soak their music into his flesh in emotional vibrations. His eyes filled when they caught sight of the anæmic flowers carried by the chapel children as tokens of love, respect, and loss, and he began to think of what his father had told him about the mad rush up the hill on the night of the explosion. He compared it to this slow-moving march down the same hill to the cemetery, and ideas tumbled over each other in his imagination as he pondered over the problem of life and death.

The hill became a symbol to him. He saw it as a belt taking live men up to the pit, then bringing them down dead to the cemetery. The pit became an ogre to him. He likened it to some inhuman monster that fed on men and spewed up their mangled bodies to be buried in the graveyard. He conjured the hill and the pit as common enemies of the people, working in connivance to destroy them. Suddenly the words of Dai Cannon recurred to him, " The good God has given and the good God has taken away," and he wondered what they meant. Did they mean that the pit was not to be blamed and that God was responsible for destroying the men whose bodies were encased in the boxes before him ? If so, he mused, then perhaps God had killed Jane, and not Evan the Overman's son, as Shane had said. His brain twirled in a vortex of conflicting and seemingly insoluble problems that made his head ache long before the funeral reached the cemetery gates, and he closed his eyes, clinging tightly to his mother's hand, letting her lead him on.

CHAPTER VII

Len starts to Work

Six months had passed since the air of the valley had been shattered by the explosion. All the bodies that could be brought up the pit had been taken by the people to the distant cemetery. The remaining hundred or so were left as cindered dust in various parts of the colliery. Imperceptibly the explosion had sunk from the surface of men's minds and become a memory, though in many homes it was a black one. The explosion distress fund that had been organised throughout the country immediately following upon the catastrophe was now declared to be running low, and the widows and orphans were informed that their relief scales would have to be reduced as a consequence.

One day Big Jim came home from his repairing work at the colliery, and after dinner casually told Shane : " Well, gel bach, we will be starting to fill coal in the old pit next week once again."

Shane turned to him. " That be good news," she said.

" Ay, but I have got even better than that. I have arranged with Williams, the under-manager, for our Len to start work with me next week."

Len sat up in his chair with a start and looked at his father with wide-opened eyes that sparkled with interest.

" Aye, aye. It be quite true. You be starting to work with me next week. Your mam wanted you to keep in school, but since you be not willing for that there be nothing left but for you to work."

The week following this brief announcement Len was so excited he hardly knew what he was doing. He told his mother one day : " I'm glad, mam, that I'm starting to work. School's no good to me, I can't learn enough there.

I want to be with dad in the pit. I'm not afraid. The other boys have told me it's not so bad when you get used to it." And, looking slyly at his mother, he added: " They get pocket-money from their mothers on top of trumps from their butties."

Shane pretended not to notice, but a tiny smile flickered for a moment on the corners of her mouth.

Len became a hero in the eyes of his schoolmates. He made them envious with tales of what he intended to do, the things he would buy, the places he would visit when he started work. He conjured up for them a romantic vista of what work meant, and the days went by so slowly he thought the week would never end. But at last the final night arrived.

His mother had bought him the usual white-duck trousers that marked the end of his boyish breeches. The large tin box and jack, to carry his food and water, were given to him by his father, who had already used them for years. Shane sent him to bed early, intending him to get plenty of sleep. Excitement and anticipation, however, prevented this and he was still awake when the first morning hooter blew at five o'clock. About ten minutes later his mother called him. She had already lit the fire and had breakfast waiting. Big Jim was half dressed in his pit clothes when Len entered the kitchen. The lad soon clothed himself in his strange rig-out, and sat down to drink a cup of tea, for food was out of the question in the state to which he had worked himself. When the half-past five hooter gave the signal that it was time they were off, Shane passionately pressed her son to her body. She kissed him tenderly and whispered in his ear, " Do everything your dad do tell you, my boy. Don't move from his side. You be starting to-day what only the grave can steal you from." She said this more to herself than anyone else and put the canvas apron to her eyes. Then shaking her head sharply, she turned to Jim.

" I know you will take care of him, James. 'Member he be only a baby after all, the only one us have got left."

With another hungry kiss she sent them into the dark, wet street with a ' Good morning ' that stuck in her throat and was never uttered.

The rain poured down as Len and his father, like a giant and a pigmy, trudged up the hill towards the pits. Jim made his son walk as closely behind him as possible. It was some time before Len realised this was done to shield him from the main force of the rain driving down the valley. His head bent to the drops that evaded his father's body, Len vaguely noticed the long string of silent men, like shadows, making their way in the same direction as himself. Each of them, dragging his feet, used the man immediately in front to shelter him from the rain.

Len followed his father across the bridge into the cabin where authoritative-looking men scanned him over curiously as if he were a calf.

" So this be the boy, James ? " asked the most officious.

" Ay, this be him," responded Jim, whereupon Len had to write his name and age in a big book.

He took a round piece of metal handed him by one of the men, who told him, " Take care of that, my lad ; it is your lamp check with your number on it."

A few further words passed between the group before Jim led the way to the lamp room, a long corrugated-iron structure containing hundreds of lighted lamps arranged on a series of trestles. Len followed his father to one of the pigeon-holes, where Jim handed in the check and received a lamp in exchange. Len did the same and at once felt himself a man, although the lamp dangling from his hand nearly touched the floor. They left the lamp room and walked to a cabin, where another man with an air of authority examined the lamps. Having unscrewed the top and blown all round the pots, he handed them back with a final twist of the bottom, to ensure that the lamps were stuck fast.

Big Jim and his son left the cabin and went straight to the pit-head. The shaft in which Len was to work was called the " upcast," because all the air from the pit was sucked

up through it by a fan of huge dimensions. To prevent the
air being drawn up before it had time to circulate all
round the workings, the shaft was closed in with heavy
wooden " droppers," only leaving a space for the rope to
wind its way through, so that when the two cages were in
the pit the air howled and screamed through this tiny outlet.

Len was rather frightened by the terrible tumult on the
pit-head, and he had to shout to make himself heard above
the din. While they were standing in the queue waiting
to go down, he felt for his father's hand and pressed
it to his side in a gesture of love and confidence, but Big
Jim, sensing the boy's mood, said nothing, thinking to
himself that the lad had to " find his own feet."

When the ascending cage lifted the wooden barriers from
the pit-top the released gusts of heated air rushed through
with a roar. Jim cautiously led his son over the little gap
between the cage and the pit edge. Eighteen other men
and boys followed before the man in charge declared that the
box was full and placed a thin iron bar across the entrance.
This was a measure of precaution supposed to prevent the
men falling out.

Once inside the cage, Len held his breath and waited.
He heard the knocker clang three times, and the tinkling of
a bell far away in the engine-house. Then suddenly he
felt the floor of the cage press against his feet as it lifted off
the stanchions that held it to the pit-head, and in another
second the breath was torn from his lungs by the sudden
drop as the cage plunged its way into the depths of the
pit.

Even in his panic Len heard the clatter of the droppers
falling into place above him, and he felt that a door had
been bolted between himself and the world. Regaining his
wind after the initial shock he put his arms round his
father's leg, finding courage in the human contact it provided in the black, falling void. Warm air rushed past the
cage with wicked squeals, and just as Len was beginning to
get accustomed to the sensation of dropping, the bottom of
the cage again pressed against his feet. This was due to the

brakes in the engine-room being applied to the great winding drums and marked the half-way line between the pit bottom and the surface. The lad felt the cage rising under him and wondered why they were returning to the pit-head, but before he had time to think it out the cage, with a few preliminary jerks, jarred on the planks that covered the water sump at the bottom of the pit.

The men slowly got out, Len behind his father. His curious eyes noticed at once that the little lamps appeared to give out a greater light here than they did on the surface, due to the more limited space they had to illuminate. He was also surprised that he could see underground as well as he could above, for he forgot there was no daylight when he left the pit-head and that his eyes were already inured to the darkness before he descended. He stumbled against a rail and glanced around the semi-elliptical passage-way that led from the pit bottom. Looking behind, he saw a similar passage going in the opposite direction, the other side of the pit, then, threading his way carefully between the long line of coal-laden trams on the one side and an equally long line of empty ones on the other, he eventually came to the end of this double roadway.

" Look where you be going to now, Len bach," advised Big Jim, as they turned off into a narrow and gloomier passage.

" There's different this place do look, dad, without no whitewash on the sides."

" Never you mind about the sides. You watch these ropes in the roadway."

Len took his father's advice and kept his eyes glued upon the ropes. Not another word was said until they came to a large cabin dug into the side of the roadway, where their lamps were again taken from them and tested.

Big Jim received certain instructions from the man in the cabin, and Len listened to their talk of " shots " and " rippings." After receiving instructions and having their lamps returned to them, Big Jim remarked to Len : " Come on. We have got a hell of a plateful for to-day, so you'll have to look sharp." Without a word Len followed his father. The roadway was becoming narrower and lower with every stride, and steel girders gave way to timber as supports for the roof.

In his anxiety to keep pace with Big Jim Len had no time for talking ; it was his father who broke the silence.

" Are you all right, Len ? "

Len started at the sound of Jim's voice. " Ay. I'm all right, dad. How much further have we got to go ? " he asked tremulously.

" We got a good bit to go yet."

" Have we come two miles so far ? "

" Thereabouts, boy bach," replied Jim, turning to Len. " You don't feel tired, do you ? "

" Of course not," bragged the lad, forgetting the tired ache in his legs and pulling himself to his full height.

Jim walked on again. " Many is the time I have tramped this old roadway," he mused. " Duw, duw, I be sure to have done hundreds of miles along it."

They proceeded in silence for a while, Big Jim thinking of the good old days that had gone, while Len thought of the days that were to come. Suddenly the former warned : " Look out by here, Len bach. This be a nasty old trip."

Len continued down the steep road that reminded him of the path leading from the mountain top.

" I 'member coming over this trip once with old Dai Cannon," said Jim, " when all of a sudden we did hear a rush behind us. Dai and me stopped like statues for a minute. But not for long. The rush come louder and louder and, muniferni, you did ought to see us jump for the side. Ha-ha ! Dai gived one howl, mun, and before I did know what was happening he fell back on 'is arse in the middle of the road. Ha-ha-ha ! Argllwydd mawr, boy, I was bound to laugh, mun, if Dai did kill me for it. Argll-wydd, you should have seed the look he did give me ! ' That's right,' he did say, ' laugh you silly beggar. Go on. Enjoy yourself although I have broked my bloody neck.' "

Jim burst out into another uproarious guffaw at the

memory. When this had subsided Len asked : " But what was the matter, dad ? "

" Why, some of the horses, coming down from the top of the trip, got a little bit restless and was stamping their feet like hell. 'Oops a daisy, we did think, the devils be running wild. Dai jumped for the side and bumped right into a low piece of timber, and that was why he did land flat on his arse. Ha-ha ! "

The descent now became even steeper. Len compared it to the sheer mountain drop near the quarry, and the thought made him long for the first time that morning to be back again in the sun. He had never dreamed of this interminable tramp in the darkness of the pit. Thinking of the world above prompted him to ask : " How far be we down, dad ? "

" They do say 'bout two thousand feet. But never mind 'bout that, now. You look after yourself ; the roof be getting pretty low by here."

Jim was walking with his body bent nearly double and Len, taking the tip, dug his chin deep into his chest and bent his head low. After a while they came to a part of the road where the roof was higher. Jim, knowing the spot, straightened his body and walked erect, but Len, fearing to raise his head, was not aware of this and walked on in solemn silence with his head bowed like a man in a funeral. The ropes beneath the lad's feet were moving when Jim called out, " Come into this manhole, boy bach."

Len hurried into the tiny hole in the side of the roadway and squeezed himself alongside his father in the limited space. " What's the matter, dad ? " he asked, thinking that something serious was about to happen.

" It's only the journey," Jim assured him. " You see those ropes by there," pointing into the roadway, where the ropes were slithering along like snakes, one sizzling along the ground while the other ripped through the air nearly to the height of the roof, " Well, those do belong to the journey."

Len hesitated a moment, then asked, as a low rumbling

sound came to his ears from the distance, " What's that noise, then, dad ? "

Jim started to explain when thirty empty trams rushed past the manhole with a deafening clatter. The terrific din sent Len cowering against his father's legs. Without further explanation, Jim caught the lad by the arm and drew him out of the hole. " Come quick," he shouted above the rattle of the receding trams, " let us get to the parting before the full journey come out."

Len did not understand the meaning of these instructions, but he obediently ran headlong after his father. Gasping and perspiring, they stopped after they had run about a quarter of a mile. Still panting from his exertions, Len noticed that the roadway had widened and was blocked by two strings of trams, one of which was empty, the other full of coal.

Safe in another manhole, the lad watched with interest two men change the rope from the string of empty trams and place it on the full ones. When the change was completed he heard a whistle blow further on, and one of the men near him responded to the signal by rasping the two thin wires above his head with the blade of a knife. The wires connected with the engine-house at the bottom of the pit. The ropes began to move and slowly tightened on the first tram of the string, then the others, attached to it with steel shackles, were drawn forward with increasing speed and clamour until the last was lost to sight in the darkness of the roadway.

Len and Jim emerged from the manhole and again continued their walk, the former beginning to think that it was to be endless. He noticed places where huge holes gaped in the roof. At other places he saw large masses of stone overhanging into the roadway without any visible support.

He turned to his father and asked in a quavering voice, " Be that safe, dad ? "

" Safe ? Ay, boy, safe as houses. It will take more than Gabriel's trumpet to blow that down."

Len was too fatigued to ask any further questions. He was glad when Big Jim stopped and said, " Here we be. Strip off and get yourself ready. A little whiff will dry up all that sweat on you."

Len's exhaustion vanished with the knowledge that the interminable trudge was over and that he was now in his father's working place. He started to pull off his coat, when Jim interrupted him testily. " Not by there, boy bach. Shift under those timbers, where you will be safe."

Len did as he was told, and putting his box and jack carefully at the foot of a strong-looking prop, he pulled off his coat and shirt. He paused at this until he saw Jim pull off the singlet next his skin ; then he did the same, and immediately felt the air beat more cool and pleasantly upon his naked chest.

" Duw, that be nice, dad," he said, revived by the contact.

" Huh," grunted Jim. " Take the tools off the bar. Here be the key."

Len did so, then, with a shovel in his hands, he followed his father on hands and knees through the coal-face. The glistening coal, reflecting the gleam from the two lamps, fascinated Len. He watched Jim crawl, practically on his stomach, up the long stretch of the coal face until only the dim light of his lamp was visible. Scared to be left alone, the lad followed, only to be gruffly ordered back.

" You keep by that empty tram and don't move till I tell you."

Len turned back and for the first time gave conscious thought to the tram. It stood end on to the clear-cut roof, or " rippings," which had to be blown down as the coal-face advanced, so that the tram could follow the coal.

A deep feeling of loneliness enveloped Len as he wondered what would happen if his father were not near and he were left entirely on his own. All round him he could hear little movements, as if the place were alive. He had an uncanny feeling that the roof was moving, and each creak of the timbers, as they unwillingly took the weight of the settling strata, sent a quiver through his body. He had yet to learn that the pit had a life of its own, that it was never still or silent, but was always moving and moaning in response to the atmosphere and pressure.

Suddenly he felt a burning sensation on his stomach. His hand flashed to the spot automatically, his fingers clutched some object and tore it away, and opening his hand he saw a huge red insect with innumerable hairy legs and hard, shiny wings. Although crushed in his convulsive grip, the ghastly legs still beat the air, and looking down at his belly, he saw a thin stream of blood running down it where the cockroach had gripped the flesh and torn it away. A sick giddiness swept over the lad for a moment, while the perspiration burst from every pore in his body, lathering it in a mixture of coal-dust and moisture, but before he could recover from the shock he heard his father crawling back. This proof that he was not alone encouraged the lad and he was smiling when Big Jim emerged on the roadway.

" We will work in the right hand cut to-day, Len bach," he said, " so that we can free the whole face for to-morrow."

Len did not understand the technique underlying the remark, but he asked with assumed indifference, " What be I to do, dad ? "

Jim replied : " You will come up the cut with me and throw the coal back towards the tram."

The lad obeyed, and followed his father, and for hours he worked on his knees with the back of his head rubbing against the roof. He began mentally counting each shovelful of coal his father cut and which he had to throw back to the tram. His arms grew heavy as lead, cramp caught him in his bent legs, and his back felt as though it were broken. The coal-dust that filled the air got into his nose and eyes. It made him sneeze and blink and, working into the sweat-opened pores of his body, set up an intolerable irritation. He felt it impossible to lift another shovelful of the coal he now detested, but somehow he kept on, until at last his father said :

" That will do for now. Let's go back and get a bit of tommy."

The lad dragged his weary, painful limbs back into the roadway, where he stretched himself full length in the dust. He saw his heart pumping against the bones of his naked chest, and felt pins and needles run through his flesh in spasms of excruciating agony.

Big Jim, sensing what was happening, urged him to his feet. " Come on. Get up before you go stiff."

With infinite care Len dragged his limbs together and slowly rose to his feet. He opened his food box and sat down. The bread-and-butter looked dirty and un-appetising, but the water in his jack was like nectar. Jim stopped him before he had emptied the tin of its contents. " Don't do that again or you will get cramp in your belly. Get on with your food."

The lad tried to obey, but the hundreds of savage-looking cockroaches that buzzed and fussed around turned his stomach, while the dust he had already swallowed curdled in his inside.

After a while Big Jim rose and made his way back up the face, telling Len : " You stop there till I shout for you. A bit of a whiff 'on't do you any harm now."

During the rest the lad slowly recovered from his exhaustion. The black dust under his body seemed softer and more sweet to him then than even the green grass on his beloved mountain, and his mind wandered to the end of the shift. Before his eyes floated a picture of the envious glances of his schoolmates when they saw him striding, black-faced, down the hill in his working clothes. He saw the glad look in his mother's eyes as he walked into the little kitchen, having finished his day's work. Already he began to count the pocket-money he would have in a fort-night's time, and speculated how best to spend it.

Deeply immersed in these pleasant contemplations, Len dozed off into a heavy sleep. Jim's deep voice seemed miles away when he shouted, " Right you are, Len bach ; come up and start chucking this coal back."

Len came back to reality with a start and made his way up the coal-face he already hated with every fibre in his body. He worked in a semi-conscious state, only faintly aware of the three or four occasions when the haulier and his horse noisily changed the full tram of coal for an empty one. When the fireman came round and chatted with Jim he waited respectfully on his knees, wishing fervently that the man would stop there till the end of the shift. But he had ceased to take any interest in what was happening. His brain was numbed with the physical exhaustion that again consumed him even though his father had been careful to limit the amount of work to a minimum.

The poor lad, accustomed to the fresh air of the mountain, felt the foul atmosphere of the pit beginning to choke him. He thought again of his mother, and now wished he had listened to her advice and tried the examination for the secondary school. Young Mary, Ezra's daughter, had done so and passed successfully, although she was no better scholar than he. Too late now, he thought to himself, half weeping ; now he had started in the pit he had to continue. He wondered if the rain had stopped up above; it seemed years since he had left its refreshing coolness. He was sorry now he had ever grumbled at the rain, and was willing for it to pour down for ever as long as he was on the surface to see it.

Tears involuntarily gushed to his eyes and he was on the point of bursting into sobs when a terrific crash shook the whole earth. For a moment he stood paralysed with fear, then he rushed headlong with a wild scream towards his father. Big Jim caught the terror-stricken, hysterical lad to him.

" Duw, duw, mun, don't ever let it be said that the son of Big Jim is frightened by a noise. That was only gas and squeeze busting inside the coal, mun. There, there, now, don't be 'fraid no more."

It took Len some time to control his quivering flesh. The crash had sent the memory of the explosion flashing through his mind, and in a split second he had seen himself in the place of the bodies he had watched being buried on the day of the funeral.

Jim made the lad rest back on the roadway again until, some half-hour later, he took him down the roadway to fetch some timber. Here Len saw another lad with his adult mate engaged in the same task. The sight of some-one his own age immediately restored his confidence. His natural taciturn unsociability evaporated with the new contact in the new environment. While the two men were chatting and selecting the timber they wanted, Len shyly asked the strange lad, " How long you been working ? "

" Oh," was the casual, off-handed reply, " a long time now, butty. More than six months, I believe, though I can't 'member 'xactly, because it be so long ago." Saying which, he took a lump of chewing-gum from his mouth and spat noisily into an empty tram near him.

" Well, what do you think of the bloody hole ? " patronis-ingly.

" Not so bad," lied Len, trying to forget the torments of the day.

" Huh. I'm only sticking it till I'm old enough to get a horse."

" Get a horse ? " queried Len amazedly.

" Ay, ay, that's it. I'm going to be a haulier."

" Oh, I see. Like that man who do bring the horse to fetch our full trams out ? "

" You got it, butty. And, by Christ, can't I handle them ! " warming to his subject. " Take a tip from a old hand, butty, never take no bloody nonsense from them. When they turn twp or stupid, a sprag will always bring them to their senses."

He accompanied these remarks with a clicking sound and a practical demonstration which left Len staring with admiration. The budding haulier put the chewing-gum back into his mouth with a grimace and remarked, " This bloody stuff be getting too weak for me now ; I will have to start chewing 'bacca soon."

Len felt he would like to have a say : " I only started to work to-day," he said hesitantly.

" Be that so ? Ah well, never mind, you'll soon get used to it when you have worked so long as me."

Their conversation was interrupted by the man with Big Jim.

" What the hell be you blabbing 'bout by there ? " he demanded. " Why don't you come and give me a hand with this blasted timber ? "

" All right, all right, keep your wool on," the lad said casually, and turning to Len, he hurriedly whispered : " That's my butty. I 'spose I'd better go and give him a hand. Come out same time as me to-night—we be working next place to you. My name is Will Evans. So long." With this he and his mate left, each with one end of a long nine-foot prop on his shoulder.

Shortly after this finishing time came and Len gathered all the tools together, his father showing him how to put them securely on the tool bar.

He dressed in quick time, the clothes sticking to his steaming body, and as he envisaged his triumphant entry into the house all his old pride began to surge through him again. To make sure his face was quite black he rubbed it vigorously with his dusty cap.

On the way out he told his father of the request made by Will, the lad in the next working place. Big Jim took him round to it, and they both waited for the others to finish ; then the two men and their boys went out together, the former in front.

Len felt elated as he retraced his steps along the roadway that in the morning had seemed like the pathway to hell. He chattered incessantly and already felt he was an old hand in the pit. His new-found mate let him ramble on for a while, then broke in with the question : " Do you know Sam Dangler ? "

Len shook his head negatively.

" Huh, you have missed a treat. That's a haulier for you, mun. You ought to see him handling the rough 'uns." He stopped half-way up the trip "This is how he do do it," he remarked, catching hold of an imaginery rein. "Whoa boy, whoa! Ah, bite you sod, would you?" giving a sharp tug and pressing his body back as though he were pulling the non-existent rein. "Take that, you bloody cow!" hitting the air with a short piece of timber. "Whoa, boy. Steady now. Ah, that's got you. Come to your senses, have you? He flung the sprag into the roadway triumphantly and remarked: "That's how Sam Dangler do conquer um, see?" A moment's pause, then: "He's a devil. All the horses do know him, and after a week he have very near got them talking. I'm going to be like him one day. He do have more trumps off the colliers than any haulier in the pit."

He broke off here to take Len on the side and whisper in his ear: "You want to watch your old man on pay day. Tell him straight from the beginning that if he want you to work he have got to give you trumps. Huh. Fathers be the worst butties going. They do think their own sons be bloody slaves and do never think of trumping 'em. Oh, no. They do pocket that their bloody selves and the old 'ooman don't have a smell of it. You listen to me," he continued sagely. "Don't let any butty make out of you unless he pay you for it, father or no father."

A voice drifted down to the two lads from the top of the trip: "Will-o! What the bloody hell be you hanging like a shirt behind there for?"

They hurriedly continued their way, and eventually overtook their mates on the pit bottom, where they had to wait a while in the queue before they were bundled into the cage.

The sound of the iron knocker, announcing to the men on the surface that all was ready, came to Len's ears like the chime of sweet-tolling bells. The cage sprang up the shaft like a projectile released from a mighty catapult, and in a matter of breathless minutes the roar of the air beating against the droppers drowned every other sound. There was a clamouring rush as the chains caught the covering and Len once more saw the light of day.

5

Although it was not a bright day, the light hurt Len's eyes, and he had to close them for a while. Will waited for him, then led the way to the lamp room, where they exchanged their lamps for the numbered metal discs. Having done this, Will led the way to some iron girders near by and began poking his fingers into the crevices. His movements became more vigorous and excited and his face grew red.

Len noticed this and asked timidly : " Be there anything the matter, Will ? "

" Matter ? Matter to hell ! " exploded Will. " Some dirty swine have pinched my fag. I put it by here this morning before going down, and now the bloody thing is gone. Ah," he grunted viciously, twisting his cap in his hands, " if I only had him by here now I'd wring his dirty neck." He gulped something down his throat and turned to Len. There was a pathetic look in his eyes when he said, " Butty, that is the worst thing a man can ever do. To pinch a fag is worse than pinching grub. Huh. Hanging be too good for a man who do a thing like that."

Some other lads now approached and listened interestedly to Will's tirade against the unknown thief. One of them eventually handed over a piece of cigarette that he had been smoking himself, and the little party made their way homewards. Seeing all the other lads enjoying their cigarettes made Len feel out of place, and he decided he must learn to smoke as soon as possible.

He took his place in the long line of men that streamed homewards down the hill, and looked surreptitiously into every window to see the reflection of his coal-blackened face. The eyes which looked back at him seemed twice their usual size in the dark frames.

When he reached home he found Shane busily fussing around with the dinner. Len never felt so proud in his life. Pulling off his coat, he put it in the box under the table and jovially remarked, " Hallo, mam. Here I be, safe and sound."

Shane did not look up from her task as she answered in a

voice that quivered a little : " Ay, I see you are, Len bach,
thank God. How did you like it ? "

Len forgot all the pains and terrors of the day when he
replied, " All right, mam. It be not so bad and I have made
a new butty."

He proceeded to retail the events of the day. When he
had finished Shane beckoned him to wash his hands in the
bowl of water she had ready. This done, he drew his chair
to the table and voraciously ate the kipper and potatoes she
had cooked him.

He had nearly finished his dinner when Big Jim came in,
and explained to Shane he had called in to have a pint of
beer to clear his throat. He always claimed, and believed,
that if he did not have this pint of beer he would be unable
to eat his dinner, because of the coal-dust that coated his
lungs.

After dinner Shane fetched in the wooden tub made out
of half a big barrel. Jim lifted the boiler from the fire
and poured its contents into the tub, while Shane cooled
it with cold water. Len quickly stripped to his waist while
his father enjoyed a smoke, and was thrilled at the fact
this was the first time in his life he had bathed with the
top half of his body over the tub.

While he wiped his head and shoulders Jim followed him
into the tub ; then, when the latter had finished, Len got in
naked to wash his bottom half. He enjoyed the sensation
of the warm water running down his legs and lingered in the
tub until Jim said : " You be in there long enough to swim
round it, boy bach. Come out and give your father a
chance."

Big Jim had hardly started rubbing soap into his legs
when the door opened and Mrs. Thomas, their neighbour
came in.

" Can you lend me a bucket of coal till mine do come from
the pit ? " she asked, taking no notice of Jim's magnificent
nude body.

" Certainly, gel fach, go out the back and fetch it," he
replied, completely unabashed by her appearance.

By the time Mrs. Thomas had filled her bucket of coal Len had dressed, and when she re-entered the kitchen he was peering at his face in the cracked mirror. The two black rings of coal-dust that circled his eyes made them show up vividly against his white face, but though he rubbed them with the towel until the rims were sore, he could not remove them entirely. Later in the evening when he walked through Main Street he was proud of the black rings, because they showed to all and sundry that he had started to work.

That night he slept without any coaxing and was still fast asleep when the hooters blasted the air with their warning call at five o'clock. Shane had to call the lad a few times before he completely awoke and slowly drew his legs from beneath the bed-clothes.

The second day in the pit was much the same as the first, but this time he took more notice of what happened during the shift. When finishing time came he was even more tired and sore than on the first day, but in spite of this he arranged to meet Will by the fountain in the evening. After dinner, however, he fell asleep while he was bathing, with his head over the tub. Shane tenderly finished washing him, after which Jim carried him to bed like a child. Although the appointment with Will was not kept, a strong friendship developed between them, which gradually forced from Len's mind all thought of Ron, his old schoolmate.

Will taught him much about the pit and its ways, and the knowledge so gained helped Len to avoid many a fright he would otherwise have had. In time he learned to hew coal and stand timber without the help of his father. He came to understand the struggle between himself and the coal-face, and he pitted his brains against the strata, using the lie of the coal and the pressure of the roof to help him win the coal from the face with the minimum expenditure of energy. He learned the exact angle to stand his timbers so that they would bear the maximum weight of roof and side, and which part of the roof to shatter with a shot to bring only what he wanted to the floor.

In this manner, quietly and stealthily, the pit became the dominating factor in his life. Each morning, wet or fine, well or indisposed, he had to struggle out of bed at exactly the same time, join the same never-ending silent flow of men to the pit, and travel the same ever-lengthening pit roadway. He came to hate the hooter, whose blast he had to obey if he were not to suffer loss of food and pocket-money. He saw the walk to the pit in the mornings as one long queue from which he dropped in the evening only to catch up with again the next day. Slowly he came to regard himself as a slave and the pit as his owner, and his old taciturnity again grew in him as he brooded over these matters in the months that followed. Not that he had any objection to the work, but the thought that he was tied to the pit horrified him. His workmates noticed the growing unsociability. They thought it due to a love affair, and cracked smutty jokes at his expense.

" Have you got a dose, or what, Len ? " Will asked him one morning.

" Dose ? What dose do you mean ? " Len replied, colouring up.

But the only answer he was vouchsafed was, " Well, if you haven't, you ought to marry the bloody wench."

Len said no more, but the conversation made him even more introspective and morose.

One evening after work Len wandered aimlessly down to the village, and, having nothing else to do, he ambled into Ben the Barber's, which happened to be practically empty. He asked Ben for the loan of a newspaper, but after scanning the headlines for a few minutes and finding nothing to excite his interest, he dug his hands deeply into his trousers pockets, thanked Ben, and shuffled to the door.

It was opened as he reached it, and a well-set-up young man about his own age entered. Len would have passed, but the stranger deliberately obstructed him.

" Len Roberts, if I am not mistaken ? " inquired the newcomer.

" Ay, that's me," replied Len, beginning to take an

interest in his well-dressed questioner.   He pulled his hands
from his pockets and drew himself to his full height.   " Did
you want me ? "

" Ah, I see you have forgotten all about your old schoolmate.   I'm Ron Evans.   Don't you know me ? "

Len stood on one side, surprise in his eyes.   " Well, well,
just fancy, Ron.   Who would have expected you ?   Duw,
you have altered a lot since our schooldays."

" Yes, and you haven't remained the same, either.   I see
you have started work and didn't go to the secondary
school after all," looking meaningly at the rims of Len's
eyes.

" Ay.   I have been working going on three years now."

" Are you going anywhere particular to-night, Len ? "

" No.   I only come down here to have a hour or two out
of the house."

" Will you come with me for a stroll, then ? " Ron
suggested.

Len agreed, and the two sauntered together along the
Main Street and up the steep stony path that led to the
mountain.

Ron talked volubly all the way, and Len was suitably
impressed by his tales of college life.   But try as he would,
Ron could not get Len to talk of the pit.   The latter felt it
would be a waste of time talking of the pit to a fellow who
was so obviously out of touch with such life.   Dusk
lengthened their shadows as the two friends retraced their
steps to the village.   Ron was jubilant at the fact he had
renewed an old acquaintanceship, and Len was pleased
because Ron had promised to give him some books to read.

This unexpected walk was the prelude to many while
Ron was home on vacation, and when he returned to college
he remained true to his promise and gave Len a number of
books which dealt with a subject called socialism.

Len had not the slightest idea what this was apart
from the occasional remarks he had heard in the pit to the
effect that socialism was some method of sharing other
people's property.   Ron sent a letter from college explain-

ing what the books were really about and what the subject really meant. The colourful manner of his explanations stimulated Len's interest. He felt here was a key to the problem troubling his mind.

Len devoted his spare time to the books, but most of the contents he did not fully understand, and those parts he could fathom only served to deepen his disappointment. Mentally he cursed the ignorance that prevented his understanding all that the books contained, yet, in spite of this, the little knowledge that he gained revived his interest in the pits and in his workmates. He dimly began to see them in a new light, although he failed to appreciate the real basis for this. And in addition there was awakening within him a vague physical urge that made him feel more sentimental and philosophical.

The hard work and long hours, combined with his mental and physical turmoil, began to take toll of Len's strength. He became dispirited and a weakening lassitude crept over his body. Big Jim noticed the symptoms in the pit when Len, though his body was steaming with perspiration, continued to shiver as if he were cold. He decided to speak to Shane about the matter.

The opportunity came one evening when Shane was swilling the wet working clothes, while Jim sat in his usual place with his legs stretched towards the fire. Len had gone to bed directly after bathing, complaining that he was tired.

" Hem," Jim started. " Have you noticed anything wrong with our Len this last few days, Shane bach ? "

Shane looked up sharply from the tub, her face red with exertion. " What do you mean ? " she asked. " Do you say the boy be bad ? "

Jim nodded assent.

Shane rose from the tub wringing the soap suds from her hands. " What make you think that, James ? "

" Oh, nothing much, only I fancy he be getting very weak and miserable. He couldn't lift a lump of coal into the tram to-day, and I do know that if he was well he could bloody eat it."

Shane said nothing and Jim went on : " Not only that, but he was sweating like a pig to-day and was shivering at the same time, as if he had pewmonia."

" Ha," interrupted Shane, " so that be why he went straight to bed, eh ? Do you think we had better send for the doctor, James ? "

Jim spat heavily into the fire before answering contemptuously : " Doctor, mun jawly ! What good would they be ? What the boy do want is a good whiff and some boiled beer. Sweat it out, see, Shane bach. That be the thing for a cold."

" I don't know so much 'bout the beer," replied Shane, " but I be sure he 'on't go to work to-morrow. No, nor he 'on't go till he be quite well." She sat down on the stool near Jim, her eyes full of tears. " I 'ood sooner have him sit by the fire by there all the days of his life," she asserted, " than to see him lie by the side of Jane bach and her babby in the cemetery."

Jim said no more.

The following morning Len did not wake till nine o'clock, four hours too late for the pit. His head throbbed even as he wondered what was wrong, for Shane had never slept late before and he could not understand why she should have done so this day.

He shouted to her and noticed that his voice was thin and weak and that it cost him an effort to raise it. He heard her shuffling feet patter up the stairs in response to his call, and she came into the bedroom with a basin in her hand.

" Here you be, Len bach," she murmured. " Mam have brought some gruel for you. Now you must drink it all down like a good boy and you will soon be well again."

Len did not like gruel, but he felt too weak to argue, and obediently swallowed the hot, thick fluid. Shane tucked the clothes around him although he was already perspiring.

" There you be," she said, " you must be a good boy for mam now, and go to sleep."

Len dozed off into a semi-conscious state.

He remained in bed a month before he was able to go down to the kitchen again. During this period Jim and Shane often quarrelled over his illness. Each day in the pit Jim received advice as to the best recipe for curing Len, the favourite one being a quart of stout, treated with a red-hot poker and thickened with nutmeg. Jim was convinced that this treatment would cure his son, but Shane was equally convinced it would kill him, and for hours they nagged each other on the matter, each trying to persuade the other.

During his convalescence Len was visited by his workmates, the younger of whom brought him fruit while the elder, belonging to Jim's circle, brought him flagons of beer under their coats without Shane knowing. But she always discovered these before Len had the opportunity of informing his father of their whereabouts.

One day when Len was well on the way to recovery, Jim saw Shane emptying one of the flagons down the sink. He jumped to his feet from the armchair in which he was sprawling and with one stride reached the back door, but when he saw the last dregs trickling from the upturned bottle in Shane's hand, he could only open his eyes in a pitiful stare. He grasped the flagon, looking at it hard for some moments while the ends of his moustache twitched convulsively, and then turning reproachfully to Shane, asked her : " Have you no shame, venw, that you pour good money down the sink like that ? "

Shane glared at him a while before replying : " Shame ? " she queried indignantly. " You talk to me of shame ? Ha-ha ! You, who did let your drunken butties bring beer to your innocent dying son and let them try to poison him behind my back ! "

Jim did not expect this outburst and retreated shame-facedly into the kitchen. " Come, come, Shane bach," he mumbled, " you have got no need to say such a thing to my face."

He would have continued but for a peevish interruption from Len, who exclaimed, " Oh, leave it there, dad. Don't

5*

start quarrelling over nothing." And at this they both stopped arguing.

Len read again the letter he had received that morning from Ron. It asked about his progress with the books and commented on certain political matters, and he spent the remainder of the day answering it.

A few days later Shane allowed him to take a short stroll up the mountain. She put Jim's overcoat over his shoulders, whence it dangled to his feet, and but for the fact that he flatly refused, threatening to remain at home if she insisted, she would have wrapped her shawl round him as well.

" I don't know what the world be coming to," she complained. " Children don't no longer trust their mothers to know what be best for them." But eventually she let him go with the warning : " Now, 'member, Len bach, if you will be longer than a hour mam will be after you." Len promised he would return within the prescribed time, knowing that if he did not she would waken the valley with long-drawn cries for " Len-n-n-n."

Each day after this first attempt he continued his excursions up the mountain. He felt his body regaining strength and in a short time began to talk of restarting work. His parents tried to dissuade him, but Len was aware, in spite of attempts to hide the fact, that the loss of his wages was playing havoc with the domestic budget and that Shane was getting more deeply into debt each week. One day he walked to the colliery office and notified the officials that he was now fit and well.

He was told to start with his father next morning.

CHAPTER VIII

The Pit claims another Victim

THE Saturday following his return to work, as he had no wages to draw, Shane agreed that Len should approach the management for an advance on the security of the work he had already performed. He did so, and was granted the equivalent of three days' wages. He was aware that the advance given was actually a mortgage upon his body, but he saw no other alternative in view of the debts that had accumulated during his illness.

Shane paid off the sundry little creditors with the money but was unable to diminish the bulk she owed Mr. Evans Cardi for groceries. The latter was very agreeable about it when Shane informed him of the position.

" I understand, Mrs. Roberts," he said. " Things will come better by and by. Perhaps you will be able to settle it next week, now that Len have started to work again."

Len was rather worried over the whole business. For one thing, he did not want his family to be indebted to Ron's father, but the main cause of his worry was the fact that, after working for more than three years, he was unable to meet the financial emergency of an illness. The books he had been reading, in addition to improving his vocabulary, had also explained why the family could not meet the obligations incurred during his enforced period of idleness. The knowledge made him very bitter, especially when, on the following pay-day the advance made him was deducted from his wages.

Tired and irritable, he mentioned the matter to his parents one night.

" It's a shame," he started, addressing both of them, " that you two have to suffer because I have been too bad to go to work."

Big Jim merely grunted. " Ho, ay. That's just how it be in this old world, boy bach. It have always been the same ever since I can 'member, and it always will be the same."

The casual, off-hand nature of the reply drove Len frantic. His experiences since starting work had made him emotionally more volatile, and he sprang to his feet with a curse, the first they had ever heard him utter. His face was white with passion.

" Holy Christ, dad," he burst out, " how can you sit by there and talk so comfortable about it ? You talk as if we are nothing but cattle, mun. Look at yourself. You have been working in the pit for over thirty years and are supposed to be one of the best workmen there. Yet what are you now ? The body you are so proud of is breaking up before our eyes, 'in't it, mam ? " he pleaded, turning to Shane, who continued to look at him dazedly without answering.

" Yes," Len went on, " and not only that, but it is breaking your spirit if your words are anything to go by."

Jim half rose from his chair at this, but Len paid no attention.

" Look at me," he said passionately. " I have been working over three years. Yet when I lose a month's work because I'm too bad to go to the pit, we get in arrears with the rent and have to owe money for food."

He paused a moment, overcome with emotion. And when he continued in a sad voice the muscles of his face were twitching visibly.

" Cattle are not treated like us. A farmer takes care of his cow when it is bad, but we be no use to anybody." His voice rose in a sudden frenzy of passion. " No, not even to our bloody selves when we fail to drag our bodies up the hill to the blasted pit."

His voice dropped. " Oh, mam. I couldn't help falling bad, could I ? Yet you have got to suffer because of it. You once said, dad," turning to his father again, " that when you came to the pits first you had five golden

sovereigns in your pocket. Since then you have spent a
hard life and have given your wonderful body to the pit.
And now, after all these years, instead of having five
sovereigns in your pocket we owe five for food and rent."
His voice began to rise again and a little quiver ran through
it. " Think of it—a lifetime of hard work ending in debt.
Mam do quarrel with you sometimes because you do have a
pint or two of beer. Christ almighty, don't you deserve it ?
Or is it only work we have got to live for."

" Oh, dad and mam," he cried in despair, " I am sorry if
I have hurt you, but think. You two are getting on and
are beginning to look back. I have got to start where you
finish, and I must look ahead, not behind."

He seemed to lose his thoughts for a minute and swallowed
hard before turning to his mother beseechingly. " Oh,
mam bach. Look at our dad. He's the finest working man
that ever went down a pit. He do take pride in his work
and do never lose a shift, but because I, his son, do go bad
for a month he have got to go in debt. It's not right. It's
not fair. There's something wrong somewhere."

He bent his head on the table and his parents looked at
him with a loving pity. Presently Big Jim spat in the
fire and said, " Don't worry, Len bach. You be not quite
right in your head after that bout of illness, yet."

And Shane broke in : " Ay, and you be reading too many
of those old books, too. They 'on't do you any good."

Jim stopped her as Len raised his head from the table.
" It be not that," he said, before Len could say anything.
" You listen to your old man, Len bach, and don't worry
your head 'bout anything. When you do fail Big Jim be
still here, strong as ever even if I do have a few pints now
and agen."

Len looked at both the old people and felt something tug
at his heart. He opened his mouth to say something, but
shut it again without speaking.

That evening he met Will, his workmate, who coaxed him
into the Royal Head, where, as he explained, he had some
winnings to pick up. Len waited until Will returned with

the man he was looking for, and the three sat down while
the bookie called for a pint of beer apiece. Len was still
feeling the effects of his outburst and only required a little
coaxing to drink up the first pint of beer he had ever tasted.
He did not like the taste, but the warm glow it sent through
his body was pleasing and helped to dissipate his anger,
and as the conversation became more lively, the first
was followed by a second and a third.

Len could drink no more after this. The stuff rose back
into his throat and the room seemed to be twisting around
him, but in spite of this physical discomfort, the glow still
pervaded his body with a languorous warmth, and his brain
moved more quickly and in pleasant channels.

He never remembered how he reached home that night
or how he got into bed, but next morning when he woke his
mouth was dry and his head throbbed.

Shane asked, " Why did you go straight to bed last night,
Len bach ? Was you bad ? "

He was thankful she did not suspect, and told her, " No,
mam ; I was only a bit tired."

Once in the pit, however, he soon sweated out the after-
math of the beer and felt really well again. At this time
he and his father were working with many other men and
boys on a long stretch of coalface called a " barry."
During the dinner break, when all the men were gathered
together, a discussion started about a shortage of timber
from which they were suffering.

" Ay," said Jim, " this be the third day now. The
fireman do know all about it, but not a bloody stick have I
seen yet."

" That's quite right," interjected Bill Bristol. " They
can't say they don't know nothing about it, because I told
the fireman myself this morning. I suppose the sods
will not send timber down till we are all buried."

" Ay," said Scottie, " and they'll not need to wait verra
long. My bloody place is just on the floor now."

Will took up the discussion. " That be true. The
whole rotten barry be on the move now, and once this top

do start to work nothing in blue hell will give us time to get out before we are all squashed flat as bloody black pats."

All the men nodded agreement with Will's crude observation as they chewed their food and brushed the cockroaches off the boxes that held it.

Len had been silently listening to the talk. The men's casual appreciation of the deadly possibilities arising from the timber shortage made him think deeply. He wondered if it were sheer bravery that made the men and boys talk so calmly about the possibility of a horrible death awaiting them in the next few hours. He pondered over this while the men carried on the conversation, and eventually came to the conclusion it was not only bravery that made them talk in the way they did. He felt there existed a callous indifference among them, bred in their knowledge that the pit held their fate in its power and that death and destruction could come suddenly in a thousand different ways. He sensed this feeling in himself, and realised that if he pondered over the possible deaths awaiting him, he would never muster sufficient courage to descend the pit again. But his thoughts were interrupted by the booming voice of his father.

" Boys," he said, " we have got to make our minds up. Either we do stop by here until the timbers come or we do shut our chops and get on with the work. I'n't that it, Len ? " he asked, turning to his son.

Big Jim was always decisive in a crisis. He divided all problems into two straight opposites and demanded the acceptance of one or the other without the slightest regard for compromise. He was precisely the same in his public-house affairs. Either a man wanted to fight or he did not. For Jim, that was the end of it.

Len knew of this characteristic, and he was wary. " Perhaps we can find some other way out for the best," he answered hesitantly. " What about one of us going back for the fireman now, before we start to work. He ought to know by now when we can 'spect to have the timber in."

" But what if he don't know ? " shouted Will. " What do you say we do then ? "

Len thought hard for a moment, then said, " I believe the best thing we can do if the fireman don't know when we can get the timber, is to sit down by here until it comes to us."

There was some discussion on this suggestion. A few of the workmen wanted to continue working, pending the reply of the fireman. Others were opposed to this. Len considered the danger to be immediate and not ultimate, and re-entered the argument with this in mind.

" If we start now, and one of us gets killed, we won't be able to use the timber when it comes."

The logic of this statement appealed to the men's humour and their common sense. Big Jim insisted upon every man voting, " so that everything be square and above board," as he explained. Two men were sent to notify the fireman of their decision. The remainder whiled away the time with obscene jokes and smutty yarns that, for some undefined reason, reminded Jim of his adventures in the Boer War.

" We was coming out of the old farmhouse," he related, " when I seed a black 'ooman, naked as a dog, on a tump 'bout hundred yards away. Duw, duw, she was the first 'ooman us had seen for years, and the sun that hot we was full of tickles all the time. We all winked to her, but she take no notice, mun. Then I shout, ' Dera-ma. Argyll-wydd mawr.' She didn't half run then. All of us did race after her like mad. But I was a good runner then, and did soon leave 'em all standing. But funny thing, mun, she did leave me standing. I did go like hell, but all I could see was her little black arse shining in the sun like a brass button, before she did turn round and shout, ' Toodle-oo ! ' "

All, except Len, enjoyed this little anecdote, but he regarded it as sacrilege for his father to talk smut. Before he had time to say anything, however, lights appeared back on the roadway and everyone became silent as they drew nearer.

The fireman was obviously uneasy. " Well, boys," he asked, " what are you doing here ? Dinner-time is up and you all ought to be back in your places."

No one answered, so the fireman resumed, this time more harshly : " You all know that the output was down yesterday and that Mr. Hicks have said if we don't get more coal from this barry we will have to shut it down."

The men looked at each other sheepishly, much of their courage vanishing at this threat to their livelihood. They would probably have returned to their working places without another word had not Will shouted out : " What the blasting hell be the barry to us ? We don't own it, do we ? Mr. Hicks do claim it belongs to him, so let him look after the bloody hole. The only thing that do belong to us is our bloody lives, and that be all we have got to look after."

This heartened the men and they maintained their stand.

Len rose diffidently to his feet. " Will have hit the nail on the head, boys. If Mr. Hicks wants to shut the barry, that be his business. What we have got to do is to watch we are not buried in the barry for ever, which we will be very soon if we don't get timber." There was an audible murmur of approval at this statement.

The fireman felt the tide going against him, and started to cajole : " I have told you that I'm doing all I can to get timbers for you as soon as possible. There will very likely be some on the next journey. Now be reasonable and get back to your work, boys bach, and I will see that everything will come all right."

" That's my eye of a bloody yarn," said Bill Bristol. " We have heard that tale before during the last fortnight. It's like the battles Big Jim used to fight in the Boer War, always finishing miles further back than where they started."

Jim started to his feet at this insult, but the fireman, exasperated by his failure to get the men back to work, interrupted. " Hell fire ! Do you 'spect me to shit bloody timber for you ? "

A voice from outside the circle of light shouted : " No. And even if you did it 'ood be no good to us, because nothing from you would be of any use to anybody."

Len felt the air grow tense, and knew the men were now in the mood for defying anything the fireman ordered. Turning to the latter, he said : " Perhaps it 'ood be better, Shenkin, if you went back the road for five minutes to give the boys a chance to talk the thing over."

The irate fireman bridled up immediately. " What," he shouted, at the top of his voice, " you want me, the fireman of this district, to go back on the road ? Never in your life ! Huh. Who ever heard of such bloody cheek ? What do you you take me for, a bloody doorboy or what ? If men haven't got guts enough to talk open and free before another man, that is their own look-out."

Again from outside the ring of light came the voice : " You be bragging hell of a lot, to-day, i'n't you, Shenkin ? Nobody said you was a man. Ach. There be no more bloody man in you than there be in a dog's arse."

This stung the fireman into a fury. " What," he howled, saliva trickling down the corners of his mouth, " cheek me, would you ? Defy me, eh ? Easy you can do that when you hide your dirty bloody face in the dark. But I know you. Oh, ay. I know who you be by your voice, don't forget. No man have ever got the better of me yet. Do you know," he asked them all, " that a fireman in a pit is like a captain on a ship ? He have got, by law, to be obeyed. The law is on his side and you men must do as I order. If you are not ready to do that, then out you go, the bloody lot of you. And don't none of you ever come back, either."

This sudden and unexpected ultimatum alarmed the men, particularly those with big families. Len saw through the fireman's attempt to split the ranks, and knew they were all in a tight corner. Capitulation at this moment would leave them no alternative but to go back to the untimbered face, hoping for the best, until timber came. And for this he was not prepared. On the other hand, if they refused there was nothing else for it but to leave the pit for good.

He looked around the perturbed men before him. They were all thinking hard and hoping someone would tell them what to do. Len glanced at the fireman and saw the triumphant smirk on his face, and for some reason or other the sneer gave him the counter-move to the fireman's threat. Turning sharply, he shouted : " Go round the other barries, Will, and tell all the men to come down by here. Tell them there be a dispute on and that Shenkin have ordered us out because we 'on't work without timber."

Like a flash the men grasped the astuteness of the move. The fireman knew that the other colliers were also short of timber and that they would follow such a lead as this. He grew alarmed. If the agitation spread there was every likelihood of all the men in the pit going on strike, and rather than face this possibility he gave way with a bad grace.

" All right. I didn't mean what I said 'bout going out, but we must have a little bit of order sometimes or everything will be upside down. You can hold your meeting, but don't be too long, and give me a shout when you are ready."

His eyes glinted viciously in the light of the lamps as he went back. The men waited until he was out of hearing before excitedly starting the discussion.

Len had already planned what was to be done. " Look here, boys," he said. " When me and the old man was going out yesterday I noticed some good timber loose on the other side of the parting. What if we tell Shenkin we are willing to go back and fetch that for the barry if he will give us an extra half-turn each for our trouble ? "

This appeared a brilliant idea to the men. It solved the immediate problem of timber and at the same time took the offensive out of the fireman's hands. In addition it meant more money on pay-day. Without hesitation they all agreed to stand for this.

Big Jim shouted for Shenkin, who soon came panting up the roadway. " Well, have you made your minds up ? What are you going to do ? I hope you are going to be sensible for once." His voice was like a rasp. Bill Bristol reported the outcome of the discussion. The fireman scratched his head for a while, then asked, " How far back is these timbers you are talking about ? " Jim told him, whereupon Shenkin said : " Very well, boys. If you fetch that timber I will put five trams of muck in for each of you on measuring day."

This was not equal to the half-turn asked by the men, but they saw the compromise as a victory and accepted. They fetched the few timbers that were available and shared them equally. All of them were elated, for this was the first time they had been together in a conflict with the officials of the pit, and the victory gave them confidence in each other.

In the minds of all of them Len was automatically promoted to leadership of their affairs in the barry.

Having had their timber, the coal face soon became a hive, each man hurrying to make good the time lost in the dispute.

Towards the end of the shift, the enclosed air of the barry shook to a sudden crash, which was followed by a loud cry : " Quick, boys, quick ! Bill is under a fall."

Flinging down their tools anywhere, the men instantly responded, tearing along in their headlong scramble to get to the scene of the accident. When they reached it they saw at a glance what had happened. Bill Bristol had been digging a hole in the floor ready for the last prop he intended standing that day. He must have been bending over this hole when the roof had crashed down upon him, and now only his feet and one clenched hand were visible. Without a moment's pause the men began tearing at the debris that had buried their mate. Big Jim worked his hands beneath a huge stone that had fallen flatwise. Straining his gigantic muscles till they stood out in knots, he gasped out : " Now, boys, put that prop under." It was the one Bill intended using to protect himself from the roof that had now fallen.

" Careful, now," went on Jim, " not too far or you might put it on poor old Bill. Right. Now, all together."

With one concerted lift the stone was heaved over in a mighty jerk. Jim flung himself on his stomach and hurriedly scraped away the loose rubble until his fingers felt the flesh of his crushed workmate. He put his arms gently beneath the poor mangled body and lifted it carefully away from the fallen roof.

The men helped Big Jim to carry Bill back to the comparative safety of the roadway, where they laid him down, tenderly as breasting mothers, on the hastily arranged coats and shirts. Two of the men ran back for a stretcher, while the others cut away the injured man's bloodstained clothing. Blood spurted from the contorted limbs as, with infinite care, they were examined by the men. The white's of Bill's eyes were turned up in a ghastly glitter, and he groaned deep in his throat. Jim gave him some water to drink, but nothing more could be done until the stretcher came. The men stood around silent and sad while Jim rested the dying man's head on his arm. Presently he groaned again, and his lips shaped as if he were trying to say something. Big Jim bent down. " There, there. Don't excite yourself, Bill bach," he whispered, with a lump in his throat as he lied : " You haven't had much, mun. Just a scratch or two, and a bruise here and there. Duw, duw, you will soon be all over the old 'ooman as strong as ever."

Bill made no movement other than with his lips, but he failed to utter anything, and all that came from his mouth was a thick stream of blood and saliva. His eyes now seemed to have become normal again, and he looked at Jim with a deep intensity as though he were concentrating all his energies and thoughts in an attempt to say something. Jim bent his head nearer the bloodied lips, but the only thing that came was a horrible gibbering of the mouth. The men looked on helplessly, their faces full of grief and sadness, until at last they saw Bill's body quiver, then suddenly stiffen. They had known after the first brief examination that his back was broken.

The men who had run to fetch the stretcher came panting back, accompanied by the fireman. The latter was given details of the accident while the body was placed on the stretcher and covered completely with coats and a sheet of brattice as a final blanket. Then four of the men grasped the stretcher in lowered hands and led the slow procession to the pit bottom, each man taking it in turn to carry the lifeless body of his mate.

As the file of stooping men made their way forward no one spoke a word until they met Mr. Williams, the under-manager.

" Who is it, boys ? "

" Bill Bristol."

" Well, well. Pity. A splendid workman, too. It's always the best that go. Pity, pity. Try not to be longer than you can help, boys, not to keep the journey waiting too long. Well, well."

The men continued their slow trudge. The whole pit seemed to hold its breath, and the usual clamour was stilled. Yet as if the warm air had whispered the news in every ear, everyone in the pit knew what had happened, and at the pit bottom everything was in readiness. All approaches to the cage had been cleared and the cage itself hung waiting. Ten men filed in with the corpse, lining it five aside like a guard of honour. The iron knocker clanged six times, announcing to those on the surface the presence of death, and the cage, now become a coffin, was drawn slowly to the pit-head. Men on the surface hushed their voices as they waited for it and stood respectfully to one side while the body and its escort came out.

Big Jim sent Len off in front of them to acquaint the widow of what had occurred. This was regarded by the men as the most unpleasant job they could undertake, and many of them stated they would sooner be on a stretcher themselves than have the task of telling someone else it was coming. But much as he disliked it, Len regarded the task as a duty that had to be fulfilled, and handing his box, jack, and lamp to his father, he ran without coat or cap towards the home of Bill Bristol.

At the corner of the street where Bill had lived he stopped, and standing for a few minutes panting and gasping, he wondered how he was going to break the news. Neighbours were already flocking to the doorways as though drawn by some invisible magnet. All of them knew intuitively, as soon as they saw Len, that an accident had occurred, and though Len tried to walk casually up the street, every woman went white as he approached. Only when he had passed did the colour come back to their cheeks and, feeling themselves spared, every woman became immediately solicitous for her neighbour.

By the time Len reached the house he was looking for all the women in the street were with him, many of them already in tears. He knocked softly on the closed door, fearing that a loud sound would advertise his message, and as he waited he felt his heart beating painfully at his ribs.

The knock was answered by a pretty young woman holding a baby at her breast, while another dragged at her skirts. Len recognised Bill's wife at once. As soon as she saw him, her face went white as a death-mask with blue streaks and black shadows painted across it. She looked slowly from Len to the neighbouring women, then back to him. His coatless form and wild eyes struck her like a physical blow.

Something seemed to choke her for a moment, but she swallowed hard and gasped : " For God's sake don't tell me something have happened to our Bill."

Len gulped back the sour saliva that gathered in his mouth before replying. " Ay. Bill have had a little tap. He will soon be all right and you have got no need to worry."

She glared into his eyes and clutched her children more closely to her. " Tell me the truth, man," she demanded. " Don't you dare to lie to me. Oh, God," she added, bursting into hysterical sobs, " Bill is dead. I can see it in your eyes. Oh, Bill, Bill ! Oh, my little babies ! "

Len said no more. The neighbours took the children from the grieving woman and led her weeping back into the house.

Meanwhile the procession of half-clothed, black-faced men from the pit grew longer with every stride as miners returning home from work fell in behind the corpse. News of the accident trickled through the doors of each house long before the mournful cortège passed it. The stretcher betrayed the dead body by the fact that the face was covered, and whispers of " Who is it ? " floated quietly from one side of the street to the other. Tradesmen drew down their blinds till it passed and publicans closed their doors. The pit had claimed another victim and everyone mourned the latest sacrifice.

Big Jim and two other men remained behind in the house to wash the shattered limbs and lay the body out on the parlour table ready for the coffin.

Next day in work the men of the barry hardly spoke to each other. The blood-spattered stones had been cleared away by the night-shift and the coal face was ready for work immediately the day-shift returned. This cold planning by the management to ensure that whatever happened to the men there should be no hitch in the production of coal drove Len frantic. Throughout the morning he kept on working without saying a word to his father, although inwardly he was impotently fuming.

During the dinner hour, when all the men were gathered together, he could contain himself no longer. He spat a lump of half-chewed moist bread from his mouth and let his temper grip him.

" Holy Christ. This isn't a pit, but a slaughter-house," he began. " The officials are more like butchers than men. They measure coal without giving a thought to our flesh. They think, they dream, they live for coal, while we die for it. Coal—that's the thing. Get it. Drag it out by its roots. Do what you damn well like with it, but get it."

" Ay," he went on more calmly, " I believe that coal has come to be greater than God to the officials, and they now measure our lives by the trams of coal we can fill for them. Can't you see it, boys ? " he asked, his passion again getting the upper hand. " Firing hell, we don't count ! If we had timber a couple of minutes sooner yesterday, Bill 'ood be eating food with us now and cracking his jokes. Instead of that he be lying dead with his body cut to pieces and the bosses have already planned how to make up for the coal they lost yesterday."

His rage overcame him and he subsided into silence.

For the remainder of the week the men plodded to work like dumb animals each morning, answering with their bodies when the hooter called. But on the day of Bill's funeral, though the hooter blasted the air as usual, no one answered its hysterical screams. It kept blowing and bellowing like an animal robbed of its food, and still no one answered, until at last its noisy shrieks faded into a wail and died out. The men had determined not to go to the pit on the day of Bill's funeral. They had to bury their dead.

CHAPTER IX

Cwmardy prepares for Action

DURING the next few months big changes took place in the valley. The colliery company had extended its interests and now controlled the other groups of pits. As a result of this transaction Lord Cwmardy called a meeting of the directors and various pit managers at the Big House. While these were assembling he looked through the open french window at the pits he controlled and the valley he dominated. His black hair carried little tufts of grey at the sides, but his square, clean-shaven face was as hard as the coal he owned. When he turned from the window and took a chair next his daughter-secretary at the end of the table, everyone present became silent. They were aware that drastic changes of policy and personnel would accompany the merger which Lord Cwmardy had so cleverly negotiated, and each of them wondered how he would be affected.

When Cwmardy spoke his words dropped into his listeners' ears like icicles on a hot body. He accused the managers of lack of interest in their work, insisting that their friendly handling of the men was ruining the pits and the company. Some of the officials tried to remonstrate, but he abruptly checked them.

" You have come here to listen, not to talk," he told them. He spoke for more than an hour before introducing to them the sharp-faced grey-moustached man who sat unobtrusively at the far end of the table.

" This is Mr. Higgins," he announced. " In future Mr. Hicks will look after the practical and technical running of our affairs, but Mr. Higgins will work in close co-operation with him and will be directly representative of the financial

interests of the company in the day-to-day operations of
the collieries. That is all, gentlemen," he concluded.
" But before you go we will drink to the future prosperity of
our undertaking," and filling their glasses, they all rose and
echoed the toast.

In the meantime Len also had developed. He attended
the night-school recently organised by the Council in order
to study mining, and most of his spare time he spent in the
bedroom with his books.

Shane warned him : " No good will come from all this
reading, Len bach. The Lord have put into your head all
that it be good for you to know, and if you go beyond that
you will be sure to land up in the 'sylum, like your poor old
uncle John, God help him."

But Len took no heed of her grave warnings. He kept
on at his studies and passed examinations which theoreti-
cally qualified him to take up a position as a colliery
manager if he so desired. But this was the furthest
thought from his mind. His heart revolted at the idea of
becoming an official, for deep in him was still the memory
of Jane's death and the official's son who was supposed to be
responsible for it. But even apart from this emotional
reaction, his experiences in the pit had embittered him
against the officials as a caste. He regarded them as something distinct from the ordinary workmen and felt it would
be an act of betrayal to his family, to himself, and to the
men in the barry if he left the ranks of his workmates.

News of the amalgamation soon spread from pit to pit
and became the main topic of discussion. The older workmen were apprehensive of the move and their feelings were
neatly summed up one night in the Boar's Head by Big Jim.

" Mark my words, boys bach," he warned them. " Old
Lord Cwmardy haven't done this for our sakes. Oh no.
You can bet the buttons on your shirt that he have got
something up his sleeve that 'on't do us any good."

The pits resounded with furious discussion each day.
Many of the younger miners were inclined to regard the
merger in a more favourable light than Big Jim, some of

them arguing that the amalgamation would eliminate competition and so lead to more wages.

One Saturday when the men were returning from work the village crier met them at the end of the bridge. Shouting at the top of his voice, he announced there was to be a special mass-meeting of all workmen on Sunday afternoon. The announcement created a stir in the valley and there were very few public-house fights that night, as the men were too busy discussing the meeting on the morrow. Many of them remembered that the last time such a meeting had been held it was followed by a strike of hauliers.

When Sunday afternoon came Big Jim and Len made their way to the huge old barn where the meeting was to be held. They found it packed with workmen, and Big Jim had to use all his weight to force a way in, Len crushed to his side in the press. Ezra Jones, the miners' leader, sat by himself on the improvised platform waiting for the hubbub to die down. The hall was thick with tobacco fumes when he rose to his feet and advanced to the front of the stage. He looked exactly as Len had first seen him at the funeral of the explosion victims. His solid, square body fitted his stern face and made a complete picture of rugged determination. There was something powerful and dominating in the man's presence, and when he raised his hand in the authoritative gesture that Len still remembered, the tumult of voices in the hall faded away. Ezra waited until everyone was perfectly quiet and then, his voice as hard and stern as his face, began to speak.

" Fellow workmen, I have taken the responsibility upon myself for calling you together to-day. You will decide for yourselves if I was justified in doing this after I have reported the purpose of the meeting. Many of us believe we should meet like this more often. Maybe what follows from this meeting may make that not only possible but necessary." Loud shouts interrupted him.

" That's right. We ought to meet more often."

" Good old Ezra ! Get it off your chest."

This was followed by a prolonged stamping of feet, but

when this had ceased Ezra went on to explain that the colliery company, through Mr. Higgins, was no longer going to pay for the small coal filled by the men. In future the only payment made would be for large coal.

" That is the exact message I have to give you from the company," he concluded, " and that is why I have called you together. You can now ask what questions you like and discuss the matter for yourselves."

With this he sat down abruptly. The hall was immediately in an uproar. Men asked each other a hundred different questions and made a hundred different statements that were lost in the general din. But eventually a voice forced itself above all the others.

" Can I ask a question, Mr. Chairman ? " it asked.

" Yes, if you want to," was the curt reply.

" Well, can you tell us how much small coal we fill in each tram ? "

Everyone became silent as Ezra, without rising from his chair, answered : " Yes. About forty per cent.—that is, nearly half."

A groan echoed throughout the hall, and another workman rose to his feet. He was tall and austere-looking, as became a deacon of Calfaria, the biggest chapel in Cwmardy and the one much favoured by the colliery management and officials.

" Does Mr. Hicks really mean to do this thing to us ? Is he serious in what he says ? It will mean a big loss to all of us, and I was thinking perhaps Mr. Hicks is going to make the loss good in some other way, maybe by giving us a bigger price for large coal."

The chairman rose to his feet. " Yes, Mr. Hicks and Mr. Higgins are prepared to consider something in that direction. On the old price-list for through and through we had a shilling for every ton of coal we filled, large and small. Now we are offered one and threepence for every ton of large but nothing at all for small coal. This means that where we used to earn a pound, the same amount of coal will now give us fifteen shillings."

The men were dumbfounded as they closely followed
Ezra's statement. As the meaning of the offer sank home
to them the hall became a bedlam, and everyone broke into
abuse.

" Dirty old swine ! "

" How the hell do he think we are going to live ? "

" Let him come and do his own dirty work ! "

" Better starve out than in ! "

" Let him get to hell and find his workmen there ! "

Len sat silent and morose. He was astounded by the
proposition. More or less subconsciously his mind searched
for favourable possibilities in the situation.

To his father's terse comment, " Only one thing we can
do, take it or fight," his only reply was, " Wait a minute,
let's see how the men take it. There might be some way
out which we can't think of for a minute."

He sensed the implications of the ultimatum, and pictured the men in the barry, already overworked on the
present basis, slogging themselves to a standstill to make
up in extra output what they lost by the lower price-list.
He saw his own home where, working full-time as he and his
father were doing, they could barely pay their way, and he
tried to imagine what domestic conditions would be like
if they failed to make good their present wages by harder
work.

A deep hush brought his thoughts back to the meeting.
He looked around and saw Dai Cannon standing on a
bench directly opposite him. The man's beer-drenched
suit and bedraggled moustache, under which the bottom
lip hung loosely, attracted attention. He stood above the
seated workers and looked a picture of disgust and defiance.
His voice was deep and booming when he spoke.

" Mr. Chairman and fellow workmen, at last the octopus
is closing his tentacles about the living bodies of our women
and children. Like a gloating vulture, the hireling of the
company is waiting to fill our valley with the sighs and sobs
of starving people." He lifted his eyes and hands to the
ceiling and went on in this strain with increasing passion and

vehemence in each phrase he uttered. The men were on their feet cheering wildly when he concluded with the words : " If we are to starve let it be in the sun with God's pure air around us. If we are to die let it be fighting like the slaves of old Rome. I stand, like Moses, for my people."

Big Jim, a puzzled frown on his face, bent to Len and said, " By Christ, old Dai is a good speaker, mun, but what did he mean by octopus's testicles ? "

Len hurriedly corrected him, without taking his eyes off the speaker. Dai knew he had struck the right note and sat down contentedly, his wet lower lip more conspicuous than ever.

Presently, when the tumult had become hushed, Ezra rose from his chair. " That's a good speech of Dai's," he said with quiet irony. " As usual he has told us what to do, but has not told us how to do it. It is quite easy for us all to get excited and enthusiastic, but that alone won't take us far against this company. Whatever we think is necessary to safeguard our conditions will have to be planned out in cold blood." He sat down again, leaving the men to think out the problem. Speaker after speaker got to his feet and contributed to the discussion that followed.

Len listened attentively to everyone. He felt there was a lot in what Ezra had said, but thought he could have been more helpfully critical of Dai's speech instead of brushing it aside as he had done. During the discussion he had already, in a hazy way, seen how the ravelled threads could be separated, but he wanted to be sure before plunging. At last he satisfied himself that the way was clear and tremblingly rising to his feet he asked for the floor. Big Jim looked at him with open mouth and was about to say something when Ezra nodded acquiescence. In a shaking, squeaky voice Len asked : " Does this new price-list affect the workmen in the other pits taken over by the company? " Ezra again nodded a curt assent, and Len's thoughts immediately cleared, for the reply showed him the counter to the company's threat. Clearing his throat, he told the meeting :

" If that is so, as far as I can see there are two things to be done if we are to succeed in this fight." His voice became more confident and resonant as he continued : " While I agree with all that Dai Cannon has said, I don't believe he has gone far enough. What I mean is this. The old price-list made it possible for us to earn some sort of a living, but the new one will make this impossible. If this be so, then we should demand from the company a minimum wage that will guarantee we won't starve under the new list." Ezra had leaned forward when Len began pro-pounding his policy, and the workmen, who grasped its import immediately, applauded loudly. Len went on : " But how to get this is the problem. We can depend on it that the company will fight, because this is a principle that affects every miner and owner in the country. That is why we must look for support right from the start, and where better can we look for this than among our neigh-bours, who are suffering under the same company as us and facing the same attack ? I believe we should send some-body from this meeting to our butties in the other pits under the company and ask them to come with us to a mass-meeting of the workmen from all the pits."

He stuttered here, tried to go on, then gave it up and sat down. For a second the hall was perfectly quiet. Then uproar broke out as the men grasped the logic of the arguments. The shouting and applause continued for many minutes, while Big Jim looked round the hall, nodding his head all the time as if saying, " There you be, you beggars, what think you of that ? Big Jim's boy, see ? "

Len, sitting next to him, hardly heard the cheering, his face was pale with nervousness and he bent his head in a vain attempt to stop the thumping of his heart. Ezra at last succeeded in restoring order.

" I think that our young friend has cleared the way for us," he said. " If fight there is to be, then we bring our allies into it from the start." He strained his eyes to peer through the smoky atmosphere. " I am not sure—the smoke is rather heavy—but I believe the last speaker is Big Jim's boy."

Again the cheering broke out, and despite Len's efforts to restrain him, Big Jim got to his feet and shouted : " Ay, ay, Mishter Cadeirid, you be quite right. Big Jim's boy."

Once the way forward was clear the men soon disposed of the steps to be taken, and the meeting closed with the singing of a Welsh anthem. The excited and chattering men streamed into the street and, breaking up into groups, continued the discussion as they made their way homewards. During the intervening week approaches were made to the other workmen in the valley, and it was agreed to hold a joint mass-meeting on the following Sunday.

Two matters now dominated the minds of the people, the coming strike, which they regarded as inevitable, and the coronation of the new king that was shortly to take place. This latter was the cause of much speculation. Will told Len, as they trudged to the pit one morning, " The new king will never be so good as his old man was."

" What makes you think that ? "

" Well," replied Will, " by all accounts the old man was a hell of a bird, a proper sport by all accounts and different to the rest of 'em. He'd have a bit of fun with the best, and they tell me he was hot bloody stuff with the gels."

Len did not seem to be paying much attention, so Will brought out what he regarded as a broadside. " More than that, your old man told me that if it wasn't for the last king us 'ood have been at war with the bloody Shermans long ago. Now he's gone it will be bound to come off one day."

Len merely murmured abstractedly : " They're all the same, Will bach, they all carry out the orders given to them by our masters."

Will snorted contemptuously. " Huh ! That be all balls."

6

His mate did not reply for a while, then said, " Don't let us bother our heads about the new king now. What do you think is going to happen in the meeting Sunday ? " and with this began an argument that continued throughout the day in the pit.

Len listened avidly to everything that was said about Ezra, and found out that he had once worked on the other side of the mountain before he was blacklisted by the company and driven from his home. This had made him bitter and cynical, but since coming to the valley his dour determination and dominating personality had made him respected and admired by the workmen.

Listening to the instances of Ezra's staunchness and loyalty related by Big Jim, Len was thrilled, for he was now of an age when his vague ideas were beginning to find a coherence. Although very emotional, he yet had a capacity for deep thinking, and what he now needed was someone who could inspire him, a person whose words and actions would serve as a focus for his thoughts, a man he could look up to as an example.

More or less subconsciously, Len began to accept Ezra as a leader to be followed and trusted.

CHAPTER X

Cwmardy goes into Action

WHEN Sunday came the weather was bright and the sky cloudless. The atmosphere was free from the weekday thrum of the pits and the smoke of the huge stacks, and this accounted for the strange hush that enveloped the valley as, up at the Big House, two men gazed silently through the window into the shimmering air that separated them from the mass of people gathered on the rubbish dump near the pit.

"They will assuredly strike," Mr. Higgins told Mr. Hicks as they withdrew from the window.

"You may depend upon that," replied the general manager, pouring himself a generous dose of whisky. "But we have one consolation. They can't remain out long, because they have practically no organisation and no finance to maintain them for any length of time. More than that, they have no leaders."

Mr. Higgins looked up at this last remark. "I don't know so much about that. This man Ezra Jones strikes me as a pretty stubborn type, and he seems to wield a great deal of influence with the men."

"That's true," murmured Mr. Hicks hesitantly. "We were warned about him before he came to the village and were very foolish to have permitted him to start work at our pit."

Mr. Higgins interrupted him rather abruptly. "What are the possibilities of placing him on the staff?" he asked.

"Absolutely impossible. The man is incorruptible. All we can do now, if the men are foolish enough to strike, is to ensure that it is a short one. We must close every possible avenue of finance to them and use whatever measures are necessary to show them how silly their conduct is. We are fortunate in this last respect, Mr. Higgins, in that we have a representative majority in both the district and county councils. This will enable us to proceed constitutionally in the desired directions."

Down on the rubbish dump thousands of miners and their womenfolk were waiting for the meeting to begin. They became accustomed to the putrid stench of decaying matter that rose from the nearby river, and it ceased to sting their nostrils. A lorry in the centre of the huge mass of people held Ezra and some other men. Presently a glorious baritone voice lifted itself from the throng in the lilting melody of an old Welsh hymn. Its strains floated over the crowd like a shawl encircling a child. The people lost their individual identities in the vibrating rhythm of the tune, which impelled their emotions into expression through bonds of vocal unity. In a matter of seconds every voice had taken up the refrain. The music rippled round the mountains in caressing billows that fell back upon themselves and then ran wistfully down the valley, the power in the men's deep voices carrying with it the tender soprano of the womenfolk.

The men on the platform stood with bared heads and took part in the singing until it finished, when they all, with the exception of Ezra, sat down. The latter waited with bent head until the last echoes ebbed into silence down the valley, then with an imperative wave of his hand he commanded attention. Each of the thousands of eyes was fixed upon him when his cold voice split the air as he reported all that had happened since the previous meeting. With steady calculation he built his case against the company and eventually concluded with the words :

" That is the position, fellow workmen, either we fight or starve. You will yourselves decide which."

For a minute after his voice had ceased the whole world seemed to slumber, then it awoke to a terrific shout that rattled and throbbed in the blood of the people present. It ascended in increasing crescendos, pushing itself up the mountain with brazen resonance until it banged itself against the windows of the Big House.

" Strike ! Strike ! "

" Better starve out than in ! "

" Strike ! Strike ! "

Ezra, white-faced and tight-lipped, stood motionless on the lorry waiting for the storm to abate. He knew the men and their moods, and was aware that no power on earth other than complete capitulation by the company could now avert a strike. But he felt neither pity for the company nor sympathy for the people. His heart had been broken with the breaking of his home, an event which had sent his wife to a premature death. His eyes looked blankly over the mass of heads before him as he unemotionally pictured the immediate future and concentrated his mind on the dominating need for defeating Lord Cwmardy and the company. After a while he raised his hand again.

" Men and women of our valley," he began, " no need to ask, is there peace or war ? You have declared for war. So be it. Now let every man and woman stand solid in the fight, for we shall need every atom of energy and determination if we are to win."

For the first time his eyes shone with hard glints as though he gloated over something long desired and now obtained. The gleam strengthened as someone struck up the strains of a Welsh battle hymn in which everyone joined. The meeting ended to the strains of the stirring song, and the people returned excitedly to their homes.

Len had been silent all the while. Overawed by the huge crowd of people and the tremendous upsurge of feeling, he had dumbly followed the proceedings, and that night he lay awake for long hours wondering what would be the outcome of the whole business. He knew the issue had now widened beyond the question of small coal and had become the vastly bigger and more important one of a minimum wage. He saw that the initiative had been taken out of the hands of the company, who were now thrown upon the defensive, and, although proud of the part he had played, he was sensible enough to realise that such a development was inevitable even had he not spoken at the initial meeting.

Next morning not a man other than officials presented himself at the pits. But in the afternoon each of them was surrounded by hundreds of men and women. The weather was beautifully fine and warm and the valley looked as peaceful as a hamlet in the Alps. The people joked with the police, most of whom they knew, while at the same time they jealously scrutinised everyone who approached the colliery. During the evening separate pit meetings were held and committees elected, from which representatives were chosen for a central committee that controlled all the pits. To this committee Len was elected.

The strike had dragged on for two weeks without any move being made by the company before Len realised that the men could not win on the present basis of operations. He had many ideas on the matter, but felt rather nervous of expressing them before the seasoned veterans of the committee. Particularly was he shy and diffident in Ezra's presence. The manner in which the latter had handled the decisive meeting greatly impressed him, and he began to look upon Ezra as the greatest man he had ever seen or read of. Despite this hesitancy, the thought persisted that something must be done, and he eventually made up his mind to seek an interview with the miners' leader. "After all," he thought to himself, when coming to this decision, "he can't eat me. The most he can do is order me out of the house."

Len's nervous rap on the door was answered by Ezra in person. The lad looked up to him for some moments as though he had suddenly lost his tongue. The elder man broke the silence.

"Hello," he asked, "what's brought you here, Len? But come in. We can talk better inside." The welcome and interest in Ezra's voice heartened him, and he felt more at ease when he sat down in a room lined with bookshelves. He had never before seen so many books at one time and would have liked to go round reading the titles, but Ezra gave him no opportunity. The man's keen, dark eyes seemed to bore into him and he again began to feel uncomfortable, but he swallowed his rising chagrin and went direct into the matter troubling his mind.

" I have come to see you, Mr. Jones, about our strike. We have now been out for a fortnight and I feel that unless we do something we will be beat." He stopped abruptly as if he had unloaded himself of all he had come to say.

Ezra tried to help him. " Well, Len, my boy. What ideas are troubling you ? I would like to know what you are thinking, because I, also, have been disturbed by the way in which the strike is drifting."

Len was pleased and encouraged by the implied compliment, and in a very short time his initial embarrassment was banished as he talked of the things he thought should be done. Ezra listened attentively until he had finished, and for some moments, that seemed like hours to Len, he sat deep in thought.

At last he rose from the chair and looked in a queer way at the young man. " I am glad you came to me, Len, and I want to say before I go any further that I don't like being called Mr. Jones. My name is Ezra to all the workmen and it is the same to you." Len looked a little startled at this but had no time to make any comment as the miners' leader went on. " There is a great deal in what you have said. Yes, a great deal. But to my mind there are even more important things than the steps you are suggesting, all of which I agree with, by the way. For instance, Len," he asked, looking directly into his eyes, " have you thought what the next move of the company is likely to be ? "

Len shook his head negatively.

" Well, you see, my boy, when you enter a fight such as we are in now we must always try to see at least two moves ahead. We must always try to anticipate what the enemy is thinking and what he intends doing. To begin with, do you think for a moment the company is prepared to let the strike drift on indefinitely without taking measures to

bring it to an end ? No, of course not," he answered
himself. " Each day the strike lasts means further loss to
the owners, and they are no more anxious than we are to
prolong the strike. Just as you have been thinking of
methods to strengthen the strike, so have they been thinking of ways and means to break it and drive our men back
to the pits. Our job is to find out how they intend doing
this. Yes, that is the problem."

Len listened avidly to all he had to say and felt the
ruthless strength of the man even in his words.

" I am glad you came to see me," Ezra concluded," and
shall always be pleased to welcome you in my house. I
know," he added somewhat wistfully, " that you think me a
hard man, but there are reasons for this. In any case I
shall always be glad to help young men like yourself who
take an interest in the affairs of the people. You had
better let me raise the matters you mention in the committee. They will have a better chance of being accepted."

Len unhesitatingly agreed to this and, after a moment's
awkward pause, Ezra diverted the conversation into other
channels. He talked of Big Jim and related little anecdotes
in an inimitable manner that simply convulsed Len, who
had never thought this stern man could be so human.
Presently Ezra called into the kitchen, " Mary, my dear,
I have a visitor here and I want you to make a cup of tea for
him."

The answer came back in a sharp girlish voice : " It's
already done, dad. Shall I bring it into the parlour or will
you have it in the kitchen ? "

There was a soft look in Ezra's dark eyes when he replied,
" Len and I will come into the kitchen, Mary."

Len had seen very little of Mary since their schooldays,
and understood she had been away from home a great deal,
although he did not know why.

He shyly took the slim outstretched hand as Ezra introduced him, and looked into her eyes. At first they appeared
too big for her small, well-defined, straight features and he
could not determine their colour. Her aquiline nose was

rather long when compared with the remainder of her face and her small body gave the impression it was an incidental appendage to her eyes. Even Len's slim body looked robust beside hers. She had very little colour except in her hair, which was a shiny brown whose gleaming sheen and accompanying shadows found a reflective pool in her eyes. Mary invited him to take a chair, at the same time sitting on a stool near her father. It was obvious they were devoted to each other, and as Ezra continued his reminiscences she joined in with occasional remarks. Len felt himself in a new world. The time seemed to fly, and when at last the time came to take his leave there was real regret in his voice as he thanked them for their kindness. They both accompanied him to the door, where he thanked them again. He felt strangely elated as he made his way home to Sunny Bank.

That night in the committee Ezra surveyed the strike situation. The committee-men realised that the strike had gone on for a fortnight without any real effort being made to organise the struggle, and there was a serious discussion as to the number of safety men permitted to work in the pits. A resolution involving the withdrawal of the safety men was agreed to. This business having been disposed of, the men considered the proposals Len had made to Ezra during the afternoon. They included sending emissaries throughout the land to gather finance and win sympathy, the establishment of food kitchens, publicity, sports and concert departments, and the organisation of methodical picketing at the pits. This latter was considered of primary importance in view of the decision to withdraw all the safety men and officials.

The decisions of the committee were given to the mass-meeting next day, at which all the adults in the valley, with the exception of the bedridden, attended. Ezra, as usual, conducted the proceedings.

Mary strolled among the women, the sun, dazzling through her hair, giving her face a brightness that made it attractive. She felt proud of her father, as she watched him focus

6*

the attention of the workers to the points at issue. He stood
perfectly still on the lorry and his face in no way betrayed
his feelings while the multitude of people roared their assent
to the proposals. After the recommendations had been
vociferously accepted, Mary heard his calm voice call out
the names of the men who were to act as emissaries in
other areas. Each name was greeted with bursts of cheering, and when the last of these had died down, Ezra
turned to where he had seen Len standing near Big Jim.

Without any preamble he announced : " I now call upon
Len, the son of Big Jim, to say a few words to us."

Len was stunned by the unexpected suddenness of
what virtually amounted to a command. His face paled
and he felt the air heavy and humid about his body. He
started to stammer something when, in the centre of the
huge grey blob of faces that confronted him, he saw Mary.
It seemed to him her eyes were filled with pity, and the
thought that this was so stung him into a frenzy. Without
further hesitation he flung himself on a flood of words into
the silence that had followed Ezra's announcement.
The words spilled from his mouth in a torrent that
left little drips of saliva on his lips, each word pulsing
with the tremor that shook him. For some minutes he
stumbled on, unconscious of the import of his remarks,
until the situation began to grip him. Then his sentences
became more coherent and started to flow with an eloquence which gained added power in the natural music of
his voice. He spoke of Ezra as one would speak of God.

" We are being led into battle by one who knows all that
the battle means and all that we must do to win it. There
in the Big House," he pointed dramatically towards the
mountain, " are the people who have brought us to this
pass. If they are looking down on us now they see us as
solid as ever."

He urged the people to be steadfast and true and to
follow Ezra with faith and loyalty, and concluded with the
exhortation : " It may be a long strike. It may be hard
and bitter, but whatever comes, if we stand together and

stick to Ezra we will be as sure of victory as we are that the sun rises in the bottom of our valley and sets over the pit." He stood motionless with his arm upraised and his head thrown back as if he were seeking inspiration from the sky. Then he burst out : " He who follows Ezra captures victory. Let those who want victory shout it till the mountains carry its echoes to those who are waiting in the Big House."

Like an avalanche the roar shook the air : " For Ezra and victory."

A sudden rush took the miners' leader by surprise and, before he could avoid it, he was lifted into the air and carried triumphantly through the streets in a spontaneous demonstration of loyalty and determination.

Later that night, while Ezra was in a deep meditation that had already lasted some time, Mary quietly asked him : " Why did you call on Len to speak, dad ? You knew he was shy and not used to it."

Her father looked quizzically into her eyes. " Why do you ask, my dear ? "

" Oh, there's no definite reason at all, only I wondered why you did so unusual a thing when you knew the men had already shown they agreed with you. In any case," she added with a little confused blush, " I don't see why you chose the man you did."

She stopped, then went on quickly before Ezra could intervene. " Don't think I'm nosey, daddy dear. I'm only concerned for your sake. You have so many enemies who would like to buy or destroy you. I know, dear, they can never buy you, but I'm sometimes afraid they will use your own friends to destroy you. That is why I want you to be strong in yourself without having to depend on others." Her head drooped on his chest and a lump rose to his throat as he ran his fingers gently through her hair and around her face till they came to her burning ears and began playing absently with the lobes, as he had always done in moments of great bitterness or loneliness when caressing his wife.

The action was now quite unconscious, but it reflected his mood, and Mary, aware of this, raised her head and murmured. " There you go again, daddy. Wandering round an empty world. But you are not lonely. How can you be with all these wonderful people who look up to and follow you ? How can you be lonely when you have me ? "

Ezra looked at her again, his eyes sad and heavy. " No, I cannot be lonely while I have you, although you are all that I have got. The people who to-day carried me on their shoulders would, with equal willingness and fervour, in different circumstances trample my body into the mud. One day, my dear," he went on slowly as if he were deeply cogitating, " you will learn there is only one way to lead, and that is the way the people want to go. Once try to take them away from this, they destroy you. When you are not prepared to go their way, they desert you. They deserted me before and left me to the mercy of enemies who smashed my home and killed your mother. That is why you are left to-day with a crusty old man as a father to take care of and worry about."

He gulped hard and abruptly changed the subject. " You ask why I called upon young Len to speak. It was because I wanted to do two things : I wanted to know how deep he is in the events of the strike and I also wanted to know the extent of my influence over him. It is necessary that I should know both these things, because the future is full of unexpected happenings and if a leader wants to survive them he must have some knowledge of their drift before they actually occur. That's all, my dear," reaching for his pipe.

The intimacy was at an end.

CHAPTER XI

Action deepens

LATE one night Mr. Evans Cardi was surprised to hear a hurried knock at his front-door. He hastened down to open it and found Mary waiting on the step.

" Duw's anwyl y byd, Mary bach. What has brought you here at this time of the night ? " asked the old man anxiously.

" May I come in, Mr. Evans ? I would like to talk to you privately if you can spare the time."

" By all means, my gel. But tell me quick, what's the matter ? "

" There's nothing the matter, Mr. Evans," Mary assured him as he led her into the parlour beside the shop.

She took the proffered chair and went into the business straight away. She explained she had just come from the canteen committee, which was anxious to start the feeding centres as soon as possible but did not have the necessary means. In view of this she had been invited to approach Mr. Evans to solicit his help in providing foodstuffs on credit till the money came in from the outside areas now being canvassed by the strikers' representatives.

Mary had little trouble in coming to an agreement with the old man, and without more ado took her leave, making the lateness of the hour an excuse for not waiting to see Mrs. Evans. She had hardly gone a hundred yards, however, when she heard someone hurriedly running behind her. As the steps came nearer, she stood still, wondering who it could be, and for a moment fear clutched at her heart and she felt like running back to the safety of the shop.

The running footsteps tip-tapped even more quickly on

the roadway and Mary was on the point of dashing wildly down the street when she heard a girl's voice gasp out :

" Miss Mary. Miss Mary. Wait for me."

Mary remained motionless as if turned to stone. She had no idea who was calling her until the runner overtook her, struggling to regain her breath, and she recognised the servant-girl from the Big House, evidently in a state of great agitation.

" Well, Lizzie, what on earth is the matter ? " she asked, her voice betraying the surprise she felt and her heart pounding madly with the temporary fright.

" Oh, Mary, they are going to do something awful to-morrow," the girl managed to say, almost bursting into tears. " Those black swine up there," pointing to the Big House, " I heard them with my own ears. They were sitting in the lounge planning what they are going to do about the strike. The hell's scum that they are ! " She was so overcome for a moment by the depth of her feeling that she stood mute and trembling, and Mary grew impatient.

" But what have they planned, Lizzie ? For God's sake let's have some sense."

" They are going to bring policemen from all over the country into Cwmardy to drive our men back to work. I heard them say it. Good job I saw you coming from Evans Cardi. You can tell your father all about it now."

" No, no, Lizzie," said Mary, beginning to grasp the situation, " you come along with me and tell father yourself." And taking the girl by the arm, Mary led her, half walking, half running, to the house where Ezra sat anxiously waiting.

It was only a matter of minutes before the miners' leader had drawn from the girl the whole story of Mr. Higgins' sudden journey to the city, of the stormy scene on his return, and the orders that all the officials were to present themselves for work irrespective of what the strikers thought or did. Having satisfied himself, he bade Mary make tea for the girl and, taking his cap from its peg, he quietly left the house.

Next morning as the sun was sending its red beams across the valley, the pickets specially selected by Ezra during the previous night surrounded the pit. Ezra, Len, and Big Jim stood together when the first group of officials approached. As usual the pickets closed in to scrutinise if they were *bona fide* safety-men, and Ezra noticed in the group four men who were not regarded as being necessary to the safety of the pit.

Accompanied by Len and Big Jim he pushed his way through the pickets and addressed the men concerned. " The decision to-day remains as it did yesterday," he remarked. " No officials below the rank of overman can go down this pit. There is no need to argue the matter. I advise those of you who are not entitled to act as safety men to return home."

Not a single official moved. The police who had been scattered loosely about drew together as though they had received a signal. The atmosphere became tense and many of the officials turned pale with nervousness. Their orders had been clear and explicit. They had to go down the pit in spite of the pickets.

One of them, noticing the movement of the police, gathered courage, and turning to Ezra said abruptly, " It is none of our business what the strikers decide. Our duty is to keep the pits in a state where they can be worked again. That is what we intend doing. I ask you to with-draw your men and let us get on with our work."

Big Jim, who was standing near, took umbrage at this last remark. " Duty! Work! " he exclaimed con-temptuously. " What in hell be you talking about, mun ? Oonly the other day you was a workman yourself, and not the best of them, too. What do you want down the pits now when we be fighting for a living ? I know these pits so good, if not better than any man. There be no need for half of you devils down there." He broke his statement off short.

One of the officials howled : " Look out there, the bloody lot of you, or I'll blow your rotten brains out." And the steel barrel of a pistol flashed in the sun like a streak of blood.

As the official advanced with the pistol quivering in his hand, the men tumbled hastily back over one another.

" Look out there ! Clear the way ! " he bellowed hoarsely. " The first man who tries to stop us will get his blasted brains splashed on the ground."

A tremor ran through the ranks of the pickets. They saw all their plans being suddenly and easily defeated, as they fell back helpless in the face of the slowly circling pistol, that seemed to leer through its bore at each of them in turn. The circle they had formed round the officials broke, and Ezra, feeling the tension, murmured, " Steady, boys, no panic and don't do anything silly."

The officials were nearly clear of the pickets when a fist, seemingly flung from nowhere, struck the man with the pistol a terrific blow that flattened him, silent and senseless, on the roadway.

A howl like the roar of a lion burst from Big Jim. " Good old Africa," he shouted his eyes glinting with excitement, " the man who can fight Boers can fight blacklegs any day." In two strides he broke through the ranks of the now frightened officials and called upon the strikers. " Hold 'em tight, boys bach. Hold 'em tight ! " His words and quick action electrified the pickets, and in a twinkling the officials were again surrounded.

The sudden movement with its complete reversal of the position made the latter think they were in danger of physical harm. They hastily dragged lead piping, wooden clubs, and other weapons from their pockets and commenced frenziedly hitting out at the strikers. In a moment everyone was fighting furiously. Grunts followed howls and screams as fists, boots, and weapons made violent contact with flesh and bone. The police tried to force their way into the centre, where Big Jim was fighting to ward off any harm to Len and Ezra. But the strikers saw the move and closed around the trio in such a way that a compact mass of men stood between them and the police.

The affray ended as suddenly as it had started. First one and then another of the officials struggled back down the hill to their homes, and in a few minutes they had all disappeared, including the one with the pistol. Big Jim, towering above the pickets, laughed happily although blood dripped from his nose on his moustache. The police had followed the officials and the strikers were left in sole command of the colliery yard, and though a few suffered from cuts and bruises no one was seriously injured.

Len's heart throbbed with excitement and pride, and he kept as near as possible to his father and Ezra. The latter, with his coat torn, and capless, stood on the steps of the colliery office, and looking around him waited for the excitement to die down a little, then said : " Well boys, we have, thanks to Big Jim, beaten the first move of the company." The strikers gave a resounding cheer, while Big Jim with a dignified gesture solemnly twirled the ends of his long moustache. When the cheers had died down Ezra went on. " We have beaten the first move, but God alone knows what their next step is going to be. The best thing we can do now is to go home altogether and hold a mass-meeting this afternoon."

Very little was said during the march down the hill, but everyone walked with a jubilant spring that seemed to repeat in every step : " We have won the first round, first round, first round."

After the wildly enthusiastic meeting that afternoon the word " blackleg " went flashing from mouth to mouth. It captured the people's imagination. No one, least of all Big Jim himself, had any idea why the term was appropriate, but it was sufficient to everyone that it conveyed to their minds in a simple manner the significance of all personal actions detrimental to their strike.

Late that night when Shane was preparing for bed she was surprised to see Big Jim and Len making preparations to leave the house. She said nothing about the unusual and unexpected procedure of the two men, but Big Jim fidgeted uncomfortably when he caught the burning look in her eyes. As they were ready to leave she asked Len in what she intended to be a casual, off-hand manner :

" Going out late to-night 'in't you, Len bach ? Be there something special on ? "

Getting no answer, she addressed herself cuttingly to Jim. " Anybody with any sense would think it was time for all decent peoples to be going to bed, not thinking at this hour of going gallivanting about the place. You can't be up to no good."

Jim blushed, but made no reply to the taunt. The silence made Shane even more uneasy. She turned pleadingly to Len. " Tell your mam, nghariad i, where be you going. Don't say that you don't trust your own mother that have reared you."

Len saw she was bravely trying to squeeze back her tears, and his love for her forced him to say, " Don't worry, mam bach. You go to bed and sleep sound. Me and dad 'on't be long, we are only going to see the boys about the soup kitchen to-morrow. You see," he added as a bright afterthought, " we have got to get some planks to make tables and benches."

Shane knew he was lying, but she said no more. The two men bade her good-night as they went through the door into the darkness. She waited a few moments after they had left, then hurriedly put the heavy woollen shawl over her head and followed them. Throughout the night she dogged their steps, and she did not return home till the early hours of the morning.

Next day when the people of the village went about their business they were amazed to see splashed upon the walls of each official's house a word painted in huge black letters : " Blackleg." On the door of Evan the Overman's house was the single word " Skab." Throughout the day the groups of men and women discussed the sensational action. They wondered how it had been so silently and effectively carried out. Many speculations were made, but no names were ever mentioned.

During the afternoon the strikers were astounded to see hundreds of police in military formation parade the streets of the valley, and the committee was again called to discuss this new development.

Ezra's pale face went a shade whiter when reports were given that police drafted from all parts of the country were being barracked at each of the pit-heads and in the public-houses. The hint given him by Lizzie the servant girl had somewhat prepared him for this, but the fact they were actually in the valley upset him. He knew it was bound to happen sooner or later, but the speed with which it had been organised took him by surprise. He listened attentively to the reports and the muttered whispers that accompanied them.

All the committee-men were uneasy. They felt that something unusual, something beyond their experience was about to happen in the valley. They had seen the strike in the first instance as a more or less sharp battle in which each side tried to call the other's bluff. Most of them had even been prepared for a long-drawn-out struggle of endurance in which victory depended upon the amount of support they could get for the strikers. None of them, apart from Ezra and possibly Len, had foreseen the possibility of this new move by the company.

Their bewilderment was summed up in the words of Dai Cannon : " But they have no bloody right to bring police in from outside. The duty of the police is to stop stealing and to catch murderers. Nobody is stealing here and no-body have yet been killed. Whoever asked for them to come here had no bloody business to do it. We know how to carry on a strike without interference from outside."

It was slowly dawning in the minds of these raw, un-tutored strike-leaders that in preventing officials from working they were hitting the owners in their weakest part. What they failed to understand was why, when the advantage was with them, the police should be placed at the disposal of the owners. They all knew that the testing time had now come. Either they must capitulate after a month's struggle or go on to victory despite all opposition and whatever the consequences. They decided to go on, and at the mass-meeting to which they announced their decision, the committee were greeted with prolonged cheering.

The weeks went by more or less uneventfully. The men in each pit had organised football and other teams. Matches of all descriptions were played every day amid scenes of great excitement and partisanship. Mary organised a dramatic society and concert party. She was particularly interested in the former, and proved herself to possess considerable dramatic talent ; and her natural appearance and moods gave life to the characters she portrayed.

These activities did much to rouse Mary from her insular subjectivity, and she watched carefully her father's direction of the strike and its reactions upon him. She got to understand him much better and noticed with perturbation that the longer the strike lasted the more moody and taciturn he became. She knew that, cynically bitter though he was, the developments in the strike worried him, but she never by word or deed tried to hasten the time when he would unburden himself to her. With the infinite patience of a mother watching over her convalescing child, she waited, happy in the knowledge that her strike activities were a source of pleasure and of pride to him.

The weather continued to be gloriously fine. For the first time in many years the sun showed itself clear and heartening in the shimmering atmosphere that quivered on the mountain-top like skeins of hair. The wearing throb of the pit had already become a memory. Pit horses, grazing and playing in the fields, oozed the content they felt, even though their pit-blinded eyes were sightless. Children went light-heartedly to school as if the world had suddenly become beautiful. The drabness of the valley no longer lived in their minds. Like the horses, they only felt the immediate ; and most of them had already forgotten how the valley looked and sounded before the strike.

Each evening parties of youthful men and women made their way up the mountain paths and drank in romance with the grass-sweetened air. The mountain became to the young people a vast bed which nestled their bodies to its breast in a voluptuous embrace. Under the star-sprinkled sky it became a bridal chamber, and when dusk at last fell the youth of the valley whispered into listening ears the innermost thoughts of their hearts and shared together the intimacies of their bodies. In the small hours of the morning their voices filled the air with melody.

At the head of the village the pit stood brooding in its enforced silence, scowling like an immobile death's head on the peaceful streets and people ; and the Big House was the scene of many confidential discussions. On one occasion a tall, uniformed man with an authoritative air consulted in secret with Mr. Hicks and Mr. Higgins for nearly two hours. But the strikers knew nothing of this. Nevertheless, one night shortly afterwards, when they were parading the streets of the village as usual, they noticed that whenever they gathered in groups for a chat or to look into the shop-windows they were gruffly ordered to move on by the police. Scores of uniformed men were moving about the streets and the least hesitation on the part of the strikers to obey their arbitrary instructions was met by the harsh command : " Now then, you there, move on when you are told, and none of your damned nonsense."

The strikers had hitherto been accustomed to a measure of affability from the police, and the suddenly changed attitude disturbed them. Harassed from point to point, they gravitated slowly towards the Square, which, as always on important occasions, became the centre of attraction. And soon, despite the efforts of the police to break up all groups and keep them on the move, it was filled with a mass of excited people.

Len, who had been spending a couple of hours with his parents at the free entertainment organised by Mary, noticed something unusual in the air directly he came out, ·but seeing nothing wrong he paid little attention. Shane stopped before reaching the Square to look in a shop-window, whispering something to Big Jim that Len did not catch. But he saw a policeman who had suddenly appeared nudge her sharply with his elbow and order them all to move on. Before he had a chance to say or do anything Big Jim's fist flashed out like a thunderbolt, and the policeman tumbled over as though he had been struck by a battering ram.

The action seemed like an electric current that set hell loose, in a moment some of the crowd began smashing plate-glass windows. Almost immediately, above the shattering crash a voice screamed, "Charge!" and as a solid phalanx of police rushed from nowhere into the Square, the crowd began to sway like wheat in the wind. Batons rose and fell with smashing regularity, and the contact of clubs and heavy boots on living flesh brought men and women in sickening tumbles to the ground. Like wildfire the fight spread down the street and into the distance, its progress marked by the crashing shop-windows and the screams and moans of the injured lying in the roadway.

That night, when at last the streets were empty and the windows darkened, posses of uniformed men paraded the back lanes. Sometimes they would burst their way into a darkened house, and their entry would be followed by the sound of curses and crashes, and then suddenly silence.

Len, tired and worried by the day's event, was just dropping off to sleep when he heard a terrific rap on the back door. He jumped out of bed and was about to make his way downstairs when Jim and Shane overtook him on the landing. " I 'spect they be after me," whispered Jim hoarsely. He crept quietly down the stairs, pulling on his trousers as he went, followed by Shane's instructions : " Make your way to Ezra's. We will keep them here as long as we can." No one heard the front door open or close as he went out, and after a few minutes Shane, grasping Len tightly by the arm, led him to the back door.

Her long flannel nightdress clung round her legs as she feverishly stumbled her way forward.

Len took the lighted candle and, from force of habit, held it up when she shouted : " Hello. Who's there this time of the night ? "

" Open in the name of the law," came the gruff answer.

" I have never in my life opened my door at this time of the night to nobody, not till I know who it is," said Shane, all the while seeking to kill time. " Who are you ? "

" The police."

" Oh dear. Oh dear," moaned Shane. " What for do you want in my house ? For more than thirty years I have lived here and not a policeman have ever had cause to come inside my door."

The rapping on the outside became more vigorous and a voice shouted, " Are you going to open this blasted door or must we break it down ? "

Realising she could save no more time, Shane fumbled at the bolts, grunting audibly the while, " Duw, duw. Can't you wait a minute dyn jawl ? "

Len said nothing, but his quivering limbs betrayed the extent of his emotions. Eventually Shane opened the door and the little kitchen filled immediately with policemen.

One, who appeared to be the chief, stood in the centre of the room and solemnly stated : " We have information that leads us to believe you have property in this house that has been looted from the shops to-night."

" What say you, man ? " flared Shane indignantly. " Do you call me a fief ? Me, who have reared my children 'spectable and tidy, thank God. Better be careful what you say, my man, or I will call the police to you for slandering my character."

Len could not help smiling to himself, but his mother heedlessly fumed on : " Never in my life have I heard such impudence ! For a man to call me a baggage and a fief before my own face in my own kitchen—it be more than any 'spectable 'ooman can stand ! "

She would have kept on, but was cut short by the curt

order to search the house.   The first man to obey was one
with an ugly cut on his lip and a big bruise on his jaw,
whom Len recognised as the policeman Big Jim had
struck when the riot started.   Although no one was seriously
looking for any stolen material, they went through the
pretence of searching the house from top to bottom, Shane,
following them wherever they went, threatening to have the
law on each of them in turn.

Failing to find what they were searching for, the chief
again approached Shane.   " Where is your husband ? " he
demanded.

" How on earth do you 'spect me to know where he be ?
Do your wife know where you be ?   No.   Once a man
have got a hat on his head he have got a roof on him, and
the good Lord knows when you will see him again.   But
there," she sighed dismally, " all men be the same."

At this the chief, giving it up in disgust, ordered his men
out, and when the last one had gone Shane hastily bolted
the door again and drew Len to her.   " Do you think your
father did get safe to Ezra's ? " she queried.

Len nodded hesitantly to reassure her, but staring towards the front door, said : " I had better go and see to
make sure."

But Shane caught him before he could move.   " Not a
living soul do leave this house to-night again," she asserted.
" If anyone go out now they will be followed by those men,
see, Len bach."

He nodded assent and they went upstairs to bed, but
neither slept as they waited for Big Jim's knock at the
door.   That night he did not return.

Shane, anxious because of Jim's non-appearance, sent Len
out early next morning to pick up what news was available.
At each street-corner he found groups of people discussing
in subdued voices the events of the previous night, everyone
adding something new to the recital, but he continued on
his way to Main Street, where he found large numbers of
strikers waiting for some word or instruction from the
strike committee.   Many of them carried bruises and gashes

that deepened the pallor of their faces, and blood was still seeping through some of the bandages. When they asked him for information Len shook his head negatively.

" You will more than likely find all the news you want in the papers," he said, and passed on to Ezra's house.

At Ben the Barber's he stopped to look at the paper. Ben watched him as he hurriedly scanned the pages before asking slyly : " What are you looking for that your brow is so furrowed ? "

" I was hoping to see something about what happened last night, but all I can see is this," Len answered, throwing the paper down. " Reports and pictures of the coronation. Have you got another ? "

" No. In any case, didn't you have enough of the riot last night without wanting to read about it to-day again ? " But as Len did not answer, Ben picked the newspaper from the floor, and pointing to some photographs, went on in a satirical voice : " Look here, what better would your eyes like to see than this beautiful coach made of solid gold. See this magnificent crown of gems and rejoice at such skilful manipulation of wealth. You talk of your puny riots and futile strike when staring at you from the paper are a hundred thousand resplendent troops equipped with arms. Talk of the justice of your case," he went on mockingly. " Read here of the million people who last night, while you and your sort were smashing up the town, were howling deliriously in support of their newly crowned monarch."

Len fidgeted restlessly, although he was aware of Ben's propensity to sarcasm. Without noticing him the barber went on : " Ay. You say your people are fighting for a living wage. Read here of how other people, who also want a living wage, spend the little that is given them in jubilation over another's power. Ach," he concluded, as he spat on the floor, " the bloody lot of you make me sick."

No more was said for some moments until Ben, as if repenting of his harsh words, said, " If you want news of your strike, look at the stop-press on the back page."

Len took the paper and his face went white as he read :

HOOLIGANS SMASH UP TOWN

Police Draw Batons in Self Defence

As we go to press reports are coming in of outrages at Cwmardy. Strikers loot shops. Much damage to property. Police persuasion fails to restore order. Wild crowds attack police. Batons drawn. Many casualties.

Ben smiled sarcastically at Len's attempts to swallow back his rising rage. " You understand what you are now and you also know what happened last night."

" But it's all lies. It's not true," Len blurted out.

Ben looked at him reproachfully. " The papers never lie, my boy. What you see in black and white is truth, and you must always believe it."

Without another word Len left the shop, and when he reached Ezra's house his temper was still burning and his mind was absorbed in the new lesson he was learning. Running through his contempt for the newspapers was a thread of worry about Jim's whereabouts. His timid knock was answered by Mary, who invited him in.

Ezra, who sat near the fire, looked around as Len entered, but said nothing until Mary had prepared a cup of tea for each of them. Then, without looking at Len, he asked : " Well, what has happened ? "

Len felt hurt by the casual tone of the query. More so because it told him that his father had not been at Ezra's during the night. He choked back the lump that suddenly rose to his throat and began relating, in a husky voice, the events of the night. As he spoke of Jim's part in the fight Mary listened attentively with sparkling eyes, but Ezra appeared to be paying no attention. The memory of what had occurred, however, warmed Len's imagination and he soon became lost in the recital. The blood pounded through his veins, and as he lived the fight again, his musical voice gave harmony and rhythm to his story. When he indignantly related the newspaper report Ezra smiled grimly, but neither he nor Mary moved for some minutes after Len had finished.

Mary was the first to break the awkward silence. Rising to her feet, she said, " Dad, we must find Big Jim."

Ezra nodded slowly. " Yes, my dear, you are right. But first things first." And, turning to Len and looking him up and down, he went on, his voice cold as steel : " You must tell all the committee-men to be at the agreed place two hours from now. Tell them to be careful how they get there and to let no one know there is a meeting. On your way back call at the pit criers' and tell them to remain at home till they hear from us."

As his words became more sharp and incisive Len felt again the overwhelming power of the man sweep over him, and without a word he left the house and proceeded on his mission.

After he had gone Ezra paced the length of the kitchen several times before pausing suddenly by the fireplace. He rested his elbow on the mantelpiece, holding his head in the cupped palm of his hand, and Mary knew from experience that his mind was now finally and irrevocably made up on some matter, and that conversation would be unwelcome. She therefore busied herself in clearing away the teacups and washing-up, and when she had finished sat patiently waiting for him to speak. Some minutes elapsed before he bent down and took her by the shoulders, looking deeply into her eyes. They looked back at him gleaming with solicitude and love, and as if to himself he murmured : " Yes, my dear. Exactly as I had expected, so it has happened. Right always has been, and always will be, determined by might. There can never be one law that is at once good for the tiger and the lamb. Neither can there be one law that binds together the interests of workmen and owners. No one can blame the tiger for using his claws and teeth to destroy his victim. Nor can anyone blame the company for using the means at its disposal to safeguard its interests. That is what both claws and batons exist for."

He broke off and resumed his pacing, without noticing the expression of doubt that flashed across Mary's face as he made the last assertion. Presently he came back to her, and she felt the familiar caress of his fingers trickle through her hair till they touched the small, pinkish lobes of her ears. She felt the love of his touch and cuddled her head between his chest and his arm.

" Go on, dad dear," she whispered gently. " Tell me. You surely haven't yet finished what you were going to say ? "

As she had anticipated, he at once continued : " If the tiger is justified in using his claws, his victim is entitled to use everything to defend itself and defeat the enemy that is seeking its destruction. Yes," he repeated, " that is so. If the company takes the initiative and uses its claws, we can't complain. What we have now to do is to see what is necessary to prevent the claws hurting us, and if we can't do this, then we have to find some way of causing greater hurt to the company than it does to us. That is the only course left to us now."

He stopped abruptly and fetched his cap and coat from the hall. Near the door he turned to her, and said : " When I come back we shall have taken decisions that will determine the course of the strike for good or evil. In the meantime, dear, don't worry about Big Jim. If I know him at all he is perfectly safe."

That evening messengers were sent around the picket-leaders with instructions that not a single man was to go down any of the pits until the committee gave further orders. This was the strikers reprisal for the attack by the police on the previous night.

Meanwhile Ezra and a deputation from the committee went to interview Mr. Hicks and Mr. Higgins. The latter, who accused Ezra of fomenting disorder, asked him : " Do you intend that the pits shall be so damaged that they can never be reopened again ? "

Ezra looked him in the eyes and replied : " The pits are no longer any concern of ours. You represent those who claim ownership and it is your business to do what you will with them. The business of this deputation is to safeguard the men and women we represent. Neither myself nor any other member of the deputation desires any harm to the pits. Too many of our men have died in making them what they are. On the other hand, we hope you desire no harm to our people. Our mission here is simple. Withdraw the police and we will permit the safety men to work."

" That," replied Mr. Higgins, " is impossible. The matter is entirely out of our hands. The police are under the control of the authorities and have nothing at all to do with the company." And, as Mr. Hicks nodded approval, he went on with a sanctimonious smirk : " Probably the riotous disorders of last night and yesterday morning, when numbers of our officials were seriously injured while attempting to do their duty, influenced the authorities and led them to take the necessary measures to protect law-abiding people."

He seemed to warm to this theme and would have continued, but Ezra brusquely interrupted with the remark : " We are not here to discuss your theories, Mr. Higgins. I think I speak for my colleagues when I say we want an answer to our offer. We are prepared to allow your safety men to work if you notify the authorities that the extra police are unnecessary and must be withdrawn. When you talk of the few bruises suffered by some of your officials, I would remind you of the scores of our people who were severely manhandled last night."

Mr. Higgins muttered an excuse and beckoned his colleague to the far corner of the drawing-room, where the two men considered the proposition put by the deputation. As they carried on a conversation in low voices, a discussion developed amongst the men. Len wanted to know how far

Mr. Higgins was correct in stating that the company was not responsible for the police, but Ezra brushed the question curtly aside. " We were sent here to get the police withdrawn, not to argue responsibility," he declared. Some of the deputation, however, disagreed with this, and one of them asked how, if the company was not responsible for bringing the police in, they could be responsible for taking them out. Ezra coldly replied : " That is not our concern. If they want safety men, it's their duty and not ours to remove the obstacles that prevent them working. Our mandate is clear. Don't let us lose sight of that in attempting to find excuses for the company."

This veiled sneer closed the discussion, and at the same time the company representatives returned from their consultation.

Mr. Higgins again took on the role of spokesman : " It appears, Mr. Jones, that your deputation is determined to give a free hand to all the unruly and disorderly elements in the valley, even if it means the destruction of the pits. In these circumstances we do not feel justified in asking the authorities to reconsider the position. You will understand, gentlemen," turning towards each striker in turn, " that it is the desire of the company, in the interests of the men themselves, that everything shall be done to ensure that the pits restart normally immediately this unfortunate dispute is ended. And I may say, as far as the company is concerned, we are adamant on this. Good night."

It was clear that further argument was useless and, without another word, Ezra led his men out.

In the valley people were still talking about the events of the previous night. Practically every street contained someone who had been more or less injured in the affray, and when Len reached home after the deputation had dispersed, he found Big Jim the centre of a group in Sunny Bank.

Len was pleased to hear his father reporting how he had eluded the police. " Ay," Jim boasted, " it will take a good man to catch me. You see, I been used to dodging Boers on their own ground, and any man who goes through that do learn a few tricks, I tell you."

" But tell us how you did it," came a voice from the crowd.

" That be easy enough. When I went out through the front door there was just enough light to see any shadows that be hanging about. I could see that there was plenty of police between me and Ezra's house, where I did think to make for, so I had to double back on my tracks. By this time the police was all over the place like black pats, and I was just beginning to think it was all up the spout when I did suddenly think of old Will Smallbeer's chicken-hutch. I gived one dive and landed in on my head. I don't 'member what shape the door is in, but it can't be very solid by now. Only two chickens he have got, but they did make more bloody noise than all the brass bands in the army. And me wanting quiet, see, not for the police to know where I be hiding. I lighted a match on the quiet and saw where they was. It wasn't long before I had 'em one under each arm and gagged 'em proper with my coat."

Everyone, including Len, laughed at this anecdote, but Jim, changing the subject, began to speak of the baton charge. It was a matter of honour to the people in the valley that the Square belonged to them and that no one could turn them from it, and a harsh note stole into his voice as he said : " We got beat on our own little dung-heap last night, by God ! They 'ood never have done it if they wasn't so bloody sly."

That night, as though by some inaudible command, most of the able-bodied strikers made their way in casual groups to the Square, but except for the more adventurous, the women remained at home. By midnight the Square was thronged with people. No one seemed to know what they were there for, yet every group of ten or so appeared to have a leader. There was complete absence of shouting and hilarity, but the night air quivered in the drone of five thousand whispering voices, and presently, without a command or a shouted order, the strikers slowly formed themselves into a procession which threaded its way like smoke towards the pits.

Every voice was now silent, even the drone of whispered talking had ceased, and the only sound that disturbed the peaceful air was the shuffle of heavy-booted feet and the sharp clang of iron hobnails on the stony road. Suddenly, when the head of the procession was already a quarter of a mile on the way to the pit, there was a rush upon those in the rear who had not yet left the Square. Hearing shouts and screams, the strikers in front turned to see what had happened behind them. The scurry of their twisting feet sounded above the din, but the darkness was too heavy to permit sight and the only news was spread by the deepening moans and the wild undulations that swept along the ranks like waves.

As the foremost strikers, pressing back upon each other, tried to force their way back to the rear, the tumult and trampling became wilder and more desperate until the pressure was eased as sections of the men broke from the main body and turned up the little side lane that circled round to the Square. Only those in the immediate vicinity saw them go, and before anyone had time to conjecture about the manœuvre, a whistle pierced the air with three distinct blasts, which were immediately followed by a roar from the front and the wild clamour of galloping horses.

For a second the men in the procession froze into immobility. They did not know what was happening. Nothing could be seen. Nothing could be felt but the increasing undulations that marked the fighting at the rear. The world at that moment seemed to be dominated by the horrifying trample of unseen horses' hoofs bearing down on the front ranks of strikers, and as the hoofs tore into their flesh the air was filled with screams. Above the moans and thuds an anguished cry, " We are trapped," swelled to a hysterical roar, and in a moment everything had become mad tumult as clubs swished down on unprotected heads. In the hearts of all the strikers there was one overwhelming desire—for light. Light to see what was actually happening. Light to fight back. Light to see the enemy.

The horses had torn through to the centre of the procession, leaving behind them a trail of bleeding bodies, and it seemed that the one-sided fight was already over when a soft red glow, deepening in intensity, dissolved the darkness. It came from the pit. It grew wider and brighter, spreading its crimson wings over the valley like a red glare from hell, and at once the men realised that someone had set the power-house on fire. They paid no attention to the fellows lying on the ground, but concentrated on the column of horses rearing and plunging in the roadway, that was bounded on one side by a high stone wall, on the other by a stout wooden fence separating the road from the pit and the burning power-house. As the glow quickly grew to a flame that showed up everything in crimson relief, the panting men and frightened horses in the centre of the procession could be seen, mixed together like dough in which the yeast was fermenting. But there was no sight or sound of the men who had turned up the little side-lane. Their existence was forgotten.

In the houses of the village lights that had been extinguished suddenly flared into new life. Women, already dressed, came tumbling out of their doorways and rushed screaming and cursing towards the Square. Above the tumult could be heard the voice of Big Jim booming instructions to tear up the fences, and in a matter of seconds every man had dashed across the road and provided himself with an improvised weapon.

Again the commanding voice rang out : " Pick your man and bring him down."

Big Jim had now assumed command, and as the strikers instinctively rallied their forces and rushed headlong down the narrow roadway towards their separate objectives, the tumult rose to even greater volume. Shouts and curses mingled with groans and cries, while cracking thuds joined in the chorus. Horses driven mad by ripping spurs reared their forefeet into the air like hammers that methodically

7

broke down the barrier of human bodies before them. Here and there bleeding men tore a rider from his mount, and his screams would end abruptly.

The pressure of the horses was too great for the strikers, and they slowly beat a track for themselves over the heads and bodies of the men. The eyes of the mounted police were anxiously fixed on the Square, and they gradually drew nearer, ready to join the ranks of the foot-police who were already in possession. If they succeeded in this manœuvre it meant that the strikers were trapped in a *cul de sac* with the police concentrated in the only outlet.

The strikers fought desperately to prevent this fusion of forces, but the sticks they had torn from the fence were too short to make effective weapons against the mounted men, and each minute the battle lasted made the trap more secure. Suddenly, however, as they were on the point of giving up hope, they heard a mad roar from the hill that led to the opposite side of the Square. They looked anxiously in the direction of the sound and saw a compact body of men rushing down the hill to fling itself with wild impetuosity upon the surprised police. The horses screamed horribly as the sharpened points of long broom-handles were plunged into their soft sides, and they kicked out frantically in all directions, dislodging their riders, who became easy victims of those who were waiting to get them on the ground. This reinforcing body of strikers was that which had slipped up the side-lane when the first charge took place. They had gathered all the children's marbles they could lay hands on and now scattered these under the feet of the horses, bringing them crashing to the ground.

The sweeping suddenness of the attack disorganised the police, who ran like rabbits for refuge in the neighbouring side-streets. But here women were waiting for them with buckets of water and slops, which they emptied on to them from the bedroom windows. Gradually the police were driven from the Square, which was left in the possession of the strikers.

Ezra at once climbed up to a precarious platform on the Fountain, where he stood supported by the great arms of Big Jim, and surveyed the scene. Jim's face was streaming with blood, but he paid no heed to the wound from which it flowed, being much more concerned about the absence of Len, whom he had not seen since the fight began. A deep silence that contrasted eerily with the previous clamour fell over the Square as the strikers waited for Ezra.

Clearing his throat, he began to speak, warning them that the battle was not yet over and that unless they stood firm it would be lost. The police were reforming their ranks, cutting them off from their own wounded. They could not allow this, and he suggested that a message should be sent to the chief of police asking that the wounded of both sides might be collected and brought to the surgery. Twenty men would be enough to bring them all in, he said, and then, raising his voice, concluded :

" If he agrees, well and good. If not, we must fight for it. Is it agreed we send a message to the chief ? "

A roar of assent swept the air like a tidal wave.

" Will anyone volunteer ? "

" Ay, I be just the man for that," shouted Big Jim above all the other voices.

Ezra hurriedly wrote a note and with this in one hand and a blood-stained handkerchief in the other, Big Jim made his way to the spot where the police were regathering and concentrating their forces. But he had only gone about two hundred yards when he was suddenly surrounded by police, who sprang upon him from the darkness of a side-lane. " Hold on, boys," roared Jim waving his handkerchief wildly as he saw their threatening demeanour and the loosely twirling truncheons that seemed to itch with desire to land on his head.

" I have got a special message for your chief if you will be good enough to take me to him."

After some muttering among themselves the police, with apparent disappointment, hemmed him in and curtly ordered him to " Get going." They led him to where the main body of police was concentrated, and as the little group approached a tall, military-looking man stepped forward.

" Who are you ? " he asked harshly.

" My name is Mishter Roberts, known to everybody as Big Jim. Old soldier. Served through the Boer War with the old 41st and proud of it. I have got a letter here from our leader."

The police chief silently held out his hand for the message. A slow smile crept across his face as he read it. As an old soldier he appreciated Jim's courage and also the request made by the strikers, and turning to one of his subordinates he remarked :

" Evidently these men regard this as a war and expect the mutual courtesies of such." Then, turning to Big Jim, " So you are an old soldier, eh ? "

" Ay, sir, and a reservist. Seven years with the old 41st, the best line regiment in the British Army and most battle honours."

He drew himself up smartly to the full height of his magnificent body and saluted.

The chief acknowledged the salute.

" Tell your leader that the request is granted. I hope to see you again in better times, Mr. Roberts."

With another salute Big Jim turned sharply on his heel and marched back through the open ranks of police.

His old war days had risen vividly to his mind. Everything that had happened during the night had assisted in reviving habits and memories of his old life, and when he reached the Square he gave a gasp of pleasured surprise as the strikers made a clear path for him to the Fountain, where he saw Len and his mate, Will, chatting excitedly to Ezra.

Both young men were black with mud and coal-dust and their clothing was in tatters, but Ezra seemed pleased with what they were telling him.

Big Jim strolled up, still in his military mood, coughed and smartly saluted before reporting : " Your request is granted, sir." The strikers around looked at him in amazement and Len stared at him with open mouth.

The momentary silence jerked Jim to his senses. " Argllwydd mawr," he roared, " be I bloody mad or what ? "

No one replied, so he turned on Len.

" It's your fault, worrying a poor man as you be.   Where the hell you been all night ? "

" Not far, dad.   I'll tell you all about it again."

This somewhat mollified Jim, and he stood sheepishly on one side while Ezra gave orders to the selected men to bring in the wounded.   All the roads and lanes near the Square were scoured and in a very short time the casualties had been brought to the little surgery which now looked like a miniature hospital.   Those awaiting treatment and those already treated were lined up in a queue of lying and sitting bodies on the road outside the surgery.   The queue was over a hundred yards long.

By the time the police had been marshalled and marched back to their barracks in the public-houses and on the pit-heads, the sun was already peeping over the mountain into the turmoiled valley, and when the last of them had disappeared, Ezra again climbed on to the fountain plinth. As he faced the strikers he felt buoyed up by their spirit of confidence and determination, and he spoke to them proudly, praising their courage.   The night that was now dying, they would remember till the day of their death. It had been a test and they had proved their strength, but it was not yet over, he warned them.

" We must not think we have now won the fight.   No ; the fight is now really beginning.   But we can talk of that later.   First we must go home with our injured ; and we will go home all together.   Remember, unity is always strength."

And in spite of their exhaustion and suffering, the strikers raised a cheer that crackled in the morning air as Big Jim and Ezra led the reformed ranks up the hill.

When Ezra reached home, Mary had a big fire and tea

waiting for him. She took his cap and coat and put them away while he washed his black hands and face. This done, he sat down and drank the tea in gulps, heedless of its boiling heat. He emptied the cup, then turned to the fire, looking into its depths as if seeking an answer there to the problems that were rising in his mind.

Mary sensed her father's mood and sighed softly. She was impatient to know what had happened. All night she had paced the little kitchen wondering if he were safe. Often during the long hours she had felt an overwhelming urge to get out into the streets to see for herself. Yet she had refrained from doing so because she knew that the sight of herself would distract Ezra's attention from the serious things in hand. Patiently sitting on the stool near his chair, she had to exercise all her will-power to prevent herself asking him questions. Presently, with a sigh, he muttered something to himself which she failed to distinguish, and, seeming to hesitate, turned from the fire and looked at her. Then, for the first time in many years, he caught her passionately to him and kissed her tenderly.

"My dear," he murmured, "I wonder where it is all going to end. How long can hungry men stand up to physical violence? The first charge last night told me how men can be out-manœuvred and how all our plans can be shattered by an unexpected action. Do you know, my dear," he continued in a soft voice, while his fingers played with her hair, "that when we fail to anticipate things it means that men's bodies, their flesh, have to suffer? Bravery isn't enough in a strike. Often what we call bravery is merely an act of desperation committed in a moment of sheer fear." He stopped short, then, as though recollecting something, went on. "But no. Not all brave deeds are acts of desperation. Big Jim last night did a brave thing in cold blood. Young Len and his mate also did something that required nerve and courage, and they did it without the stiffening of noise and company." Mary fidgeted on her stool, but kept on listening without interrupting. "Yes. All of them fought and all of them are brave. But to what end ? What has been started must be continued in one way or another, and right will work itself out on the basis of might. The company will not give way after last night's events ; they will continue trying to force their officials into the pit." He jerked his head spasmodically : " Yes. That's the word, ' force,' " he said, as if he had discovered a solution to the problem troubling him, and again he looked into the flaming depths of the fire. The word seemed to conjure up a picture in his mind that found life in the leaping flames, and he suddenly sprang from his chair.

Mary watched him pacing the kitchen. She felt a vague ache in her heart. Her mind bubbled with involuntary questions, one of which continually posed itself before her. " Is he weakening ? " she asked herself, and immediately tried to brush the thought from her mind with a toss of the head.

Ezra stopped his pacing and stood with his dark, gloomy eyes burning into hers. When he spoke the words rattled in his throat.

" I wonder where it is all going to lead. We should have known in the first place what was bound to happen sooner or later, that we could never carry the strike through peacefully. My own experience should have told me that the company would move heaven and earth to defeat the men. The owners don't care that we are only fighting for a livelihood, and will use any means to their hands to get us back on their own terms. What matters it to them the months of misery, pain, and suffering that our people have endured ? To them these are added weapons with which to break us."

His voice became a snarl as he talked of the company. He stopped, and Mary flung her arms round him as she searched his face through her tears. " Dad," she said, with more confidence than she felt, " our people will win. They must win. Right and justice are on our side."

Ezra smiled bitterly. " The company claim the same thing, my dear, and are prepared to prove their argument by force. What worries me is the future. Dare I continue the strike and all that it means indefinitely, and at the end be forced to accept perhaps even worse terms than are offered now ? Or had we better give in and avoid further injury and misery ? "

Mary looked at him, alarm large in her eyes. It was obvious to her that the suspicions she had tried to banish were being confirmed. " No, no, dad," she cried. " You must *not* give in. I know our people are suffering. I know they are short of food and aren't strong enough to stand up to these monstrous policemen that are being imported. But we've not lost yet. You know the support our men are winning all over the country. Money is coming in greater amounts for our food kitchens. No : we can carry on a long time yet."

Ezra looked at her intently as she spoke, and he seemed to gather strength from her words.

While this discussion was taking place, Len was sitting at home listening to Big Jim telling Shane of the riot. " What a lovely fight ! Nearly so good as one I 'member 'gainst the Boers when we put the old farmhouse on fire." He twirled his moustache and looked quizzically at Len before asking, " Who put the power house on fire, boy bach ? ".

But, receiving no reply, he went on : " That be a clever move, Shane, who ever done it. It comed just when us was all beat and the jawled horses was trampling our brains out. Duw, duw ! You ought to have heard the row, gel bach ! 'Nough to make your hair stand on end."

Shane looked at him admiringly, but Len was absorbed in his own thoughts. His mind flashed back to the climb over the high fence when neither he nor Will, his mate, dared whisper as they dropped the other side. He wondered again, as he crawled in memory through the river, if each shuffle forward would end in a hole from which he would never rise. Dread of the possibility even now made him shudder. He remembered whispering to Will, " Are you there, Will bach ? " and receiving a grunt, followed by a muffled " Blast it," in reply, as Will's knee jerked into a stone.

He smiled at the memory, and Shane, observing his expression, asked, " What be you laughing at, Len bach ? "

Len readily related the story of his adventures to his parents, who listened with deep attention.

" When we got over the fence to the side of the river nearest to the pits, me and Will was right out of breath. We sat down for a bit to get it back. I could hear Will draw it in through his teeth as if he was sucking water." They all laughed at the analogy, and he continued : " Will asked me quietly, ' Which bloody way now, Len ? ' I told him. But all the same I wasn't quite sure myself, and I was wishing we had a bit of light."

" Ay," broke in Jim, " that is what we was short of, too."

" Well, we crawled on our hands and knees to the pit. I remember both of us shivering with fright when we got near to it. Rats ran under our legs and we could see their eyes shining wicked and cruel when they peeped from between the timbers on the colliery yard. I put my hand on one of them and squashed it flat before I knew what was there. Ugh! It was cold and wet. I gave a little scream, I couldn't help it, when I heard the rat go ' squelch ' under my hand. Will jumped into the air and called me everything under his breath. At last we came to a big building that was blacker than the night. Both of us knew that this was the power house, and now we was close to it we was more afraid than ever in case there was some policemen left inside to watch it. Will crawled round and squinted in through the windows, none of which had glass in them. When he came back I knew everything was all right.

" The two of us knew exactly what we had to do, but neither of us, somehow, was willing to start. At last Will gave a shaky, squeaky little laugh and said to me, ' Well, us might as well get it over, Len bach.' I didn't answer him for a minute. From over the river we could hear the sounds of the battle. They floated to us like waves in the wind. The screams made us shiver, and Will

7*

said to me, ' Cold, 'in't it, Len ? ' We crawled inside the
power house, more to get away from the noise of the riot
than anything else. When we came back out flames
followed us with wicked crackles as if they was laughing at
some big joke."

Len said no more. He was torn between pride in what
he had done and fear that the wrong people would find out
who had done it.

CHAPTER XII

Soldiers are sent to the Valley

ONE day shortly after the riot on the Square a conference was held in the Big House at which four people were present : Lord Cwmardy, Mr. Higgins, the chief of police, and another man with wheezing breath and a thick gold chain across his stomach. Lord Cwmardy was pointing out to the others that once the strikers succeeded in stopping the safety men the company would have no alternative other than to grant their demands, and he added, " I need not tell you, gentlemen, that this would have disastrous effects upon our undertaking and is a project we dare not face." Then, turning to the man with the chain-imprisoned paunch, he went on, " To give way to this display of intimidation and force, Alderman, would be tantamount to condoning anarchy and disorder. Such a thing is inconceivable, and that is why, with the consent of the proper authorities, I have asked you here to-day."

" Quite right, my lord, quite right," wheezed the alderman. " What do you say, chief ? " turning to the police chief.

The latter stood up and shrugged his shoulders. " I am here to see that the peace is kept and to ensure that those men who desire to work shall do so without molestation. That is what my men are for."

Then, as Mr. Higgins did not say a word, Lord Cwmardy nodded his head sententiously and said in a tone of finality : " Well, gentlemen, it seems we are all agreed and all that remains is to work out the precise steps necessary to preserve peace in the valley."

While this conference was taking place the pickets on their way to the pit-head found for the first time that their entry was barred. Scores of police were cordoned across the road, while each group of officials was escorted by posses of additional police. As the latter passed through the streets they were greeted with cat-calls and shouts from the women and children, " Blacklegs ! " " Scabs ! " " Traitors ! " being the favourite epithets. The officials walked with lowered heads between their uniformed escort. They were ashamed or shy, for they had worked among these people all their lives and it now hurt some of them that they had to act as open enemies of the strikers. But they could see no alternative. They had to obey instructions or lose their positions, while many of them felt the strikers should not have gone to the length of wanting to leave the pit to the mercy of the waters.

The strikers, however, appeared to think differently as they waited for the guarded officials who were silently escorted as far as the first rank of the picket lines, where they halted while Ezra and his colleagues consulted the officer in charge.

Big Jim kept his eyes on the man who had drawn the pistol on the first occasion. The argument between Ezra and the police-officer ended abruptly when the latter suddenly snarled, " Make way there."

Not a striker moved, and the policeman lifted his hand high in the air as a signal. His men immediately obeyed, and, drawing their dangling batons, began hitting down the strikers nearest them without the slightest warning.

Big Jim saw Len and Ezra tumbled over, and, setting up a howl, he threw himself bodily towards the stricken men. In a flash the colliery yard became a battle-ground, the police trying to force the officials to the pit while the strikers fought to prevent them. But slowly the pickets were pressed back by repeated police charges until, with one accord, as though the same thought had struck each of them simultaneously, they broke up and rushed headlong over the bridge towards the pit.

For a moment the police stood stock-still in stupefied amazement, then they gathered their forces together and, with the officials in the middle, made a concerted dash after the strikers. For fifty yards they raced across the bridge without meeting any opposition, but just as it seemed the strikers were making for the mountain and leaving the way clear for their pursuers, they suddenly stopped and began hurriedly clambering up the walled coal-heaps near the end of the bridge.

The police rushed on with wild, exultant shouts, confident that the strikers were now trapped, but before they had gone a further ten yards they were met by a fierce shower of coal lumps that smashed into their faces and their bodies. Numbers of them dropped to the ground like logs. Others, blood streaming down their faces, staggered to the rear screaming with pain and fury. When the charge was halted the strikers were still between the officials and the pit where, in spite of several efforts made to dislodge them, they remained. The men now knew they were in an impregnable position and were determined to hold it at all costs. This fact eventually forced itself upon the police chief and he reluctantly ordered his men to pick up the injured and retire.

The roar that accompanied their retreat ran down between the mountains like rain, and the strikers, arming themselves with pieces of timber and iron scraps that littered the colliery yard, marshalled their forces and marched down the valley, picking up their own wounded on the way. Their jubilation was increased when they discovered that no one was seriously hurt and their battle-song electrified Cwmardy with news of the victory. Women and children, together with the pickets on other shifts, poured into the streets and swelled the volume of marching feet. Tramp, tramp, tramp they went, down the valley to the Square.

Outside the house of each official on the route the people stopped for a while, shouting and singing, after which they reformed their ranks and proceeded on their way. There was no leadership now and everyone did what the mood impelled. By the time the demonstration reached the house of Evan the Overman he was frantic with fear and injured pride. He watched the procession from his bedroom window and cursed wildly as it slowly passed his door. But the fact that no one seemed to take any notice of him drove him mad and he howled at the top of his voice : " Get back to your kennels, dogs, and leave decent men rest."

For a fraction of time the people stood in petrified silence. Then a shower of stones darkened the air and crashed through the windows of the overman's house. A moment later a dozen young strikers forced their way through the front door, to return in a very short time with a quivering, white-faced man helplessly squirming in their midst.

" I didn't mean anything," he screamed when he saw the mass of set, stern faces before him. " Oh, God, think of my poor wife and children."

The people were very quiet now. They silently opened their ranks to make way for the wailing official, and he was led right to the centre of the throng, where Shane and Big Jim stood like statues awaiting him. From the back of the crowd burst a sudden cry : " To the river ! Take him down to the river. He should have thought of his wife and kids before."

The cry became a shout that grew in volume and spread until it seemed to empty from the sky : " To the river . . . the river."

As the threat penetrated Evan's twitching senses he turned piteously to Shane. " Don't let them drown me. Oh, don't let them drown me," he gasped in a whisper, the words oozing out slowly with the saliva that stuck in frothy bubbles on the edges of his moustache.

Shane's face was as pale as his own. She looked at him scornfully, her eyes blazing with contempt, then, turning to the crowd, she shouted in a shrill falsetto that sounded like the dry " gawk " of a vulture sighting its victim : " Don't anybody touch him. Wait till I come back. He do belong to me." She tore up the street towards her own house, the people spontaneously making way for her, and in a few minutes she returned, panting for breath and carrying something white in her clenched hand.

" Here," she cried, " don't hurt him. Don't no one of you dirty your hands with such muck. Help me to put this shimmy on his stinking body, then we can march down the street agen," and she held up the night-dress she had fetched. The idea fired the imagination of the strikers, and willing hands helped to place the garment over the head of the shivering Evan, so that it covered him from his shoulders to his feet. Then the ranks reformed again with Shane and Big Jim on either side of the white-draped, shame-faced figure. Shane gurgled in her throat and she felt her heart swell with every stride the demonstration made as she soaked in the full measure of her vengeance. She had grasped the possibilities in the situation immediately she saw Evan in the hands of the strikers, and the night-dress in which she had robed her enemy belonged to the dead daughter his son had besmirched. With burning eyes she stooped down to look into his face, stimulating his dragging feet with taunts.

" Proud man you did ought to be to-day, Evan, wearing my Jane bach's night-dress. Let your eyes see it. Don't it look nice and white and clean, like her little body did be before you and yours did send it rotting to the grave." The helpless official shivered in the blast of her words. Something gripped her by the throat and she stopped to cough, then, with greater bitterness, went on : " You do 'member, Jane bach, don't you, Evan ? She did used to pass your house to chapel. Yes, of course, you be bound to 'member her."

When Evan made no reply she changed her line. " Look you, mun," she rasped through her teeth, " what revenge you have now. Often have your wife's night-dress covered the naked backside of Williams the manager ; to-day Jane's do cover your body over your clothes." Big Jim listened in silence, biting the drooping ends of his moustache, but when the overman quivered beneath this last taunt he felt in his heart that Shane was too cruel, yet he dared not try to thwart her in her present mood.

Oblivious to everyone but her prey, Shane continued : " They do tell me that your son be going to get married. Well, well. How nice it will be for his wife." She paused a moment and blinked, something hot was burning in her eyes, then bent her head again till it was level with Evan's face. " I wonder if the poor gel do know that her coming husband did send my daughter to the grave with his baby lying cold by her side in the coffin."

The overman stumbled and Shane hastened to put her hand under his arm to help him along. " There, there, Evan bach, perhaps you be a little bit tired or perhaps you can see again poor Jane's body as it did pass your window on its way to the grave."

The memory forced the tears to her eyes and she suddenly loosened his arm and turned her head away from him. She could say no more, and Big Jim, taking her by the waist, solicitously led her on.

The strikers paraded every street with their exhibit, but no attempt was made to injure him in any way, and very few of the jeering shouts and cat-calls were directed to him personally. When at last the strikers retraced their steps to Evan's house the noise of their coming floated before them, and as they reached their destination the door was violently drawn open to reveal a dark-eyed, comely woman trembling with passion. She gave one flashing glance at her husband to make sure he was safe, then, grabbing him by the arm as one would grab a cat by its scruff, she spat viciously towards the strikers and screamed to the women among them : " It would be fitter if you stopped at home and washed your dirty faces, you stinking cows !" Then she slammed the door against the people as they rushed towards it.

Shane pushed her way through the crowd of women who were angrily beating the door with their boots and fists, and, putting her mouth to the key-hole, she shouted with all the strength of her cracked voice, " We have brought your bread-basket safe back home to you. Take care of him now that you have got him. Your bed-warmer will come later on, when no one be looking."

This sneer placated the angry women, who looked upon it as a vindication of their personal honour, but the people remained some time longer outside the house, singing and shouting, before they finally dispersed to their homes.

Len did not accompany the others. He and Will accepted Ezra's invitation to call at his house for a chat. The older man's interest in the two lads had deepened since the firing of the power house and Len was frequently summoned to the house and taken into his confidence.

For the greater part of the evening Ezra sat back and smiled quietly at the eager chatter of the young folk. Len and Will were anxious to talk of the demonstrations and battles, while Mary was equally anxious to talk of the food-kitchens that were now in operation. Will, with his usual irresponsible exuberance, eventually dominated the conversation for a time with a tale about the concert party that had been touring the surrounding towns gathering support for the strikers.

" Ay," he said, " our Ianto went to Pantglas with 'em. He be a pretty good singer, you see, and have won prizes at the Eisteddfods."

" Never mind about the prizes," broke in Mary eagerly, " get on with the story, Will. Tell us what happened at Pantglas."

" Well, they did have it pretty tight all day and there wasn't much hopes of sending much back to the soup-kitchens, so they did hold a meeting and made their minds up to go round the streets singing like as if it was Christmas. They gived the collecting-box for our Ianto to go round the doors with. They went to one grand street and sang till they was blue in their faces, but not one answer did Ianto get at the doors. At last a kid come up and told him he 'ood have to go round the backs because the kitchens where the people lived was behind. So round the backs they went, cursing all the way ; then they sang all their songs over agen, our Ianto knocking at a door till he rubbed the bones out of his hands. But no answer came and they all got their hair off. ' Open the bloody door, mun, and go in ! ' they bawled. So my brother rises the latch and steps in bold as brass, and where do you think he found hisself ? . . . In the bloody lavatory. Ha, ha, ha ! "

They all laughed at the crude narrative. " I would have liked to see Ianto's face," chuckled Mary. " Do you know, I saw the funniest thing to-day. You remember those barrels of apples sent to the canteen yesterday ? Well, we decided to ask some of our women to make jam from them, and this morning when I was going down the canteen I saw little Maggie Coch sitting in the gutter hugging an armful of jam-jars. ' Hello, Maggie,' ' I asked, ' where have you been ? ' ' Down the cemetery to fetch these pots for mam to put jam in,' she answered."

They continued to cap each others' stories for some time longer, until Will jumped to his feet in a flurry and announced, " Duw, duw, I must go. I got to see the boys 'bout sticks for the canteen fires."

" I must be off, too," said Len, also rising, but Ezra stopped him.

" If you have nothing important on, Len, I would like you to stop here with Mary while I do a little business."

" Perhaps," said Mary slyly, when she noticed Len's hesitation, " he has a sweetheart somewhere he wants to see."

The blood rushed to Len's face. " No-no, Miss Mary ; I have no time for girls. There are bigger and more important things than that facing us now," he retorted with such vehemence that Mary was completely taken aback. But Ezra, looking at the young couple with a queer, half-sad smile, beckoned Will to follow him, and left the house.

Mary soon recovered her composure and, standing boldly before him, she asked in a challenging voice : " Perhaps you don't think women worth bothering about, eh ? "

Len started forward at what he knew was an accusation,

but he pulled himself together and twisted his lips into a
smile. " No, it is not that. I love my mother. I loved our
Jane. I love all those women who are with us in the strike.
Who could help loving them ? " he demanded passionately.

There was a moment's silence during which the only
sound was Len's heavy breathing. Neither dared look at
the other during this tense pause until Len, regaining a grip
on his emotions, slowly raised his eyes and, seeing the sad
expression on Mary's face, said in softened tones : " But
to go courting is another thing."

She looked at him directly, her sympathy encouraging
him to continue, and he went on : " I know our boys do go
courting up the mountain and in the back lanes. My
butties have told me all about it, but that isn't all there is to
love, is it ? " he asked, as if beseeching her assent. Mary
made no reply, so he continued : " I have seen my father's
dog, which is the best scrapper in the valley, follow a
bitch about all day and let her do as she like with him.
But that isn't love, is it ? "

The essential innocence of Len's words appalled her,
even while for some reason unknown to herself she thrilled
at their significance, and her eyes melted when she asked in
a low voice : " Well, what do you think love is, Len ? "

He looked at her for some moments as though he were
trying to see through her eyes into her mind. His mouth
became dry and he ran his tongue over his lips before
hesitantly replying : " I don't know. It puzzles me.
Sometimes I feel something burning me up and I can't
sleep. As I lie awake in the nights and think, all the
time, do what I will, my mind goes back to all the girls I
have known." He seemed to be talking to himself.

Mary asked timidly : " But isn't there one girl who comes
to your mind more often than the others ? "

Len turned his eyes away from her and swallowed hard
before replying : " Yes. There's one girl I think about
more than anyone else. But what is the good of
talking about that ? " he asked petulantly, trying to
shake something from his mind. She waited for him to go

on. " I am not much of a scholar since I left school, but
the strike is teaching me lots of things I would never have
learnt without it. The boys in work talk of girls as the
owners talk of us. The owners make us slaves in the pit
and our men make their women slaves in the house. I've
seen my father come home after a week's work and chuck
his small pay on the kitchen table, chucking his worries
with it at the same time. My mother had the job of
running the home and rearing him and me on money that
wasn't half enough to pay the bills. Yes. A man's worries
finish in the pit. Once he comes home it is the woman
who has to carry the burden."

Mary listened attentively, intrigued by the new direction
of his thoughts. " Ay," he went on, " I have heard my
butties talk about women exactly as if they were cattle—to
be taken up the mountains and then laughed at in the pit.
If that is love, I don't want it." His next words came
with a rush that was pregnant with pride and indignation.
" Look at our women to-day. They are on the picket lines
with us, they are in the riots. It is they who give our men
guts to carry on. And it is because of this I love them all.
You ask if I think more of one than the others. Yes, I
do." His voice became stern. " I think of you night and
day, in the meetings and on the pickets. You haunt me
like a spirit. But not in the way men talk in the pit.
I want to be with you so that we can talk about the strike
together. There is so much to be done and I am so weak
when I am by myself. I feel if you were with me all the time
both of us could do so much more just because we were
doing it together. Sometimes when I am lonely I think of
you, and my body goes warm as I imagine that you are
close enough for me to whisper in your ear all the thoughts
that crowd into my mind. Ach," he concluded lamely,
" what's the good of it all ? You are only laughing at me."

Throughout the recital Mary had listened in amazement,
but now she pulled herself together. Unconsciously she
had drawn nearer to him and had to look up to see his face.
" I am not laughing, Len. What you have said is too

serious for that. You have made me think a lot by what you've said, and I don't quite know where I stand."

She hesitated, and was glad when a knock, which she knew was her father's, sounded on the door. As he came into the room he glanced at the young couple, and Len, mumbling an excuse, quickly left the house.

Once outside the door Len, in a maze of emotions, stumbled down the street unaware of any direction until he found himself facing Shane in the kitchen. His mother was obviously agitated. " Oh, Len bach, thank God that you have come. Me and your father have been worried awful 'bout you," she greeted him.

" Why worry about me, mam ? But there, you are excited after getting your own back on Evan the Overman."

" Don't poke fun at your old mam, my boy. You are laughing all right now, but you 'ont laugh when the soldiers be here."

Len straightened up in shocked surprise. " Soldiers ? What soldiers ? " he asked excitedly.

Shane turned appealingly to Big Jim. " Tell the boy, James, not sit by there as if you have lost your tongue." Jim rose from his chair, crossed to Len, and laid a great hand heavily on his shoulder.

" I thought you 'ood have heard the talk in the village, boy bach. They do say that the sodgers is on their way to Cwmardy," he said, adding with greater vehemence : " But I don't believe the bastards. I don't believe them."

Shane chimed in spiritedly : " What do us want sodgers here for ? Sure to goodness, haven't us got 'nough old police here now ? "

Len grasped the situation but said nothing to further agitate his parents.

Some days later the committee sent Ezra to make inquiries why the troops were being sent to Cwmardy. His return was anxiously awaited, and long before the train was due a huge crowd of strikers had gathered at the station. Len caught sight of Mary and they kept together while they waited. A restless, impatient excitement

ran through the crowd when the puffing train was heard in
the distance.   Ezra's face was more stern than usual
when he stepped from the carriage, and although the strikers
gave him a rousing cheer, for some reason this soon died
down and a queer kind of half silence followed as he led the
way through the crowded station.   The people's exuberance
sounded flat and hollow as they marched through the Main
Street, whose shop-windows, covered with corrugated iron
sheets, looked like bandaged eyes.   When the procession
reached his house Ezra instructed the committee-men to
enter and, turning to address the main body of strikers,
advised them to go home quietly.   They silently obeyed,
and throughout the valley the air seemed to breathe a
deathly sort of menace that caused children to cry and dogs
to howl without apparent reason.

The committee sent Len to fetch his father, and in a
short time both entered the parlour where the meeting was
to be held.   Big Jim proudly twirled his moustache,
nodding familiarly to those present, before taking the chair
that was offered him.   No one objected to Mary, who
shyly took a stool near her father, while Len stood erect
with his elbow on the mantelpiece.   When everyone was
settled Ezra rose from his chair at the end of the table.
His face was haggard and his voice was deep and heavy
when he reported the result of his interview with the
authorities.   Once he was interrupted by a murmur that
sounded more like a snarl, and Big Jim, rising to his full
height with inflated chest, solemnly declared: "I have fought
and died for my King and country, and I 'ont let any man,
whether he be a Home Secretary or any other kind of
secretary, call me a hooligan."

Ezra quietened him with a glance and continued his
report.   "They told me the whole British army would be
used if necessary to restore law and order in our valley,"
he said.   He waited a moment and felt Mary's hand steal
softly into his own.

Big Jim gave a sarcastic guffaw.   "Ho-ho.   If it did
take the devils a regiment of sodgers with cannons to shift

Peter the Painter from a house, they will want more than all their army and bloody navy too to shift us, muniferni ! "

A general laugh followed this remark, but Ezra did not participate. He scrutinised the faces of the committee-men and lowered his voice to announce that Lord Cwmardy had made a final offer of an additional threepence per ton of large coal. Having done this he passed his hand slowly over his brow, then, rising suddenly from the chair, he left the table, saying to the bewildered men as he walked towards the door, " Now make your minds up quickly as to what you are going to do."

A momentary silence followed before Len's voice, sounding far away and strange, broke the awkward stillness. " But, Ezra, you can't leave us like this. You haven't told us what you think we should do."

A muffled chorus of " Ay, let's hear what you have got to say," followed this appeal, and all eyes turned expectantly towards Ezra, who had stopped at the door.

The miners' leader turned round sharply and faced them almost accusingly. " Isn't it time you started to think a little for yourselves ? " he snapped. " I am sick and tired of your ' See what Ezra says,' ' Go and ask Ezra.' Now Ezra asks, what do *you* think ? "

His voice broke, but after a moment he recovered himself and faced the astonished men again. " Forgive me, boys. I didn't mean all I said. You see, the responsibility is too great for one man. Here we are, offered more than the Company intended to give us. If we don't accept it the soldiers will be used against our people and after weeks or months of further misery and fight we may be forced back without the extra threepence even. I cannot take the responsibility. That's why I ask you to decide for yourselves."

None of the men said a word, and it was again left to Len to be their spokesman. He walked slowly towards Ezra. " Look here, Ezra, we have followed you faithfully during the strike, have always obeyed your orders, carried out your commands. Don't tell us now that you are going to desert us when we need you most." Ezra's head sank on his chest and his voice appeared to come from deep in his stomach.

"Very well. I will tell you my opinion. I believe we should accept. Half a loaf is better than nothing." His mouth closed with an audible snap.

Len quietly made his way back to the mantelpiece and spoke to the crestfallen, despondent committee-men. His voice was a little high and carried a tone of sadness: "Friends, don't take any notice of what Ezra says. He is tired and worried after all he has done. But we, who have not done or worried half so much as him, can see the the whole position differently. I believe the offer the company is now making is a sign of their own fear and despair." His voice became more strong and spirited. He outlined the steps the company had taken to break the strike. "But in spite of it all, our strike is still solid," he said.

"Hear, hear, Len," his listeners applauded as they showed signs of renewed confidence.

Len continued : "I believe, friends, this new offer is a bribe ; they want to buy us back to the pit on half of what we ask. We asked for bread and butter and, in the words of Ezra himself, they offer us half a loaf."

Ezra, again seated by Mary, shuffled his feet uneasily, but Mary's dilated eyes were on Len.

"Bah !" he said contemptuously. "Not one of us dare to tell our women ' The strike is over. Half a loaf is better than nothing.' No ; if we did such a thing they would turn us from the door in scorn. They would tell us that we were afraid of a Home Secretary we have never seen. Who is this Home Secretary," he asked in a sudden outburst of passion, "this man who calls us hooligans and savages ? Is he a working man ? Have he ever worked down a pit ? Have his mother been put in a county court because he have been too bad to work for a week or two ? Not on your life !" he answered. "He don't belong to us, that's why he sends his soldiers here to drive us back to the pit. Ha. But he'll never beat our men that way. If we are to die, let it be fighting in the clean air that the pit has robbed us of for so long. Better to die like that than as Bill Bristol did, or die of starvation by an empty grate in the back kitchen."

His voice now rose into powerful resonance as he drove home his convictions. " They claim they own the pits. All right. Let them come and work the coal themselves if they want it. Let them sweat and pant till their bodies twist in knots as ours have. Let them timber holes whose top they can't see and cut ribs in coal like solid steel. Oh, boys," he exclaimed confidently, " we have no need to be downhearted. They will do none of these things. While it is true our bodies belong to the pit, so also is it true that this makes us masters of the pit. It can't live without us. When we are not there to feed it with our flesh, to work life into it with our sweat and blood, it lies quiet like a paralysed thing that can do nothing but moan. The soldiers are here. Good. Let the company use them to work the pit. Soldiers can shoot. Soldiers can kill. But soldiers can't drive us back to work if we all stand together. My father has been a soldier, yet none of us are afraid of him, because we know he is one of us. Neither need we be afraid of the others. Let us tell our people to have no fear. Let us tell the soldiers the justice of our case and we will beat the company yet."

As Len finished his passionate indictment the room became electrified. Ezra raised his head from the table on which it had drooped. His eyes were heavy and bloodshot as though from loss of sleep, and his voice was hoarse when he said : " I think we can all learn from the spirit of Len's words. There is hope even now. Let us get on with the business, with no more talk of calling the strike off. We have nothing to be ashamed of and nothing to fear. Forget the words I used just now. I was tired and a disheartened man, but now I have new life and strength. I take it we all agree to urge our people to remain solid and staunch as ever ? "

A loud " Ay " came from everyone present, and with this the meeting came to an end. The committee-men hurried to the canteens for their tea, but Len was too much

concerned about Ezra's attitude to think of food. He
took the path to the mountain, where he could find the
loneliness he desired to help him solve the problems
tumbling in his mind.

Ezra's outburst at the committee had given the young
man a terrible shock. He felt that the miner's leader,
whom he had regarded as the greatest man in the valley,
had been prepared to betray the strike. He would have
staked his life on Ezra's honesty, but could not help the
doubts that rose to his mind. He wondered what was
wrong and asked himself if Ezra had lost faith in the
power of the men to win the strike. Failing to find a
satisfactory answer, his doubts multiplied and his confidence became weaker. He wished he could talk to Mary
about the matter, but knew she would curl up like a hedge-
hog immediately he broached the subject.

Still hounded by these thoughts and chased by his fears,
he was wandering aimlessly over the grassy slopes when,
arising from a dingle, he heard voices lustily singing :

> " We are strikers from Cwmardy,
> Fighting for a living wage,
> And we do not mean to surrender
> To the terror of the age."

Before the strikers' song had ended Len found himself
facing the singers, Will and three other young men from the
village, who were obviously unnerved at being confronted
so unexpectedly. Fidgeting uneasily, each tried to conceal a sack under his coat, but Len saw their confusion and
the peculiar bulge along the leg of Will's trousers.

His curiosity prompted him to ask, " What are you up
to, boys ? "

Will, to whom they all turned, answered : " Nothing,
Len. We be only out for a stroll."

Len shook his head disparagingly. " Come on, Will,
you can't kid me."

" Well, if you be so bloody nosey as all that, why not
come with us ? You will soon see for yourself."

Len asked no further questions and with Will in the lead

the little group made its way up the mountain side until it came to one of the numerous mine levels that scarred its crest. Here they stopped for a while and as the dusk was beginning to settle on the valley one of them began laying a trail of potato peelings outside the mouth of the level. Another lengthened the trail inside, while the third hid nearby. Without a word Will led Len into the cavern, and in perfect silence they all waited.

Len had not the faintest idea what all these careful and secretive preparations were for, and was about to ask Will for an explanation when the latter, as if anticipating his words, whispered, " Sh-h-h-h. There's something coming." Looking towards the level mouth, which looked like a circle of dim light, Len saw the dark shape of a sheep slowly following the trail of potato peelings. He held his breath as in a flash it came to him what the expedition was for and what was to be done.

The sheep drew steadily nearer the level as it chewed its way forward, oblivious to the eyes that watched its every step with eager excitement. Suddenly there was a wild rush as the watchers outside the level flung themselves head-long towards the surprised animal, which turned head-on to meet the rush. Someone gave a pained gasp, " Hold his bloody head, mun ! Turn him back or he'll be away. Ah-h ! "

Will flung himself upon the animal in a rough rugby tackle, grasping its legs and, with a sharp twist, threw it upon its back.

The young men dragged the poor animal, gasping and snorting, into the level near Len, one of them lighting the miner's lamp he carried on his belt. For some minutes they sat on the sheep, waiting to recover their breath. At last one of them said, " Come on, boys. Let's get on with it or we'll be here all blasted night." Unable to turn his eyes away, Len saw the gleam of the flame on the knife that Will drew from the leg of his trousers, and as Will drew the blade across the sheep's throat, it seemed to be beseeching him with piteous eyes that glared glassily in the glow from the lamp. The poor beast struggled as the steel bit more deeply into its neck and blood poured from the opening wound as Will, ignorant of butchering technique, sawed and hacked at the mutilated throat. The animal's struggles were unavailing, and when the knife eventually cut through the wind-pipe they ceased entirely.

Len felt faint, and sharp dazzles swirled before his eyes. He wanted to be sick, but fear of ridicule helped him to swallow back what had risen to his throat, and presently, when the sheep had been cut up and dripping bundles of meat had been shoved into sacks, the entrails were buried in the level and they all went outside. On the way down the mountain they met other groups of men laden as they were, and next day the strikers had roast-mutton and potatoes for their dinner at the canteens.

Towards the end of the week Cwmardy resounded to the rhythmic march of military feet. The people watched the impressive parade without comment, their faces hard and bitter as they saw the glitter of naked bayonets in the sun. The soldiers were camped in the spacious grounds of the Big House.

Hardly had the resentful excitement aroused by the arrival of the soldiers died down when news arrived at the committee that strike-breakers had been introduced into one of the pits. On one of his early-morning rambles Big Jim made the discovery, and at once communicated the knowledge to Len, who conveyed it to Ezra. A secret meeting of the committee was summoned, and it was decided that on a particular day all the strikers should march to the pit.

This sudden and unexpected development made Len forget all his previous doubts and revitalised his blood. He shared the work of preparation for the march with the other men, and went from door to door to acquaint the strikers of the final plans.

When the day arrived Ezra and Big Jim were the first on the Square, where they waited while the strikers sauntered in casually, most of them, remembering past experiences, carrying mandril shafts and other improvised defensive weapons. The streets leading to the Square soon became packed with people, and the excitement rose as the mass became more dense. Len kept near his father and Ezra, who, despite his habitual coldness, looked haggard and hot, with his lips drawn tightly across the teeth.

By common, though unspoken, accord, the women had been kept in the side-streets off the Square, and presently without a warning word, the miners' leader and Big Jim led off towards the pit where the strike-breakers were working. The towering head of Big Jim, visible to everyone, was recognised as the mark they were to follow, and steadily the human mass, hemmed in by the walls that skirted the road, made its way towards the bend that hid the pit from sight.

The strikers heralded their approach with loud shouts :
" Out with the blacklegs ! "
" Down with the scabs ! "
" Clear our valley of strike-breakers ! "

The slogans rang like cannon salutes up and down the ranks, pounding tumultuously at the air.

Len felt the deadly power of the weight behind him. It gave him strength and courage until the first ranks, with quickening impetus, swept round the bend and confronted the deep cordons of police, batons ready poised, drawn across the road. Then he felt himself hesitate with an involuntary checking of his stride, but the pressure lifted him forward and burst him, with the others, through the solid cordon like a hot ray of the sun through snow. He sensed rather than saw batons rise and fall with deadly precision and regularity, and heard the dull thuds that followed each descent. Before he could completely grasp all that was happening the air was full of screams and groans from stricken men. In the mad, chaotic whirl of bodies he lost sight of Big Jim and Ezra, and his eyes went dark as he fought frantically to get back to the thick of the strikers. Something struck him on the cheek, cutting it to the bone, but he paid no heed to the blood that followed the blow. Dimly he saw a poised baton falling. He ducked his head sharply, but staggered as it met his shoulder with a crack that seemed to crush the bones. Staggering on his knees, he felt a muscular paralysis run down his side, deadening his arm and leg, but, dazed and blinded, he forced himself to his feet and weakly fought his way back.

Vaguely above the din he heard the roar of his father's voice. The sound gave him greater strength, and in a short time he was again at Big Jim's side in the midst of the strikers, although he never knew how he got there. By this time the police had reformed their ranks and once more stood between the strikers and the pit. They made repeated charges in an effort to drive the people back to the Square, each charge being fiercely combated, but inch by inch the police gained ground, the narrowness of the street giving them every advantage, because the main body of strikers could not actually enter the fight. In spite of this, the resistance grew more determined and frenzied, and it became a hand-to-hand fight in which everyone had to fend for himself. Police and strikers grappled with each other when the pressure became too great to strike blows. All who fell or were struck down were trampled upon in the mad fury of the battle, until the roadway was covered with still and squirming bodies.

Just when it seemed the police must give way to the tremendous weight their ranks suddenly opened and disclosed a large body of soldiers running forward at the double, rifles clenched tightly to their sides. The strikers fell back before this new threat and, without any resistance, allowed the troops to reach the Fountain where, as though he had dropped from the clouds, Mr. Hicks, closely guarded by police and soldiers, drew a long paper from his pocket and began to read. Though they could not hear a word the strikers knew he was reading the Riot Act. With a wild howl of rage they rushed for the Fountain, drowning the words of the general manager in a snarl of fury and hate. In a moment the battle became more intense and bitter than ever. The officer in charge of the troops was seen to open his mouth, but no one heard what he said. The only sound that came to their ears was the sharp crack of the volley that the soldiers fired. Twice it smashed the air round the Square to fragments, before the echoes bounded from mountain to mountain as though seeking to escape from Cwmardy and to soften the thud of the eleven strikers who fell to the earth as if struck by gigantic sledge-hammers.

In the long, deathly silence that followed the volleys one of the shot men rolled, with weak, funny squirms, over on his side. His fingers tore into the roadway as, with infinite slowness, he twisted his head and looked at the dumbstruck mass of people. A geyser of hot blood squirted from his neck and sent thin veins of steam into the still air.

Len, who was standing quite near, gazed fascinatedly at the squirming form with its white, blood-stained face. He saw the lips slowly shape to the word " mam " before the limbs relaxed and the body flattened to the road. Something snapped in Len's brain. With a wild, inhuman scream he flung himself beside the prostrate striker, and he remembered no more until he felt himself being lifted by the arms and led up the hill, to the accompaniment of a low wail from the people.

The latter, as soon as they had recovered from the shock of the shooting, had picked up their dead and wounded and were now marching away from the Square. The dragging rattle of their hobnailed boots harmonised with the moans of their dying comrades.

They took the dead and wounded to their respective homes, then, motivated by a common silent urge, the people made their way to the banks of the mountain. When they arrived at their destination the committee-men, led by Ezra, walked quietly to the centre, like mourners in a funeral. Ezra's head was bowed and his shoulders hunched as he confronted the men and women he had led for so long. His white face twitched. The man's mind was focused on the shooting and the bodies he had seen lying still in the dust of the road as though already asking to be buried in the earth. Not even in his most calculating moods had Ezra anticipated such an outcome to the strike.

Lifting his heavy head he looked slowly about him. Horror and grief were stamped on the faces he saw. Tears were tumbling down Len's bloody face, making his wounds burn, and Ezra, seeing them, sensed that they sprang from an overpowering temper and not alone from grief. With a superhuman effort he forced himself to speak, but his words, when they came, were those of a man who had lost grip upon himself. They were words squeezed from a broken heart. The roar of the volley had blasted his confidence and shattered what faith he had in the ability of the men to win the strike.

"My poor friends," he said in a low, sad voice, "we have arrived at the saddest moment of our lives. The strike which we began with so much hope and power, with so much confidence and faith, has brought us nothing but misery, injury, and, now, death. The forces against us are so many and so great that they can smash our determination by bludgeon and bullet in the name of law and order. I don't know what we can do. We must have time to think. I don't believe we can carry on much longer."

His voice broke and came to a halt, but the silence that followed Ezra's statement seemed to electrify Len. Swaying slightly, he raised his arms excitedly in the air.

"Never say die," he shouted at the top of his voice, yet hardly hearing himself. "We can't expect to fight a battle without suffering hurt, and we can't expect to win the strike without beating the company and all that it brings against us. We can grieve for our poor butties who have been battered and shot, but to give in now will be to betray all the principles for which they have suffered and died." A sob rose to his throat, but he struggled on. "Let them blow and blast, but never let them force us back to the pit without what we have fought for." Then, finding it impossible to continue, he openly burst into tears that were lost in the roar from the people: "To the end! To the end! No giving way now!"

Later that day Mary found her father in the parlour with his head pillowed on his bent arms which rested on the table. Deep sobs shook his shoulders and, hearing them, she withdrew and left him alone with his grief and shadows.

In the weeks that followed the initial bitterness of the shooting wore away and the strikers began to fraternise with the soldiers. In the public-houses and on the streets the latter shamefacedly tried to excuse their action, and for the most part their explanations were accepted. Strikers' daughters took to the mountains arm-in-arm with the young soldiers and told them all about the strike.

While this was developing some of the strikers had banded themselves together and each night raided the houses of particular officials. No trace of these men could be found next day after the injured man or his relatives had reported to the authorities. No striker asked questions. Even Shane no longer paid attention to the nightly absences of Len and his father, and she refrained from questioning when they returned in the early hours of the morning. The raids took place in the most unexpected quarters and never at the same times, so that the guards placed round particular houses were useless, as the raids always took place elsewhere.

Gradually the officials became stricken with fear and the management failed to persuade or coerce them to the pits, with the result that the directors had to reconsider the whole position and decided to grant the men's demands rather than lose the pits entirely. A conference was held at the Big House to which the committee was invited. Here Lord Cwmardy grimly announced that the men could restart as soon as they were ready and that the government was introducing a minimum wage act. This was in the tenth month of the strike.

News of the victory was conveyed to the people at a mass-meeting on the rubbish dump where they had first declared for strike. The roar that followed the announcement swept the news down the valley like a raging fire, and the windows of the Big House quivered in the victorious tremulo.

8

CHAPTER XIII

The Pit throbs Again

EZRA in the period following the shooting had aged considerably, and he was no longer so assertive and cynical. The people greeted him with a storm of cheers that continued for many minutes before culminating in song. The joy of victory was boiling in the strikers. Thunderous applause and wild flinging of caps into the air followed the reading of the terms.

Ezra finished with a peroration : " We are left as victors, but some of our friends and mates will never work or live among us again. Yet if they could only see us now they would pride themselves, for they have played a determining part in winning the fight for those they have left behind."

Mary, who had refused to go on the platform, listened in silence to her father's words. They appeared enigmatic to her when she related them to other words she had heard him utter. Nevertheless, her eyes glistened with pride as she felt the power and control of the man. She stood on her toes and tried to look over the dense throng. A man near by sensed her need and lifted her small body in his arms so that she could get a better view of the teeming mass of people. Her heart stirred when she saw the lined and haggard faces covered with smiles, and she felt the victory more than counterbalanced the tribulations that preceded it. The friendly worker lowered her to the ground as a further roar of cheers announced the conclusion of the meeting. The Big House frowned down upon the exultant mass as though disapproving of its wild, victorious exuberance when the people lined up for the march to their homes.

From the pits a deep throb was already beginning to beat

through the valley, as if the engines were starting to laugh because the men were coming back to work.

For the next few days the people of Cwmardy celebrated the victory while the pits were being made ready for their return. All the chapels held special services, the public-houses gave free beer for one night, and Mary organised a victory concert. Everyone was consumed with the desire to help and please.

Even Big Jim succumbed to the general mood, and accompanied Shane to the little tin chapel where Dai Cannon was preaching a sermon on the text " Render unto Cæsar the things that are Cæsar's." The sermon lacked nothing in fervour and vehemence from the fact that Dai and Jim had spent the previous night in the Boar's Head drinking everyone's health at the expense of the landlord. The schools closed for a day and the children, spotless in their specially washed linens and voiles, paraded the streets, their teachers marshalling the procession. Shopkeepers hailed the victory with bunting which transformed Main Street into a bright and colourful thoroughfare.

It took a week before the examiners completed their scrutiny of the workings. The people anxiously awaited the final report. They regarded the pits as living things and wondered how they had fared during the long stoppage. The report showed that very little harm had been done, and in a very short time the valley began to vibrate again as the pit developed its old life and power. The sun once more became a thing of the past, an orb that shone some-where above the murk that was Cwmardy's heritage from the pit. But the people enjoyed this transformation, for the smoke and throb meant work, wages, life.

After full resumption of work had taken place the weeks soon lengthened into months, but the passage of time did not eradicate the great lessons of the strike from the minds of the men and their leaders. Ezra and the committee took full advantage of the fruits of victory to draw the men into permanent organisation. Ezra told Len one day : " The committee can only hold power and control when it is directly representative of the men. The seat of strength is not on the surface or in our meetings, it is in the pit itself." Len's doubts of Ezra's integrity and motives were once more dispelled by the manner in which the latter had smoothed out the complications following upon the strike and his dynamic drive to keep the men organised. The man's spirit and determination spurred Len on.

A few nights later Len held a conversation with his father as a result of which Shane was instructed to call them very early for work the next morning.

They were first on the pit-head, and the fireman who tested their lamps was very curious. " Early this morning, i'n't you, boys ? " he asked.

" Ay ,mun," Jim replied casually. " The old 'ooman was in her tantrums and me and Len was glad to get out of it."

The official appeared to accept the explanation as *bona fide*, and said no more. In a few minutes the two men were down the shaft and on their way to the district in which they worked. Instead, however, of proceeding as usual direct to their own barry, they remained on the four-railed engine parting, to which all the coal trams filled in the district were drawn by horses. This parting was wider than the ordinary roadways and contained two parallel sets of rails. Here all the trams were shackled together in journeys of twenty to thirty, and hauled to the pit bottom by the three-mile-long wire ropes attached to the haulage engine. The various headings and roadways in the district branched off from this parting, and it was, therefore, the farthest point towards the coal-face which all the men working in the district had to pass. Here father and son waited.

The restless squeaking of the roof-pressed timbers, the hurried scuttling of mice and cockroaches, the tiny avalanches of rubble that trickled down the sides reminded Len of his first day in the pit. He felt again that the pit had life, that it was always moving and muttering. His eyes tried to pierce through the darkness that edged on the brief rim of light cast by the safety-lamps, and he wondered if the grave held a heavier pall than that solid blackness. A horrible feeling of loneliness engulfed him in a tight grip, although his father was near placidly chewing a lump of tobacco and squirting its juice at the mice which came within range. Len tried to tear himself from this mood and started to think of the interminable roadways and passages that intersected the pit like knotted arteries. In a short time, he mused, men would be circulating in these like blood, giving a hurried, palpitating life to the pit that now seemed restlessly sleeping. His meditations were disturbed by a hum of voices heralding the approach of miners through the black, encircling belt. The hum was soon followed by a glow, and in a very short time some men were looking in surprise at Len and his father.

Will Smallbeer, the pit-battered, crotchety old miner who for many years had made it a matter of personal honour to be first workman down the pit, broke the short silence.

" Well, I'm damned," he gasped, his deep Welsh accent emphasising the deep resentment he felt at this trespass upon his rights. " Are you two living here now ? Didn't you go home last night, or have you no bloody home to go to ? "

Big Jim immediately took umbrage at his tone. " What be the matter with you, mun ? " he demanded spitefully. " Think you that you do own the bloody pit ? "

Len intervened before Will could take up the implied challenge. " It's all right, boys," he said. " Me and dad have come down early to-day at the orders of the committee. They want us all to hold a meeting this morning before we go on to our working-places."

Will Smallbeer grunted. " Huh. Why in hell didn't Big Jim say that, then, instead of making a long speech ? "

Jim's jaw dropped in sheer surprise. " Argllwydd mawr ! " he roared, but he caught Len's eye and closed his mouth with an audible snap.

Will turned with an air of triumph to the other men who

had come with him. " May as well sit down by here, boys, till the other lazy beggars come, I s'pose," he mumbled.

They all, with the exception of Big Jim, sat down on the damp roadsides. Jim strode backwards and forwards, his hands behind his back, muttering what sounded like curses under his moustache. Len watched him carefully, fearful that he would precipitate an argument with Will. If Jim had this in mind he was prevented from putting it into effect by the arrival of more men, who, after a brief consultation, also squatted down. Within half an hour all the men working in the district were gathered on the parting. Hauliers, holding their horses's heads, stood on the outskirts of the circle when Len got into an empty tram and started to speak.

" Fellow workmen," he began, his voice ringing in the confined space, " it has been decided by those who led us through the strike that we must now hang together in such a way that an injury to one is an injury to all." He stopped a moment while he tried to recollect what followed in the speech he had carefully prepared and which he had repeated to himself a dozen times. Failing to recall it, he cleared his throat to give the impression that the pause was due to something sticking there, then went on. " What I mean is this. We won the strike because we were united and organised, but we can easily lose all we have won if we go back to the old way of every man for himself."

He was interrupted by a shout. " Spit it out, Len bach. Tell us what you be trying to say."

Big Jim took up the cudgels. " Don't you try to be clever against my boy," he shouted threateningly. " Haven't you got sense enough to see he do want us to join the federashon and for us to pick a man to be our re—re—rep—— " He failed at the word and finished " Our spokesman on the committee, mun."

A cheer greeted the end of his remarks and the men agreed they should all join the union. Will Smallbeer said nothing one way or another. This matter settled, Len asked for a representative upon the committee.

Immediately pandemonium broke loose. The hauliers at the rear demanded a special representative for themselves on the plea that they were key-men. Tom Morgan, their spokesman, put the case. " Where would you colliers be," he asked, " if it wasn't for us hauliers ? You do know you would be all to hell. We have only to take our horses back to the stable and you colliers can put your tools on the bar and clear off home." The other workmen saw the truth of this, and after a heated discussion during which many hard and personal things were said it was decided that Len and Tom Morgan should represent the district upon the committee.

Len, pleased with what had been accomplished, was about to make a laudatory peroration when the fireman and Evan the Overman, panting and fuming with rage, pushed themselves through the crowd.

" What the flaming hell is this ? " asked the latter. " A bloody circus or a pit, or what ? " No one answered him, and this infuriated him still further. " Hi," he shouted at Len, " you in that blasted tram. Who in firing hell do you think you are ? Since when have you become the manager of this pit, eh ? "

Still there was no reply, and the only sound was a shuffling of feet as the men drew nearer. The fireman, who had left all the speaking to his superior, grew nervous when he noticed the movement. He looked around and saw faces as shadows rather than features in the light of the small-flamed lamps. But the overman, oblivious to everything but his temper, continued to fume and threaten. " Come on," he ordered Len, " get out of that bloody tram and up the pit you go. I won't have none of this damn nonsense here."

Len started as though the words were a physical blow. From his vantage point he looked at the white, shadowy faces of his workmates. Something in their demeanour gave him courage. " All right," he shouted. " You heard what he said, boys. I am to go up the pit. Good. How many of you are coming with me ? "

In a flash every lamp was lifted into the air, and babel broke out with the action. Through the clamour a staccato voice shouted :

" Let's put the old bastard in the water-bosh before we go. We've had enough trouble with him in the strike. Now we can get a bit of our own back." The cry was taken up and the overman hurriedly scrambled into the tram to avoid the rush that was made.

Len, shouting himself hoarse, at last managed to quell the noise. " Don't do anything rash, boys," he begged. " It will only make matters worse if we hurt him."

The men stopped and one of them shouted : " Ay, that's right. Getting our own back be like pissing against the wind."

A loud shout of laughter greeted this sally, during which Len began to leave the tram. He already had one leg over its side when the overman grasped his arm. " Do they all mean to go out ? " he asked, his voice hoarse with incredulity.

" Of course they do," replied Len. " You watch them and you'll see."

But before he could draw his other leg over the side Evan the Overman again spoke. " But what in hell for, Len bach ? " He paused, then started to plead. " Come, come, Len bach. I was only joking, mun. Ha-ha. Fancy taking me serious. Ho-ho. Well, well, Len bach, I thought you had more sense than that, mun. Tell them everything is all right and they can go on to their work." His words tumbled over each other and his laughter sounded flat. Len looked at him for a moment, thinking the man had gone mad, then, suddenly realising that the men's determination to return home had smashed the official's pugnacious authority, he got back into the tram.

His arms waved wildly and his voice broke with excitement as he yelled : " Fellow workmen. The overman has withdrawn his words and all of us can go to our places. From to-day on we will know what to do, and this parting shall be our meeting-place where the trouble of one shall be the trouble of all." A wild shout followed his words, and the men excitedly made their way to their working-places.

That evening after work Len could not eat his food and bath quickly enough. Shane scolded him for his haste. "You will get cramp in your stomach, sure as God is in heaven, one day, gulping your food down like that."

Len smiled. "It's all right, mam. It will take more than a bit of grub to hurt me."

Shane tossed her head when she retorted : "Hmm. I don't know so much about that, indeed, my boy. Your poor old mamgu was a much stronger body than you, but it was pitiful to see her the last days. God help her."

Jim squirmed restlessly in his chair, being always afraid of something starting Shane off on reminiscences of her long-deceased mother. Len finished eating as quickly as possible and, with his dark, wavy hair still damp, made his way to Ezra's house.

With shining eyes he looked into Mary's big grey ones as he asked for her father. Her emaciated body looked even smaller than usual and a pain tugged at his heart when he followed her into the kitchen, where Ezra was reading some papers.

The shadow cast over Len by Mary's appearance was soon dissipated in the bubbling enthusiasm with which he related the events of the day. At the end of the recital Ezra nodded his head in satisfaction.

"Very good, Len ; you have now seen where power lies and what it is."

Mary made some hot tea while the others were conversing. This and Len's contagious elation thawed the elder man's taciturnity. Stretching his feet towards the fire and running his fingers through Mary's hair, he began to speak in an unusually soft voice.

"Yes, my children, power is both great and terrible. It is great when it is held by yourself, but it is terrible when it is held by your enemies."

8*

The two young people looked at each other, neither of them quite following the drift of his mood, but they said nothing as Ezra went on, more to himself than to them : " There were some occasions during the strike when I feared power was passing out of our hands into those of the company. On the night of the big riot and the days following the shooting, I felt it would be better to capitulate to power than be crushed by it."

Mary's eyes widened at these remarks and, although she had not the slightest doubt of his ultimate courage, they reminded her of his favourite adage : " Always think two moves ahead before you make a single move yourself. Always try to find out what the enemy is thinking."

Len was more emotional than Mary, and when in the presence of someone who could dominate his impulses, he was less inclined to critical analysis. His mind was now concentrated on Ezra's words and their import in relation to the day's events, and he failed to link them up with incidents that had disturbed him during the strike. He had carried many gods in his life, but never one had he held to with the tenacity with which he held on to Ezra.

When he returned home Len ate a frugal supper and went straight to bed with a simple " Good-night " to his parents. As he tossed about in his bed, Ezra's words kept recurring to his mind, preventing sleep. Through them, like a burning thread, ran thoughts of Mary. He wondered what was the matter with her and longed to see the body under her clothes. He likened her to Jane, but failed to imagine the small body carrying robust breasts like his sister. At such intimate thoughts he felt his face warming as the blood went pounding to his head. At length he fell into an uneasy sleep and dreamed that he and Mary were walking over the mountain hand in hand. He saw Jane waving to them, beckoning them on. They started to run, but Mary stumbled and fell. Stooping to pick her up, he saw her clasped in the arms of Evan the Overman's son, one breast hanging loose and flaccid through her blouse. Len moaned and tossed in his sleep as the dream gripped him, and he woke the next morning feeling heavy and lethargic, while his head throbbed painfully.

During the weeks that followed the main topic in the pits was the " federashon," as the men called it. Most of them had already joined, but a few of the older ones remained independent and adamant to all approaches. Will Smallbeer, now working in the same barry as Len and his father, was one of the most stubborn. To all Len's enticements he replied : " What think you, Len ? Do you think I slog my guts out every day in the week, first man down and last man up, in order to keep lazy beggars in collars and ties idle on top of the pit ? Huh, not me."

Len tried to point out the value of organisation and the lessons to be learned from the strike, but he was always met with : " Don't you worry 'bout me, boy bach. I have always looked after myself, ay, before the napkins was off your backside, and I will do so till me and the old 'ooman peg out. I have got no man but myself to thank for anything. Let those who want a federashon have it, I say. But I be one of those who can manage by myself, thank you."

The old man's attitude worried Len, and he reported it to the committee. As a result of this he went to work early the next morning and visited all the men of the barry in their working-places, but he passed that of Will Smallbeer without saying a word, though the old workman shouted, " Good morning. How be ? " as he passed. Will spat on a heap of small coal, then turned to the man in the next working place and asked conversationally : " What be the matter with him this morning ? Got out of bed the wrong side, I 'spect." The man thus addressed did not answer.

Will looked up from the huge lump of coal he was hoisting to his knees, preparatory to jerking it into the empty tram, his body naked from the waist up sweating and shining with the strain. " Huh," he grunted. " Everybody bloody deaf this morning or what ? " Still receiving no reply, he swore at the top of his voice. " Be you all bleeding mad ? But perhaps you do think to worry me with your quiet.

Huh. Don't forget old Will Smallbeer have beat better men than you before breakfast in the morning. Ay," he howled into the silence, " and spit 'em out as easy as that," retching a prodigious mass of mucus from his chest and spitting it into the tram.

Big Jim started his way up the barry at the challenge, but Len caught him in time and drew him back to his own place, and though Will's curses continued to dribble down the barry no one paid any heed to him. Everyone was concentrated on filling his tram of coal in the shortest space of time. A number of horse-drawn empty trams rattled and clanged in the distance. When the haulier arrived with these he unhitched the horse with a " Whoa. Come here back," and began pulling the full ones singly out of the barry.

When all the full ones had been withdrawn the men came down the barry to help each other shove the empty ones up the steep incline to their respective working-places. Will Smallbeer worked the top place but one, and when it came his turn to have a tram the men left it at the working-place below his without saying a word.

Will, his eyes bulging with amazement, the sweat pouring off his nose and down his moustache, looked dully after the retreating lamps. Carefully turning so that his bare back was against the cold iron of the tram, he spreadeagled his feet and, jamming them against a sleeper, waited for the men to return, thinking they had made a mistake. In a short time he heard the clankety-clang of the next tram being pushed up the barry. This again stopped lower down, and the men once more made their way back for the next.

" Hi, boys, you have made a mistake, my tram isn't in the right place," he howled, but no one paid the least attention. Will tensed his body to the weight of the tram he was holding and his muscles swelled with the effort. Sweat and fury bathed him, and the tram felt so cold on his back that he was convinced it was burning a hole through his body.

Yelling helplessly after the men, a deep suspicion slowly grew in his mind. " Ho-ho. So that be it, is it ? " he screamed. " Not satisfied with putting muck on a man, you want to rub it in, do you ? " Putting all his strength and weight into his back, he straightened his legs and tried to press the tram up the incline, howling all the while, " Think I'll bend to ask for help, eh, you lousy lot of useless bastards ? "

Squeezing and straining, he at last felt the tram move a little. This and his fury urged him to greater efforts, and he pushed it another yard, when the weight forced his feet back down the slippery roadway and they again jammed against the sleeper where they were when his mates left him. Panting and gasping for breath he was forced to stop, his efforts for a while. He heard the men shove the last empty tram to its place, but was too proud to ask them for help after what they had done to him.

Will closed his eyes to ease the smarting of the sweat that poured into them. He kept them shut for a while till he heard a sudden bang in the tram resting on his back. Startled out of his wits, he turned his head by twisting his neck, and saw two men throwing coal into the tram as if their lives depended upon the speed with which they filled it. His eyes bulged glassily at the sight, and, horrified to the point of tears, he bawled, " Hi there ! What in bloody hell be you doing ? Do you know this is my tram ? " His voice was hoarse and cracked with fatigue, passion, and self-pity.

The men continued their frenzied filling, apparently deaf to Will's howls. He felt the strain on his back become greater with every lump and shovelful of coal, but he knew if he tried to get away from the tram its weight would over-come him and smash his body to the ground. Impotent and fuming, his only hope was to keep his feet tight against the sleeper and maintain the burning pressure of the cold iron on his back until the men released him. It seemed hours to Will before the tram was filled, but at last it was full. One of the men went round it chalking a number

on the sides. When he came to the front he gave a
surprised start when he saw the wet, straining body
of Will.

" Duw, duw, butty, look what I have found by here ! "
he cried in feigned alarm. His mate hurried to the spot and
both of them looked at the suffering Will for a moment
before shouting loudly to the barry, " Come up quick,
boys, and see what we've found."

A scurry of pattering feet followed the shout. Forcing
his way to the front, Big Jim looked pathetically at the
figure before him. " Well, well," he murmured com-
passionately, " it is poor old Will Smallbeer. Pity, pity.
I wonder what he is doing by there."

One of the other men replied : " Poor old dab. Gone off
his head sudden, I 'spect. Pity, too, mun. Only yesterday
I was telling him he was bound to go one day with all the
beer he be drinking."

This infuriated Will and sent the strength oozing back
into his body. " You lot of dirty whoremasters," he
screamed, " pull this bloody tram off my back, then see if
you can insult me."

Big Jim looked at him, a pitying look on his face.
" There you are, boys," he said sadly, " that do prove he
have gone in his head. Fancy him holding a tram by there
all this time and there be two sprags in it."

Will gave a squeal and jumped to the side as if impelled
by an electric shock. The tram did not budge. Wide-
eyed and motionless he looked at it for some seconds, then
broke through the surrounding men like a thunder bolt,
frothing and howling incoherently. They heard him
hurtling back with gruesome threats of " I'll chop your
bloody heads off," and scattered before the whirling, razor-
sharp hatchet in his hand. The impetus of his stampede
carried him past them, and before he could turn Big Jim's
huge arms were round his belly. After a short, sharp
struggle Will was subdued. Tears of mortification filled his
eyes while the men sat round him in a ring.

Len was the first to speak. " Well, boys," he said

quietly, " this is the first test of strength between all of us together and one who is not willing to be with us."

Will struggled to his haunches as he grasped the import of the words, and Len went on : " No man can be strong enough to do what we all don't want him to do. You remember the blacklegs in the strike ? " he asked.

" Ay, ay," the men replied in chorus.

" Well, the other side of that is no man can refuse to do what we want him to do. One man in our barry thought he could stand by himself against us all and bring disgrace on us in the eyes of the other workmen in the pit. If he still believes this, that is his own look-out."

Will, much less cocksure after his experience, broke in : " Say straight what you do mean, mun. You do want me to join the federashon, is that it ? "

" Yes," all the men shouted together.

" Do the federashon mean that workman have got to fight against workmen ? "

Len replied this time. " Yes, when a few stubborn workmen go against what is good for the majority."

" Huh. If that be it, then I give in, muniferni, and will join next Saturday. But mind you," he added hastily, " no man be going to make on my bloody back and no man can rub muck in me, either."

The workmen cheered this speech and Will was allowed to rise to his feet. They all helped to fill an additional tram to make good the one he had lost, and this satisfied Will, although he threatened to have the blood of any man who tried to " simple " him.

CHAPTER XIV

Len and Mary organise the Circle

ABOUT this time Len found himself becoming more and more interested in books, particularly those lent to him by Ron, but though he spent much time with them, they remained as inscrutable as ever. As usual when he was in an intellectual or emotional difficulty, his thoughts turned to Mary and Ezra. Knowing the latter was absorbed in the affairs of the federation, Len did not want to worry him with his troubles, but he wished he could gain the confidence of Mary and break down the cold barriers she placed between them. At last, after pondering over the matter for weeks, he decided to approach her.

Standing outside Ezra's door, he felt the same perturbation as on the first occasion, but plucking up his courage he knocked timidly. Immediately he had done so he regretted it and forgot all he had planned to say, but before he could recover his composure the door opened and Mary confronted him.

She looked stronger and brighter than when he last saw her, and this made him glad. For some moments he remained silent, his eyes unconsciously fixed on her face. But presently, realising that she was blushing under his stare, he pulled himself together and, coughing in an embarrassed manner, he asked if Ezra was in.

" No," answered Mary ; " dad has gone away since this morning and won't be back for some time. Can I give him any message ? "

He paused a second and dropped his eyes before answering : " Yes . . . er . . . well, no. I didn't exactly come to see him, Miss Mary. I wanted to ask you about something that is worrying me. But it doesn't matter now," he concluded hastily.

Mary looked at him in surprise. She knew he was shy and diffident, but she had never before seen him so completely at sea, and his uneasiness touched a sympathetic chord in her.

" Well, if you have something to talk to me about," she said, less brusquely than she usually spoke to him, " why not come in and chat it over, since you are here ? "

He followed her through the passage into the kitchen, his heart beating in his throat. Inviting him to take the arm-chair where her father usually sat, she took her favourite stool near the fireplace. Len noticed that her big eyes now looked blue.

He swallowed nervously and began to explain what was troubling him. " You see, Miss Mary," he said, " ever since your father started telling me about books and the way newspapers are used to tell us what other people want us to know, instead of what we ought to know, I've been trying to learn what exactly we *should* know." He felt he was tying himself into verbal knots, but went on desperately : " Ron, of the general store, told me a lot of things before he went to college and gave me some books, but I can't make head or tail of them."

He stopped, hoping she would show in some way that she appreciated his difficulty, but she continued to look at him gravely without saying a word. Her silence made Len more confused than ever. He felt he could explain no further and decided to come straight to the point.

" I was thinking," he stuttered, " that perhaps your father could spare time to teach some of us young chaps all the things he knows." And as this sounded lame and insufficient, he plunged on : " What I mean is, perhaps he could take a class of us youngsters same as they do in school. Only he would teach us about the working-class."

He stopped here, completely at a loss for words, and for some time not another word was spoken. Then Mary said, " I think I know what you have in mind, Len." Her rather hoarse voice sounded very sweet in his ears and he quivered at her use of his name. She did not notice this, however, and went on : " What you want is someone to teach politics to a group of young men like yourself who want to learn things but are groping in the dark for want of direction ? "

He nodded his head dumbly, and again both remained silent for some time. Mary was once more the first to break it.

" I don't think dad has the time for such a thing," she observed. " And in any case I don't think he would be of great use to you, because he's a man of action rather than of words."

Len stirred in disagreement but said nothing, and she continued : " What you should do is to get your chaps, and some of the young girls if you can as well, into a kind of little circle where you can share your problems and discuss them together each week."

Len immediately saw the possibilities in her suggestion, and feeling suddenly full of confidence, said : " Good. You've hit it right on the head."

They began at once to make a list of the people who might come to such informal meetings, but Len found that his temperamental unsociability left him with very few suggestions. Mary, however, made up for this deficiency. She seemed to know everyone in the valley, with their tendencies and idiosyncrasies, and between them they worked out a list of over a dozen names, confident that Ezra would be able to add to the number. Mary agreed to interview Ben the Barber, to see if the " Circle," as they decided to call it, could meet each Sunday in his little back room.

Having concluded these arrangements, Len got up to go, but Mary invited him to have a cup of tea. Shyly but readily, he assented and sat down again, while she busied herself with the dishes. Watching the movements of her body, the dream he had had of her in the arms of Evan the Overman's son again flooded his mind. He pictured the loose breast hanging from its bodice and wondered if her breasts were really like that. A pain shot through him at the thought that, perhaps, she was courting some young man. He knew Ezra wished her to become a school-teacher eventually, and the knowledge maddened him, for he felt that it entailed her moving in circles superior to his own.

He was jerked out of these morbid thoughts by Mary handing him a cup of tea and offering him a biscuit. Ashamed of his thoughts, he stuttered his thanks, but self-consciously he avoided her eyes for fear she should read his mind. She seemed, however, to be oblivious to all he had been thinking, and while they sipped the tea they were both silent. But the turmoil in Len's heart increased with every moment, and suddenly, raising his eyes to hers, he asked : " Do you remember the night you teased me about love ? "

Mary was startled for a moment, but she managed to retain sufficient composure to murmur : " Why, yes. Of course I do. You mean the night you ran away like a little baby ? "

Her words hurt Len's dignity. " I don't think I ran away. You were asking me questions I didn't know how to answer, so I thought the best thing I could do was to get out."

Mary looked at him more sympathetically, but though she knew he expected her to speak, she found herself at a loss for words.

He waited a while, then, getting no response, continued in a lower voice : " But since then, I believe I am beginning to learn the truth about myself and about you."

She looked at him, her eyes filled with doubt and wonder, but let him continue uninterrupted : " All through the strike, whenever I was worried about anything, my thoughts used to turn to you. Sometimes I thought I hated you for your snotty, cutting ways to me. Then I would always apologise to you in my mind for thinking such things." Mary lowered her eyes, and he went on, more to himself than to her : " Ay. Just like that. Often I dream of you, and always they are dreams which make me angry and miserable." He turned to her with a quaint

little shrug and asked : " I wonder if what I feel for you is
love ? "

Mary rose from the stool, and, unconsciously imitating
her father's habit when he was disturbed or worried,
began pacing up and down the room. The restless action
brought to Len's mind a comprehension of what he had
said. Immediately nervous and penitent, he sprang to his
feet, saying : " Oh, forgive me, Miss Mary. I had no
business to say such a thing to you. I'm sorry." His face
was flushed with embarrassment and shame. Mary ceased
her pacing, and standing directly before him, looked deep
into his eyes.

" Sit down," she said ; and was glad when he did so,
because, looking down at him, she felt stronger. Then,
slowly and distinctly, she spoke to him, her voice very soft
and her eyes becoming moist : " There have been times
when I've really hated you, because I thought you were
robbing me of dad. But now I know I was wrong ; that
you are just a boy groping for something you are not even
yet aware of. You probably think what you do of me
merely because you have felt my antagonism. Now that's
all gone ; I see you as a friend and a comrade, who can
help me to help dad carry out all he has in mind. Your
words tell me you are too sentimental ever to be a serious
menace to dad's position. But," her eyes flashed, " you
must never talk to me again of love. I don't think I am
capable of such a thing. Besides," she added sadly,
" there are good reasons why I should put any such ideas
out of my mind even if they were to arise there."

Len's head sank lower on to his shoulders while she was
speaking. He felt the world was suddenly being torn from
him, and sensing his mood, she put her thin hand, soft as
a butterfly's wing, on his head.

" Don't worry, Len," she said. " You have many more
years before you than I expect I have, and if you follow
dad and your real impulses there will be thousands to love
you, thousands whose love will be much more precious to
you than mine could ever be."

Tears trickled down Len's cheeks, and he swallowed hard. But before he could say anything, a knock sounded at the door.

" That's dad," said Mary, in her normal voice, and a moment later Ezra entered the kitchen. He found Len on his feet ready to go.

" Why the hurry ? " he asked.

" Oh, I've been here a good time," was the answer, " and I ought to be going or my mother will be getting worried." And with a brief " Good night," he left father and daughter alone.

During the following weeks Len did not have much time to brood over Mary's words. He had been made secretary of the Circle, into which Ezra and Mary had succeeded in drawing the most varied elements, and they began organising lectures and debates, bringing in speakers from outside the valley. Slowly the members of the Circle gathered confidence and began lecturing to their fellow-members, each taking his turn.

The subjects ranged from philosophy to music. For the latter a piano was borrowed from Mr. Evans Cardi and Mary collaborated with the lecturer, the son of Williams the under-manager, illustrating his points by playing for him. Watching her fingers move in obedience to young Williams, Len was consumed with jealousy, and though he joined in the applause at the end, his clapping was false and hypocritical. When he heard the lecturer ask Mary if he could take her home, he burned with fury that she should consent with a smile.

At work next day he hardly spoke to anyone, and only grunted in response to his father's occasional queries. They were standing some huge thirteen-foot timbers underneath a great hole in the roof, and Big Jim swore there had been grass on some of the soil that had been shifted from the fall. Len, being more light and sprightly, straddled the cross-timber, or " collars," at the top of the upright props, while his father lifted up to him the smaller six-foot timbers. They were wet and slippery and Len, whose feet hung unsupported, had to take the weight in his arms and the small of his back. The strain on his body was terrible, even though Big Jim assisted him as far as possible, cracking jokes all the while in an attempt to raise him from his despondency. Turning his lamp sideways so that the gleam lifted and added to the light from the lamp Len held in his mouth, Jim commented :

" Argllwydd mawr, you do look funny up there, mun— 'sactly like a ape."

Len took no notice. His breath hissed through his teeth, clenched on the heavy lamp. The strain of handling the long, heavy timber, that twisted in his hands like an eel, began to exhaust him, and he jerked it in an effort to get the further end fixed on the timbers opposite. But it fell short, and swearing under his breath he twisted and strained in the effort to control it. But its slippery wet surface, added to the leverage of its length, defeated him, and forgetting the lamp in his mouth, he shouted : " Look out, dad ! "

The lamp clattered to the ground thirteen feet below and though his father sprang back like a panther, Len heard him moan. A cold chill ran through him.

He looked down and saw Big Jim squatting on the side, rubbing his naked chest vigorously and muttering : " Oh, my poor tits."

The sheer incongruity of the scene amused Len, and looking down from his high perch, he began to rock with laughter. But suddenly his father, ceasing his wails, jumped to his feet and roared out :

" Ifarn daan ! Not satisfied with nearly killing your poor old father, you now make fun to him ! "

Len, however, made no effort to control his laughter, and this enraged Big Jim. Running back a short way, he picked up the huge fourteen-pound sledge-hammer, and swinging it above his head like a broom-stick, he howled :

" Out of that bloody timbers ! Come on. Down you come before I hit the bloody lot out." Then, giving the upright prop a hard blow as an earnest of his intention, he continued threateningly : " By Christ, you can muck on me, but no man can rub it in.   Dangerous man I be when I lose my temper.   I have kilt men for half of what you have done to me.   Just shows what comes of spoiling your children ! "

In a leisurely way, and still laughing, Len began to scramble down from his perch, when suddenly a rattling sound came from the timbers above, and before he could drop to the ground a stone struck him glancingly on the head.   Without a murmur his limbs relaxed and he fell headlong, but Big Jim caught him in his huge, sure arms before he touched the roadway, and carrying the inert body some distance back, he laid it gently on the side.   Feverishly he examined the sweat-bedewed head.   Len's eyes were closed, and, finding no wound or sign of blood, Jim was frightened.   A dread shot through his mind that the lad's neck was broken, and drawing him to his body like a mother cuddling her child, the old worker began to cry piteously.

" Oh Len bach, I didn't mean what I was saying.   Open your eyes and look at your old dad again," he pleaded. But there was no response.   Len lay limply, his features immobile, and Jim's voice became more pathetically vehement as he begged : " Come, Len bach, let me hear you laughing at me again."

Presently Len's eyes twitched, and, Jim, placing him tenderly back on the roadway, ran for the big tin jack of water.   He upturned the neck of this to Len's mouth until the water gushed over the lad's face and chest, bringing him back to consciousness with a shudder, and seeing that no vital harm had been done, the old man began to upbraid him.

" There you are," he scolded.   " That do just serve you right.   That's what you get for poking funs to people older than yourself."

Len's hand wandered to his throbbing head, and at once Jim became solicitous again.

" Is your poor little head paining ? " he crooned as if he

were talking to a baby. Len nodded, but said nothing. Fortunately the stone had struck him flatwise. Had its edge caught him it would probably have fractured his skull.

He tried to struggle to his feet, saying, " I'm all right now, dad, let's get on with those timbers or we'll never finish."

But Big Jim was adamant. " You sit here for the rest of the day," he insisted, wrapping Len in shirts and coats. " There is a day after to-day. I can go on cropping the sides ready for to-morrow, then we can finish the whole job." Len gave way because he knew it was useless arguing and he still felt giddy and sore.

A few Sundays after this incident a stranger attended the Circle. He had a letter of introduction from Ron, who had promised to lecture, saying that he was unable to come, but had sent a substitute much more efficient and interesting than himself.

It transpired that the lecture was to be on " Sex, its purpose, problems, and diseases," and Len, shocked by the title, took old John Library, the chairman, aside and suggested that the girls should be asked to leave in case they should be offended.

John looked at him quizzically.

" You've still got a lot to learn, Len bach. Why shouldn't the girls have the benefit of this lecture, if there is any benefit to it, as well as yourself ? "

Len, taken aback by the old man's answer, could only blurt out : " There are some things we can't talk about before women." And then, as if this closed the matter, he added : " It isn't right."

But John merely walked to the front of the room and without more ado opened the meeting.

Len kept his eyes on the picture of " Bendigo in Fighting Pose " that faced him on the opposite wall, occasionally giving a sly squint at the charts the lecturer produced, but hurriedly averting his eyes. His face went red and white in turns and he felt an insane desire to get up and order Mary out. He was not so much concerned about the other girls. " If they are brazen enough to stay here, that's their own business," he thought. He fought the desire back. When the lecturer spoke of the diseases, Len was amazed and horrified. He had never realised that people suffered from such ghastly things. He remained throughout the lecture wishing all the time that Mary were not there.

That night in bed he could not rid himself of the terrible pictures drawn by the lecturer. It appeared to him that everything connected with sex left one open to putrefying diseases. The lecturer had stated that syphilis (Len had always heard the men in work call it " pox ") was brought into the country hundreds of years ago by the Crusaders, and that eighty out of every hundred people now had it in one form or another. But when Len thought of Mary and his own father and mother, he could not believe that any of them suffered from such a thing. His whole being revolted at the idea, and he tried to forget the hideous subject. Nevertheless, his sleep was disturbed by dreams that left him moist with a cold sweat.

The village was now more prosperous than it had ever been. The pits never ceased their throbbing night or day. The " foreigners " had inter-married with the natives, their children, now young adults, creating a new cosmopolitan population in the valley. Street and mountain fights were no longer so frequent, but the continually extending police-station housed more police than it ever had. Each of the four groups of collieries had its separate federation lodge, linked together by a Combine Committee. Mr. Evans Cardi, together with most of the other little tradesmen, extended their premises and their business at the same time. A new theatre was built near the square. Every Saturday the men and women of the village followed their rugby football team into the neighbouring areas, and the game sometimes turned into a battle of fists. A new railway was laid through the valley to deal with the flow of coal that was too great for the railways already there, and the city by the sea into which this coal was poured became one of the greatest ports in the world. Beautiful houses and buildings sprang up in it. The number of its millionaires increased with the increased number of ships that left its docks with coal for the four corners of the earth. Lord Cwmardy became so wealthy that his daughter could afford to travel the country demanding rights for women.

Early in the spring a joint meeting of the pit committees was held in the Boar's Head, where the inquest on the explosion victims had been held. The big room was packed to suffocation, reeking clay pipes filled it with black acrid fumes, and huge jugs of beer were shared out in little tots among the men.

Feeling stifled by the thick atmosphere, Len drank his in a single gulp, and going out into the bar for fresh air, bought himself another pint, which he took back with him to the meeting-room. Putting the mug under the bench, he began to listen attentively while Ezra explained the purpose of the meeting and the need of striving for a majority on the local council. As the speech concluded, a murmur of applause came from the men present and they began chatting among themselves.

For a while Ezra let them go on, the hubbub adding to the density of the atmosphere, but at last he tinkled the empty glass on the table before him. " Now boys, we will have a little bit of order and start the discussion. Who's going to begin ? "

There was a long pause before a middle-aged man from one of the neighbouring pits got to his feet, and coughing nervously, began : " Mr. Chairman. I must be quite honest to you all. I don't see what good can come to us if we begin to potch about with these old politics. To me politics is something for rich people who have got plenty of time to spare to play about. We have got our federashon and I do think that is enough for us to go on with, without bothering our heads about things that are no use to us. I do agree that it is all officials and what not is on the council now, but what difference do that make ? Haven't they always been there ? No," he went on more slowly, spitting on the floor before he continued, " I do say let well alone. We are all right now. Don't let us spoil everything by poking our noses into things that have got nothing to do with us."

He sat down amid some applause, and another coal-scarred veteran jumped up, who, speaking in a high-pitched, excited voice, agreed with the first speaker. As he worked himself up, a little globule of moisture gathered at the end of his nose. This fascinated Len. He watched it growing longer as the old man continued, and held his breath as every nod of the speaker's head threatened to break the grip of the wet blob and drop it on the old man's chin. Unheeding, the latter went on.

" Ay, boys, you can take it from me that the best thing is to stick to our own last and let everybody else stick to theirs. I also do agree that it is all officials and their butties be up there now. But let them be, say I. It do give them less time to run after the firemen's wives."

A roar of laughter greeted this last sally, and he sat down, wiping his nose on the back of his hand. Immediately three men jumped on their feet simultaneously, each claiming the floor, and began quarrelling as to who was first on his feet. One twitted the other : " You say you are first ; why, mun, you are too slow to be the first of twins."

This drove the slandered man, who happened to have a twin brother, into a frenzy.

" Say that again," he howled, " and I'll knock your bloody face to the back of your dirty bloody neck ! "

The man thus challenged made no reply, but rushed past the intervening benches, pulling off his coat as he went. The delighted committee-men made no effort to stop him. They cleared the benches out of the way and formed a ring round the fuming contestants.

In a flash the meeting had split into two groups, who were all mixed up in a tumbling mass of fighting bodies. As benches and tables went crashing to the ground and blood was splashed about the room, Ezra remained still and silent in his chair, but the tumult brought men rushing in from the bar, Big Jim leading them.

Jim caught a glimpse of Len standing white-faced and trembling near the door, and without waiting to ask questions, he jumped to the conclusion that the lad had been hit. Roaring like a bull, he flung himself into the mass of bodies, hitting indiscriminately at everything that came near him. Dai Cannon rushed after his mate and met a crack on the ear that tumbled him over before he had struck a blow. Holding his ear tenderly, Dai slowly crawled to where Len was standing watching the scene with eyes that betrayed his fear.

Len smiled, despite his alarm, at Dai's comment. " By Christ ! They're hitting hard here, Len."

For some minutes the fight continued, but at last the men began to tire and, as one by one they dropped out, others began to drag the chairs and benches back into place. When this was completed and the men once more seated, Ezra continued with the meeting.

" Now you have all enjoyed yourselves," he said, " perhaps we can go on. Who wants the floor next ? "

The same three men who had started the row at once sprang to their feet, but before the argument could begin again, Ezra said : " Tom Davies has the chair," and the other two immediately sat down.

Wiping the blood from his nose with his coatsleeve, the speaker started : " Mr. Chairman. I don't agree with the other two speakers, much as I respect 'em. What I want to know is, why for should the company have all the say in our valley ? When we was on strike it was the council who brought the police here. I have always said this and no man can make me believe different. If Ezra is good enough for us in the Federashon he is good enough for us on the council or anywhere, I do say."

This speech had the loudest applause of the evening. The reference to Ezra seemed to focus the whole matter for the men, and they saw the issue no longer as an abstract thing between themselves and the Company, but as one between Ezra, their leader, and Mr. Hicks, the representative of the Company. It turned the tide in favour of fighting the elections, and after Ezra had still further explained the matter, a vote was taken, and all the men, except those who had spoken against, put up their hands for contesting, Big Jim looking around to see what Len was doing before raising his.

More jugs of beer were sent for and shared in the little tots among the company. But, although Ezra went out immediately the meeting was concluded, Len remained behind with his father, for fear he might start another fight. In spite of some critical moments, however, the night passed off without further disturbance, and presently an impromptu concert had started.

Everyone present was expected to contribute to the programme or sacrifice the price of a pint of beer for the pianist, and by the time Len's turn came he had drunk sufficient beer to shatter his usual shyness. He felt he could sing better than any who had performed before him, and at last the self-elected chairman, his eye already black from a blow he had received in the fight, announced in a grave, urgent voice : " And now gentlemen, with your kind attention, I am going to call upon our great friend, Big Jim's boy, to oblige the company."

Len blushed and fidgeted in his seat, as he had seen the other artistes do. Big Jim shifted a lump of tobacco into his cheek and buried his nose in his pint mug ; and the pianist struck up a preliminary chord that ran from one end of the piano to the other. When Len still hesitated, the crowd grew restless and the chairman shouted : " Order, gentlemen, please, the singer is on his feet. Give him a clap, boys." Big Jim hastily replaced his pint on the table to participate in the encouraging applause, and Len walked self-consciously to the piano. Bending his head, he turned his back to the audience and hummed a tune into the pianist's ear. The latter's fingers ran over the keys, but he failed to get the pitch of Len's voice. Finally he muttered : " It's all right, kid. Kick off. I'll follow you." Len turned round and faced the noisy, smoke-filled room. Again the chairman raised his hand warningly.

" Now gentlemen, please, the singer is on his feet. Now then, Dai," he continued, addressing someone at the back, " if you can't 'preciate good singing, there is a room downstairs where you can drink your beer without disturbing nobody else."

This statement was greeted with loud applause, and the pianist again struck up a chord while Len, swaying slightly, clasped his hands before him and fixed his eyes soulfully on the ceiling. Something in the back of his mind told him this was the correct posture. Drawing his breath in deeply he began to sing, " A fair-haired boy in a foreign land at sunrise was to die," and finding he had pitched it too high had to force himself to the top notes, each of which threatened to burst the veins in his neck.

Big Jim gazed at him with open mouth ; he thought he had never heard such a beautiful voice. As Len slowly entered into the mood of the ballad, his voice sank naturally to its proper pitch. In his drink-hazed brain he pictured the incidents on which the words were based. He saw himself in the condemned lad's place, and a quiver of self-pity gave his voice a pitiful vitality. Then as he imagined his mother in Sunny Bank, weeping for him as he sat in the death cell, he felt manly and brave, and his voice echoed the mood. In the last stanza, where the pardon came too late, he saw his mother and Big Jim bringing wreaths to put on his grave.

When the last quavering tones were silenced, a burst of applause greeted his effort. Tears flooded the eyes of the men present. Loud shouts for encore rose from all parts of the room to be drowned in the stentorian shout from Big Jim.

" No, no. Blast an encore. Let us have the same song again."

The chairman appealed for order. " After that very fine rendering," he said, " I am sure you all agree with me that we ought to ask our young friend to oblige us again."

Len was embarrassed. He did not know any other songs, except hymns, and the words of these even he had forgotten. He felt very proud of his first effort, but was at a loss how to accede to the request.

Turning from the piano, his face flushed and eyes burning, he looked at the people before him. Their features, shrouded in a thick haze of smoke, looked blurred and indistinct, but when the chairman again called for order, Len gave a little preliminary cough and said :

" Fellow workers, I don't know any more songs, but if you like I will recite a poem entitled, ' The Oration of Spartacus to the Gladiators.' "

Loud applause greeted this announcement, and Len continued :

" It tells of a band of Roman slaves who escaped from their masters and hid themselves in the mountains where, for three years, they beat back all the attacks of the whole Roman army."

The pianist struck a low chord and Len commenced the oration. His brain was now so muddled that he forgot half the words, and he substituted anything that came to his mind. At the end neither he nor any of the audience knew what he had said, but the latter applauded as if this made no difference.

Later that night Big Jim and Len returned home. Both felt very happy until they reached the house, where Shane was awaiting them.

One glance at their faces showed her what had happened.

" For shame," she said to Jim, " teaching your young son to drink ! "

Len went straight to bed. He lay down and felt the ceiling falling. When he closed his eyes the room ran madly round him, and his stomach turned with it. He swore never to drink again.

CHAPTER XV

War

As summer melted into autumn, Len and Mary devoted themselves with even greater assiduity to the Circle. The subjects they discussed took on an increasingly Socialist bias, and under the guidance of John Library the Circle organised private and public lectures at which well-known Liberals and theoretical Socialists spoke. The experiment proved very popular, and political interest and discussion began to develop in the valley.

Large numbers of young men joined the Circle, the cleverest among these being Tom Morris, who came from the neighbouring valley. Eventually lack of space made it necessary to close the books to many who would have liked to become members. The informal homeliness of the whole proceedings, together with the camaraderie between the members, made new-comers anxious to remain.

Discussions commenced in the Circle were carried into the pit in such a way that the Circle became a big factor in the life of the valley. Marx and Socialism slowly became the chief topic of discussion and debate, and many of the Circle members, led by Tom Morris, were ready to believe that Marx was God's second name. Len was voracious for information and knowledge. He began to comprehend a little more of the books given him by Ron.

Ezra advised him to leave Marx alone. " Besides being out of date," he said, " his books are too heavy and dry for you." And Len took his advice.

One Sunday Mary suggested that the Circle should have a holiday-fund for the purpose of spending one day a year together at the seaside. This was agreed to, and each week the members subscribed to this, and it was decided to go to Blackpool on the following August Bank Holiday. Len and Mary were delegated to look after the arrangements, and when at last the day arrived, beautiful and warm, each member of the Circle put on a red tie or scarf as the symbol of their vaguely defined beliefs.

The journey and the scenery reminded Len forcibly of his first excursion to the seaside. The long train journey made him depressed and morose, but Mary, who seemed more sparkling and lively that day than he had ever seen her, tried to lift him out of this despondency.

Someone in the carriage pulled out a large bottle of whisky from his case, and the spirit was offered round. Len felt it would be churlish to refuse, particularly when he saw Mary swallow her portion in a single gulp, and as the fluid ran through his veins like mercury, his eyes began to shine and his taciturnity was dissipated by the softening influences of the liquor.

During the day Len, for the first time in his life, met girls who had not been reared in the valleys : robust, boisterous women from the factories of Lancashire and elsewhere. Their free-and-easy camaraderie bewildered him and, noticing some of them linked arm-in-arm across the street and looking the worse for drink, he asked Mary shyly if they were loose women. She gave him a biting, scornful glance and replied shortly :

" They are hard-working girls having a hard-earned holiday, exactly the same as you are to-day. The only difference is that they are enjoying themselves and you are not."

Len subsided at the snub, and soon the company began to break up.

Mary refused many invitations to join particular groups, excusing herself on the plea of a headache, and eventually she and Len were left alone.

She suggested a stroll, and they wandered away from the crowds. The sparkling sea fascinated Len, and he became absorbed in emotional daydreams which led him gently and logically to Mary walking at his side. They sat down at a

9

spot from which they could look out over the ship-speckled sea, soaking its rim in the vast impenetrable horizon.

Len felt intoxicated with the scene and the proximity of Mary, who sat clasping her knees and staring into the distance. The heat rose in little hazy bubbles before his eyes. It oozed into his body, and he started to speak, but closed his mouth before uttering a word. Turning on his side, he looked at Mary. Her profile was straight and delicate, reminding him of pictures he had seen in books. Without turning her head she remarked, each word like a soft tinkle of a bell in his ears : " Isn't it lovely here ? The world is a beautiful place, and worth living in after all."

The last phrase startled Len for a moment.

" Why do you say ' after all ' ? " he asked.

She made no reply, and Len, rising from her side, crawled on his knees until he was facing her. He looked deep into her eyes and brought them back from the limitless distance which had for the moment stolen her from him. He saw his own eyes look back at him from hers, and his bones turned to liquid and his muscles to steel. He leaned sharply forward, his face slightly moist, his body vibrating.

" Mary," he said, and in his voice was the essence of his desires. " Mary, dear, why do you lose yourself outside a world which you say is good to live in ? " But before she had time to answer, he rushed on as if each word spontaneously gave birth to a hundred others. " The world is beautiful, my dear, because of the people, the children. Because of you." A slow blush dyed his face, as Mary looked at him. The sunbeams in her hair burned Len's body through his eyes. Something hard and impelling quivered in his nerves, and taking hold of her hands, he drew them from her knees, disarranging her skirt as he did so. He squeezed the thin, delicate hands to his chest, which heaved spasmodically in the tumult of his emotions.

" Mary, my love," he whispered, " I want you."

She did not answer, but lay back upon the long grass that curled around her. Len looked down on her, his eyes stripping her body of its garments, and tiny bubbles of froth gathered at the corners of his mouth. His elbows either side of her head, he lay on her body, his own vibrant with desire.

His voice was low and husky when he whispered : " You are my love. Now I know what has been tormenting me. I am not complete without you. I want to squeeze you to my body, into my heart, until we become one."

His hand stole slowly to her blouse. He undid the buttons and thrust his hands through the opening until his fingers touched her flesh, and a tremor ran through him at the contact.

Mary looked at him with dilated eyes. His pulsing fingers sent trickling electric currents racing over her, and slowly, like a thief before a newly-opened safe, his hand crept forward until it closed on her breast. She gave a momentary sigh, closed her eyes, then sprang up at the burning touch, rolling him to one side. Panting for breath, she allowed the sun to kiss away the burn of Len's hand as, unwilling to release what it had found, it drew her bosom free from its sheltering blouse. The pink, crustling nipple made him giddy, but as he leaned towards it, she halted him.

" I'm sorry, Len," she said quietly, in spite of the throb in her voice. " It was all my fault. I shouldn't have forgotten and led you on. Forgive me and forget if you can that I have been so foolish."

Len looked at her amazed. " But you've done nothing," he exclaimed. " If there is anyone to blame it is me. But I don't see what wrong we have done. Oh, Mary, why do you turn from me like this ? I'm sure you loved me for a moment just now. Then you break from me as if you were snapping a chain. I can't help wanting you. It's no disgrace, unless," he added quickly, as if the thought had suddenly leapt to his mind, " unless you don't think I am good enough for you."

Mary started. Slowly she covered the taunting breast before looking him in the eyes.

" Len, if you want to remain friends with me, you must never say that again. You were born to our valley and are one of our people, therefore you are good enough for anyone."

Len started to apologise, but she waved his words aside and continued : " In this world there are many reasons why we must sometimes crush back our desires. As long as my father lives, I belong to him and he belongs to the people. And if that isn't enough," she burst out with a sob, " feel this."

She caught his hand savagely and placed it on her chest beneath her bosom. He felt the cavity beneath the loose skin, and her ribs were sharp under his fingers.

Without removing his hand, he looked into her face. His eyes were soft with unshed tears, but the tumult of his emotion was quieted and his voice was calm and soothing when he said, " I understand, dear. Don't let that worry you. Instead of carrying the horrible burden by yourself, we can carry it together. People have got better, although they had the same thing as you. We must try to make you well."

His voice failed and he could say no more. Silently he circled her head with his free arm and drew it down until his lips were pressed to hers. Gently, without passion, he kissed her, all his body melting into the caress. And when he released her, he saw little shining imps playing happily in the depths of her eyes.

They rose, and sauntered, arm-in-arm like a pair of children, back to the crowded town, and for the remainder of the day they were inseparable.

They heard the paper-boys shouting the news, but they paid little attention. It was only in the train that they learned from the other passengers that Germany had forced Britain to declare war in defence of Belgium, and though everyone was excited, it was the general opinion that it would be a very short one.

The journey back was slow and tedious. On innumerable occasions the excursion train was shunted into sidings or held up in other ways for hours, while trains full of khaki-clad men were given the right of way.

The sight of these men, shouting and singing, stirred something in the hearts of most of the people in the carriage, except a short man with bright eyes and black, bushy hair, who had sat quietly in the corner throughout the heated discussions that had raged in the carriage. Looking out of the carriage window at a passing troop-train, he murmured audibly : " Poor boys. Food for the guns."

Everyone in the carriage stared at him, and he began to address the carriage in general. " Those men, now singing and happy in the belief they are going to have an extended holiday, will soon be lumps of clay rotting in the soil of a foreign land."

A member of the Circle challenged him heatedly. " Don't you think it right," he asked, " that Britain should go to the defence of a little country that is being trampled underfoot by one of the greatest military powers in the world ? Don't you think it is the duty of Britons to defend those weaker than herself from the jack-boots of militarism ? " He looked around triumphantly when he finished, as if saying : " That's taken the old geezer down a peg or two and put him in his place."

Len, though he was deeply interested, said nothing. With the others in the compartment, he felt that the Government could do nothing other than declare war in the circumstances that had been forced upon it. He instinctively believed in the altruistic motives of the Government and thought it only right that England should put a stop to the challenging Germans. In common with most of his own age, he had been taught to despise the Germans as a sly, jack-booted people who spent most of their time hatching plots and spying upon other countries. He was therefore inclined to agree with the second speaker, but no more was said on the subject.

When they arrived in the valley they found it full of excited, gesticulating people, and during the following week nothing was talked of but the war. The pits became battle-grounds. The police-station was turned into a recruiting office. All reservists were called to the colours, and they left the valley in a special train, to the sound of band music and cheers. The streets were decorated with bunting and house-windows were plastered with cheap, gaudy prints of the foremost generals.

Shortly after the declaration of war, Big Jim and his cronies sat drinking in the Boar's Head. Jim retailed tales of the Boer War, painting a romantic, glamorous picture of the campaign.

Dai Cannon in a surly voice asked, " If it was so nice and cushy as that, why the hell don't you join up now ? "

Jim, already half drunk, sprang to his feet, shouting, " Think you I be 'fraid to fight measly, square-head Shermans ? If so, Dai, you make a bloody mistake, muniferni. Huh. One Englishman be worth ten of the bleeders. But there," he questioned sadly, " what can you 'spect from a man who is forced to fight ? That is the beauty of our country," he continued, " only those who do want to fight is taken."

The other men joined in the argument, one of them remarking, " Ay, boys. After all, our little country is still the best of the bunch. If Big Jim do think it worth fighting for, I be with him." Dai felt the tide against him and said no more. Actually he felt rather sorry he had spoken at all, because he knew his words had put into Jim's head an idea the latter would surely carry out.

And sure enough, later that night Jim and four of his drinking pals marched arm-in-arm down the street towards the police-station. The constable on duty nervously jumped to his feet at the intrusion. He was alone, and feared their intentions. In a conciliatory manner he asked : " Hallo, boys, what do you want here this time of the night. Not lodgings, I suppose ? " He laughed at his own wit, and the others joined in.

When the laughter had subsided Jim said, " No. We be not come here for lodgings. Ha-ha. We be come to fight for our King and country."

The policeman immediately grasped the situation. " Sit down for a minute," he invited. " The recruiting sergeant will soon be back. He is only just gone down the road a little way."

Jim and his mates seated themselves on the bench while Jim regaled them with reminiscences of the numerous nights he had spent in different cells in all parts of the world.

A considerable time passed before the recruiting sergeant returned. When he at last entered, he was staggering a little and his face was flushed. He sat heavily and suddenly in the nearest chair and commenced to snore immediately. The constable leaned over him and whispered something in his ear, shaking him at the same time and bringing him to his feet with a jerk.

" Eh ? " he gasped, while his bleary eyes roved the room. " Men want to join the army of Hish Majeshty the King ? Where are they ? "

He caught sight of Jim and his pals, and strode unsteadily towards them. " By Christ," he shouted, " what splendid figures of men ! The King will be glad to see you, boys. I suppose, like all the others, you want to be in the same crush. Good. I'll see to that. Now come over here so that I can fill in particulars."

The men followed him, Big Jim in the lead. The latter was the first to be questioned.

" What's your age ? "

" Thirty-two."

" Eh ? I asked your age, not the size of your waist."

" Don't bloody shout at me," yelled the irate Jim, " and don't you dare to call me a liar, butty. Don't forget I have seen more service than you have seen years. I was fighting and dying for my country when you was hanging to your mother's tits."

This outburst cooled the sergeant a little.

" All right, mate," he said pacifyingly, " don't take no offence at me."

Some time later all the men were signed up, given a shilling each, and informed they would receive instructions. Jim went jubilantly up the hill to Sunny Bank, where Shane and Len were awaiting him. They heard him singing before they heard the rattle of the latch. He came in beaming, lifted Shane in his arms and danced a crazy jig round the small kitchen. Shane struggled strenuously and forced him to put her down, then stood for some moments gasping for breath. Jim turned his attention to the silent Len.

" Well, boy bach," he said, " proud you ought to be this night with your old dad."

For a moment Len did not grasp what he was saying, but Shane, as if sensing what was coming, stared at Jim with wide-open eyes.

" Proud ?   Why proud ? " she asked suddenly.

" Well, my gel," he answered sheepishly, taken aback somewhat by her evident lack of enthusiasm, " 'in't it something to be proud of that your old man have joined up to fight for his King and country ? "

Shane gave a cry and drew the hem of her canvas apron to her eyes.

" I knowed it," she moaned.   " O God, why did I give you money to go out to-night ? "   Her voice broke in a sob.   " I ought to have knowed you would get drunk and do something daft."

She turned on him fiercely.   " Don't you think a man of your age have got something better to do than to go trapezing round the world while I got to struggle by here alone to rear the children ?   What have the war got to do with us ? " she continued despairingly.   " We did not make it.   Let those who did fight it out between themselves, not take men from their wives and children.   All my life I have been tormented with you.   First you run to the Boer War and leave me alone with little Jane bach, now in her grave, God bless her, and Len, by there. Now you are going to leave me again and go God knows where. Shame on you, James. How can you ever hope to find forgiveness at the hands of your Maker for doing such things ? Sure as God is my judge, you will come to a bad end."

She wept bitterly, wiping her dripping nose on the rough apron that left it red and chafed. Then she continued with greater vehemence, while Len and Jim looked on speechlessly : "For King and country indeed ! I have never seen no king, and the only country I know is inside the four walls of this house and between the three mountains of our valley. What have Belgiums got to do with us ? I have never done nothing to them and they have never done nothing to me. And now my home is to be broken up again because him who did ought to be caring for me do think more of other people."

She broke down completely and Len led her to the chair while Jim attempted to defend his action. "Duw, duw, venw," he said, "haven't you got no heart, mun ? If we don't stop those Shermans getting through little Belgium, mun, they will come over here sure as hell. And think what that will mean. Us 'ont have no homes then. We will have to go and live like dogs in the levels on the mountain-sides. Do you think I want you to go through that, Shane bach ? No. I would sooner lie stiff and cold, with ten bullets in my heart, than see any Sherman having you, ngyhriad bach y."

This somewhat mollified Shane. Raising her red-rimmed eyes to his, she said, "But, James bach, don't you think you have done enough ? You did go all through the Boer War. What more can anybody want ? Why don't you let the young men go ? " she concluded.

Jim felt her last retort was unanswerable until he caught sight of the whitening face of Len, who had not missed the significance of his mother's words. Shane sensed in a flash the error she had made. The lad's features looked drawn and haggard in the dim lamp-light. The words made him feel he had betrayed his mother, for if he

9*

had only joined up his father would have been forced to remain at home. He turned to Shane.

" I'm sorry, mam," he said. " If I had joined up, dad would have stopped at home. It's all my fault." He looked into his mother's worried face. " Don't nag him any more." His head bent lower. Shane jumped to his side and pressed his head to her body.

" Don't you dare never again to say such a thing to your mother," she scolded. " Your dad is much more able than you to carry a gun and fight. He is used to it and his body is big enough to bring him back safe. Don't you worry your little head, Len bach, and don't pay any heed to my old tongue. It is like a snake's sometimes, but I don't mean half of what I do say. Huh. You join up, indeed," she concluded, with a deprecating shrug that settled the matter in her mind.

Next day Big Jim's exploit was the talk of the pit. Will Smallbeer snorted, " Fitter if his son did the clean thing and let his poor ole man stop in the pit for a change."

Len choked back the lump in his throat, but made no reply. Big Jim, however, took up the challenge. Flinging his pick to the ground, he strode up the barry.

" Well," he asked threateningly, " what have you got to say about our Len ? "

All the men in the barry stopped working in anticipation of some excitement. " Nothing much," replied Will. " Only I do think it only fair that the young uns should have a go at this lot and not leave it to us old uns all the time."

" What in hell be you talking about, mun ? " was Jim's retort. " You have never done any fighting in your bloody life. The only soldiering you have ever knowed is the militia. Bah ! Toy soldiers ! You don't know what you be talking about, and I be just as daft as you to waste my breath on you." He spat heavily, and putting a huge lump of damp tobacco into his mouth, returned to his own place.

That evening Len hurriedly bathed and was preparing to leave the house when Shane stood with her back to the door.

" Where be you going ? " she demanded, her voice quivering with dread.

Len looked at her a moment in surprise before he realised the reason for her fear.

" Don't worry, mam," he reassured her, " I am only going up to Ezra's house. Before I ever do what you are thinking I will be man enough to come to you and tell you first."

Swallowing her tears, the distracted woman withdrew from the door, warning him : " 'Member now, Len bach, not to be late. I will be waiting for you."

Len proceeded direct to Ezra's house. Both Ezra and Mary were in. The former looked anxious and worried, but nothing was said until the usual cups of tea were ready and Mary took her seat near the fire. Since the eventful day at Blackpool the young people had seen very little of each other, although both instinctively felt they were in the other's thoughts. Mary opened the subject first. " It seems," she said, " the war can't last a long time with the number of men that are joining the forces. Oh," she added impulsively, " I wish I were a man and able to go."

Len felt the blood rush in waves to his head. He became momentarily giddy, then pulled himself together as Mary's voice seemed to come to him from a distance. " How splendid it must feel to fight for something that is good and honourable, to fight in defence of someone weaker than yourself." She looked at Len and stopped when she saw the agony in his face.

" What's the matter ? " she asked solicitously. " Are you ill, Len ? "

Ezra glanced up from his brooding at this remark, before he could say anything Len spoke in a quiet, strained voice.

" I came to you to-night to help me. I feel I have been a great coward. My father has joined the army and everyone is now looking at me as if I'd committed a crime, but I'm not a coward," he cried hysterically. " I didn't know what my father intended doing ; if I did I would have gone before him. I know that Mary is right when she says that all the young men are joining up, but what can I do ? " he asked helplessly looking from one to the other. " Dad is going this week. If I go as well, my mother will be left alone and she will break her heart." He turned and spoke directly to Mary. " Tell me. What am I do to ? You say you glory in someone who fights in defence of one weaker. I am ready to fight for you or my mother, but," he added in bewilderment, " I don't see you in any danger from the war."

Ezra looked at him in sudden surprise, but Len hurried on, his words bubbling over each other.

" I don't want to go to the war, although I know I ought to. I hate brutality. It hurts me to see men wilfully maiming each other for no purpose."

The silence of the other two oppressed him. He asked a straight question to both.

" Do you believe I should kill men I have never seen ? "

Ezra hesitated a moment, then replied with another question. " You say you detest physical violence, Len, but what do you think strikers should do to blacklegs who insist on attempting to break their strike ? Take our own strike, for instance," he added. " Do you think our men did wrong? Or, again, were our men who fought in the riots wrong when they used physical force and violence to defend themselves ? "

Len felt himself in a trap and turned his eyes mournfully to Mary.

" What am I to say ? " he asked. " Of course our men were right in what they did." Then he added more brightly, as if struck by an afterthought. " But it was different then. We could see them face to face. Now we are asked to kill men we have never seen and never known."

He swallowed hard, and Ezra interjected : " Yes. Isn't it better that we should stop those who want to do harm, before they come here to do it ? Isn't it better to stop blacklegs leaving their own homes than it is to fight them on our own doorstep ? Not that I believe in war," he went on hastily. " In my mind most wars are made by competing capitalist nations, but this time there can be no doubt that we have to defend our own country against a set of capitalists who are more brutal than our own. When a country violates treaties she has solemnly entered into, Len, then we have no choice but to teach her a lesson." He closed his mouth with a snap.

Len had a deep underlying feeling that the arguments were not real, but he could find no words to express his doubt. His mind wavered, but it seemed to him that Ezra's words were so logical that they were unanswerable, and he bent his head low.

" All right, I'll join up to-morrow."

Mary started to her feet, but he was gone before she could say anything.

Pain tugged at Len's heart the remainder of that night. His vivid imagination took him to the battlefields even before he had volunteered. Before going to bed he told Shane there was no need to call him for work in the morning. The startled woman looked up from her supper.

" Not going to work ? " she inquired, her voice echoing the mental anxiety that immediately gripped her. " For why be you not going to work, Len bach ? Be you bad ? "

Len shook his head sadly. " No, mam bach," he said, not daring to look her in the eyes.

" I am all right." His shoe scraped awkwardly on the floor. " I am going to join up to-morrow."

Shane gave a little scream and jumped from the table. She staggered to the foot of the stairs and shouted hysterically.

" James, James. Come down quick as you can. Something awful have happened to our Len."

There was a quick scamper in the bedroom overhead and in a moment Jim rushed down the stairs. He arrived in the kitchen with his trousers in his hand, his short, flannel shirt barely reaching his knees.

" What's the matter ? " he growled.

Shane sat in the armchair sobbing. Len replied for her.

" Nothing much, dad ; only I'm joining up to-morrow."

Jim stopped pulling the trousers over his bare legs.

" What ? " he shouted. " Tell me what you be saying again, boy."

Shane looked up at the tone of his voice. " That will do, James," she said sharply, while the tears rolled unheeded down her drawn cheeks. " Don't you shout at the boy like that ; he is not a dog."

Jim looked from one to the other in amazement, then finished putting on his trousers, grunting to himself the while. Shane began to moan.

" Not enough for me to lose my gel and then to get my man to leave me for the sodgers once again, but now I have got to lose my son. O dear God ! Pity you did not take me to the grave when you did take Jane and her baby bach. My life have been nothing but work and misery ever since I did first come to know James. Better if I had died in my poor mother's arms before I see the light of day." She sprang to her feet, shouting to Len. " But you shan't go. You are not twenty-one yet, and the law do say I have got control over you till then."

At the look in Len's eyes, she started to wheedle. " Why for do you want to leave your mam by herself in her old age, Len bach ? Have I not been a good mother to you ? Haven't I worked my fingers to the bone to put food in your little belly ? Haven't I often gone without a shimmy to my back to rear you 'spectable and clean ? " She hesitated as her love conquered her self-pity. " You can't go ! " she exclaimed. " You aren't strong enough to be put about like your father. You have always been a delicate child. Three months of sodgering will kill you. You won't have a nice soft bed to yourself in the army. No, you will have to sleep with bad men and drunkards who do not know what a decent home is. You won't have your mother to get up at four o'clock in the morning to light the fire for you and warm your pants before you come down." She exhausted herself and wept quietly in the corner.

Jim took up the cudgels. "Your mother's right," he said. "The army is no good to boys like you. You have got to be strong and tough, like me, to stick it. And, mind you, once you jib in the army you are finished, because the men will make your life not worth living. You stop at home, my boy. If there is any fighting to be done, Big Jim will do it for you. I am used to it. You listen to me. Your old man won't tell you wrong."

Len wilted at the pathetic attempts to win him from his resolution. His heart responded to all they had said, but his mind was made up. Mary's silence when her father had challenged him had been the deciding factor, stronger even than the loneliness he felt when he saw all the other young men of his own age leave the valley for the war.

"Your words grieve me," he said to his parents. "But I must go. Everyone else is already gone and very soon people will be calling me a coward, as Will Smallbeer did to-day."

"Who the hell is Will Smallbeer, anyhow?" broke in Jim. "He have never done any real sodgering in his bloody life. It do only prove what I have always believed. If there is any killing to be done, let the old uns go first; they can be spared better and they won't be missed so much." His big, thickly veined hands clenched. "Don't worry about a useless old snot like him, Len boy. 'Member I have joined up for you, and if you go now it do mean that you let your father down."

This new line of action galvanised Len.

"What?" he shouted. "Do you mean that you joined up so that I could stop at home?"

"Ay, of course," answered Jim without hesitation.

Len persisted. "Tell me the truth, dad, did you and the other boys join up when you was all drunk?"

Jim struck a dignified posture. "I never thought," he said reproachfully, "that I would ever rear a son who would tell me to my face that I be a liar, and that Big

Jim do not know what he be doing after he have had a pint
or two." He sighed deeply as if the thought were too
heavy a burden to bear.

Shane came to his rescue. " That be it, Len bach," she
said excitedly, ignoring the latter part of Jim's statement.
" Your father did join the sodgers for you to stop at home.
It wouldn't be fair for the two of you to go, and the gov'ment
ought to be satisfied with one of you. There now, let's
leave the nasty old business there. Come to bed and forget
all about it, Len."

Each argument they adduced strengthened Len's belief
that he had no business in the war, but he was too weak to
face up to the situation that would follow his refusal to
volunteer. He pulled off his boots and made for the bedroom, saying, " It's no good, mam and dad. I have got
to go. Perhaps you will understand one day."

Next day he found that his father also had remained
from work. The only reply Len received to his query on
the matter was a brief, " I be coming with you, Len, to see
fair play. If you are bound to go, then you must come in
the same crush as me, so that I can look after you."

Shortly after breakfast both men presented themselves
before the recruiting sergeant at the police station. A long
queue of other young men was there before them, and they
waited their turn, Len listening vaguely to the conversations taking place around him. He knew practically all
the men and marvelled at their breezy nonchalance, on the
verge of what they regarded as a new life, but for himself
he was nervous and fidgety. Eventually he and Jim
were welcomed by the doctor who had attended Jane before
she died. The sight of him brought sudden tears to Len's
eyes.

The office was crowded with young men, many of whom
were stark naked. Len's mind revolted at what he saw and
heard. The recruiting sergeant, with a satisfied smirk,
brought him back to the work in hand with the words :
" Ah, a fine young man ! I can see now you are going to
be a credit to the forces." He asked Len for his name, age,

and address, then handed the lad over to the doctor, who
curtly bade him undress. Len unconsciously looked around
the crowded room as if mutely asking for some privacy,
but no one took any notice of his appeal, and he began to
strip. The doctor kept him waiting a while, then thumped
his body about, and after a lengthy examination, grunted
to the sergeant : " No good. Cardiac and traces of lung
trouble."

In a maze and hardly knowing what he did or what was
happening around him. Len dressed and went out with his
father. He felt a sudden despair tear at him, for he was
the only one among all those he knew who had been turned
down. His repugnance of the army suddenly evaporated
and he wanted, more than anything, to become a soldier
with the others. A strong feeling of inferiority began to
consume him as he walked slowly, without a word, back up
the hill to Sunny Bank.

Jim broke the news to the weeping Shane, who had not
moved from her chair since they had left the house. Her
eyes immediately brightened up and a soft smile played
around the corners of her mouth.

" I knowed it," she said triumphantly. " Something
told me they wouldn't take my boy away."

" Huh," grunted Jim. " You can thank me for that.
If I did not give a tip to the doctor he would have passed
the boy all right, never fear."

Both Len and Shane knew he lied, but neither contra-
dicted him. That night in bed Len wept tears of sheer
impotence. He wondered what Ezra and Mary would
think of him, and pictured the valley denuded of all young
men except himself, scorned and despised by the women and
the older people. For the first time the glamour of the
war began to grip him. He imagined himself performing
valiant deeds that won Mary's approbation and the applause
of all the people. He felt himself an outcast, and his old
taciturnity grew on him again.

Before the week was out, Jim and his mates were called
up. After the leave-taking in their separate homes, they

proceeded to the Boar's Head, where they all got drunk before making their way to the railway station. Even the staunchest adherents of the chapels gave them bright greetings as they made their way singing and staggering down the hill. Len, however, did not accompany his father. He could not bear a parting in which he thought he should have been the central figure, so having bade his father " Good-bye and good luck " in the house, he went up the mountain and for hours wandered there aimlessly, like a person who has lost all interest in life and merely drifts on.

The days that followed were like a nightmare to him. The newspapers published reports of the horrible atrocities being committed by the Germans, and his blood ran cold when he read in one account that they had crucified a baby to a door. But the horror that filled him was turned to rage when he read later that the Germans were slicing the breasts off the living bodies of the Belgian women they captured.

One morning Mr. Hicks rode to the colliery-yard and called upon all the men below the age of forty—he was forty-one himself—to join the colours and avenge the atrocities.

Scores of men reponded to the appeal, marching down the hill behind Mr. Hicks, and next day a recruiting office was opened at the end of the bridge leading to the colliery.

The following Sunday the big theatre was taken over for a recruiting-meeting. Len was drawn to this like a fly to a web. All the week the streets and the pits were buzzing with talk of the revelation of atrocities and cruelties that were going to be made. Huge placards covered the hoardings and sidings of the valleys, and empty trams came down the pits with chalked slogans advertising the meeting.

When Len arrived a long queue was already formed half-way up Main Street. He noticed Mary, who beckoned him beside her. They found the huge theatre a mass of flaunting Union Jacks, and photographs of stern-looking men in military uniforms. On the platform were a well-known Trade Union official in the uniform of an officer, a short, fat clean-shaven man who edited a famous journal and was later imprisoned for swindling, the bishop in his robes, Mr. Evans Cardi, a few local preachers, the vicar from the church, Lord Cwmardy, Mr. Hicks, and some military officers, together with a man in a blue-flannel nondescript uniform who had been brought specially from the military hospital a hundred miles away to be presented at Cwmardy as one of the first heroes wounded in the war.

The meeting opened with the singing of the National Anthem. When this was over the Trade Union official stepped to the front of the stage.

" Men and women of the valley," he said, swelling out his chest, " I want you to show our distinguished visitors how you can sing the ancient hymns of Wales. Put your hearts into ' Hen Wlad Fy Nghadia,' boys." He began the tune himself, his beautiful voice filling the hall and stirring the audience into emulation. At its conclusion Mr. Hicks and Ezra stepped forward as joint chairmen of the meeting, and the latter having outlined the procedure, continued :

" I am on this platform to-day not because I believe in war but because I believe in right. When right is threatened, then we are justified in using might to protect it. If this were a war of aggression on our part I should oppose it with all the strength in my power, but as a man and a worker who has suffered, I cannot stand aside and see all the democratic traditions for which men have died being trampled underfoot by unscrupulous rulers of other nations. If the people of these nations cannot see how they are being misled, and take up arms at the behest of their rulers, then our reply must be sharp and emphatic. For every one of them who takes up arms against right and justice, we must have two to defend it."

When the cheering had subsided, Ezra called on the editor to address the meeting. " You have all heard or read of our famous friend," said Ezra in his introductory remarks. " Therefore I have no need to explain who he is, other than to say that his fearless exposition through his journal of all that is unfair and unjust demands the appreciation of every decent man and woman of our valley."

The fat man stepped forward to a storm of applause. His greasy face shone in the glare of the footlights and his breath came in wheezy gasps from the strain imposed on his overfull paunch.

"Ladies and gentlemen," he said, wisely clearing his throat, "I am indeed pleased to know my little efforts in the sacred cause of humanity are appreciated by you. To-day that humanity is in the melting-pot. An octopus of horror creeps over the world in the guise of men. Heartless monsters rape the virgin soil of Europe with obscene jack-booted feet. To-day our country is called upon to defend humanity, to defend righteousness and all that is good and pure from the onslaught of Hunnish barbarians. I have come specially this night with proof for every word I utter."

He kept on for an hour retailing tales of torture and lust inflicted on innocent people by the Germans. His eyes glistened and his jelly-like flesh quivered in an ecstasy produced by his own words and thoughts. The speech lifted the men and women in the meeting to a pitch of furious indignation. Howls of execration and sharp cries of bitterness and hate filled the hall as he unfolded horror after horror.

Mr. Hicks took the chair at the conclusion of the speech and immediately called upon Lord Cwmardy. The latter made a brief statement during which he remarked, "All those of you employed in the pits of my company—and that means all the pits in the valley," he added as an aside which met with responsive applause—"well, those of you, I repeat, who do your duty to your King and your country in this time of common danger and crisis need have no worry about your homes. More than this, every man who leaves my pits for the war will have his place in that pit sacredly safeguarded, so that when he returns home he can step back into his work as if he had never left it." A storm of clapping greeted him at the end of the speech.

The Trade Union leader was next called upon. Solemnly holding himself as erect as possible in his uniform and holding the sword with untrained hand to his side, he marched to the front of the stage to the accompaniment of wild cheers. The people rose to their feet, singing and shouting. Red-faced and awkward, the speaker waited until the tumult had subsided before saying, slowly at first, then with increasing tempo :

" Men and women of this glorious valley, the civilisation and freedom built up by the untold sacrifices of the forefathers of our land is being menaced by the iron heel of war and destruction. The whole world to-day is looking at our country, and every eye in the country is looking at this valley. Shall it ever be said that, for the first time in our history, we have been found wanting ? I say no, a thousand times no. Our nation is to-day united as it has never been before. All sections are blended in the common desire to save democracy in the name of our holy God. To-night on this platform you see me with Lord Cwmardy, my Lord the Bishop, and the other good friends. What is it that has brought me, a true son of the people, into the same harness as those we used to think our enemies ? It is the common human urge, my friends, to sink our petty little quarrels when the cause of justice and freedom is threatened. After all, when danger threatens it is then we realise that we are all brothers. To-night, in all humbleness and sincerity, I am asking every one of you who is eligible to join up with me. Let me lead you on the battlefield as I have led you at home. I do not ask any of you to do what I am not prepared to do myself. The King has graciously given me a commission, not in honour to myself, but in honour to you whom I represent. ' Go,' said His Majesty to me, ' back to those wonderful people in your vales and in your pits. Tell them the Empire is calling them to its defence.' Yes, friends, our empire, our country, our homes are in danger. Who will follow me in defence of all they love and hold dear ? "

His voice lifted into a dramatic tension on this last appeal.

For a moment there was breathless silence, then a roar of " I will " surged through the hall as a mass of men rushed down the aisle towards the platform. In a second the recruiting sergeant, blazoning with medals, sprang from the wings to the stage. The bishop beckoned to Mr. Hicks, who, after a few whispered words, walked to the edge of the platform and held up his hand. It was several minutes before a measure of calm asserted itself and the long line of men on their way to the stage halted.

" Hem," began Mr. Hicks, " our bishop thinks that so solemn an occasion should not be allowed to pass without thanking the Lord for putting courage into the hearts of these men who are now ready to defend the faith and asking Him to extend to them His grace."

All present bowed their heads while the bishop stuttered a prayer interspersed with hiccoughs. This over, Mr. Hicks proceeded, " As our men are joining up in the army of justice and truth, it is the bishop's wish we should give praise by singing the hymns ' Onward Christian Soldiers ' and ' Abide with Me.' "

The Trade Union leader lifted his voice in the opening notes, and as everyone took up the hymn, the men were swept towards the recruiting sergeant who, sweating and silently swearing, took their names and addresses. He was overcome by the numbers and called upon the other people on the platform to help him. Before the meeting concluded, Lord Cwmardy again walked to the front of the stage.

" It is fitting," he announced, " that I should report that five hundred and ten men have volunteered in this meeting to enter battle on the side of the just and the right."

Both Mary and Len were overcome by the fervour of the whole proceedings. The lights, emphasising the glamorous colours of the decorations, seemed to dance in the vibrations of the mass-singing and swept the people forward on waves of hysterical emotion.

CHAPTER XVI

Len works for Peace

WHEN Len returned home he missed his father from the usual chair and, without thinking, asked Shane :

" Where's dad, then ?   He's late to-night, i'n't he ? "

Shane looked hard at him for a moment, then began to cry. Len realised his mistake and tried to soothe her. But to no avail.

" Your dad be gone, Len bach," she moaned.   " Perhaps he will never come back to us.   The good Lord alone knows what he have gone for.   I don't.   They do say the Shermans are cruel.   Perhaps they be ; I don't know.   But wasn't our own sodgers cruel that night they did shoot down our men for nothing ?   Them was supposed to be our own flesh and blood, but that did make no difference.   When their guns went ' bang,' our men did drop just as sure as if it was Sherman guns."   She lapsed into silence, but her words brought Len back to himself.

The vague revolt in his heart seemed to find a focus-point in her words.   He began to wonder vaguely how the country could be in danger when the supposed enemy was the other side of the water.   He brought back to mind incidents he had witnessed during the strike, and pondered the difference in men when they wore different clothes.   He thought to himself that his mother was right when she questioned the distinction between English bullets fired at Englishmen and German bullets fired at Belgian people. He was not quite clear or fixed, but nevertheless he was beginning to find a mental balance.

In the weeks that followed he came to see the situation more clearly, and he was helped by a lecturer who came to the Circle to explain what the war meant.   The lecturer stated it was a fight between robber states, each of whom was intent upon exploiting its own people and each other. He used the words " cannon-fodder " and this reminded Len of the dark-haired man in the excursion train. The lecture as a whole made a great impression upon Len's outlook, and a new vista of thought and understanding opened up before him. He learned that the young lecturer called himself a revolutionary and believed that nothing would come right until this revolution had taken place. He had heard of revolutions before, but never in such a positive way as that presented by the lecturer, and at the conclusion of the lecture he asked :

" What does the lecturer actually mean by the revolution ? Does he mean that we have got to have a civil war and slaughter each other ? "

The lecturer smiled. " Not quite so crude as that," he answered. " What I meant is that the workers will have to be armed in order to overcome the resistance of the capitalist class, who will never give up their power by peaceful measures. Even if we had a majority in Parliament," he continued, " the capitalists would use the armed forces of the State against the government of the day, if that government was against their interests."

Len failed to see how this contingency could occur. He believed that the government was the final authority and that whatever measures it decided were final and binding upon everyone. He did not agree that it would be necessary to have a mass slaughter in order to maintain the conditions of the workers. He was appalled by the thought of his fellow countrymen doing to each other what they were all now doing to the Germans. But in spite of Len's opposition on this matter the lecturer had cleared, to a large extent, the fog of doubt that assailed him in relation to the war.

Later in the evening John Library suggested that the Circle should organise a public meeting at which the lecturer could put his point of view against the war. This was enthusiastically agreed to, and Len and Mary were deputed to make the necessary arrangements. They failed to get the theatre for the meeting and had to content themselves with the huge baths that were hidden in a corner of the valley practically inaccessible after dark.

Len continued to ponder the problem of the war. He began to mentally query how Ezra could find it possible to stand on the same platform as Mr. Hicks and Lord Cwmardy after all they had done against the workmen during the strike. In Len's mind nothing could wipe that out. He felt Ezra's action to be an insult to those victims of the soldier's bullets who now lay resting in the cemetery. He kept brooding over the matter and thought to raise it with Mary. But he feared risking her displeasure, because he knew once the subject was broached it could only end in a condemnation of Ezra.

Despite his introspective doubts the arrangements for the public meeting went on apace. Mary painted attractive posters to advertise it, which Len pasted on the hoardings and the walls in the early hours of the morning.

Two days prior to the meeting Len received a message in the pit that Mr. Hicks would like to see him at the end of the shift. Throughout the remainder of the day Len wondered why he was wanted. He finished a little earlier than usual and was among the first to ascend the shaft. He proceeded direct to the colliery office, the lamp swinging on his belt.

Rapping on the inner door that led to Mr. Hicks' private room, he waited nervously. He heard a cough and a rustling of paper inside, followed by an authoritative " Come in."

Hesitantly Len opened the door and walked towards the smiling Mr. Hicks, seated at a desk in the centre of the room. He heard the door close behind him and glanced around abruptly. The police-inspector, his back to the door, stood facing him, and Mr. Hicks greeted him with the remark :

" Well, my boy, how are things going with you ? I hear you have a pretty good place now."

Len nodded without saying a word.

"Hemm," went on Mr. Hicks, "I am glad to hear that, because nothing pleases me more than to know that my men are contented. By the way," he added, "I understand you are one of the youngest men we have working a place of his own."

This pulled Len together. "That may be so," he answered, "but I don't think it necessary to call me into the office specially to tell me that, Mr. Hicks."

"Quite so, quite so," commented the latter. "As a matter of fact," he added, "I didn't send for you for that purpose at all. Inspector Price would like to have a chat with you."

Len turned to the huge man who was now sitting on the chair near Mr. Hicks.

"Yes," said the Inspector. "Just a few words, Len, without prejudice to anyone. They tell me that you were a pretty big figure during the strike."

Len did not reply, and the other went on as if he had made no pause. "Yes. I was told you did a lot of things then that in ordinary times some of us would have to take notice of. But we must let bygones be bygones, eh? Now, what I want to speak to you about is this meeting I'm told you have in the Baths next Sunday. Something to do with the war, isn't it?" Len made no answer, but the reason for his summons to the office slowly dawned on him.

"Well, well," went on the Inspector. "Fancy you mixing up with things like that, Len. Indeed, I'm surprised at you. I'm sure your mother would be shocked to know your intentions, especially when your father is risking his life at the front to defend all the good things you are now enjoying."

Len could stand it no longer, his blood was at boiling-point.

"Look here," he burst out, "what are you driving at, Inspector? Why don't you tell me straight what you have got in your mind instead of beating about the bush like this?"

The Inspector was taken aback for a moment, but soon regained his urbane equanimity.

" Yes, that's it," he said quietly. " Let's have it straight, and here it is. A young man like you, working in a good place with good money, while men old enough to be your father are fighting and dying, has a right to ask for things straight. But," he flashed out, " they should not have the right to organise meetings for the purpose of spreading sedition and adding further danger to those now fighting. One would think that a man like you would be satisfied to skim the cream off the good things other men die to give you."

Len went white. He tried to stutter a reply, but the Inspector hurried on, his voice getting louder and more threatening with each word.

" You ought to be damn well ashamed of yourself, skulking here at home when you should be carrying a gun in defence of your country ! "

Len braced himself. " What about yourself ! " he retorted. " You are bigger and more able than I am to carry a gun and you are much younger than my father, who is already there. I tried to join in the first week, but they refused to accept me because of my heart and chest."

His effrontery infuriated the Inspector, who sprang to his feet and shouted :

" You bloody little whippersnapper, how dare you talk to me like that ? For two pins I'd make you glad to stop in bed for a month ! "

Len cowered before the huge, raised fist, but the Inspector recovered himself before the blow fell, and Mr. Hicks drew him to a corner of the room out of Len's hearing. For some minutes they talked rapidly, and when they returned to their places both were smiling again.

" Excuse me losing my temper, Len," said the Inspector. " I have not been too well lately and my temper is a bit short. Actually I have taken a liking to you. I wouldn't, for instance, like to see Mr. Hicks throw you out of a good place because you are mixed up with a gang who are using you for their own purpose. No," he went on, " nor would I like see the military authorities grabbing you in spite of your health and drafting you straight to the war with very little training. Think, Len. If you carry on with this meeting you will only land yourself in trouble and I won't be able to help you. Remember, I cannot be responsible for anything that happens in the meeting if you persist in it."

No more was said, but Len understood what was implied. He turned and left the room, his heart throbbing against his ribs. In his perturbation and excitement he could not even wait to go home and bath before seeing Mary, but went straight to her house. She gave a little gasp of surprise when she saw his blackened face and pit clothes.

" Great scott ! " she exclaimed. " Has anything serious happened, Len ? "

" No, no," he assured her hurriedly. " In any case, nothing very serious, but something very important."

She led the way to the kitchen without another word and laid an old newspaper on a chair for him to sit on. Gingerly seating himself, Len related all that had transpired. Mary listened in silence. When he had finished, she paced the kitchen agitatedly.

" I never thought of such a thing," she murmured. " They as good as called you a traitor to your country, Len, if you continued with the meeting."

" Ay. But they did more than that, Mary. They said that you and other members of the committee were bigger traitors than me and were using me for your own ends."

This had not struck Mary until Len's words brought it to her mind with a jerk.

" No man can call me a traitor to my country," she blurted out indignantly. " I agreed to the meeting because I believe it fair that everyone should have the right to their opinion, even if it happens to be against my own. I believe in this war," she continued more vehemently. " Who can read of those poor babies and those helpless nuns being slaughtered by the Germans and think they shouldn't be stopped, whatever "—she quoted the next phrase from the recent speech of a famous statesman— " whatever it may cost in blood or treasure ? "

Her bosom rose and fell under the pressure of her emotions. Len felt her magnetic strength pull him, as it always did in moments of excitement, but he checked himself.

" I don't agree with you," he said bravely. " The Germans are only men like those who have gone from our pits to fight them. I can't believe that any men, whether they are Germans or no, can do the terrible things we read about."

She turned on him with a sneer. " Perhaps you think all the papers are saying lies, that all the preachers and parsons are liars, that only you yourself know what the truth is." The pain that suddenly lined his face checked her. " Think, Len," she pleaded more softly, " you saw that man in the meeting showing us photos and other proofs of what is being done." She snatched a paper from the little sideboard as if she wanted to excuse her words yet convince him he was wrong. " Look at this, where it says the Germans are boiling down the corpses of their own dead soldiers to make grease for the guns."

Len looked and sickened. His faith in his own opinion wavered.

" Well," he asked unsteadily, " what shall we do about the meeting ? " She hesitated to give a definite reply. Something told her she had been on the verge of appearing a coward in his eyes.

" Perhaps we had better wait till dad comes home," she answered cautiously.

He assented, saying he would go home for dinner and bath and return when he was clean.

Mary's words had startled him, but even in the turmoil of conflicting thoughts he began to feel himself more strong and firm. He felt confidence and a determination welling up in him. The feeling was something new. Always, in the past, when he had been unable to answer arguments or solve problems he had capitulated either to Ezra or to Mary. Now he began to question earnestly whether he had been at fault in blindly following the opinions of others.

Shane met him at the door, her face was haggard and her eyes looked weary and heavy.

" No letter to-day again, Len bach." Her voice had in it a tone of hopelessness. " Something must have happened to him. He have never kept me so long without writing before."

Len tried to console her. " It's all right, mam," he said, although he hardly knew what to think himself at the fact that not a single letter had yet been received from Jim. " There is nothing wrong with him. I expect they are pretty busy out there now and they haven't got much time for writing letters. You can venture, mam," he added, " if there was anything wrong we would hear quick enough."

" Let's hope you are right. Many is the time I've nagged him over nothing," she murmured, weeping softly into her apron.

Len did not take long bathing, and was soon back at Mary's house, where Ezra was already waiting.

" Well," commenced the latter, when Len was seated, " I understand you and Mary have been having a squabble over the war."

" No, dad," broke in Mary, " I didn't say we had a row."

" Well," said Ezra, " let's say you had a few words. Now let me see, as far as I can gather the police desire that your meeting on Sunday should be called off. You and Len disagree on this. In am of the opinion that the meeting, for Len's sake, should be abandoned. What is the position ? " he continued. " In the present state of public opinion any statement against the war, in which so many of the men from our own valley are engaged, would result in a riot. The people who would be held responsible for anything said would not be the ones who actually said them, but those who organised the meeting. Will Morris can say what he likes and get away back to his home, but you, Len, will have to remain here and face the music. No, apart from anything else, I think for your own safety you should call it off. You will understand that in these circumstances I can't allow Mary to risk being a party to this. I'm very serious about the whole matter, Len, and I hope you have sufficient faith to believe that what I'm telling you is for the best for everyone concerned."

Len looked at him a moment, then turning his eyes to Mary, said to both of them : " I think you are wrong. Although I don't know what it is and can't explain it, something inside me tells me that we must let the people know the two sides of the war. Wherever we turn now we only hear one side. Everybody is wrong and terrible and cruel except our own people. I can't believe this. There are bound to be some decent people among the Germans. We are told that they do this, that, and the other, but I can't forget what our own soldiers did to us during the strike. No," he added, as if soliloquising with himself, " I love and respect you both, but I can't do something which I don't believe to be right. I hope," he pleaded " you won't think any the less of me for this."

A strangely warm light crept into Mary's eyes at the words, but neither she nor her father said anything more as Len, with downcast eyes and bent shoulders, made for the door.

The next evening Len saw John Library, and as a result of their chat went across the mountain to the other valley where Will Morris lived. The latter was very pleased to see him, and they discussed the meeting until late in the evening. When Len left it was dark as death, but he knew the mountain better than he knew his own mind and arrived home safely.

Shane's pain-shadowed eyes told him she had received no letter from Jim, but she made no remark while Len ate the frugal supper. When he had finished she asked him if he would wait in the queue for the pound of margarine ration allocated to them. Although he was tired and anxious to go to bed he immediately assented, and putting on his overcoat, he bade her good-night. The night seemed blacker than ever as he made his way towards the main street. When he reached the general stores of Mr. Evans Cardi, some fifty or sixty men and women were already queued up. This was not the first time Len had kept the queue all night for his mother to get the rations in the morning. He sat on a window-sill tucking his arms round his chest to keep it warm. Soft snowflakes were beginning to spangle the black air, and seemed to quiver in the throb from the pits before they finally settled on the ground. Soon everyone in the queue was covered by a snowy surplice. Many of them had learned, after much practice, to fall asleep on their feet, but the cold that penetrated his clothes prevented Len from doing so. He shook the snow from his sodden garments and found its absence made him feel colder. His feet and face went numb, an excruciating pain gripped his toes and he felt the muscles of his face tighten into rigidity. He tried to loosen them by working his mouth, but a slow shiver spread from his legs until it seized his whole body. The pain became intolerable and he gave himself a vigorous shake, which sent pins and needles rushing through him. Clenching his teeth, he began rubbing his legs, but the damp cloth in contact with his flesh made him more uncomfortable than ever. He had an insane desire to leave the queue and go back home. He pictured the kitchen and its big fire warming the armchair, which had become his favourite seat since his father had gone to the war. The thought of a cup of hot, unsweetened tea and a slice of warm, unbuttered toast moistened his mouth and nearly drove him frantic. Unconsciously he moved forward, but with an effort of will he restrained himself, for he knew that if he returned home Shane would take his place in the queue.

Throughout the night he waited with the others. He started to count the minutes and dropped off into a standing, half-conscious doze in which he saw Mary looking at him from the curb, and at last, about five o'clock,

Shane and other women came to relieve their men. Peering at every face, Shane eventually spotted Len sitting erect against the wet window pane. She gave him a gentle shake.

" Come, Len bach," she ordered. " It's time for you to go back up the house and change for work. I have left the toast lovely and warm in the oven for you and the tea-pot is on the hob. All you got to do is put the water in it."

Len felt unable to get up from the sill. He desired more than anything in the world to remain where he was without moving, and it required all his mental strength to drag his body away. His chest burned and thick mucus stuck in his throat. He coughed and spat it into the gutter.

" Take care of yourself, mam," he bade her. " Put the shawl over your head. Good-morning."

When he reached Sunny Bank his breath came in gasping sobs that hurt him. He thawed his body before the huge fire Shane had left him and drank the tea, but he could not eat the dry, toasted bread. It crumbled like dry sawdust in his mouth, nearly making him sick, and he spat out the half-masticated lump that looked like a black pebble in the grate. His shivering fingers drew on the pit-clothes, disturbing the dry coal-dust on them, which blew about in a little thin cloud. Putting his hand in his trouser pocket he felt something squirm, and he pulled out a huge red cock-roach, which he immediately threw on the fire. He gazed abstractedly at its brief, futile struggle and at the tiny green, crackling flame that forced its way with a hiss through the red glow, then stooping under the table he picked up his boots. Immediately there was a rush of squirming black beetles. The floor became black with them as they headed for their nests, and as Len squashed them with the heel of his boot, each blow made a wet-sounding squelch. He caught the broom from the corner and swept the black patches towards the grate, but their white entrails remained on the floor and he left these for his mother to remove.

Throughout the day he had to fight to keep his eyes open in the pit, afraid to sit down for dinner in case he fell asleep.

10

Most of the other men in the barry were in the same predicament. His movements were those of an automaton, and at the end of the day he did not know how many trams he had filled or how much work he had done. He felt no desire to leave the pit, all he wanted was to lie down and sleep. Dragging his feet behind him, he followed the long trail of tired, silent shadows making for the pit bottom. The air on the surface, sweeping over the slushy black snow that covered the valley, revived him, and his feet became lighter as he hastened down the hill towards Sunny Bank.

Shane was sitting near the fire, her head bent on her hands, when he entered.

" Hullo," he said in surprise. " What's wrong, mam ? Have you heard from dad ? "

Without looking up she answered, " No, Len bach. Not a word have I had from him yet."

He tried to comfort her, but he felt himself a hypocrite and a liar even as the words passed his mouth. He knew that each morning she waited, full of forced, happy anticipation, for the sound of the postman's feet entering the street, that she followed each step with a bursting heart, her breath coming more quickly as he approached, but ceasing entirely for a moment as he passed the house. If he paused a moment for some reason outside the door she would quiver in a flutter of excited agitation, but when he passed her whole body would relax. Len knew that every woman in the street dreaded the sight of the old man who carried telegrams and that when he entered a street everyone was overcome with nervous anticipation.

Shane brought him from his thoughts.

" It is not that this time," she said. " You know I did take your place in the queue this morning. When half-past eight come, Mr. Evans pulled the shutters from his window and started to serve the people who was waiting. Before he had served half of us, he said that the food was nearly all gone and that he wouldn't be able to serve us all till more was sent in. Everybody did look stunned for a minute, then, before I knowed what was happening somebody behind gave me a push and in a flash everybody there was pushing and shouting and rushing. Like wild animals they was, Len. I be 'shamed of them. They broke the window and stole ev'ry scrap that was in the shop." The tears again filled her eyes.

" Never mind, mam anwyl," soothed Len. " We will manage somehow. Perhaps he will have some more rations in by to-night, and he is bound to give us what is coming to us on our ration cards." Even while he spoke a pang of hunger tore at his stomach, giving him spasms of giddiness.

Shane looked up from her shawl. " Oh, it's not so bad as that. When they did rush, I did not let them have all their own way. Oh no. I was never a woman to stand being pushed about. So I did push with them, and when they broke the window I was close enough to have this packet of saccharin and some margarine."

Len smiled a little at her words and sat down to drink the potato soup she had made for his dinner. The saccharin made his tea sickly and left a bitter after-taste in his mouth, but it was better than no sugar or sweetening. On Shane's advice he ate dry bread, because she thought she had discovered a method of turning a small quantity of margarine into three times as much butter.

After Len had bathed he helped her bring out the large earthenware pan in which she made bread. She put the lump of margarine into this and poured about two quarts of milk on top of it, then stirred the mixture vigorously with the wooden spoon that she used to turn the clothes in the boiler. When her arm got tired and heavy she handed the spoon to Len, and for hours they kept this up, until at last Shane declared the flaccid, greasy-looking yellow mass in the pan was butter. Len was glad to hear this for his back felt as if it were broken and his arms were like lead.

The days that followed passed slowly. He heard no more from Mr. Hicks or the Inspector about the meeting, nor had he seen Mary since the day he declared his intention of carrying on. The arrangements were now completed and from scraps of conversation he picked up in the streets and in the pit he knew it would either be a packed meeting or that there would be so few present that it would have to be cancelled.

When the Sunday arrived, Len was quivering with excitement. He put on his best suit, which he had not worn since the excursion with the Circle, and in the late afternoon John Library and the speaker came to the house. Their appearance flustered Shane, who immediately began dusting the chairs with her apron, at the same time apologising because she had nothing nice in the house to offer them.

" But at the same time," she averred, " you are welcome to what ever we have got."

The two men calmed her flurry and in a short time they rose and went off with Len to the meeting. When they arrived at the Baths they found the doors had been smashed in and that the huge place was packed to suffocation with a mass of people singing patriotic songs at the top of their voices, their faces hidden in a cloud of blue tobacco smoke.

John Library took the chair. His snowy white hair glistened in the light, throwing a dignified halo around his thin, austere face. Ben the Barber, whom they met near the entrance, insisted upon coming on to the platform, and just as Len was settling himself in the chair he heard a whispered voice calling his name from the front. His heart gave a leap as he peered through the smoke and saw Mary sitting in the front row of seats beckoning to him shyly. He quickly went towards her.

" Something forced me to come to-night," she said softly, not looking at him. " I felt I couldn't remain away and leave you fight this out alone, even though I still believe dad is right."

Len caught her hand in his and pressed it to his chest, suddenly forgetting where he was and oblivious to everyone but himself and Mary. He tried to say something, but it stuck in his throat. Instead he bent his head and looked

her straight in the eyes with a glance that burned into her
consciousness the pleasure her presence and words had
given him. But a cough from behind brought him back
to the meeting, and he resumed his seat.

John, speaking quietly, opened the proceedings.

" Fellow working men and women," he said, " we are met
here to-night to listen to a speech on a matter that concerns
every one of us." A deep silence of expectation fell over the
audience at his first words. " I know that in many parts
of the country it would be very dangerous to hold a similar
meeting to this and say what is going to be said here. But
I have faith in the people of the valley. I believe that
even in your sorrows and worries, even in your love for
your country you are sensible enough to listen to every
sincere point of view, even if that point of view should be
opposed to yours at the moment. The strike has proven
that there is a very strong sense of fair play among our
people and that we always incline to take the side of the
weak and defenceless. Already young Len here, who has
done a lot to make this meeting a success, has been threatened by certain people. He has been told that if the
meeting goes on he will lose his job in the pit, will be drafted,
in spite of his health, to the war, and that possibly physical
violence will be done to him."

Loud cries of " Shame " from all parts of the hall greeted
this information, and John continued : " I don't believe
our boys across the water are fighting and dying for such
things as that. They are there, rightly or wrongly is not
for me to say, defending democracy and freedom, where
every man has the right to his own opinions and liberty to
express them. You will have noticed that not a single
policeman is near our meeting to-night, whereas if it had
been a meeting to recruit our boys to the war, they would
be all over the place." A gust of ironic laughter and shouts
of " That's so " swept the hall. " But although they are
not here in uniform," continued the chairman, " among us
is a stranger in ordinary clothes who has been sent specially
to take notes. We welcome him and hope he will put down

what is actually said by the speaker and not what he would like the speaker to say."

A thin thread of applause circled the audience when the black-haired young man with a cadaverous face and self-confident manner walked to the front. " Comrades," he said, " I have been warned and advised that if I came here to-night it would be the last meeting I would ever speak at, and that I would be taken out feet first. If such is to be my fate, if I am to be maimed at the hands of my fellow workers, so be it. I shall be content to know that I die for principles that are dear to my heart and at the hands of people whom I love. All that I ask you to-night is that you listen to me patiently when I am speaking. When I finish the matter is in your hands."

Sympathetic applause broke out, mingled with shouts of " Good kid. Spit it out straight ; you won't be hurt here."

The speaker paused a moment and put his right thumb into the armhole of his waistcoat, leaving the other free to gesticulate. He spoke coldly and dispassionately of the causes of the war as he saw them. Then he began to warm up as he came to the war itself. " What is actually happening ? " he asked. " While the papers and the propagandists are patriotically howling in the names of God, King, and humanity for the defence of their country, while the business people of the land are shouting of the sacrifices they are making, the capitalists of this country, anxious to make profits wherever they can and however they can, not caring how many die, are selling munitions to the very countries we are fighting against. Our men are left torn and mangled on barbed wire exported from our country to the enemy. Preachers declare that God is on our side—and our men are rotting in the swamps of Gallipoli, shot down by bullets made in England."

This statement was followed by a wild hubbub throughout the hall. The speaker waited till the noise died down, then went on. " The war is a war of competing capitalists and conflicting interests. We are merely pawns in the horrible game ; flesh and blood whose very destruction becomes

profitable. Each bullet that finds a bed in a human breast
is a bullet that carries a profit. In order that our minds are
prepared to take our bodies to the slaughter, our emotions
are whipped up into a frenzy. Every lie, every distortion
that can help to achieve this mad end is used in press and
on platform, ay, and in pulpit. They try to prove to us
that God is on our side, just as the German capitalists are
telling their people that the same God is on their side.
Our rulers strangle freedom in the name of democracy, they
kill Christianity in the name of religion ; they slaughter
millions of the cream of the world in the name of peace.
Oh, my friends, can you not see that these vultures prey on
us living and dead ? "

He paused in the dead silence, his chest rising and falling
visibly with emotion, before he concluded, " I want to say
that I would sooner die here and now, at the hands of my
own people, than I would carry a gun to destroy my
fellow workers, in the interest of our joint enemies."

The fervent force of his words captured the people ;
it shocked and startled them. For some moments there
was complete silence, which was eventually broken by
isolated claps here and there that rose higher in increasing
numbers until the applause was taken up by everyone.
It seemed that the spell which had gripped the people ever
since the war had started was broken by the words. The
very thing he had accused the capitalists of doing he had,
consciously or unconsciously, done himself. He had
appealed to the people through their emotions, had played
on their feelings and their deep subconscious desire for the
war to end. But, after lifting them to heights of emotional
enthusiasm, he had left them dangling with no foundation
for their feet. He had not told them what they could do
to end the war. His speech had been a declaration of
personal faith and not an exposition of policy, and though
everyone in the meeting was thrilled, when they left they
were completely in the dark as to what they could do.

Len was elated that nothing untoward had occurred and
that the speaker had not been heckled or interrupted. He

had followed every word of the speech avidly and, like everyone else, had been shocked at some of the horrible implications of the speaker's remarks. He felt half satisfied, like a starving man who eats a small sandwich ; and the problem of how the war could be stopped confronted him more sharply than ever after the speech.

On the way home he asked Mary how the speech had affected her. She told him :

" I felt horrified when he said that the capitalists are selling munitions to our enemies. I cannot believe that men can be so inhuman. I believe the speaker was quite genuine and believed all he said, but that he is being misled and makes desires into facts."

Len made no retort for a while. His arm was round her shoulders. Occasionally a harsh cough shook her and he felt her tremble beneath his arm. His own body responded as if to an electric shock, and pressing her face to his shoulder, he murmured incoherent caressing endearments into her ear. After a while she asked what he thought about the meeting. He took a little time to gather his thoughts before he replied : " I think the speaker spoke the truth ; that every word was gospel. But what worries me is how can we stop it all ? Oh," he wailed, turning her round till she faced him and both stood still, " how can we stop these men of ours being slaughtered as they are ? Day after day more of them are killed, and the post office has had to put extra boys on to carry the telegrams from the War Office."

Mary rested her head on his chest. She felt lost in a maze of contradictions. She wanted to believe with her father that the war was in defence of all that the people held dear, but Len's convinced attitude and the words of the speaker had shaken her more than she cared to admit even to herself.

" Even if it were true," she remarked, " it wouldn't make the war wrong or our cause less great and worthy."

Len nodded in silence, but did not feel capable of arguing the matter out. He was himself floating in a mental whirlpool, unable to find equilibrium, and though they did not discuss the matter further that night it remained the chief thought in their minds.

In the pits next day the speech was on everyone's tongue. It had sent a wave of horror through the valley, but the resentment was not so much against the war as against the people they were told were making a profit out of it. Len however, heard no more of the threats that had been made. He knew that John Library's exposure of them had made them too obvious and glaring to be put into effect. For both Mr. Hicks and the Inspector had anticipated and desired a different outcome to the meeting.

CHAPTER XVII

The War draws to an End

A FEW days later Len heard that the speaker had been arrested at his home the previous night and had been tried for sedition that morning. John Library told him that he had been given the alternative of paying a £20 fine or doing two months in prison, and his old eyes shined brightly as he added : " When he heard the magistrate pass the sentence, he lifted his chin in the air and said, ' You may as well take me down now, because I shall never pay twenty pounds for speaking the truth ! ' "

Len was proud he had been associated, if only for a few hours, with such a man. He felt it was the same action he himself would have taken in similar circumstances, and the fact that the other had already done it and issued his challenge in open court thrilled him.

Mr. Hicks and the Inspector organised another recruiting campaign in the valley. The chapels took the matter up, and for a whole week special prayers were offered for victory on the battlefields. Preachers called upon the men to join up in defence of God's laws, that were being violated so ruthlessly by the Germans, and girls sent white feathers through the post to the few young men who were still at home. Len, who received a few of these, felt they were doubly unjust because, as he reasoned, even apart from his growing convictions, he had offered himself for service during the first week. In spite of this he failed to console himself when he saw boys of fifteen and sixteen joining up. The terrific campaign that was waged for the war made him, as it made most men still wearing civilian clothes, feel guilty of something cowardly, and in spite of his reasoning he could not rid himself of the feeling.

At last, when this campaign had practically denuded the pits of all young, able-bodied men, a famous man, sent specially from London, appeared in the valley. He told the people they had served their country well and that no more men could be taken. " The pits," he declared " have become part of the battle-front and are as important as the first-line trenches. You can all regard yourselves as soldiers fighting on the side of right against might. You can look upon your working clothes as uniforms of honour and the pits as key positions."

This change of attitude considerably encouraged those who were left at home, and they redoubled their work in the pits. They were told to regard every lump of coal as a bullet, and the more bullets the country could have the sooner would the enemy be defeated and the war ended.

Presently Len began to notice the abnormal number of strange officials and under-officials who were started at the colliery. Most of them were young men, and he inquired from John Library who they were. The old man, with a twinkle in his eyes, answered : " Oh, they are the sons and other relatives of the people who are urging our men to the front. Mr. Hicks' son is among them, and so is Lord Cwmardy's."

One day when he handed his pay over to Shane she grumbled : " I don't know what I am going to do with this. It isn't half enough to go round."

Len looked at her in amazement. " Why, mam," he said reproachfully, " I am earning more money now than I have ever earned, and I am not getting half the food I was having when dad was home."

Shane bridled at the insinuation she thought she saw in his remarks.

" Think you I be wasting your money ? " she demanded. " Because if you do you can put it out of your mind now. I do know you are bringing in more, but it do take a lot more than the extra you do have to pay for the little bit of food we are allowed. Everything is gone up three and four times in the last months, and I can't stretch the little extra to meet it all."

Len was immediately sorry for his words. He saw how he had neglected her since Jim had gone to the war and how he had left her to her own devices, with the result that he did not know how things were going in the house. He thought it peculiar that, following upon this conversation with his mother, he should notice for the first time that most of the talk in the pit centred on the question of the cost of living. Week after week it was the same. Will Smallbeer summed the matter up nicely when all the men were having dinner back on the roadway one day. " By Christ," he said, " a pound note do go under your bloody nose now. All you got to do is to buy three penny apples and it is gone."

" Well," remarked another, munching a lump of black dried bread that looked like half-chewed tobacco, " we can't 'spect to be in a great war like this without knowing it."

Len felt impelled to intervene. " That's all right," he said, " but I bet the rich people are getting everything they want, high prices or no, and in spite of all rationing cards. If our wages have been highered it is nothing compared to the way which the cost of living have gone up. Not only that, but the company are now charging more than five times extra for coal and we don't get twice as much pay for filling it. Once the price of coal rises everything else follows, and the little bit of extra money given to us is swamped before we have it."

The men in general agreed with these sentiments, and that night Len called on Ezra and reported what he had heard in the pits, suggesting that a meeting of the men should be called to discuss the whole matter. Ezra pondered a moment before saying :

" I agree with you, Len, that something should be done, but I don't see where a meeting of the men could help us in any way. The matter, you see, is now in the hands of the Federation Executive and the Government. We cannot go over their heads in any way at this critical stage in the war."

" I don't see where that is against us," retorted Len. " The owners use the war to force up the price of coal and I don't see why we can't use it to get more wages. They have got us like soldiers as it is. We work like dogs, and they have made our committee into a ways and means committee for getting more coal instead of what it used to be during the strike."

The bitterness in his voice surprised Ezra.

" I can't understand you, Len," he said. " Only recently you declared you were in favour of producing more coal to end the war quickly. Then you said you were not concerned who won the war. Now you want to use the war to improve wages—in other words, for your own ends. I can't see what is in your mind."

This linking up of statements he had made staggered Len, for it showed him to have been inconsistent. He bowed his head a brief moment, saying :

" I never thought I was such a twister. Yet," he added, in a puzzled way, " I have been sincere in everything I have said and I have really believed and felt every word. I can't understand it."

Ezra helped him. " It's merely because you don't understand things yet. You just see things as you want them to be at the moment and don't face up to things as they are."

Len was flustered by the severity of the blow and made no more mention of the subject, but he persisted in asking for a meeting of the men. Determinedly he told Ezra that if he were not prepared to call a mass-meeting then he would himself hold a meeting of the men in his own district, on the parting where meetings had been held immediately following the strike. Ezra capitulated to this threat, knowing Len's obstinacy in matters which he felt keenly.

The meeting was held in the theatre. Len looked around from his seat in the gallery and was amazed to see how few of the "natives" were present, while large numbers of strangers, who had started at the pit since the outbreak of the war, filled the places of those who had been recruited.

Ezra opened the meeting with a brief explanation of its purpose, and immediately he had finished men jumped up from all parts of the hall. The chairman singled out one man and permitted him to speak, assuring the others that they should all have their turn. All the speakers were vehemently in favour of demanding an increase in wages, but Len, who was the last to speak, wanted to test the feeling of the men before he put his point of view.

"I agree with all those who think the time has come when we have to get our wages nearer the cost of living," he said. "What is the good of five or six pounds if it only buys a quarter of the necessities we had with our smaller wages before the war? It is nonsense for anyone to say that the company has no money. All of us here can remember when our Federation leaders offered the Company that if they wouldn't raise the price of coal during the war, we wouldn't ask for an increase in wages. What was the owners' reply to this patriotic offer, made for the sake of the old country that the owners claimed they loved so much? Their answer was that they couldn't possibly think of not using the war to raise the price of coal. In other words, my mind tells me, rightly or wrongly, that the owners saw the war as a chance to get very big extra profits for themselves. No one inside or outside of this meeting can say that they have not succeeded in this."

His voice rose louder as he entered into the spirit of his words. Everyone in the meeting listened to him intently. "No; patriotism to them is a very paying thing. The longer the war lasts the more money they make out of it. I know they will say that we are traitors to our country and that we are betraying our boys at the front if we ask for more wages. I know they will do a hundred times more against us now than they did during the strike even, but we have got to face it some time or other. As it is now, we are slogging ourselves to a standstill for a lot of shillings that don't buy half of the food we need to give our bodies strength to keep on working. I say," he concluded, " that our leaders should put it to all the miners in the country that we should be prepared to strike if we cannot have more wages. Why should we work and starve and our brothers at the front fight and die while other people are piling up mountains of money from our sacrifices ? "

Ezra put the resolution that the Federation executive should organise national strike action in the event of wages not being increased in line with the increased cost of living, and it was carried unanimously.

At the end of the meeting Ezra called Len to him, and they walked up the hill together. With biting sarcasm Ezra informed Len that the speaker in the meeting against war who had made the defiant gesture in the police-court had paid the £20 fine out of his mother's savings. The shock stopped Len in his stride.

" What ? " he gasped. " You don't mean to tell me honestly that he has betrayed his principles ? "

" Just that," retorted Ezra calmly. " Either he lied in the meeting when he propounded what he said were his principles or he couldn't face up to the test."

Len said no more. He had thought of making an excuse to drop in at Ezra's purposely to see Mary, but changed his mind when he learned of the new development. He felt at the moment that all men were liars and that such things as principles did not exist. He brought back to his mind Ezra's exposure of his own culpability in this regard and, feeling ashamed, began to look for excuses. They came to him readily after he had realised his own weaknesses and vacillations when it was a matter of weighing up fundamentals. He remembered Ezra's words, " You see things as you desire them to be at the moment instead of as they actually are." Here, he felt, was the key to the whole problem, if he could only understand it and work it out in his own mind and emotions. He began to realise that he was more of a nervous being than a consistently thinking individual.

When he reached home he found Shane awaiting him in great excitement. The sheet of paper she waved in her hand gladdened his heart, for he guessed immediately that his father had written at last. Hastily taking the letter, he read to himself the hardly decipherable words. Shane interrupted him sharply.

" Think you, Len bach, that your dad have only wrote to you ? Read out loud for your old mam, my boy."

Tears of joy made her tired eyes soft and misty.

Len read aloud :

" Dear Shane and Len and all at home,

" Just a few words hoping they will find you all well as it leaves me at present. I am very sorry being so long writing to you, but I have been very busy. My old general is out here. When he did hear that I had joined up he told his orderly, ' Now, 'member, sergeant, as soon as Big Jim do land tell him I do want to see him ! ' Now, Shane bach, what do you think to that ? You 'on't half be able to swank to Mrs. Thomas next door now. Don't worry 'bout me. Everything in the garden is lovely out here. The only things I do miss is the beer in the Boar's Head and those cakes you used to make for tea every Sunday. Nobody can make cakes like you, Shane bach. The general did tell me only yesterday, ' Don't forget, James, when the missus do send you cakes I want some of them.' True as God is my judge he did say that. Tell Len when he is writing back to let me know how the old place is going. I do miss that old barry somehow or other. He will never have 'nother butty like his old dad. What say you, Shane ? Well, I must close now, with love and kisses to all at home from your ever loving

" James and father,

" JIM.

" P.S.—I hope you are getting the army 'lotment all right. We are short of fags out here."

When Len had finished, Shane was openly sobbing.

" What a lovely letter your father do write, Len bach.

Anybody can see he is a edicated man. Fancy the General 'membering him. But there, James was always like that ; everybody do take to him as soon as they see him."

The letter helped Len to forget for a while the mental turmoil of the evening. He felt relieved now that he knew his father was safe.

That night, as he lay awake thinking over the events of the past few weeks, it suddenly struck him that the letter had probably been written at least a week or a fortnight before it was delivered and that he was no more certain that his father was alive now than he had been before receiving the letter, but he resolved to tell Shane nothing of this.

The heavy work in the pit together with the terrible food he had to eat was beginning to take toll of his health. He developed a racking cough very similar to that which tore Mary on occasions. Strangely enough, this did not alarm him. He accepted it as something that drew Mary nearer to him, and felt he was now in a position to bear her burden. Despite this mental reaction, he found the hurried drive in the pit to fill more and ever more coal telling on his strength. His face grew gaunt and yellowish, while his body became more thin and bony. He dreaded his mother's call in the mornings, and he had to exercise all his determination to respond to it. Each morning the long procession of black-clothed, silent shadows up the hill became an ever greater nightmare. He rarely went out in the evenings now, and often fell asleep with his head in the bathing tub. On these occasions Shane would tenderly try to swill his naked top half without waking him.

Ezra noticed the symptoms and urged him to take a rest at home. Len thanked him for his sympathy, but pointed out that it was impossible if he and his mother were to eat.

Ezra knew the truth of this, and said no more.

One evening Len went down to Ben the Barber's for a hair-cut. As soon as he entered the shop Ben looked up from the face he was shaving and, as if he had been expecting Len, remarked caustically :

" Would you like to know what other people think of you and your sort ? "

Len was aware of Ben's quaint mannerisms of speech and knew that deep down the man was a rebel against all conventions.

" No, why ? " he asked casually.

" Well, just look at that newspaper over there. No, not that one on top ; the one underneath," and with this Ben went on with his shaving, whistling quietly as the razor flashed in his hands.

Len sat down and read the paper. He turned over the numerous pages and pictures dealing with the war. He was sick of reading about the perpetual and ever-recurring great victories that were being won each day, none of which seemed to bring the war any nearer an end. He found he had opened the paper in the middle and so he turned the pages back. Ben watched him from the corner of his eyes, still whistling and wielding the razor over the lathered face. Suddenly Len's face went white. In a streaming headline across the front page he read :

" MINERS BETRAY SOLDIERS AT THE FRONT "

" At the moment of our country's greatest peril, certain elements in the ranks of the miners are advocating a strike for an increase in wages. While men are laying down their lives in defence of the nation, these people talk in terms of cash and threaten to deprive the navy and the gallant forces who are so heroically fighting of coal. If the perpetrators of such an agitation lived in one of the enemy countries they would be shot offhand as traitors. We cannot believe that the miners are themselves responsible for this. Rather do we think they are being misled against their desires by people who are no friends to this country and who are prepared to go to any lengths to ensure the defeat of our glorious army and navy."

Len read the remainder of the article, becoming more indignant with every word. When he had finished he raised his head and looked at the chuckling Ben. The latter spoke casually.

" Now you know what you and your tribe are, and what you should be getting."

" But it isn't true." A flush died Len's face. " Our men are not against those who are fighting. All we are asking is that the coal-owners sacrifice a little for the war as well as us and the forces. I agree we have got to make sacrifices to draw the war to an end, but let it be sacrifices on everyone's part, and not only us bottom dogs."

Ben intervened with a grunt.

" Huh. What's the good of talking like that. This is a war in which there are no classes. If the Germans conquer, what have you got to lose ? Nothing. Absolutely bugger all. But look at the owners. If the Germans win the war they stand to lose their pits and everything they have sacrificed so much for in the past. Don't you think they deserve a little compensation now in face of the risk they are running ? Let me put it to you like this. If we lose the war you lose nothing unless its your life—and that does not alter the fact you lose nothing. The owners, on the other hand, stand to lose everything : therefore they have got to insure themselves against this. So it's only right and fair they should get as much profits as possible now in case they get none later on. See ? " he concluded quizzically.

Len said nothing. He knew Ben's penchant for sarcasm and was aware of his cleverness in argument, for Ben's irony intrigued him.

Some time after this Big Jim and some of the other men of the valley came home on leave unexpectedly. Len saw them walking up the hill from the station. They were all drunk. Their puttees hung in dirtied, bedraggled strings round their legs. Their hungry-looking, pinched grey faces were shadowed by the rims of steel helmets, and they carried their deadly-looking rifles in their hands. Singing bawdily and staggering from side to side of the pavement, they attracted the respectful and awed attention of all

the people who saw them, and when they met a group of
men standing on the corner of the street directly facing the
main entrance of the Boar's Head, the soldiers immediately
entered, followed by the others.

Len was torn between two desires. He wanted to hurry
home to tell Shane that Jim was home. Yet he wanted to
let her have the full joy of surprise when Jim would
walk in the house. But, lest the shock of Jim's sudden
appearance would upset her too much, he decided to tell
her without delay.

When he reached home he asked casually :

" When did you get the last letter from dad ? "

" Well, well. What be coming over you, boy ? " she
asked, giving him a queer look. " You ought to know that
without asking me, mun. You did read it out for me in
this very kitchen."

Len pretended to recollect himself.

" Ay, of course I did, now I think of it," he said. " Only I
was wondering perhaps he have sent you a sly one and Mrs.
Thomas next door read it out for you. But never mind.
Duw, wouldn't it be fine, mam, if he was to walk
into the kitchen now, without letting us know he was
coming ? "

Shane hesitated as the tears bubbled in her eyes.

" Ay, it would be," she said. " How I would like to see
him ! It be nearly three years since he did leave us, and
he have not been home once. 'Tain't fair. Nearly everybody else have been home four or five times already. But
there, I would forgive everything if he was to walk in now.
Many a time I have nagged him for nothing, Len bach.
I do regret it all now and often wish I could draw many a
word back. Poor old James. I 'ood have to go a long
way to find a man half so good as him." She lifted the
canvas apron to her eyes.

Len interjected quickly :

" Well, mam, there is no need for you to cry. Dad is
home already."

Shane jumped to her feet like a leaping rabbit.

" What say you ? " her voice was incredulously high.
" Don't you dare to tease your poor old mother, Len."

" Mam," Len faced her reproachfully, " you know I
wouldn't do that for my right arm. I spoke the truth.
Dad is home and he is now in the Boar's Head having a
little drink with the boys before coming up."

Shane's eyes flashed.

" In the Boar's Head before coming to see his only wife,
the 'ooman who have reared his children for him ! What
do you think of that, Len ? He don't think more of your
mother than mud."

Hastily putting her shawl over her head, she opened the
door and made her way down the hill. Len made no
attempt to prevent her. He knew that her temper would
evaporate when she faced the exuberant Jim, but it was
hours before he heard his father's voice raucously singing
some obscene ditty. All the people in the street came
to their doors or their bedroom windows at the noise.
They shouted greetings to Jim, who waved salutations to
them, totally unaware that they could not see him in the
darkness. Shane kept exhorting him to be quiet, but
the only answer she received was : " Quiet, muniferni ?
Let the world know that Big Jim have come back home,"
followed by his trying to sing louder than ever.

Shane felt proud as she held his staggering form erect.
He wanted to enter every house in the street and she only
prevented him after calling for Len's assistance. Eventually
they got him to the house, and he sank with a bang into his
armchair. Len had stoked the fire, and its gleam threw
Jim's bloodshot eyes into sharp, glaring relief before he fell
asleep. Between them, Shane and Len pulled the uniform
and other military paraphernalia off the recumbent,
snoring body, Shane sobbing the while :

" Poor boy. I 'spect he be fair worn out with what he
have gone through."

Len felt a thrill run through him when he grasped the
rifle. He felt an insane desire to pull the trigger and hear
the explosion of a shot. He suggested they should take

Big Jim to bed immediately, but Shane was opposed to
this.

" No," she said. " He must be waking when he come
to bed or he will be thinking in his sleep that he is not back
in his own little home."

She poured hot tea between the clenched teeth while
Len rummaged through the haversack and other bags that
Jim had brought with him. From the depths of the
former he pulled out a dirty paper bag greasy with half-
melted butter, some uncovered sausages with grains
of sawdust sticking in their skins, and a tin of corned
beef. The sight of the food immediately set his stomach
turning and bubbling with hunger. Saliva filled his
mouth in spite of his attempts to swallow it back, and
suddenly feeling faint, he went to the back-door to get
some air.

When he returned to the kitchen Shane had succeeded
in waking Jim. Len thought his father looked even more
huge than before he went away. He noticed long red
streaks such as are made by vigorous scratching on Jim's
chest. Jim made long smacking sounds with his lips.

" Ah," he said thickly, " it is good to be home, mun."

His eyes roamed longingly over Shane's body.

" Duw, duw. You do look more beautiful than ever,
Shane bach. Ay, indeed you do. Better than the gel in
the 'staminet."

Shane perked up at this.

" What gel be you talking about, James ? "

" Oh," he replied, dimly realising the mistake he had
made, " just a ole bag of a 'ooman, you know, Shane,"
confidentially lowering his voice, " a common ole cow. Ay,
that's it. An old tart who do live by robbing the boys."

" Hush, James bach," Shane's voice was thin and her
expression shocked. " Don't say that 'bout any 'ooman.
'Member your mother was a 'ooman."

Shane cooked some of the sausages for supper. For the
first time in years a feeling of satisfaction rippled through
Len's body, sending warm glows through his blood.

After supper Jim vociferously asserted he was remaining in the kitchen for the night.

" No bloody bed of feathers for me," he declared. " Me an my ole love will sleep by here on the floor better 'n any bed, an' a damn sight more helfy."

" Sleep on the floor ? " Shane stared at him aghast. " Duw, duw, man. Have the beer turned your brains ? You do know that as soon as we put the light out the black pats will cover the kitchen floor with their dirty, crawling legs. And more than that, James, you ought to know after what happened once before that black pats be very fond of beer and will always go for where they do smell it, and you do know very well that you do sleep with your mouth wide open."

Jim rose unsteadily to his feet, holding on to the brass rod under the mantelshelf for support.

" Black pats ! Black pats ! " he said with slow dignity, inflating his enormous chest. " What be black pats to me, who have slept with millions of rats as big as dogs every night that God sent for the last two year or more ? Black pats, indeed ! " he said contemptuously drawing his hand from the rod to strike an imposing attitude and falling ignominiously backwards into the chair. Although neither Len nor his mother said a word, he shouted : " Don't think I be drunk and don't know what I be doing. A man who have killed hundreds of square-headed Jerries do always know what he be doing. Where is Shane ? " he asked suddenly.

She immediately came to his side and without further fuss she and Len took him upstairs to bed.

It was many hours before Len went to sleep. Groans, grunts, and creakings from the next room were hardly intercepted by the intervening wall. The sounds made him think of Mary, and again he felt the soft contact of her body, as he had felt it tha⁺ day at the seaside. Little flushes of heat ran through his flesh at the memory. Then his thoughts turned to the bayonet his father had brought home. He shuddered as he recollected the rust on it, which he thought must have been blood. He imagined the point sinking into a man's body and the entrails being drawn out with the suction of the grooves at the sides. He felt a peculiar kind of blood-curdling pleasure at these imaginings, but at last, with the creakings and groans still in his ears, he slowly drifted to sleep.

The next morning Len was surprised to see how the street was decorated with gay bunting bearing in bold letters words of cheer and welcome to the local heroes who had so unexpectedly returned on leave. Bright flags hung from the windows of the ugly houses making cheerful splashes of colour.

For some days he had no opportunity to talk with his father. He was in bed when Len went to work in the mornings and in the Boar's Head when he returned. But on Sunday, after breakfast, he had a chance to raise the matter that was foremost in his mind.

" Well, dad," he said, " what do you think of the war ? " He tried to make his voice as casual as possible, but its quiver betrayed the intensity of his emotions.

Stretching his long legs to their full length, Jim broke wind and lit his pipe before replying, after Shane had scolded him for his lack of manners. He addressed himself first to Shane :

" Wherever you be," he quoted sententiously, " let your wind go free." After this shattering remark he turned to Len and rolled off on a long recital of the heroic deeds he had performed.

" Ay," he said, " us in the front lines do do all the fighting and the dying and some little puppy-dog of an officer, with goose-down on his face instead of whiskers, do come along behind the lines and pick up the medals and the leave."

Len was interested.

" So it is very much like the pit," he asked, " only instead of being called workmen you are called soldiers and the officials are called officers ? "

Jim gave a loud guffaw. " Haw, haw, haw," he roared,

and it took some time for him to recover sufficiently to say : " Not quite like that, Len. We can tell the officials to go to hell. You tell that to an officer and you get to hell first. Officials be sometimes wrong, but officers are never wrong."

Jim monopolised the conversation for the remainder of the day, Shane and Len listening interestedly to the account of his many varied experiences. This was the last occasion on which Len had an opportunity of talking to his father, for Jim spent the greater part of the few remaining days of his leave in the Boar's Head.

When the day came for him to return to the front Shane clung to him like a baby, and cried. She wanted to accompany him to the station, but both Jim and Len were adamant, and they bade good-bye on the doorstep.

During the months that followed life in Cwmardy became a monotonous routine to the people. The owners granted the demands of the miners and so averted a strike. But the cost of living immediately jumped up and balanced the advance.

One evening a telegram was stuck on the window of Mr. Evans Cardi's stores :

" GERMANS ASK FOR ARMISTICE. THE WAR IS
ENDED."

Huge crowds of people tried to force their way to the window to see the telegram with their own eyes. Having seen it, they dashed off in all directions to spread the news. Musical instruments appeared from nowhere, and in a very short time the whole valley rang with music, laughter, and noise.

CHAPTER XVIII

FINALE

Cwmardy teaches Len a New Lesson

INSIDE twelve months after the conclusion of the war most of the miners in Cwmardy who had gone to the war and had returned were again at their places in the pit.

On his first day down Big Jim told Len, "Duw, duw, boy bach, being down in the old pit agen do make me feel as if I now be home real, mun."

Len laughed. "Ay. It is funny how the pit gets hold of us and we are not satisfied when we are away from it. Must be something in the air, I suppose."

It was not long before the men had adapted themselves again to the life of the pit, but their experiences in the war had made them carefree and assertive, and they took little heed of the officials, who did not dare to question their conduct.

Meanwhile the Company was introducing mechanical methods of cutting and conveying the coal, Len's barry being one of the first to be put on the new technique. The conveyor consisted of a number of long iron troughs, bolted together and fastened to a tiny engine driven by compressed air, which took the coal in bucking jerks from the coal face to the trams. And in this way the men were able to more than double their output.

One day the men, naked to the waist as usual, were crawling up the long conveyor face, squirming their way like snakes, sometimes on their bellies, sometimes on their sides, until they reached their working places. Whenever their bodies touched the cold, damp roof it seemed like a burn upon their hot flesh, and the tiny lumps of loose coal and stone on the floor rubbed into their sweating flesh like pins, so that they were not anxious to have more of this than was absolutely necessary. Once they had reached their places they stayed there till the end of the shift unless some urgent reason obliged them to move.

When they had all arrived, the workman at the top end sent the order down the line of crouching men, " Right you are. Let her go." The order passed from mouth to mouth until it reached the man at the bottom end, who responded by jerking a little lever attached to the engine, which, after coughing and rasping for a few minutes as if clearing its throat, gathered power, and presently, with a clatter and a clang that deafened the men's ears to everything else, the iron troughs of the conveyor had begun their spasmodic bucking jerks. The loud and regular "phot-phot, phot-phot" of the blast engine beat time to the rattling clamour of the conveyor, and conversation became impossible in the tumult.

The men got to work with their picks and shovels. Resting on their knees to give greater power to their arms, they tore great lumps of coal from the solid face, and breaking them into smaller pieces, heaved them with a turn of their shoulders and a twist of their arms into the conveyor But however much coal they put in, the conveyor was always empty when they turned to it again.

" Duw," said Big Jim, " it be like throwing coal down the pit and losing it."

Gradually the rhythmic, discordant din gripped the men's muscles and their movements began to keep time with the noise. Streams of perspiration oiled their joints and made them operate smoothly, and within an hour after the conveyor had started the men were immersed in a universe of coal, sweat, and clamour. If anything happened to stop the machinery they felt that the world had suddenly become void, and their ears would be filled with a strange blobbing sound, so that they were glad when the tumult began again. The silence felt like something tangible pressing on their skin, and it was on their sense of touch that they had to depend to ascertain if the roof were weakening.

After five hours of this Len felt as if his spine was on fire and his limbs had been amputated. To save moving

his body too much he tugged and strained to tumble a
larger lump of coal than usual into the trough, but each
time he got it on the rim the jerking edge tore it from his
grasp and threw it back to the ground. Len cursed and
grunted under the strain, which was all the greater because
the limited space did not allow him to use his full strength.
The coal put on by the men above him kept dancing and
jigging before his eyes as it bucked downwards towards
the tram. Big lumps, small lumps, funnily-shaped lumps
pranced noisily before him like a rushing, rock-strewn
river. The glittering mass fascinated him and made him
giddy, and the thought flashed into his mind that the strain
had driven him insane. He bent until his face almost
touched the jumping coal, staring until his eyes bulged in
glaring concentration. Then he screamed wildly, his sharp
hysterical falsetto cutting through the mechanical clamour
like a knife. The thin piercing agony of the notes rose higher.

"Stop it ! Stop it ! For Christ's sake, stop ! "

With the speed of a flashed signal the words passed from
mouth to mouth till they reached the ears of the man near
the engine, and in an instant the coal face became deathly
silent. Men looked at their nearest neighbours in mute
query, to meet the dumb echo of their own bewilderment.
Len was now scrambling like a madman in the coal on the
conveyor. His hands tore at the gleaming lumps until his
nails hung loose. Big Jim sprang forward to see what was
the matter, and in a few moments they had uncovered a
naked arm that had been ripped out of its shoulder socket.
The two men gave one horrified glance at the limb, then
frantically turned and squirmed up the conveyor face,
shouting at the top of their voices : " Quick boys, quick.
Something awful has happened up above."

Men who had become momentarily lifeless with amazement flung themselves into revitalised motion at the call.
Their sweat-slimed bodies gleamed like oil and outshone the
brightness of the coal as they frenziedly slithered past it.
Len and his father were the first to reach the scene of the
accident, the latter gasping and heaving with the mad rush

in the enclosed space that was too small for his huge body.

Alongside the still conveyor they saw the silent form of a young lad who had only recently started work. His body twisted and squirmed as if with convulsions, and his wide-open, staring eyes glittered queerly in the light of the lamps that showered their beams on him. His lips kept moaning : " Bring my arm back, bring my arm back. Why did you take it from me ? "

Len caught the lad to him, cuddling him like a baby across his chest. The single arm kept flailing helplessly, emphasising the empty socket where the other had been. The gleaming bone winked wickedly through the blood that spouted from the shreds of torn flesh.

By the time the other men appeared, panting and gasping, the lad had ceased his weak struggles, but Len felt the nerves still quivering like soft jelly in a shaken dish. The boy turned his head and asked in a low, supplicating tone : " Did one of you bring my arm back ? "

Big Jim swallowed something and blew his nose before replying, " Never you mind 'bout your arm, now, boy bach. That be all right, you can venture." He took the frail body from Len and stretched it out along his own, so that the men could quickly press their fingers and thumbs to the torn arteries, to prevent the blood pouring away.

The boy remained conscious all the time they were waiting for the officials to bring the first-aid material, and though he seemed more satisfied about his arm, he insisted upon seeing it.

Big Jim tried to dissuade him. " What for do you want your old arm, boy bach ? There be plenty of time for that, mun, when the doctor do see you. Duw, duw, he will look at it and look at you, then he will tell you to shut your eyes quick like, and when you open them again your arm will be back on."

The lad did not seem to hear him, and began to moan : " I want my arm. I want my arm." Len whispered to one of the men near by, who crawled away, and in a short time returned with the dismembered arm sticking out from beneath his own. The ghastly sight turned Len's stomach, but he could not take his eyes from Big Jim as the latter took the limb and tied it to the boy's body.

" There you be," he said, in what he intended tu be a jubilant voice. " There be your little arm, boy bach, safe and sound with you agen."

The boy sighed heavily, then asked, " Will I be able to play football any more, Big Jim ? "

The latter, still on his back with the lad lying on him, laughed boisterously. " Ha-ha-ha. Ho-ho. Now what do you think to that, boys ? What a question to ask ! Ha-ha. Play football agen ? Of course you will, mun. You will be captain of your team a hundred times yet, 'on't he boys ? Duw, duw. You be worth ten dead men, easy, mun." Jim turned to the other men, tears bubbling in his eyes, and they all hurried to confirm his words. The lad seemed satisfied, and settled himself more comfortably on the body that held him. His eyes closed and he seemed to drift into a sleep.

The officials fussily hurried up and the lad was tied and bandaged in preparation for the journey home. They tried to select the men who were to carry him out, but no one took any notice as they all put their clothes on and left the conveyor to itself.

That evening Len could not remain in the house. The horror he had felt when he saw the arm still filled his mind. He wanted to be violently sick, but his stomach would not respond. The arm dangled like a monstrous marionette before his eyes, even when he shut them. He paced the small kitchen like a tom-cat in a storm, and eventually decided he could stand it no longer. Leaving the house, he curtly informed Shane he would not be long.

Len's thoughts cleared a little in the fresh air, as, quite unconsciously, he walked in the direction of Mary's house. When he reached the door he looked up in surprise and paused for some moments while he argued with himself whether he should go in. Before he had made up his mind the door opened, and Mary and Ezra came out.

" Hallo," said Ezra, " if you've come to see us you
are unfortunate, as Mary and I are going for a little walk
up the mountain." Len felt that such an excursion would
soothe him, and he shyly asked : " Would you mind if I
came with you ? I can't bear to be inside after what
happened to-day ! " Mary looked at him sympathetically
and nodded a glad assent.

The three made their way slowly up the rugged breast
of the mountain till they reached the summit. Here they
sat down and watched the smoke from the pit drift and
spread until it covered Cwmardy with a filmy blanket. The
glow from the furnaces shot streaks of red into the black
smoke, and for some reason the scene made Mary sad.

" Isn't it awful that we have to spend our lives with
smoke to breathe and coal-dust to eat ? " she asked.

For a while neither of the men answered her.

Although they had heard the remark both appeared
engrossed in their own thoughts. But at length Ezra turned
to Len. " That makes me wonder how far the atmosphere
of the valley is helping to break your father. Have you
noticed how thin, bent, and slow he is becoming, Len ? "

" Yes. I have noticed him in work. But there, what
can we expect ? When a man works over thirty years in
the pit it is bound to tell on his body in some way or
another."

A hooter from below sent its wailing note up the mountain. Len started, as if the sound were strange to him.

" There it goes," he muttered bitterly. " Hear the whip
crack ? I wonder if all those who respond to its lash
to-night will come back up in the morning."

" That is a matter for fate to decide," said Ezra.

Len sprang to his feet excitedly. " Fate, fate ? What is
that ? Do you say that fate tore that boy's arm out this
morning ? Was it fate that blew our men to bits in the
explosion ? Did fate smash Bill Bristol to a pulp ? No ;
I can't believe that, Ezra. It wasn't fate that brought us
into the strike or into the war. You did the first and the
capitalists did the other."

Ezra betrayed no emotion at this sudden outburst, but Mary rose to her knees. " I agree with Len," she said. " We are ourselves responsible for what happens. The pity is that we follow events instead of trying to determine and mould them. Our fate is in our own hands. Take Russia, for instance. In spite of all that the papers say, I would like to see how those people are shaping their future. Whether they succeed is another matter, but at least they will have made the attempt, which is more than we are doing."

Len was encouraged by this support although he did not entirely agree with the sentiments. " You can't say we aren't trying to better things," he said. " What was our strike but a battle by our people to improve conditions ? "

Ezra broke in. " Yes, that's right. It was part of a war, a war that will never end while there are masters and men in the same world." He pointed his finger to the pits where the red glow was becoming deeper in the encroaching dusk. " Who sunk those pits and mined them ? Who made those lines into rivers of coal ? No one but our people. And what have they in return ? Nothing but poverty, struggle, and death."

The three got to their feet and watched the little pinpricks of light that were beginning to stab the darkness over Cwmardy.

" You are right," said Len slowly. " But if our people have the power to win strikes even against bullets and batons they have the power to do away with their poverty, to put an end to the struggle and begin to live clean, healthy lives."

Ezra looked at him as he caught Mary's arm, and they began the descent. " Hmm," he said. " When you two have lived so long as I have you will learn there are some things in life the people can never abolish. The struggle for a living is one of them."

There was no reply, but as they carefully negotiated the rocky path that led back to Cwmardy, Len, unseen by Ezra, squeezed Mary's arm with a warm confidence.

THE END